the yadayada *Prayer Group* GETS DOWN

a Novel

neta jackson

INTEGRITY®

PUBLISHERS

Nashville

Copyright © 2004 by Neta Jackson.

Published by Integrity Publishers, a Division of Integrity Media, Inc., 5250 Virginia Way, Suite 110, Brentwood, TN 37027.

HELPING PEOPLE WORLDWIDE EXPERIENCE *the* MANIFEST PRESENCE *of* GOD.

Published in association with the literary agency of Alive Communications, Inc., 7680 Goddard Street, Suite 200, Colorado Springs, CO 80920.

Scripture quotations are taken from the following:
        The Holy Bible, New International Version. Copyright © 1973, 1978, 1984, International Bible Society. Used by permission of Zondervan Bible Publishers.
        The New King James Version, copyright © 1979, 1980, 1982, Thomas Nelson, Inc., Publishers.
        The Holy Bible, New Living Translation, copyright © 1996. Used by permission of Tyndale House Publishers, Inc., Wheaton, Illinois. All rights reserved.
        The King James Version of the Bible.

This novel is a work of fiction. Any references to real events, businesses, organizations, and locales are intended only to give the fiction a sense of reality and authenticity. Any resemblance to actual persons, living or dead, is entirely coincidental.

Cover design: The Office of Bill Chiaravalle | www.officeofbc.com
Interior design: Inside Out Design & Typesetting

Library of Congress Cataloging-in-Publication Data

Jackson, Neta.
The yada yada prayer group gets down / by Neta Jackson.
   p. cm.

ISBN 1-59145-074-8 (tradepaper)

1. Women—Illinois—Fiction. 2. Female friendship—Fiction. 3. Christian women—Fiction. 4. Chicago (Ill.)—Fiction. 5. Prayer groups—Fiction. I. Title.
PS3560.A2415Y335   2004
813'.54—dc22   2004005456

Printed in the United States of America
04 05 06 07 08 09 PHX 8 7 6 5 4 3 2 1

To Pat Hall

— the real "Bandana Woman" —

who is now my friend and sister in the faith

Prologue

CHICAGO'S LABOR DAY WEEKEND, 2002

*T*he southbound elevated train squealed to a metallic stop on the trestles above Morse Avenue, and its doors slid open. On the street below, a slim figure slouching in the recessed doorway of the Wig Shop squinted intently through her wraparound shades at the train platform spanning the overpass. The commuter cars looked full, but only two women got off and started down the stairs to street level.

The woman in the doorway swore, sending expletives like a stream of spit toward the sidewalk. Three trains had come by already, and she hadn't seen an easy mark yet. Not with today being Sunday and tomorrow the Labor Day holiday. Mostly young folks heading downtown for the Jazz Fest in Grant Park— or coming back. The northbound would arrive soon, disgorging a handful of teenagers in baggy pants returning after a long day along Chicago's lakefront, noses burnt and ears plugged into their music. Maybe a few haggard parents who were smart enough to leave early with strollers, backpacks, and whiny preschoolers.

If only it was a workday! A bunch of skirts and suits would be coming home, tired, not so alert, twenties and fifties in their purses and wallets. Once they separated and headed onto the side streets of the Rogers Park neighborhood toward the brick apartment-buildings-turned-condos or the old two-story homes jammed between, hitting on a mark was usually just a matter of smooth timing.

But she couldn't wait till Tuesday. She needed some cash now. The ten blue Valium pills she'd washed down with a glass of vodka that morning hadn't suffocated the depression that was pulling her down, down into a bottomless black hole, threatening to swallow her, body and soul.

She had to get some smack. Soon.

The southbound pulled out overhead as the two ex-passengers spilled from the doors of the Morse Avenue station on street level. The figure in the doorway straightened, eyeing the pair. The first was a young woman, tall, nicely dressed in a white tailored pantsuit, straight black hair pulled back into a ponytail, a black handbag slung over her shoulder. And an older woman, her dark hair wound into a bun, wearing a navy skirt, red blazer, and sensible shoes with low heels. Their faces seemed long and flat, foreign. Asian. The watcher pulled back into the doorway as the pair crossed the street and passed right in front of her.

"Don't worry about your traveler's checks, *Mama-san*. See that drug store? It's got an ATM. I'll get some cash." The younger one took her companion's elbow as though to hurry her along, but the older woman shook off her hand, rattling off strange words that seemed to come out her nose, nasal and sharp.

A tight smile pulled at the corners of the mouth in the doorway, all that could be seen of a face masked with the wraparound shades and a red bandana tied tight around her head and knotted at the nape of her neck. She'd heard enough. *ATM.* She'd seen enough. *Two skirts at odds with each other, distracted.*

She waited a few seconds until the two women passed. Then, clutching the stiff paper bag with its long, hard object stuffed beneath her faded jean jacket, she stepped out onto the sidewalk behind them. *Watch ya feet, girl . . . don't bump inta no nickel feeders . . . be cool . . . don' call no 'tention to yo'sef.*

The two dark-haired women turned into the parking lot of the Osco Drug Store and disappeared inside. The woman in the jean jacket, skimpy tank top, and tight jeans leaned her backside against the corner of the store and fished out a nearly flat pack of cigarettes. She had to clutch the hidden paper bag with her elbow in order to light the cigarette with both hands. The long, flat object inside the bag made her feel confident. She wouldn't have to use it—just scare them. No problem.

The cigarette had burned only halfway when the pair came out of the store, but the woman flipped it into the street. So what if it was her last cigarette. She'd get some smack *and* a whole carton. Ha. Come right back here to this store and buy a carton straight up.

Or die. Didn't really matter.

She knew she couldn't keep this up—hooked on four habits. She'd tried to kick the heroin, signed up for that methadone program at the hospital. Yet all she'd done was pick up another habit. Most days she did all four—a handful of Valium washed down with vodka, a trip to the hospital for a slug of methadone, then back out in the 'hood to roll some sucker for money to pay for a bag of smack.

But none of it was keeping her from sliding deeper and deeper into that big black hole. It was going to come down on her one of these days. Maybe today.

She let the pair get several yards down the sidewalk before pushing off from the store wall to follow. She'd only taken a few steps when a loud voice behind her yelled, "Hoshi! Hoshi Takahashi! Wait up!" The mark—the young, tall one—turned and looked straight past her, a smile lighting up her long face.

The watcher swore under her breath. She couldn't stop now; she had to keep walking, right past the two women, who had now both turned back toward the running feet and yelling voice behind her. Why had she thrown the cigarette pack away? She needed something, some excuse to stop, to keep an eye on her mark. Desperation bubbled up in her throat. This had to work. Or it would go down—badly.

Her shoe. She'd retie the brand-new Nikes she'd lifted right under the nose of that stupid clerk at Foot Locker. She bent, untied one shoe, pulled it off, and shook out an imaginary piece of grit, rubbing the bottom of her bare foot and tipping her head slightly so she could keep the trio in her line of vision. Best thing about wraparound shades—you could watch people, and they didn't know you were looking.

A black woman, small boned, beaming, had joined the two Asian women, and the tall one was introducing the newcomer to the older woman. "You Hoshi's mama?" said the newcomer, pumping the woman's hand. The older woman smiled tightly, pulled her hand away, and nodded politely. Now they were walking again, right toward the woman bent over her shoe.

"Ain't this the bomb?" the newcomer crowed as the trio drew near, absently skirted the bent figure, and then passed on. "Yada Yada goin' to be blessed outta their socks to meet your mama. You just get off the southbound? I just rode up on the northbound, had to stand the whole way—on a Sunday evenin' too!" She laughed, a crown of tight coppery curls bouncing on top of her head. "Well, that's what happens on holiday weekends. So glad I ran into somebody from Yada Yada; don't have to walk by myself . . ."

The woman behind them straightened and swore again under her breath. Taking on three wasn't going to be so easy. The two foreigners—they'd give it up like melted butter. But this new one looked street-smart.

It was too late to wait for another mark. She knew they had money on them.

Two or three—didn't matter. It was do or die.

1

I bolted upright in the bed, soaked in sweat. *That face! Caught in my headlights, eyes round with fear. An eternal second...*

My thudding heart gradually slowed as the bedroom, bathed in early morning light, came into focus. I lay back down, begging the hands on the bedside clock to move because I did not want to close my eyes again.

Denny stirred on the wrinkled sheets beside me and cracked his eyes open mere inches from my face. "You okay, Jodi?" he murmured, slinging a heavy arm over my body and pulling me close. He kissed the back of my neck. "Happy anniversary, babe." Then he roused on one arm. "Gonna be a hot one, I guess. You're sweaty already."

I said nothing. The nightmare was still lurking beneath the surface, threatening to yank me back into its dark embrace. I forced myself to focus: our anniversary. Twenty years.

I'm so blessed. In spite of . . .

"I dreamed about the accident again." I wanted my husband to know how it haunted me, but could he ever know? How could anyone know what it felt like to have killed a child?

"Oh, Jodi." Denny pulled me closer against his bare chest. "I'm so sorry." He said nothing for a long while, just held me. And gradually his comfort eased my tense muscles like a long soak in the tub.

We slept again—maybe only ten, fifteen minutes—but this time when I awoke, Willie Wonka, our almost-deaf chocolate Lab, was licking my hand. His polite way of saying, "Don't you dolts get it? I gotta go outside—now!" Peeling Denny's arm off me, I limped out of our rear bedroom in my bare feet—boy, it felt good to walk without those annoying crutches!—circled through the dining room and kitchen, and let Willie Wonka out into the postage-stamp backyard of our two-flat. Sparrows darted and chirped in the trees along our back alley, but the usual crows were strangely silent. The West Nile virus stalking the Chicago area this summer, courtesy of ornery mosquitoes, had decimated the crow population.

Not that I missed them.

I waited at the back door for the dog to finish his business and grinned at the irony of this particular Wednesday. Getting married in *mid-August*, when the humidity in the Midwest can hover near tropic conditions, ranked as one of our stupider decisions—right up there with scheduling my two-month checkup after the car accident *today*, on our twentieth anniversary.

Though right now I didn't care. The nightmare had retreated into its dark hole and the day beckoned. I had a surprise for Denny he was going to love.

DENNY TOOK THE DAY OFF from his summer job coaching kiddy sports for the Chicago Park District to take me to my one o'clock doctor's appointment. At first I protested. "Josh can take me!" After all, what good is a seventeen-year-old with a driver's license if he can't chauffeur his parents around? Besides, a park district job doesn't have "personal days"; it's no-work-no-pay, and we were still waiting to hear if Denny's coaching contract at West Rogers High would be renewed for the 2002–2003 school year. Stupid politics.

But Denny just poured himself another cup of coffee and leered at me. "What? Work on my anniversary? Did I work on our wedding day? This family's not gonna starve if I take the day off—not till next week anyway. Besides, I want to hear what the doc says."

I took a long shower, letting the warm water run over my head long after the shampoo had rinsed out. *Thank You, Jesus, that I can wash my own hair again!* Frankly, I was doing pretty well, considering that I was minus one spleen and had a metal rod in my left leg. I didn't mind the scars on my leg so much—one about an inch long on my upper thigh and another down near my knee. Yet I was still self-conscious about the puckered pink line that ran from my

3

sternum down to my pelvis, especially when Denny and I made love. It made me feel ... damaged. And I still didn't know the consequences of walking around without a spleen. Didn't I need it? But so far I hadn't stopped breathing or anything, though Willie Wonka did look at me funny when I hobbled around the house with my stiff left leg.

And thank You, Jesus, that I didn't end up in prison! Did they have hot showers in prison? Green-apple shampoo? It had never occurred to me to wonder about that before I got charged with vehicular manslaughter. The prosecution tried for gross negligence, but the charges were dropped when no witnesses showed up at the hearing.

Grace. That's what it was. Only God's grace. It was an accident, yes. The boy had run out in front of my car in a pouring rain. Yet God knew I'd been driving angry. I was grateful—oh, so grateful!—that God had offered me mercy, forgiveness, and a legal acquittal, but . . . it was hard to forgive myself. After all, Jamal Wilkins was still dead; a mother was still grieving—

"Mom! Hurry up. I gotta baby-sit for the Fitzhughs today." I could hear fourteen-year-old Amanda rattling the bathroom door handle.

I turned off the shower, wrapped myself in a big towel, grabbed the hair dryer, and opened the door. "And happy anniversary to you, too, Mom," I said brightly in my best Amanda voice.

"Oh yeah. Happy anniversary, Mom." The tousled butterscotch hair disappeared behind the bathroom door, and I heard the lock click.

Teenagers. Amanda would be turning fifteen next week and starting her sophomore year at Lane Tech right after Labor Day. Josh would be eighteen next month, a senior. Where did the summer go?

I limped into the bedroom, toweled my wet hair, and pulled on some underwear. I knew where the summer had gone. My whole family—Denny, Josh, Amanda—had spent the last eight weeks getting Mom through surgery, through a court hearing, through recovery. My family . . . and my sisters in the Yada Yada Prayer Group.

I studied my reflection in the full-length mirror on the back of our bedroom door as I pulled on a jean skirt and white T-shirt. Who would've thought that motley prayer group from the Chicago Women's Conference last May would prop up Denny and me through the biggest crisis of our lives? *Florida Hickman* —"five years saved and five years sober!" *Avis Johnson*—the no-nonsense principal of Bethune Elementary School, where I taught third grade last year, and also the worship leader at Uptown Community Church, where Denny and I attended. *Yo-Yo Spencer*—ex-con and bagel chef, who was raising her two teenage half brothers. Plus several more "sisters" just as unlikely to end up in each other's living room.

I snorted and grinned as I flicked on the hair dryer. Only God could have put us together—and then kept us together. So far being part of the Yada Yada Prayer Group had been like riding a roller coaster without the lap bar. More than once I'd felt the group was on the verge of spinning off the planet—like when

Delores Enriques's son was shot by gangbangers while we were still at the women's conference. And when Ruth "Jewish Mama" Garfield had a falling-out with Florida Hickman over whether a foster child (Florida's daughter, to be exact) should be returned to her natural parents after such a long time. Not to mention Ms. Full-of-Herself Leslie "Stu" Stuart, a real-estate agent who had a talent for getting on my last nerve.

And then there was Adele Skuggs, big, black, and sassy, who could reduce my knees to Jell-O with one withering quip from her sharp tongue. But somehow God's hand always managed to bring us all back safely to the landing zone. So far.

I put down the hair dryer and held up a lock of limp, brown, shoulder-length hair in front of the mirror. Couldn't remember when I'd last had a haircut—before the accident anyway. Should've gotten a trim or something before my "anniversary surprise" for Denny this weekend. Oh well.

DR. LEWINSKI gave me a pretty good bill of health, but he scheduled me for physical therapy to build back the muscles in my left leg and gave me a lecture about the increased risk of infections now that my bodyguard spleen was pickled in a jar. "Bacteria that can cause pneumonia are normally filtered and killed by the body's defenses in the spleen," he said, peering over his reading glasses, which threatened to slide off the end of his long, thin nose any second. "We keep children under sixteen on prophylactic penicillin to protect them from severe life-threatening infections after a splenectomy, but"—he shrugged—"it's not routinely done for adults."

Hey, I thought. *I'm only forty-two. I'm not ready to go quietly with the "old people's friend,"* which is what my father called the pneumonia that took my grandmother. Dr. Lewinski simply cautioned me to drink lots of fluid and get plenty of rest during flu season, call my primary-care doctor if I suspected any chest congestion, and to "take care of yourself."

I'd given Denny a look. Primary-care doctor? We'd only moved to the Rogers Park neighborhood of Chicago a year ago, and finding new doctors hadn't been high on our priority list. Fact is, we hadn't seen the doctors we used to have out in the 'burbs for years. Who needs doctors when your kids are healthy teenagers and you're in your prime?

Me, I guess. Now, anyway.

Well, at least that was over. Now we could enjoy our anniversary. I glanced slyly at Denny, who was humming at the wheel of the borrowed car we were still driving while we waited for the insurance to settle on our wrecked minivan. I was sure he would take me out to dinner tonight, though he hadn't said anything about it yet. I hoped so, even though I knew our money was tight. I wasn't about to cook my own anniversary dinner—and besides, I needed a special atmosphere to spring my surprise on Denny.

I knew what he was going to say. "Jodi! We can't afford that right now." And I'd smirk and tell him I was doing sewing projects for some of the working moms at church to pay for it. But if he said, "You? Sew?" I'd throw a buttered roll at his forehead, like David bringing down Goliath.

I was so busy playing out that little scene in my head that I didn't notice we had kept going straight on Clark Street instead of turning off on Touhy Avenue. The street we lived on—Lunt Avenue—was one-way-going-the-wrong-way from Clark, which meant we always had to do this little square dance on one-way streets to get to our house. Instead, he had continued south on Clark Street, stopped, and was backing into a parking space.

I looked around at the plethora of small ethnic shops up and down Clark Street. "What's up?"

"Just be a good girl and don't ask questions." Denny came around to my side and opened the door of the old, rusted sedan.

"Okay," I grumbled, thinking this was way too early to be going out to eat—it was only two-thirty, for goodness' sake!—and besides, I didn't have my surprise along to give him.

He offered me his arm. "Close your eyes and trust me."

Oh, right. But I closed my eyes obediently and took Denny's arm, realized we were crossing the street—not at a crosswalk, because I heard horns blaring as he hustled me across—then walking down the other sidewalk at a good clip.

We stopped. I felt him pull open a door and heard a little bell ring. Where had I heard that little bell before? Yet it was the smell that gave it away—like the Tonette perms my mother used to give my grandmother back in Des Moines. What in the world?

I felt Denny's mouth brush close to my ear. "You can open your eyes."

8

I flicked open my eyes and jumped as several voices yelled, "Surprise!"

Adele Skuggs—owner and chief cosmetologist of Adele's Hair and Nails—stood smirking from behind the first chair of her shop, her hands encased in thin, plastic gloves. In the chair, Florida Hickman's hair—which for the past four months I'd only seen in perfect cornrows, braids, or tight ringlets all over her head—was sticking straight up like a bush of used Brillo pads, framing a big grin. Avis Johnson—my fifty-something boss—was sitting on Adele's vinyl couch under the front window, a copy of *Essence* on her lap and managing to look elegant even in her white slacks and embroidered denim shirt. And Leslie Stuart, otherwise known as "Stu"—the only other white woman I could see in the shop—sat in the corner chair next to the coffee cart, holding a mug of coffee and a slice of pound cake from the cake server.

All four of them were laughing at me. "Close your mouth, girl, before you trip over that bottom lip," Florida snickered.

Stu looked me up and down and shook her head. "You're right, Denny. She needs lots of help."

Oh, thanks a lot, Stu. Just what I need coming from Ms. Perfect herself. Stu wore her own straight hair long and blonde.

"Well, she's all yours, Adele." Grinning, Denny pushed me forward and backed toward the door. "Give her the works—hair, manicure, pedicure, whatever-cure. I'm taking her out on the town tonight!"

"You go, Denny!" crowed Florida as I heard the little bell over the door tinkle behind me.

2

I stood there, unsure what I was supposed to do, alternately feeling pleased at Denny's surprise and annoyed that he hadn't warned me. I should've scrubbed my feet while I was in the shower! The bottoms always got so tough and cracked in the summer from wearing sandals—

"You can sit down, Jodi," Avis said, patting the vinyl couch beside her and giving me her I'm-the-principal-but-I'm-not-going-to-bite-you look. "You're next."

Adele's big, gold earrings—like quotation marks around her short red 'fro—jangled as she resumed applying hair-straightening goo on Florida's head with a paintbrush.

"Yep." Stu washed down the last bite of her slice of pound cake with a swig of coffee. "Just relax. Don't worry about a thing." She smirked, which didn't comfort me at all. "We've already picked out your hairstyle and your nail colors."

"You're kidding, right? That's supposed to make me *not*

nervous?" I collapsed on the couch beside Avis, realizing my knees suddenly felt wobbly.

"Have some faith, girl!" Florida leaned forward in the beauty chair but was jerked back with a firm hand by Adele. "You ever see anybody walk outta here lookin' worse than when they walked in? My, my, my. You gotta trust your hairdresser."

Well, Adele wasn't exactly my hairdresser. I'd only been to her shop once before—to get my nails done on the spur of the moment. (Forty-two and I'd never had a manicure before!) Frankly, I didn't have a hairdresser. Amanda sometimes trimmed my hair, or I shelled out twelve dollars at Supercuts. Yet I had to admit that the women in Yada Yada who had started coming to Adele's Hair and Nails after we all met at the Chicago Women's Conference looked pretty spiffy after they got their hair done.

Adele peeled off her plastic gloves and said, "Leave that fifteen minutes—you watch the time." Florida grabbed a magazine and popped over to the other beauty chair in front of the long wall mirror. "In the chair, Jodi," Adele ordered.

I stood up, eyeing my friends suspiciously. Surely Avis wouldn't let Stu and Florida choose a really far-out hairdo for me—would she? "What about these guys?" I waved a hand at Stu and Avis. "Aren't they next?"

"In the chair, Jodi." Adele held the black plastic cape with all the patience of a mother counting to ten. I sat.

"I'm just here as a consultant." Stu grinned and tossed her long blonde hair over her shoulder, revealing the line of small pierced earrings running up the side of her ear.

Avis held up the back of her hand toward me, fingers spread out. "Nails. Soon as Corey gets done with her other nail appointment." Corey must be Adele's manicurist. I sucked in a tiny breath of relief. At least I didn't have to face Adele getting down and scrubbing my feet like she did the last time, which unnerved me no end.

Adele put on new plastic gloves and began wetting my hair with a spray bottle.

"Uh-huh," I said. "And how did you all *just happen* to be here all at the same time?"

"Denny thought you might need a little moral support, seeing as how we're doing a makeover here." Stu got in my face with a digital camera. "Smile! This is the 'before' picture."

When I stopped seeing stars from the flash, I glanced in the mirror. Adele was now running her fingers through my hair, holding up various lengths, and frowning, as though studying a serious scientific problem. "What happened to your other customers?"

"Huh. I can schedule whoever I want on today, 'cause I'm the boss." As though to prove her point, Boss Adele swung the chair I was sitting in away from the mirror.

"What? You're not even going to let me see what you're doing?" My protest was meant to be lighthearted, but I felt slightly panicked. Did Denny realize what he'd gotten me into? I mean, didn't Adele specialize in black folks' hair?

Adele allowed a big, rumbling chuckle. "Not to worry, Jodi. This hair can only get better. You've let this mess go too long."

Well, she had a point. Taking care of my looks hadn't exactly

13

been high on my agenda the last two months. I closed my eyes, letting myself enjoy the cool spray wetting my head and Adele's firm fingers sectioning my hair and sticking clips here and there to hold it back while she started to cut.

"So has Denny told you where he's taking you tonight?"

I popped my eyes open at Stu's question. "No." I caught looks passing between Stu and Avis and Florida. "Don't tell me he told you guys."

"Uh-huh. Sure did," they chorused.

"So tell me! Yada Yada knows where I'm going on my anniversary before I do? How fair is that?"

"Uh-uh. Sorry. Promised Denny."

Adele's firm hand pushed me against the chair back. "Sit still, Jodi, or I'll cut something you'll wish I hadn't."

Stu grinned. "No problem. You could just give her a mohawk then. Or shave it. Women do bald now."

"Sheesh," I muttered. "Some moral support you guys are. You're making me a nervous wreck."

Adele left me in mid-cut to rinse Florida's head and condition it. When they came back, Florida was wearing a perky plastic cap, and Adele stuck her under a hair dryer, cap and all. Adele picked up her scissors once more.

"Avis Johnson?" A voice called out from behind me. "Corey says you're next."

A young teenager with glowing brown skin and braided extensions passed my chair on her way out, her nails not only painted but decorated with delicate flourishes, like so many tiny flowers.

14

"Thanks, Corey," she called toward the back. "Bye, MaDear!"

"Tell your mama hi," Adele said. "And remind her to bring me that mango salsa recipe she was tellin' me about."

"I will. Bye, Miz Adele." The bell over the door tinkled as the young girl went out. Avis got up from the couch, gave me an encouraging smile, and headed toward the manicure tables in the back.

"Speaking of MaDear, how's your mom, Adele?" I tried to make conversation as snips of dark brown hair kept falling to the floor.

"Mmph. Same. Same. She's all right. Doc gave her some new kind of medicine. Makes her sleep a lot—dozin' in the rocker in back. Kinda miss the ol' spitfire, but it's easier to manage the shop when she's not so hyper."

I could well imagine that. The last time I was here, MaDear had nearly escaped out the door with her walker, muttering something about the "lousy service in this here rest'runt." The spry little woman was quite muddled in her head, though Adele wasn't sure if it was Alzheimer's disease or plain ol' dementia.

Remembering the comical scene, I almost missed what Adele said next.

" . . . just as well. She's had a hard life. Needs to rest."

I didn't know whether I should ask what she meant by "a hard life," but just then Adele walked away, so I sneaked a peek at my haircut in the mirror. Still basically shoulder length, though the ends definitely looked fresher. So that was it? Just a trim?

Adele came back with a box full of pink plastic curlers. I couldn't remember the last time I'd had curlers in my hair. Who had time for curlers? Wash, blow-dry, bye-bye—that was my motto. But I was curious. What style had this conspiracy dreamed up? Would Denny like it? Would *I* like it?

"You goin' to let my head burn off?" Florida complained from under the dryer, scratching her head through the plastic cap.

"Yep." Adele calmly began rolling strands of my hair on the big pink rollers, anchoring them to my head with long clips. "Time I get Jodi here under the dryer be just about the right time to get back to you."

I had to admit it was fun getting fussed over, sitting under one of those serious hair dryers, looking no doubt like Marge Simpson with her beehive hairdo. Then—curlers still in my hair—the young woman Corey, who was maybe all of twenty, tall and slender with cocoa-rich skin, soaked and scrubbed my feet. Then she cut my toenails and painted them a daring rich burgundy.

"Whoo, some toes." Stu eyed me critically. "You'll have to wear open-toed shoes tonight. Do you have any open-toed heels?"

By this time, everybody was hanging out in the back part of the shop, and Adele was taking a break to spoon some yogurt into her mother's birdlike mouth. Open . . . spoon . . . swallow. Open . . . spoon . . . swallow.

"Um, no. Even if I did, not sure I could wear heels yet." I was only two weeks off my crutches. The very thought of teetering on high heels made me feel unsteady.

"Oh. Right. Of course." Stu backed off. She studied my hands as Corey patiently shaped the nails, put on a base coat, stuck them in the nail dryer, and then carefully began to brush on the wine-colored nail polish. "But seems like for your twentieth anniversary—I mean, good grief, that's a real milestone!—you ought to do something really special, not just go out to dinner. Take a cruise or something."

My turn to smirk. "We are."

That got even Adele's attention as the spoon she held paused in midair. Four voices chorused, "You are?"

"Well, not a *cruise*. Though I've been planning my own surprise for Denny."

"What? What?" Florida pulled a pout. "Girl, you shouldn't be keepin' anything from us."

"Oh, right. You should talk," I shot back, but I was grinning. Even Avis was still looking at me, waiting for the revelation.

"If any of you dare breathe a word of this to Denny . . ."

"Us? Breathe?" Florida looked offended. "Did we tell *you* about Denny's makeover surprise?"

Had to admit they'd kept me in the dark. In fact, I still didn't have a clue what my hair was going to look like or where Denny and I were going tonight.

"Well then." I took a triumphant breath, smiling at my own secret. "I have reservations at Starved Rock Lodge out near Utica for this weekend—two nights in one of their cozy log cabins, breakfast and dinner in the rustic lodge. Plus a swimming pool, hiking trails—it's gorgeous out there. We camped in Starved Rock campgrounds when the kids were younger, and I've always wanted to go back and stay in the lodge . . ."

I realized all four of my friends from Yada Yada were just staring at me. "What?"

Florida screwed up her face. "Girl, you tellin' me you takin' that hunk man of yours to a *log cabin* for your anniversary?" She turned to the others. "Now I know Jodi Baxter is outta her mind."

"What's wrong with that? Denny will love it!"

Stu rolled her eyes. Avis's mouth twitched. Adele just shook her head and slid another spoonful of yogurt into MaDear's mouth.

"Girl, now, you shoulda axed us for some advice." Florida, her head full of small, finger-size curlers, folded her arms across her small bosom. "For your anniversary, you go to one of them downtown hotels—"

"Like the Wyndham or the Drake," Stu cut in.

"Yeah, one of them fancy ones. You ask 'em for the honeymoon suite; you soak in the spa . . ."

"If you want 'back to nature,' you can take one of those horse-drawn carriage rides around the Magnificent Mile." That was Adele's contribution.

"All right, all right. I get it." But I was unmoved. "You wait and see. Denny will love my surprise and will promise to adore me for another twenty years."

For just a flicker of a second, a hint of pain clouded Avis's eyes, and I winced at my thoughtlessness. Avis and her Conrad had celebrated their twentieth anniversary with a cruise to the Caribbean, but he had died of cancer a few short years later. There would be no fortieth anniversary for the Johnsons. Yet the cloud passed and she jumped up, reaching for the almost-empty carton of yogurt. "Let me do that, Adele. Let's see what these beauties look like when you do the comb-outs."

With maddening casualness, Adele put Florida in the chair first, took out all the little curlers, and swept up a cascade of coppery ringlets on top of her head, anchoring them firmly with a crown of pins. Florida preened and strutted in front of the mirror then heaved an exaggerated sigh. "All dressed up and no place to go."

"Move, girl," said Stu. "Let's see what miracles Adele hath wrought with Jodi."

Once again, Adele swung the chair so my back was to the mirror. I could feel my hair spring and bounce as the curlers came out. Florida, Stu, and Avis stood front and sides, tilting their heads sideways, saying, "Mmm-hmm" or just nodding, making me as nervous as a turkey in November.

Then to my surprise, I could feel Adele twisting the sides and top of my hair, anchoring whatever-it-was with pins, then brushing and arranging and spraying the back. After thirty nerve-wracking minutes, she turned my chair around, facing the mirror.

I could hardly believe my reflection. Some other girl—yes, *girl*—from another lifetime looked back at me. Not the haggard Jodi Baxter who'd recently had major surgery, who woke several times a week from nightmares related to that awful accident, who'd worn the same basic hairstyle for the last ten years.

No, this Jodi was almost youthful . . . and pretty, even if I was only a month shy of my forty-third birthday. Little rows of twists—not braids or cornrows—covered the sides and top of my head, then a small crown of sparkling pins announced the rest of my hair falling in soft waves down to my shoulders.

"Wow," I said.

Stu grinned. "You look great, Jodi. You really do." She fished out her camera. "Hold still for the 'after' picture."

"Wait!" Florida made a beeline for the front window. "Ain't that your wreck parking across the street, Jodi? Denny's coming!"

My heart actually started to pound like a sixteen-year-old about to meet her prom date.

"Get that cape off her," Stu ordered Adele, which was kind of cheeky, but Adele pulled off the plastic cape and let me stand up. "Come on, come on, Avis! Denny's coming."

"Don't let him in till I get there," Avis called from the back. "I'm bringing MaDear with me."

It was all too silly and funny and . . . wonderful. Would Denny like it? He had to! It was his idea. And to be honest, I hadn't looked this gorgeous in years.

Avis and MaDear joined the rest of us just as the bell tinkled over the door and Denny walked in, grinning foolishly, just like he had on our wedding day. "Oh my," he said. "Oh my, Jodi, you look absolutely—"

Denny never got to finish his sentence, because just then MaDear let out a horrible howl, like a cat with its tail slammed in a door. "You! You!" she screeched, raising her thin arm and pointing a shaking claw at Denny. "Git 'im outta this house!" With lightning speed, she grabbed a brush from Adele's supplies and hurled it through the air at Denny's head. The brush found its mark before Denny had time to react, cracking him on the forehead before it fell to the floor.

"MaDear!" Adele grabbed for her mother, but the old lady shook her off.

"Ain't you caused enough trouble, boy? How *dare* you come back here—an' with po' Larry hardly cold in his grave! Out! Out! Git out!" Adele's mother grabbed another missile—a hand mirror this time—and let it fly.

3

This time Denny did duck, and the hand mirror shattered against the front door. The blood had drained out of his face, and his mouth hung open.

The rest of us stood glued to the floor, stunned. Adele finally got her big arms around her mother in a body lock, but MaDear was putting up a good fight. "Git 'im out! Git 'im out!" she continued to screech, flailing her bony arms—and then she started to cry. "No-o-o . . . noooooooo. Not agin . . ."

Thoughts skittered like water bugs through my brain. *What's she talking about? What set her off? Why Denny? Who's Larry?*

"Everybody just leave," Adele ordered gruffly, wrestling the tiny woman toward the back room. "Go on. *Go.* 'Cept Avis. Avis, come on back and help me."

"But . . ." Denny reached for his wallet, his face stricken. "I haven't paid for . . . for—"

Florida stepped toward Denny and stopped him. "Don't worry

23

'bout that now, Denny. Come on, do what Adele says. Come on Jodi . . . Stu." Florida pulled open the door of the beauty salon and practically pushed Denny outside. Stu and I grabbed our purses and followed on their heels.

The four of us stood on the sidewalk, just out of sight of the salon's front window, and looked stupidly at one another. Denny gingerly touched the red mark on his forehead where the brush had clipped him. "What happened in there?"

Stu shook her head, mouth twisting in disgust. "It's just MaDear. She's nuts."

"Maybe." Florida's eyes narrowed. "But I think somethin' else was going on."

"Like what?" My initial shock was starting to thaw, and anger was bubbling up in its place. *Thanks, thanks a lot, MaDear, for ruining Denny's makeover surprise.* And, *That woman's dangerous! Adele should put her in an institution—under lock and key.*

Florida shook her head, setting her new crown of little ringlets dancing. "I dunno. She's confused, sure 'nough, but there's somethin' . . . somethin' real behind what just happened. Know what I'm sayin'?"

No, I didn't know what she was saying. MaDear's little tantrum had popped my bubble, and I was having a hard time getting back my enthusiasm for the day. Our day. Denny's and mine . . .

I looked at Denny. His shoulders were hunched, his hands shoved in the pockets of his Dockers, looking for all the world like one of Peter Pan's lost boys, in spite of the gray flecks in his dark hair. My anger softened. "You okay, Denny?"

He pinched his lips together and nodded, but he didn't look okay. He looked . . . distressed. Troubled.

"So, Denny." Stu shifted gears. "What do you think of our girl?" She took hold of my shoulders and turned me around. I almost shrugged off her hands, but it worked. Denny's face relaxed a bit into a smile.

"I like it. You . . ." The smile got bigger. "You look great, Jodi. Really great."

"All right!" Florida gave Stu a high-five. "Didn't I say you gotta trust your hairdresser? And your friends."

"Yeah," I admitted. Denny's sweet words soothed my ruffled spirit. "Yeah, thanks a lot, you guys."

"No problem, no problem." Florida laid it on thick. "Anything to help a friend. And you sure did need help, girl."

"Enough already, Florida! Stop while you're ahead!" I pulled a face, making her laugh.

"All right, all right." She grabbed Stu and started off down the sidewalk. "You two lovebirds have a good time tonight, ya hear?"

I watched them go, realizing that Stu had to go all the way back to Oak Park, west of the city, and Florida must have come straight after getting off her shift at the post office. They'd really put themselves out for me today. Avis too.

Denny checked his watch. "Hey, it's already past five. I got dinner reservations for seven. We better get home so I can make myself presentable. Don't want people thinking, 'What's that chick see in that old man?'"

I giggled like a teenager, flattered by the silly compliment—

and suddenly realized how patient Denny had been with my banged-up self the last few months. "So where are we going, Mr. Tambourine Man? You're full of surprises today."

The color had returned to his face—the dimples, too, creasing the sides of his face when he smiled. "Oh, thought we might go to the Bagel Bakery where Yo-Yo works, try out their kugel—ouch! I'm kidding!"

He deserved the punch on the shoulder. "I mean, where are we going *really?*"

Denny took my elbow and propelled me across the street, prompting another horn-blowing serenade. "Wouldn't you like to know? Guess you'll have to come with me to find out."

I WAS WORRIED that Denny might think he had to spend a hundred dollars on a five-star restaurant to make it a special date—especially since he didn't know yet that I'd already charged the Starved Rock Lodge on our credit card. The last time we'd tried out one of those super-fancy restaurants downtown (our tenth anniversary?—probably), we tried not to stare open-mouthed when the tuxedoed waiter put a huge plate in front of each of us with three long green beans artistically arranged on one side, a two-inch-thick "steak medallion" the size of a cookie cutter ("But wrapped in bacon!" Denny had pointed out), and half of a twice-baked potato, whipped up like a Dairy Queen. The food—what there was of it—had been melt-in-your-mouth tasty, but we decided the chef must be a former magazine editor who liked lots of "white space." Only the check came with generous portions.

So I was relieved when Denny ushered me into the Ethiopian Diamond Restaurant on Broadway Avenue. I should have guessed. Some of our friends had been recommending it for months. ("The food is to die for! And the portions are huge!" "So authentic! Lots of atmosphere.") The waiters were all Ethiopian, flashing bright-white smiles, and eager to explain the menu, which offered appetizers like *sambusas* (dough shells stuffed with vegetables or meat) and entrees like *gomen watt* (collard greens simmered in garlic and ginger sauce) and *kitfo* (seasoned steak tartare). There were no utensils on the white tablecloths, and I soon realized why by watching other diners, who were tearing off pieces of a pancakelike bread ("injera," our waiter informed us) and dipping it into the various bowls of stews and vegetables.

Denny and I held hands across the small table in the corner of the main room, where we had a good view of the five large paintings around the walls depicting scenes from different parts of Ethiopia. "This is great." I grinned. "Good choice." *Except for the eating-with-our-fingers part,* I thought, wondering if my newly painted fingernails would survive the meal. Denny looked delicious—open-necked black knit shirt, tan pants, and a wheat-colored sport coat setting off the even tan he got running around blowing whistles at peewee soccer players all summer. I wore the black slinky dress I'd borrowed for the Chicago Women's Conference last May but never got to wear. At least this time I got dressed up for my man, not for five hundred women I didn't even know. Even Josh had whistled at my new look. But Amanda said, "Mo-om! Didn't you borrow that dress from Sheila Fitzhugh? You better give it back *soon*, or she's gonna dock it from my babysitting money!"

I felt guilty for about one second. Yes, I would return it—tomorrow. Tonight I was going to enjoy feeling like a "babe."

Our waiter, whose name sounded like "Belay Wuhib," set down the steaming bowls of spicy lamb, strips of marinated steak, hummus, and vegetables we'd ordered, along with the ever-present injera flat bread and small dishes of cucumber and lentil salad in spicy vinegar, and we fell to. Between dripping bites, I prattled on about our wedding weekend twenty years ago when Denny's sophisticated Episcopalian parents from New York met my very conservative mom and dad in Des Moines, Iowa, for the first time, somewhat akin to a summit of East meets West. *Now* it was funny, but back then, it was hard to tell who was more shocked: the New York Baxters, trying without success to envision a wedding reception in the basement fellowship hall of the plain, nondenominational church my family attended, or the Midwestern Jennings, stuttering in dismay when Denny's folks offered to purchase the wine and beer for the reception "dinner." "Oh, uh, that won't be necessary," my mother had spluttered. "We're, um, well, there's not really a dinner, just simple refreshments with Red Zinger Tea punch—it's really good." I almost choked on a piece of injera bread, remembering how Denny and I had howled later.

Denny didn't smile, just nodded absently and said, "Uh-huh." In fact, I realized that for the past ten minutes I had been doing all the talking.

I picked up the cloth napkin and wiped my mouth. "Earth to Denny." At least that got his attention. "Are you okay?"

He leaned back in his chair and sighed. "Sorry, babe. It's just . . ."

I waited, but he'd already retreated behind his eyes.

"Denny, talk to me." I reached across the table and took one of his hands. "Is it what happened this afternoon at Adele's shop?"

He sighed. "I just can't get it out of my mind. She was so angry at me, and I don't have a clue about why."

"Well, it's obvious—I mean, she's got you mixed up with some-body else. It's not *you* she's mad at, Denny. I know it's upsetting—we were all upset—but you can't take it personally." *Or I'll get upset that a little old woman suffering from dementia is messing with our anniversary.*

"I know that—in my head, anyway. But *who* is she so angry at—and why? And why does she think whoever-it-is is me?"

I didn't want to think about MaDear and her problems—prob-ably part of her "hard life" Adele referred to this afternoon. Whatever it was, it was past, nothing to be done about it—at least, nothing *we* could do about it.

I patted his hand, feeling more like Mother Hen reassuring Chicken Little than Denny's lover-friend-wife of twenty years. "Look, we'll call Adele tomorrow and ask if she's figured out what's going on with her mother, okay? Maybe that'll help you put it aside."

Denny nodded, though he didn't seem at all sure. I decided it was time to spring my surprise. Hopefully that would take his mind off MaDear's tantrum this afternoon.

I reached into my shoulder bag, pulled out an envelope, and slid it across the table. Denny looked at the envelope then looked up at me. "What's this?"

"Open it." I smiled, feeling impish and smug that I'd managed to pull off a surprise, too, in spite of crutches and being stuck in the house most of the summer. God bless Web sites that let you make reservations online.

Denny pulled out the paper and unfolded it. A good fifteen seconds went by as he read. I sucked in my breath. Maybe he didn't like the idea after all, like my Yada Yada "advisers" today had predicted. Then Denny looked up . . . and grinned.

"You rascal. When did you plan this?"

I let out my breath. "Several weeks ago—soon after the trial. I wanted to do something special to thank you for . . . for standing by me through, you know, everything."

His eyes registered pain. "Oh, Jodi, don't. Don't thank *me* for anything." He leaned forward and took both my hands, looking in my eyes so intensely I could almost feel their heat. "I've been to hell and back because of that stupid fight we had that day. But God has seen us through, *is* seeing us through, and you've forgiven me and . . ."

"Oh, Denny. You're not still blaming yourself, are you? It was *me* . . ."

We both just looked at each other, overwhelmed at the memories and feelings that were still healing. A stupid fight . . . me, late for a Yada Yada meeting, driving angry . . . a drenching thunderstorm . . . and now, a boy was dead. Charges had been filed against me: manslaughter with gross negligence. If the Yada Yada Prayer Group hadn't held both of us and showed us how much God loves us, even when—*especially* when—we don't deserve it, we might not have made it even this far.

"If you want to thank somebody, Jodi, thank God." Denny's voice was husky. "Where would we be without grace?"

I swallowed. The waiter cleared our dishes while we sat holding hands without speaking. "Coffee?" he asked. "Dessert?"

"Just coffee." Somehow the simple words dislodged the lump in my throat. We had to go forward, and forward at this moment meant Starved Rock this coming weekend—just Denny and me, no kids, no dog, no laundry, no cars gunning their engines at two in the morning, no apartment buildings crowding out the sun.

"Okay, my thanks go to God," I agreed, "but it's *you* I'm taking to Starved Rock Lodge. Deal?"

This time he laughed. "Deal."

4

*D*enny was up early and back to work on Thursday, leaving me with a second cup of coffee and a quiet house—momentarily at least, till the kids got up. I sat on the back porch steps, enjoying the relative coolness of early morning in the wake of a nighttime thunderstorm, mentally reviewing what I needed to do in the next two days in order to be gone for the weekend. I'd made the reservation for Friday and Saturday nights, but the earliest Denny could get off would be five o'clock on Friday. Day camps started early and ran late as zillions of Chicagoans parked their kids in summer programs—sports camps, arts camps, drama camps, sailing camps, a little-bit-of-everything camps—filling every moment of every day with activity.

Whatever happened to lazy summer days watching ants on the sidewalk, sucking "Popsicles" your mom made in little plastic freezer molds, or playing question-answer games with your best friend while swinging on the deserted school playground swings?

Probably a myth by now, created in simpler times when kids had daddies, and moms stayed home. Summer day camps were no doubt better than all those kids sitting in front of the television all summer.

Denny and I had always been grateful we both had school-year jobs that let at least one of us be home when the kids were out of school. Yet now that they were both teenagers, it drove me a little nuts that Josh and Amanda could easily sleep till noon if we let them. I wasn't a big fan of hanging out at the mall either. Denny solved that little problem by stopping their allowance in the summer. Any spending money they wanted they had to earn.

So far it was working pretty good with soon-to-be-fifteen Amanda. She kept up quite a cash flow with baby-sitting and "mother's helper" jobs—mostly families from Uptown Community Church. She enjoyed the independence of buying her own clothes and not having to beg us for money when she got invited to Six Flags Great America.

Josh was a different story. By the time he and Amanda got back from the youth-group mission trip to Mexico in July, most of the available summer jobs had been taken. Denny got him on as a sub at the park district, but so far that had only averaged one day a week of actual employment at pitiful wages. And the ancient garage behind our house had only so many sides that could be painted in one summer. I loved my tall, gangly son, but Willie Wonka was plenty when it came to inert bodies lying around the house.

One good thing: my recovery from the accident and lame leg

finally forced the kids to do their own laundry. We probably pushed up the water bill doing it that way instead of combining loads, but it was worth it. I'd been guilty of either nagging them to death about their laundry or finally giving up with an okay-I'll-do-it-myself martyr complex. But now? Couldn't do it; I couldn't do the basement stairs. If *they* didn't do their laundry, they had to wear it dirty. Ha!

Sometimes I wondered why it took a big crisis in my life to get some simple stuff straight, like not doing chores my kids should be doing.

On the other hand, they'd be happy doing some things for themselves I wasn't ready for yet—like staying home alone this weekend while Denny and I went away for our anniversary. I knew they'd both nix the idea of having somebody come to stay at the house. I could hear them now: "Mo-om! We're too big for a baby-sitter!"—though Amanda might acquiesce if I suggested Edesa Reyes, the black Honduran university student in the Yada Yada Prayer Group who tutored her in Spanish. Amanda and Edesa had hit it off big-time, but Josh was just old enough (seventeen) and Edesa just young enough (a very attractive twenty-one) that *that* didn't seem appropriate. Not for a whole weekend. I decided against it.

I heard the bathroom door bang back in the house. Shoot. I'd missed my chance for a leisurely shower. I better get off my duff and get on the phone. "Come on, Willie," I said to the dog, who was already into his morning nap on the back porch. "Let's put some rubber under these wheels."

TEN DISCOURAGING PHONE CALLS LATER—was everybody we knew out of town this weekend?—it was Amanda who came up with a solution that made everybody happy. Well, almost everybody. "Edesa said I could come spend a weekend with her sometime, Mom. I'd love to visit her church—it's in Spanish! And I'd get to see the Enriques kids too. Just ask her. I'm sure she'll say yes."

I couldn't help but smile. Amanda had quickly taken on the role of honorary "big sister" to several of the kids whose mothers were part of Yada Yada. Maybe this would work, though I felt a little nervous at Amanda spending a whole weekend on the Near West Side. José Enriques, Delores's teenage son, had been shot in a park in Little Village—only a mile from where Edesa lived— while we were at the Chicago Women's Conference, an event that solidified our ad-hoc conference prayer group into an ongoing prayer filibuster. Yet I knew Avis or Florida would say, "We can't live in fear!" So I dialed Edesa's number.

By the time Denny got home that evening, I'd walked over to the Fitzhughs' to return Sheila's dress, Edesa had agreed to keep Amanda for the weekend, and Josh had argued reasonably that he should stay home because "somebody's got to take care of Willie Wonka." Which was true.

Denny thought it was a good plan—until I told him Edesa offered to bring Amanda back on the El Sunday afternoon. "She and Delores are coming up anyway for Yada Yada—we're meeting at Nony's house." Denny frowned. "Uh, I offered to give Edesa and Delores a ride to Yada Yada after she brings Amanda back—

it's the least I can do." Nony Sisulu-Smith was hosting Yada Yada's bimonthly meeting this week at her home in north Evanston near Northwestern University, where her husband was a professor. I wanted to see where she lived. The only other time Yada Yada met at Nony's, I never made it.

Denny's frown deepened. "Did Dr. Lewinski say you could start driving yet?"

I shrugged. To tell the truth, I didn't want to get behind the wheel again ever, but I had to sometime. "Isn't the wreck we're driving an automatic? I should be okay. There's nothing wrong with my right leg."

"Going to Yada Yada just seems a bit much after a weekend away," he grumbled.

Ah. So that was it. I let it pass. Denny had apologized for getting jealous of our diminished Sunday evenings together, now that the Yada Yada Prayer Group had decided to meet every other week, but he still struggled.

After supper, Josh took off for Touhy Park to shoot some hoops, and Amanda had another baby-sitting job. I was feeling pretty accomplished lining up the weekend when Denny asked, "Did you call Adele today?"

I looked at him stupidly. I'd totally forgotten.

He winced. "This is important to me, Jodi. Maybe I should just call her myself."

I could tell he was frustrated—even more so when he had to go hunting for the phone, which he finally found in Amanda's room. I got him Adele's number and apologized for forgetting to call—

but to tell the truth, I felt relieved he was going to do it. What would I have said anyway? *"Say, Adele, got any explanation for why MaDear went off on Denny yesterday? Nice little fiasco."*

Denny dialed Adele's number, but I could tell from the tone of his voice that he just got her answering machine. "Uh, Adele? Denny Baxter here. Could you give me a call? I need some help understanding what happened yesterday with MaDear. I hope she's okay. Thanks." He hung up and stared at the phone.

"I'm sure she'll call you back," I encouraged, rubbing his shoulders. I certainly hoped so—tonight, while he was still home.

Yet Adele hadn't called by the time Denny left for work the next morning, taking Josh with him, who'd gotten a call at 6:30 a.m. to sub. So he asked if I'd please call the beauty salon and talk to Adele.

I thought of a half-dozen things I *had* to do before I could call Adele, but I eventually ran out of excuses. I picked up the phone.

"Adele's Hair and Nails," said a young voice. Sounded like Corey, the girl who did nails.

"Um . . . hi, Corey. Is Adele available? This is Jodi Baxter."

"Just a minute."

I could hear a CD playing in the background and indistinct voices. Then Corey came back on. "She's with a customer right now."

"She's with a customer right now." That was it? Not, *"Can she call you back?"*

I stumbled. "Uh, okay. I'll try again." *Dolt!* I scolded myself. *You should have left a message for her to call.* Well, I hadn't, so I'd just have to try again later. But how did I know when she'd be free?

I was packing the clothes Denny had washed last night when I heard the phone ring and Amanda pick up. "Mom! For you."

Whaddya know, I thought. Adele had called back after all. Yet when I said, "Hello? This is Jodi," it was Avis on the line.

"Hi," she said. "Just wanted to say good-bye before you and Denny take off for the wilderness this weekend. Will you be back in time for Yada Yada Sunday evening?"

"Yeah, planning to." I rattled off our weekend plans, including driving Edesa up to Nony's after she brought Amanda home. "You can pray for me! First time behind the wheel since—you know."

"You'll be fine." There was a slight pause. "You and Denny okay after what happened Wednesday?"

"Yeah." *Okay, Jodi, be honest.* "Well, maybe not. Denny is still pretty upset. He tried to call Adele last night to talk about it but only got her machine. He wants me to call today. I did once, but she was busy. Was going to try again in a while."

Another pause. "I'm not sure that's a good idea. You might want to give it a rest for a few days—at least till you get back from Starving Lodge or wherever you're going. Adele might be ready to talk about it then . . . but I'm not sure."

At any other time I would have guffawed at Avis's misstatement about Starved Rock, but something in her hesitation to have us talk to Adele set off alarm bells in my brain. I mean, I thought Adele would probably apologize for her mother's tantrum, assure Denny that he was just a victim of his mother's dementia, and say that MaDear didn't even remember it had happened. Surely that's what Denny needed to hear. So why . . .

"What do you mean?" My tone was sharper than I intended it to be. Then it suddenly occurred to me that Avis knew. She'd stayed behind to help Adele with MaDear; now she was urging us to "give it a rest" and not push Adele on it. "Avis, what's going on? Why did MaDear freak out when Denny showed up at the shop? Why doesn't Adele want to talk to us about it?"

"I think Adele should be the one—"

"You just said Adele doesn't want to talk about it," I was dangerously close to shouting, "but that leaves Denny and me hanging, filling in the blanks with . . . with . . . I don't know what!" I had no idea what she was talking about, but knowing my active imagination and Denny's despondency over what happened, I was pretty sure we could work up a pretty good stew over it.

"All right. I'll tell you what Adele told me, but promise me you won't try to talk to Adele about it just yet. Give her some time."

I tried to control my voice. "Okay. I promise."

As Avis filled me in on what happened after we left Adele's Hair and Nails last Wednesday, I slowly slid down the doorjamb of the kitchen doorway that I'd been leaning against until I was sitting on the floor, my elbow on my knee, my head in my hand.

When she finished I hardly knew what to say. Finally I whispered, "Okay. Thanks, Avis." I clicked the Off button and just sat in the doorway, hardly noticing Willie Wonka's wet nose in my face.

How was I ever going to tell Denny?

5

*I*t took us almost an hour to get out of Chicago that evening—and that was *after* we dropped off Amanda at Edesa's apartment on the Near West Side.

Denny walked Amanda into the apartment building, carrying her sport bag of clothes for the weekend while she clutched her pillow and threadbare Snoopy dog she still slept with at fourteen. I watched from the car, double-parked in the street, as she waved and disappeared into the foyer. A few minutes later Denny was back. "Everything okay?" I asked.

"Uh-huh." He eased the clunker down the on-ramp into traffic on the Eisenhower Expressway as we headed back toward the Dan Ryan, where we would pick up I-55 heading south.

I bit my lip. Didn't he know when I ask if everything is "okay," what I really want to know is what Edesa said when they got to her door, and what he said, and did Amanda say good-bye or send any messages back to me? Did she seem nervous or anxious about us going away?

Probably not. What was one measly weekend when she'd weathered two weeks in Mexico without Mom and Dad just fine?

Friday night traffic was snarly as usual, with construction on I-55 backing things up for miles. I doled out turkey sandwiches and carrot sticks as we crept along behind a big truck, reading and rereading the stupid little sign on the back that said, "How's my driving?" and an 800 number.

"Did you bring your cell phone?" I asked.

"Uh . . . no. Why? We don't need it, do we?"

Denny had gotten the cell phone when I came home from the hospital so I could reach him anytime if I needed him during the long weeks of recovery. We hadn't used it much. I didn't think he even took it to work anymore.

"Oh, just thought I'd call that 800 number on the back of the truck. Do you think anyone ever does?"

Normally Denny would have laughed out loud at that. Even handed over the phone if he'd thought to bring it. But he just said, "Oh" and sank back into the silence that had hunkered in the car with us ever since we dropped off Amanda.

I rolled down the window, trying to catch what little breeze was created at fifteen miles per hour. My own mood that day had alternated between excited, worried, and ticked off. I'd really been looking forward to getting away with Denny, had been planning this Starved Rock getaway for weeks. But right now I felt like Pigpen in a *Charlie Brown* comic strip, walking around with a rain cloud over my head. A *big* rain cloud.

When Denny got home from work, I'd had stuff for the weekend all ready to go—two duffle bags, books to read, Bible and journal, swimsuits, Josh's portable CD player, sandwiches for the car, a cooler of lunch food so we didn't have to eat in the lodge dining room for every meal. I knew Denny still had to shower and change clothes before we could take off, but Amanda was raring to go, which helped. I dreaded the conversation about Adele and MaDear, arguing with myself all afternoon whether I should dump it all in his lap and get it over with, or put it off as long as possible. I knew I should feel bad for MaDear, but mostly I felt mad that we had to deal with this at all.

The first thing Denny did when he got home was ask if the mail had come. What he meant was, did he get anything from the Board of Education? School would be starting in a couple of weeks, and he still hadn't heard whether he'd been cut or retained. Didn't blame him for being frustrated. He'd started putting out résumés, but I could tell his heart wasn't in it. He was still hoping to go back to West Rogers High and pick up with the guys in the sports programs he'd been coaching all last year.

Yet Friday's mail had only contained the usual weekend ads, the gas bill, more medical bills from my surgery, and a note from my mother, saying she was feeling better now and maybe they'd come to visit for my birthday.

At least that was a good month away. I'd worry about that later.

As we had loaded the car, I'd decided to take the initiative. *"Oh. Tried to call Adele at the salon, but she never returned my call."* Denny frowned, but I'd just left it there. It wasn't a good time to tell him about Avis's call anyway, not with Amanda in the car.

Whatever was eating Denny obviously hadn't been left behind with the dirty pile of clothes he'd stripped off before his shower. He punched on the car radio, filling the moody silence with WBBM news discussing the latest tense negotiations with Iraq about UN weapons inspections. I waited till we finally made it onto I-80 heading west, where traffic opened up, the speedometer climbed, the air began to cool, and the sinking sun colored the high cirrus clouds like children with sidewalk chalk. When a string of commercials announced the top of the hour, I reached over and turned off the radio.

"Denny? Talk to me."

He glanced sideways, a rueful smile breaking his stony expression. "Sorry, babe." He jutted his chin toward the horizon. "Don't get to see a sunset like that too often. S'pose we could catch a sunrise over Lake Michigan, if we got up early enough, but—"

"Denny." I nailed him with a look. "I mean, talk to me about what you're thinking. This is supposed to be an anniversary getaway, but I feel like I'm riding with a robot, and you're"—I waved my hand in little circles—"off in la-la land."

He sighed. "Sorry, Jodi. Don't mean to be a wet blanket. It's just . . . I don't know. I feel like I should be home combing the want ads, searching the Net, sending out résumés, whatever. I'm kicking myself that I've waited so long to look for another job, but I kept hoping that no news was good news."

"I know." I turned my head away, watching golden cornfields zipping past. Half my mind wanted to scream, *It's just two measly days! If you wanted to sit home with the want ads, what about last weekend?!"* The other half of me realized I'd been ignoring the whole looming job disaster too. No way could we make it as a family on just my salary teaching third grade. Not with college on the horizon for Josh next year. Even without college! But, just like Denny, I'd kept hoping.

Behind the wheel, Denny cleared his throat. "And don't take this wrong, but . . . gotta admit I'm worried about the money—for this getaway, I mean. It's a great idea," he added hastily, "but I didn't know you were planning something, and with the 'salon surprise' and dinner at the Diamond and all . . ."

I put my smile on high beam. "Aha. That's one worry you can cross off your list. I'm paying for this weekend myself, with sewing projects I've been getting from some of the busy moms at Uptown—mending, table runners, curtains, stuff like that. Already got enough to pay for one night. One to go."

He turned to me, jaw dropping. "You? Sew?"

I grabbed a carrot stick and would have thrown it, but I didn't think braining him was worth sending the car across the median and piling into oncoming traffic.

"See?" I teased. "Twenty years married and there's still stuff about me you don't know."

He laughed then, and the last of the uncomfortable silence blew out somewhere on I-80. I scooted over as close as my seat belt and the console between the seats would allow and kissed the dimple on his cheek. Now maybe we could enjoy this weekend.

Yet one nagging thought tugged at me. I still hadn't told him about my talk with Avis about Adele and MaDear.

A CARVED SCULPTURE OF A BALD EAGLE greeted us as we drove into the lodge parking lot around eight-thirty, a half-hour before the dining room closed. Two dinners were included in our weekend package, so I convinced Denny we should take advantage of it before we even checked in. Didn't work. We had to have dinner vouchers from the front desk. So I left him to order salads and entrees in the rustic pine dining room while I hustled to the main desk and got us checked in.

When I came back with the vouchers, he was sitting at a small wooden table, lit only by a dimly burning candle lamp, sipping one of two glasses of red wine. I hesitated. Did I forget to tell him that drinks *weren't* included? And besides, this would be the first time alcohol had appeared on our table since the argument that led—

He cocked an eyebrow at me, reading my mind. "I know. Drinks not included. This is on me." He grinned and raised his glass. "To us. Twenty years."

I sat, wishing he hadn't, but he reached across the table and took my hand. "Thanks, Jodi, for . . ." He glanced around the lovely room, almost empty of diners now, with its big stone fireplace, wooden rafters, wilderness paintings, and stuffed game heads. "For this. We've needed to get away. Even with the job thing hanging over my head. This is good."

I relaxed. This was good. Even the wine was good. Our celebration. And no one had to drive anywhere.

Our waiter—a suntanned college-age kid, probably working at the state park for the summer—hovered over us, whisking away every dish the moment the last bite made it into our mouths. They wanted to close up. When we shook our heads at the dessert menu ("Dessert not included"), he seemed visibly relieved. We let him clear the table, and Denny paid for the wine, but still we lingered.

Suck it up, Jodi. You can't avoid telling Denny much longer.

"Denny?" I hated to break the mood, but carrying it alone was starting to eat at me. We needed to be able to talk about it. "I called Adele at her shop, like you wanted me to, but they said she was busy, and she didn't call back."

"I know. You told me."

I forced myself to keep looking at his face, even though I was twisting the starch out of the napkin in my lap.

"But I did learn something. Avis called. So I told her we'd been trying to call Adele but hadn't connected yet—remember Avis stayed behind to help Adele with MaDear after she freaked out? Avis got kinda funny, suggested we let it rest for a while."

Denny's eyes narrowed. "Why?"

"That's what I wanted to know, but you know Avis; she doesn't want to gossip. I told her that put us in a hard place—Adele doesn't want to talk to us, but we don't know why. Like it was our fault."

"And?"

I folded and unfolded my napkin. Anything to postpone saying what I had to say.

"Jodi. What did Avis say?"

"She said . . . she said that when MaDear was a little girl down in Mississippi, only her name wasn't MaDear, of course. Sally, I think. She was only ten or eleven, and her older brother . . ." *Oh God, help me.* It had been hard enough to hear the words, but saying them

. . . I could hardly push them out of my mouth. "A bunch of men—white men—came to their farm one night and dragged her big brother—his name was Larry—out of the house, yelling something about talking disrespectful or uppity or . . . or something. The family was terrified, and the next morning they went looking for him. And they found him, in the woods . . . strung up in a tree. Only fifteen. Lynched."

I dared to look at Denny's face. He didn't seem to be breathing.

After a few silent moments, he croaked, "And the other day, MaDear thought . . ."

I nodded, feeling miserable. "Thought you were one of the men who killed her brother, come back to get her—little Sally."

6

*D*enny spent the rest of the evening in a numb silence. I didn't blame him. What was there to say? I finally gave up the idea of cozy conversation and fell asleep over the novel I brought along.

When I woke up the next morning, sunlight and leafy shadows were dancing through the windows of the log cabin that was ours for the weekend. I stretched . . . and realized the other side of the bed was empty.

I sat up. "Denny?"

No answer. And the door to the tiny bathroom was wide open. I raised my voice. "Denny!"

"Out here." His muffled voice came from the other side of the cabin's one and only door.

My left leg ached with its usual morning stiffness as I pulled on a pair of shorts under my sleep shirt and limped outside in my bare feet. Denny was sitting in a rustic Adirondack chair, cradling a large Styrofoam cup of coffee.

"Here." He reached down beside the chair and came up with a second Styrofoam cup. "Hope it's still hot."

Now this is nice. I lowered my body gingerly into a second wooden lounge chair and took a sip of the black coffee. The "Pioneer" cabins—as opposed to the "Deluxe" cabins—had no stone fireplace and no TV, and they were farther away from the lodge, but I figured, it's August! Too hot for a fireplace. And we had better things to do than park ourselves in front of a television. Besides, these were cheaper.

None of the cabins had kitchenettes, though. "Where'd you get the coffee?"

"Coffee shop."

We sat in silence for a while, with just the sound of the leaves whispering secrets and bird songs dipping and trilling.

"Did Avis say anything else?"

Denny's question shot out of the blue, like time had collapsed and we were still in the lodge dining room, still talking about Avis's phone call. It took me a minute to transition from peaceful-morning-with-coffee to the shadow that had obviously been lurking in Denny's soul all night.

"Anything else?" I repeated.

"Like why she thinks we shouldn't talk to Adele about it."

"Oh." I tried to remember. At the time, I'd been so shocked I couldn't say for sure if there'd been anything else . . . except—"Yeah. She said something about 'dealing with MaDear's memories was bringing up a lot of old demons for Adele.' And Adele couldn't deal with those and worry about our feelings too."

Denny's jaw tightened, and he just stared into the trees for several long minutes, his coffee forgotten. I battled my own feelings: sad for MaDear, who lived through such horror at a young age, worried about why this was so heavy for Denny, and irritated that it intruded so heavily on our weekend. *You gotta help me, Lord. What are we supposed to do with this? Can't You just make it go away for a couple of days?*

Pray. That was it. Why did it still take me so long to get to the first line of defense when upsetting things happened? Avis . . . or Nony . . . maybe even Florida . . . if they were here right now they'd be circling our chairs like warriors doing battle with fear, confusion, disappointment, anger. All those sneaky spiritual fiends out to trip us up. Hadn't I learned anything in the last several months, riding life with the Yada Yada Prayer Group? I could just hear Avis say, *"It's not your battle. It's the Lord's!"*

"Denny?" I reached out for his hand. "Let's pray about all this, okay?"

I HAD NEVER THOUGHT of prayer making me hungry, but Denny and I were both ravenous by the time we let go of each other's hands, wet with sweat and tears. Somehow we were able to "leave it there" in God's lap and enjoy our day.

After showering in the tiny shower stall and breakfast at the

Starved Rock Café, we hiked up to the actual "Starved Rock"—a huge flat-topped pinnacle at the edge of the Illinois River, where a historical marker told the grim story of a band of Illinois Indians who starved to death on top of the rock, surrounded by enemy warriors below. Hard to imagine all that fierce drama now as we made our way up a walkway with safety railings leading to the top.

Still, that little hike did me in, and I chose to soak my leg—okay, all of me—in the hot Jacuzzi next to the indoor pool while Denny hiked a longer trail. By the time he came back an hour later— muddy, sweaty, and grinning—I was sure this was the perfect treatment for what ailed me, not those physical therapy sessions Dr. Lewinski had ordered. I said so to Denny, but he merely showed off by swimming thirty laps in the pool.

We made love in the cabin in the afternoon, trying not to giggle as sightseers roaming the grounds walked past our cabin and tried to peer in the windows. "Wonder what these cabins look like inside?" called a woman's brassy voice. Fortunately, we'd drawn the muslin curtains. Still, it made me feel weird, like a couple of teenagers caught making out. *Really* making out.

The sightseers kept poking around, which put a damper on passion. "I could go to the door," Denny murmured, nuzzling my ear, "and ask, 'Can I help you?'" The thought of Denny confronting strangers at the cabin door, buck-naked, ended all restraint. I belly-laughed till I cried, and Denny laughed too. Loudly. The snoopers beat a hasty retreat.

Oh God, it feels good to laugh. Don't let the laughter die.

WE DIDN'T TALK MUCH on the way home the next afternoon, but it was a different silence than the tension that had filled the car on the way out of the city Friday evening. We both knew the job thing was still unresolved and Denny would have to hit the ground running to find something at this late date. And MaDear's confusion . . . neither one of us knew how to compute that one, so we just kept praying all weekend. That felt good, just admitting, "We don't have a clue what to do, God," and "Heal her hurt, Jesus," and "Make a way out of no way about this job thing." It felt good praying together. Why didn't Denny and I do that more often?

As the Chicago skyline loomed out of the horizon, I smiled to myself, thinking about our personal "worship service" that morning in the cabin. Too bad the snoopers hadn't come back—they would've gotten an earful! We played some gospel and praise music on Josh's CD player and tried to sing along. Okay, it was a little hard to keep up with Kirk Franklin and the Family, but it was fun anyway. And our prayers changed when I said, "You know what, Denny? I always thank God *after* He's answered my prayers, but when we pray at Yada Yada, Avis and Nony and some of the others—they're always thanking God *before* He answers. Like, 'Thank You, Jesus, because we know it's already done,' or 'Thank You for what You're going to do.'"

So Denny and I tried it—just started thanking Jesus for what He was going to do—but it was hard to hang on to the richness of our weekend as our borrowed car joined the ever-increasing herd of semis, delivery trucks, cars, and minivans funneling back into the city. We'd left Starved Rock at noon on Sunday to give us plenty of time to get back home before Yada Yada, which started at five. But as I-55 slowed to a crawl, I wasn't so sure. Even weirder, I felt an odd relief. I might have a perfectly good excuse not to go tonight. . . . Why was that?

Deep down I knew. It would be awkward to face Adele at prayer group. Did she know Avis had told us about MaDear? How could it *not* come up? Not only Avis, but Stu and Florida had been at the shop that afternoon too.

Yet I'd promised Edesa I'd give her and Delores a ride—

My meandering thoughts were jolted by a thunderous roar overhead that felt like it was going to take the car roof right off. "Wow! Did you see that?" Denny shouted, poking his head out the driver side window and twisting his neck to look behind us.

"What?" I couldn't see a thing.

"A stealth bomber! I totally forgot—this is the weekend for the Air and Water Show."

Oh, great. Just great, I thought. *We'll never get home at this rate.* "Is it too late to take the Dan Ryan and stay west of the Loop?"

"No, no!" Denny's eyes practically glowed. "Let's take Lake Shore Drive. We still have time. Might get to see some of the air show!"

7

As it turned out, Denny and I got to see a lot of the air show as we crept up Lake Shore Drive. He tuned in WBBM radio, and a sportscaster's voice identified the low-flying planes screaming overhead—breaking eardrums if not the sound barrier—as an F-16 Falcon . . . an Apache helicopter . . . the Red Baron Squadron . . . and a finale by the Blue Angels. Guess we'd missed the aerobatics and parachute teams, much to Denny's disappointment. What did he expect? The show had been going on all day.

"I bet Josh is in that crowd somewhere," Denny moaned, scanning the thousands of bodies, shades, and sun hats populating the lakeshore. I was tempted to kick him out on the curb and drive home myself.

We finally pulled into our garage around four-thirty. *Sheesh.* Not early enough to freshen up before Yada Yada; not late enough to stay home. Oh well.

Amanda was already home, serving glasses of ice water for Edesa Reyes and Delores Enriques, who had come up on the El together. Left to themselves, Edesa and Delores often spoke rapid Spanish to each other, the younger woman obviously adoring her motherly mentor. It was easy to think of them as mother/daughter—except that Edesa had the rich, dark coffee-bean complexion of her Honduran heritage, while the Enriques family was "Mexican latte."

Willie Wonka was beside himself with joy that his family was back. He kept running from one to the other, leaving wet kisses on our knees and ankles. Denny was right; a note from Josh on the dining-room table said he'd gone to the air show. I hated to take off again without seeing him, but . . . *Hey,* I reminded myself. *At least he left a note.*

I splashed water on my face, dabbed on another layer of deodorant and a whisk of blush, and then came back out to the living room where Amanda was raving about worship at Iglesia del Espirito Santo that morning. "I understood a lot of the Spanish, Dad!" Our budding beauty then pounced on me. "Mom! Yada Yada *has* to go visit Edesa's and Delores's church! And when you do, I want to go with you."

Delores Enriques's round face beamed. "Why not next week? It's the last Sunday in August—time for Yada Yada to do another church visit. We can invite the others tonight." The older of the two women gave Amanda a warm hug. "Amanda, Amanda . . . she suits her name, *si?*"

Edesa laughed at Amanda's red face. "Amanda means 'lovable' in Spanish."

Amanda blushed. "Mom! Don't tell Josh. I'll never hear the end of it!"

Lovable. Well, my daughter could be at times. And to tell the truth, I'd rather stay home right now with my "lovable" daughter than get back in that clunker car again. Yet I held out my hand to Denny for the keys and turned to my Yada Yada sisters. "Ready?" I smiled, hoping I sounded more cheerful than I felt.

"Are you sure?" Denny mouthed at me as we trooped through the dining room on our way out to the garage. I gave him a half-hearted shrug and left him sorting through Saturday's mail.

I MADE IT FINE to Nony's house, even though my fingers tensed on the wheel as we approached the intersection at Clark and Howard streets, where I'd had the accident. Today was hot and sunny—nothing like the downpour that day, which had matched my ugly mood. For a brief moment, Jamal Wilkins's startled face rose up in my mind's eye, like a hologram—there but not there. The light was green, but I crept cautiously through the intersection, looking both ways, and then finally let out my breath. Edesa and Delores probably didn't even realize we'd just passed the site of the accident.

Evanston picked up where Chicago left off, and the Sisulu-Smiths lived on the north side near Northwestern University. We found Nony's home easily enough, a lovely two-story brick home on Lincoln Avenue with beds of impatiens hugging the house, and ivy clinging to the bricks and framing the windows. The house was modest by North Shore standards, but it was roomy enough for raising a family and "tastefully decorated," as Denny would say.

Nony met us at the door in a loose, caftan-type dress and gold-strap sandals, still managing to look like a *National Geographic* cover photo of African royalty even in her at-home attire. She led us past the polished wood stairs, through the spotless kitchen where Hoshi—who had been staying at the Sisulu-Smith home since NU dorms had closed last June—handed us glasses of iced tea on our way to the family room in the back, which looked out over a nice-sized yard with sturdy wooden play structures, big pots of flowers, and a tall hedge all around.

I sighed. Willie Wonka would *love* that backyard.

Most of the floors in Nony's house were polished wood, covered with patterned area rugs I presumed were African designs. On a trip to the bathroom I peeked into the dining and living rooms, both of which looked untouched by living human beings. I mean, did anyone dare sit on a white damask-covered couch?

Avis was already there, with Ruth Garfield and Yo-Yo Spencer. "Whoa," Yo-Yo sputtered. "Look at Jodi's new hairdo!"

After four days, I knew my hair didn't look quite as good as when I got out of Adele's beauty chair, but the little twists had held over the top and sides, and I'd actually rolled the back on some big curlers that morning to give it some bounce.

"Well, look at *you*," I tossed back. "Your overalls in the wash?" It was one of the few times I'd seen the twenty-something Yo-Yo in anything *but*. Tonight she had on khaki shorts and a rumpled

Bulls T-shirt. With her short, spiky hairdo, she looked like an ad for preworn Gap casuals. Yo-Yo just smirked.

"A picture she is! Denny had to beat off the competition, yes?" Ruth Garfield beamed at me from beneath her own frowzy bangs and planted a big kiss on my cheek that I was sure left red lipstick marks. "So!" she went on, giving me a big wink. "You and your *bubbala* had a—you know—great anniversary?"

The front doorbell ding-donged just then, and a moment later Florida Hickman and Chanda George tromped in. "Jodi! You back, girl?" Florida plopped down on a big floor cushion. "I thought maybe you lovebirds would still be at it." She grinned up at me.

"All right you guys, lay off. Denny and I had a great weekend, and that's all you're going to hear about it." I settled myself on the large, comfy couch beside Avis, knowing that everybody thought they knew what I meant. Truth was, I didn't want to admit that the incident with MaDear had threatened to derail our weekend big-time.

As it turned out, I didn't have to worry about prying questions, because Chanda had been practically dancing ever since she came in. "You gotta go to the bathroom, girl?" Yo-Yo butted in. "Go! You makin' me nervous."

"Nah, nah." Traces of Chanda's Jamaican accent spiced up her persona, which tended to be on the dumpy side, like the shapeless skirt and sweater hugging her extra pounds. A grin practically split her round face. "Nobody askin', so I'm a-tellin'." She paused for dramatic effect then squealed, "I won! I won!"

We all gaped. None of us took Chanda's weekly lottery tickets seriously, and the only time I'd worked up the courage to suggest she use her money more wisely met with unabashed optimism.

Ruth reacted first. "What are you now, a millionairess?"

"Nah," Chanda's smile was nonstop, "but I matched me t'ree numbers in the Pick T'ree game and got a hundred sixty dollars! Whoo-oo!" She did a little victory dance on Nony's African rug. "Me and the kids uppin' to Great America next weekend."

"That's *it?* A hundred sixty bucks?" Yo-Yo shook her head, probably thinking the same thing I was: *Bet you spent more than two hundred bucks winning that hundred-sixty.*

Chanda shrugged and sat down, still beaming. "My luck turnin' now."

Avis's eyebrows raised a hair—a twitch that usually meant, *Not going to go there. I have to pick my battles.*

Stu was the last to arrive, but she had the farthest to come, all the way from Oak Park. At least her silver Celica would be relatively safe in this neighborhood. "Aren't you tired of all that drivin' yet?" Florida wagged her head at Stu. "You goin' to church at Uptown, and you drivin' an hour each way to Yada Yada. You need a crib in the city, girl."

"Maybe when I change jobs." Stu took a seat next to Chanda, crossing her long, slender legs. "Right now most of my real-estate showings are in Oak Park—*what?*" she said to Chanda, who was grinning at her. "You win the lottery or something?"

Chanda's mouth fell open. "How'd you know?" Everybody cracked up.

Yet as I watched Chanda, something niggled at my mind—

besides the fact that she'd cleaned my house from top to bottom after my accident and wouldn't take any pay, even though cleaning houses is how she made her living. Then I realized what it was. Chanda had come in with Florida, which meant she'd ridden up on the el. Didn't she usually get a ride with Adele?

Adele wasn't here.

Avis must have had the same thought, because she said, "Guess we should get started. Adele's the only one missing. Anybody hear from Adele?"

"Yah." Chanda sighed. "I call her for a ride, but she say she not comin'. So I met up with Florida."

"She not coming" hung in the air for only a heartbeat, but I felt my mind pull two ways. Relief that Adele wasn't coming. But *why* wasn't she coming? Was she upset? At who?

I felt guilty—and resented the fact that I felt guilty.

Avis opened her Bible to the Gospel of Luke and read the passage in chapter 22 about the Pharisee who asked Jesus what was the greatest commandment of all. To which Jesus replied, "Love the Lord your God with all your heart and with all your soul and with all your strength and with all your mind, and love your neighbor as yourself."

"What?" Yo-Yo, who rarely brought the Bible I'd given her, grabbed Ruth's Bible off her lap. "Let me see that." She silently read the verse Ruth pointed out and then smacked her forehead. "You mean I gotta love my neighbors? But I *hate* my neighbors. I think they ate my cat for Thanksgiving!"

We couldn't help it. Every single one of us totally lost it. Nony's boys stuck their heads around the corner, no doubt wondering why all these women were laughing so hard. Even Avis's shoulders shook with helpless mirth. Florida kept howling, "I love it! I love it!" Yo-Yo was barely on the other side of her decision to "do the Jesus thing," and frankly, she didn't dress up her words any more than her clothes. *When was the last time I was honest enough to admit I didn't like my neighbors?* It wasn't the kind of thing a "good Christian girl" from Des Moines said out loud.

When we'd finally dried our eyes, Avis encouraged Yo-Yo to read the rest of the story when she got home, the story of the Good Samaritan who *did* love his rotten neighbor, but suggested that right now we move on to prayer.

I opened my mouth to ask for prayer about the messy situation with MaDear and Denny—after all, half the Yadas had been there when MaDear threw a fit; why shouldn't the others know about it?—then closed it again. *MaDear is Adele's mother, not mine. Maybe it isn't my story to tell.* On the other hand, Denny was my husband, the victim of mistaken identity—so wasn't it my story to tell too? I opened my mouth again, like a goldfish mouthing underwater O's. My hesitation cost me, because I heard Avis say, "Hoshi, have your parents arrived yet from Japan?" I closed my mouth and swallowed a sigh.

Hoshi was probably the quietest person in the Yada Yada Prayer Group, but her story had come out in bits and pieces. She had come to the U.S. a year ago to attend Northwestern University as a history major, ending up in a world history class taught by Dr. Mark Smith—Nony's husband. At a student reception for history majors, Nony invited the Japanese student to visit their home and also invited her to their "church of all nations" in Evanston, the Worship Center. Now Hoshi's decision to follow Jesus was about to be tested: her Shinto parents were coming from Japan to visit their daughter, and we'd been praying for Hoshi to have the courage to tell them about her newfound faith.

"No," Hoshi replied to Avis, "but soon." She was fairly tall, with silky black hair often pulled back into a simple ponytail at the base of her neck, and she had a tendency to nod a lot while she was speaking. "My parents—they will be coming in three days, for my birthday next week. Two weeks they will stay." A pink flush appeared on Hoshi's smooth cheeks. "I am scared so much to tell them that now I love Jesus. They will . . . feel very bad, very hurt. Maybe not speak to me again." Her eyes glittered with unshed tears.

"What are the names of your mother and father, Hoshi, so we can pray for them?" Delores's tender question broke Hoshi's reserve, and she started to cry.

"Takuya Takahashi, my father . . ." The tears slid down her cheeks. "And Asuka, my mother."

Nony moved quickly to the side of the student she had befriended and simply started to pray. "Thank You, Jesus, that You have said You will never leave us nor forsake us. We are bought with a price, therefore we glorify You in our bodies and in our spirits, which belong to You . . ."

I recognized the scripture Nony was paraphrasing, but as usual, I couldn't pinpoint the reference. I'd have to look it up in the concordance when I got home.

Several other sisters prayed for Hoshi, then Avis suggested we take turns calling Hoshi during the next two weeks to encourage her, to pray with her. Stu, of course, had a "better" idea. "Why don't you bring your mother to the next Yada Yada Prayer Group, Hoshi? To meet your new friends. If that seems like a good thing, of course."

"Oh, I don't know . . ." Hoshi was wide-eyed. "Please, I don't mean I am ashamed of you, but, I don't know. My mother . . ." She shook her head.

I wasn't sure it was a good idea either. The culture clash in our group could be pretty overwhelming, even for women who shared Christian faith in common. And somebody's mother, visiting from a foreign country, steeped in a foreign religion—it sounded like a recipe for disaster to me. But Avis said, "Well, you know she's welcome if you decide to bring her, Hoshi."

We moved on to the latest news in Florida's efforts to get her daughter, Carla, back from foster care. She'd been taken away before Florida got "saved and sober." Nothing could get Florida's eyes sparking like the subject of Carla. "I keep tellin' them that school is starting in two weeks, and it wouldn't do no good to Carla to start her in one school then transfer her to another, you see what I'm sayin'?" Her crown of copper ringlets bobbed as she jabbed a finger in the air. "Then they have the nerve to say, well, then, maybe Carla should stay with her foster parents another year. Almighty Jesus! Sometimes I am so tempted to lose my religion, just long enough to punch that social worker in the nose."

I didn't blame Florida one bit. I could hardly imagine all the red tape she was going through now that Carla had been located—so close, and yet still so far from "coming home." We prayed, stirring up a good storm in the heavenlies, binding Satan, rebuking red tape, and praying a hedge of protection around eight-year-old Carla.

As the prayers for Florida and Carla were winding down, I glanced at my watch. It was almost time to close, and nobody— not Avis or Florida or Stu—had brought up what happened at Adele's beauty shop last Wednesday. I wished *somebody* besides me would bring it up. Denny and I felt caught in the proverbial Catch-22 and certainly could use some prayer. Or would that be "telling tales" since Adele wasn't here? But all Avis said was, "Any other things that need prayer?"

"Yeah," I jumped in, but I chickened out about MaDear and offered up something safe. "Denny hasn't heard yet whether he still has a coaching job at West Rogers High. We're feeling pretty desperate."

"T'ree weeks till school be startin' and him still not know? Or it only be two? Well, no matter." Chanda shook her head. "Mm-mm-mm. Next t'ing they be tellin' us is the teachers on strike and our kids not goin' ta school."

The prayers of my sisters wrapped around my anxiety. Maybe this is what we needed to pray about anyway. First Ruth blurted, "Shake loose this constipated school system, God," which provoked a few chuckles. Then Nony prayed, "Oh God, the psalmist said he had never seen the righteous forsaken or their children begging for bread, so we ask You, Lord God, to be with Denny and Jodi right now, to provide for them beyond their expectations . . ."

I felt a hand on my shoulder. It was Nony's husband. Mark held up a cordless phone. "For you," he whispered.

I felt awkward leaving the group when the prayers were for Denny and me, but I slipped into the kitchen with the phone. "Hello?"

"Jodi." Denny's voice. "Sorry to bother you in the middle of your prayer time, but . . . we got some good news."

"Good news?" My heart leaped. *His job!*

"Yeah. The mail that came while we were gone? The insurance company sent us a check to cover the car. Won't cover a new one, but—"

"That's the good news?" I couldn't believe it. "You called me in the middle of our prayer time to tell me we got the insurance check?" I mean, of course I'd be glad to get rid of that borrowed clunker we'd been driving, but it could've waited.

"Partly, but thought you might also want to know I got my letter from the high school. Since Yada Yada was probably praying about my job tonight."

I sucked in my breath. *Uh-oh. Here it comes. The good-news/bad-news bit.*

"Somehow it got sent to the wrong address—can you believe that? Anyway, I was supposed to get it weeks ago." I could almost hear him break into a smile on the other end of the phone. "Good news, babe. They renewed my contract to coach another year."

8

enny's news got a round of whooping and hollering when I came back into the family room grinning from ear to ear. "Thank ya, Jesus!" Florida cried. "Ain't that just like God—right on time." She punched the air in a victory salute.

More like right under the wire, I muttered to myself, remembering how much Denny had been sweating it out all summer. Yet I wasn't about to complain. At this point *any* job sounded like good news to me, and to be able to coach the same kids he'd had last year? Icing on Denny's cake.

We had a few more rounds of prayer and praise before Avis closed us out, and in the hubbub of everybody talking and leaving, we somehow also managed to agree that our next church visit would be at Iglesia del Espirito Santo this coming Sunday, and the next meeting of Yada Yada would be two weeks from today at my house.

I dug in my tote bag for my datebook to jot it down and realized with a jolt that two weeks from today was Labor Day weekend.

Chicago schools would begin right after Labor Day, and I hadn't even started to prepare.

Huh. I was gonna need prayer for *sure.*

THE NEXT WEEK rushed at me like a NASCAR video game—especially when it hit me on Monday that Amanda's birthday was only three days away, and I'd been so busy trying to pull off my Starved Rock surprise that I hadn't planned a thing. But while furiously sewing a set of curtains for a family at Uptown Community—I was going to pay off our Starved Rock getaway before school started or die trying—I got an idea: I'd make new curtains for Amanda's room for her birthday; maybe get her a new comforter too. The bedrooms in our two-flat were rather small and dark. Maybe she'd like to paint it a sunshiny yellow—though they probably called it "lemon chiffon" or "sunrise mist." Maybe I could talk Josh into helping me with painting.

Denny thought it was a great idea, though I'm not sure he really heard me. Every spare minute he wasn't at the high school getting ready for his new coaching year, he was looking in the *Tribune* for a good, used minivan. Besides, I knew he'd probably get Amanda a little something "just from Dad." He always did that. I'd be thinking our Christmas gifts to the kids were from both of us, and then little things we'd never discussed would show up under the tree "from Dad."

Monday night was the first evening we'd sat down to supper as a family in four days. I made chicken fajitas—tasty and easy, twin requirements for a five-star rating at the Baxter household. "Oh, Mom," Amanda groaned, holding up a store-bought flour tortilla that I'd lightly seared over the gas flame on the kitchen stove. "This is truly pathetic."

"Pathetic? I thought you loved fajitas."

"I do. Did." She flopped the thing onto her plate. "But that was before I ate *real* tortillas in Mexico." She pronounced it "Meh-he-co," showing off her new aplomb at conversational Spanish.

"You don't want that?" Josh reached across the table with his fork and speared the lonely tortilla on his sister's plate, flopping it next to his own overflowing fajita.

"Give it back!" she screeched.

"Hey!" Denny yelled. "Josh, give the tortilla back to Amanda. Amanda, eat—and spare us the food critique."

Denny and I exchanged looks. These two were supposed to be young adults?

I passed Amanda the chicken fajita filling. "Speaking of food, what would you like for your birthday dinner?" For years that had been a safe question, since the answer was usually pizza or spaghetti. Last year, though, Josh had requested shrimp kabobs and twice-baked potatoes. I might have to ask for three choices and pick the one I could actually cook.

By now Amanda had stuffed half a fajita into her mouth. "Oh! Could I invite Edesa and Emerald to my birthday supper?" At least, that's what I think she said. It came out rather garbled. She swallowed. "And ask Edesa for her recipe for enchiladas. She made them for me this weekend, and they were *sooo* good."

That was different. Usually Amanda wanted a sleepover with some of her friends—but that had been back in Downers Grove, where she'd practically grown up with the same pack of girls from kindergarten through middle school. Last year at this time we had just moved to Rogers Park, and she'd settled for just one friend from our old church to come spend the weekend.

Now she was asking for her Spanish tutor and Delores Enriques's daughter, who was two or three years younger, to be her birthday guests. Was this the same teenager who'd been on the verge of failing first-year Spanish just a few months ago?

"Sure, but I'm not making any promises about the enchiladas." I caught Denny's eye again. *"Go ahead, tell them,"* I mouthed at him.

Denny cleared his throat. "Got good news," he said, refilling his own plate. "My contract at West Rogers High has been renewed."

"Great," Josh said. "Is there any more chicken?"

Denny opened his mouth then closed it again. Obviously the kids hadn't wasted any time worrying about it.

After supper, Josh took Willie Wonka for his evening walk, Denny and Amanda went out to look at used cars, and I tackled the final set of curtains for the Gage family. When would I be able to get to Vogue Fabrics up in Evanston to get some material for Amanda's curtains? Denny had preseason soccer practices at the high school, which meant no car during the day. Maybe tomorrow evening—if I could interrupt the car hunt—and then I'd have to find time to sew when Amanda wasn't around.

This might be more complicated than I thought.

I was almost done sewing the rod pockets when Denny and Amanda came in. "No luck on the car," he said and disappeared into the kitchen. A few minutes later he was back in the dining room, where I'd set up the sewing machine. "You about done?" He held up two sweating glasses. "Decaf. Iced." He headed for the back door with both coffees. "Come on out to the back porch when you can."

I sighed. I wasn't quite done, but Denny obviously wanted to talk. I turned off the sewing machine. Probably a good thing. My leg and midsection were starting to throb.

Denny was sitting on the back steps sipping his iced coffee. The cicadas were putting on a thunderous concert—if you call sawing away on one note a "concert"—but I liked it. Nature's refusal to take a backseat to urban noise.

He handed me my glass as I lowered my aching body to the steps. "Did, uh . . . did Adele or Avis say anything to you last night about MaDear?"

I shook my head. "Adele wasn't even there. Made me feel funny. Like she was staying away on purpose. I kinda hoped somebody would bring it up—after all, Florida and Stu were there too. But nobody said anything, so I didn't either."

Denny spit out an expletive under his breath. "Well, I'm gonna call Adele. It's driving me nuts. I feel bad for MaDear—but it's killing me, her thinking I'm some redneck racist who killed her brother. We gotta set this straight somehow." He stood up.

"Now? I mean, it's kinda late." I squinted at my watch. Nine-forty, to be exact. I wanted Denny to call—and didn't want him to call. Adele wasn't the easiest person to "get real" with.

Denny went inside to call Adele, and I prayed fervently into my iced coffee. *Jesus, we need some help here. Give Denny some peace about what happened—maybe erase MaDear's memory again. Wouldn't that work? Don't let Adele blame us for something that's not our fault—*

The back screen door banged. "No answer." Denny sat back down beside me. "I left a message." His shoulders hunched as he leaned his elbows on his knees. We both knew she wouldn't call back.

WITH AMANDA'S BIRTHDAY COMING UP, my sewing projects to finish, and school just around the corner—which meant shopping for school supplies and clothes for the kids, getting my classroom ready, updating my lesson plans, and attending the obligatory Professional Development days next week—temptation pulled me in two directions the next morning: roll over and go back to sleep, or hit the floor running.

Willie Wonka helped me decide by licking my hand and face—whatever skin he could reach with his doggy tongue—then clicking rapidly on the wooden floors toward the back door for his morning pee.

Okay, so I was up. As I waited for Willie Wonka to finish his business, I faced my next daily struggle: grab my to-do list or grab my Bible? Avis constantly reminded the Yada Yada sisters that the busier we got, the more we needed to "stay in the Word" and to pray. I knew for a fact that a morning devotional time would be hard to come by once school started, so as the dog came back into the house I muttered, "Okay, Willie. I'm gonna slow down these last two weeks long enough to get a half-hour for Bible reading and prayer before the rest of the family gets up. Hold me to it, okay?" Not that the deaf-as-a-doornail dog could hear my vow, but it felt good to tell *somebody*.

With a mug of fresh coffee in one hand and my Bible in the other, I draped myself in the recliner by the fan in the front window while Willie Wonka plopped down at my feet to start work on the first of his many daytime naps.

Prayer . . . It was still a challenge for me to get beyond my laundry list of "Dear God, bless so-and-so and please do such-and-such," a prayer routine perfected by family devotions as a kid, not to mention forty-plus years of Sunday school and church. Avis and Florida had given me several gospel and praise CDs when I was laid up after the accident, and that helped me focus on who God is and do some praising. But I couldn't exactly play loud praise music at six o'clock in the morning, or the neighbors upstairs would be knocking on the floor with a broom handle. And turning the volume low enough not to bother anybody didn't do justice to Donnie McClurkin or CeCe Winans.

My other challenge was a mind that skipped around like a pinball—and today was no different. *Two weeks till school starts—sheesh.*

I'm sure not ready for that emotional marathon. I tried to tell myself that I enjoyed teaching, that I loved third graders, but my first year at Mary McLeod Bethune Elementary hadn't exactly been a stellar experience. Half the kids in my room spoke something besides English at home, which made parent-teacher conferences like a debate at the UN—without the headphones and translators. *If* the parents bothered to show up. The no-show parents really made me mad. Out in the suburbs, I'd been used to a close partnership between school and home, but here, a good percentage of kids came to school without the supplies they needed. Or breakfast. A few of my students could barely read or write, but the school district seemed to push them along year after year, regardless of skill. And classroom management—don't even get me started.

My primary saving grace had been Avis—"Ms. Johnson" to the staff—who was the principal of Bethune Elementary. Yet she couldn't hold my hand all the time; she had eight grade levels and a large staff to oversee.

Trying to corral my thoughts, I opened my Bible to the Gospel of Mark, which I'd been reading in bits and pieces over the summer. Several of the women in the Yada Yada Prayer Group could quote reams of Scripture promises from the Old Testament—even from those pesky Minor Prophets—but my motto tended to be: "When in doubt, check out what Jesus said. And did." And right there alongside the little black ribbon that marked my place was the story of Jesus blessing the children: "'Let the children come to me!' . . . Then he took the children into his arms and placed his hands on their heads and blessed them."

Sudden tears filled my eyes. I'd read that story a zillion times at least. This week, though, it seemed like Jesus was giving it to me because I needed to carry it with me as I started my second year at Bethune Elementary.

The phone rang. So early? I could hear the shower running—Denny must be up—but someone answered, so I just shut my eyes, squeezing tears down my cheeks. *Okay, Jesus, You love the children. I guess that's why I'm at this school, so You can love them through me. But it was hard to love some of those kids last year, and now I'm going to have a whole new class. Everything from "sweeties" to "beasties." You're going to have to help me big-time—*

"Mom?"

I opened my eyes. Josh, pushing six feet, towered over my chair in a T-shirt, sweat shorts, and bare feet.

"Uh, Pastor Clark is asking if I'd take some kids to the beach today. He's helping their mom get signed up for Section 8 housing or something. I know I said I'd go with you to pick out paint for 'Manda, but . . ." He stared at me. "You okay?"

I gave him a bleary smile. "Yeah. God's just getting me ready for school."

9

*A*manda's birthday dinner was a great success. At least if you count that we laughed a lot. Edesa brought Emerald, who seemed delighted to be the only member of her large family invited.

My enchiladas, however, didn't measure up to Edesa's, even though she gave me her recipe—I could tell by the way Amanda politely said, "Good, Mom." Usually what I got from Amanda when I tried something new was either, "Eeewww, gross!" or "This is *so* to die for!" Guess company brought out her manners.

I'd taken the El up to Main Street Evanston to get material for Amanda's new curtains from Vogue Fabrics, and Denny and I got out to Home Depot in the evening to choose paint on the way to look at another used car. "Are you sure she'll like yellow?" Denny had asked—*after* the clerk had already mixed two cans of "summer sunflower."

I glared at him. "She better."

I had hoped to shop for a matching comforter, but Denny wanted to look at a promising Dodge Caravan he'd seen in the paper. The Caravan was only a couple of years old and in great shape, but the family who was selling it had decided they "only" needed two cars. "Understandable," Denny had said with a straight face. We bought it on the spot and drove it home—well, Denny drove it, and I followed in the clunker. By the time we returned our borrowed car to the Uptown family—bless 'em— who'd kindly loaned it to us after I totaled the Voyager, it was too late to shop for a comforter.

So I just made a coupon—"Good for a New Comforter!"—and stuck it in Amanda's birthday card. Josh paid for one of the cans of paint and promised to help paint her room—though I had a momentary heart palpitation when she said, "Can I exchange the paint? I was thinking of doing my room in red." But she gave it up when we said she'd have to pay for *that* herself.

My "fruit pizza" dessert with fifteen sparkle candles *did* go over big, as did Edesa's birthday gift: a Spanish-English New Testament. Emerald, looking like a Latina Alice in Wonderland with her thick mane of dark hair tied back with a baby blue ribbon, gave her a cloth bookmark that she'd stitched herself with Amanda's name. The way Amanda carefully put the bookmark in the Spanish Bible then hugged the book to her chest, I knew Amanda's fifteenth birthday would be held in her heart a long time.

And of course there was the "little something" from Denny: an ankle bracelet. How cool was that?

Denny and Amanda gave "The Two E's"—Josh's shorthand for

our guests—a ride home in our "new" minivan while I cleaned up the kitchen. Emerald gave me a hug before she left and whispered, "When *I'm* fifteen, my parents will give me a *quinceañera*—a big fiesta. You will come, *si?*"

"*Si,*" I replied, which used up my entire Spanish vocabulary, though I could only guess what a *quinceañera* was. "See you Sunday?" Emerald nodded happily before scurrying out the door after Amanda.

Visiting Edesa's and Delores's church on Sunday would be a treat. *Wonder who else from Yada Yada will show up? Does Adele even know about it?* I was usually the communicator to folks who missed a meeting, but I hadn't e-mailed Adele yet.

I gave the kitchen counter a last swipe with the dishrag, turned out the kitchen light, and limped into the dining room. My leg was *really* tired today. Maybe that physical therapy tomorrow would be good stuff. I lowered myself into the chair in front of the computer, turned it on, and called up our e-mail.

I scrolled past several birthday greetings for Amanda and the usual spam that made it past our blocker. Then I called up a note from Nony.

To: Yada Yada
From: BlessedRU@online.net
Subject: Hoshi's parents

Dear Sisters . . . By the grace of God Hoshi's parents arrived Wednesday. Mark and I and the boys (Hoshi, too, of course) picked them up at the airport. We offered our guest room to them during their stay, but Mr. Takahashi bowed quite formally and said they had instructed Hoshi to make reservations at the Orrington, so we just took them to the hotel.

Well, that made sense, since the Orrington in downtown Evanston was within walking distance to Northwestern's campus. On the other hand, so was the Smiths' house. Nony didn't sound offended, but it made me curious. Had Hoshi told her parents that her mentors were African-Americans? If this was their first visit to the United States, they were probably already in a state of culture shock.

The rest of Nony's e-mail was just a reminder to pray for Hoshi and to remember her birthday next week.

I called up a new message and typed in Adele's address:

To: Adele Skuggs
From: Jodi Baxter
Subject: YY church visit this Sunday

I stared at the blinking cursor for several minutes, wondering what to say. Just tell her about the church visit? Say nothing about MaDear? We'd left at least three phone messages for her, asking her to call. Surely she knew we wanted to talk about what happened last week. And why hadn't she come to Yada Yada last Sunday?

God, why does this feel like a minefield? I don't know what to say. I need some help here!

It took me ten minutes of writing, deleting, and rewriting, but I finally ended up with:

> Hi, Adele. Jodi here. You were missed Sunday evening! Delores and Edesa invited Yada Yada to visit Iglesia del Espirito Santo this coming Sunday (last Sunday of August). Can you make it?
>
> Also, if you get a chance, Denny and I would like to talk about what happened last week at the shop. Avis told us a little bit about why MaDear was so upset. We are truly sorry your mom experienced such a tragedy in her past, but it feels bad to just leave it as is, given such a huge misunderstanding about who she thinks Denny is. Let us know when would be a good time to talk. Thanks.

I read it over at least twenty times . . . and finally hit Send.

SUNDAY MORNING wasn't too bad for Chicago in August: heading for the low eighties and humid. I had no idea what kind of church building Iglesia met in, but I tucked a couple of bottles of water in my tote bag along with my Bible and notebook just in case. Uptown Community wasn't air conditioned, just ceiling fans, and sometimes all those bodies in that second-floor room on a hot day could get stifling. *And* rather smelly if it was potluck Sunday, which always drew more street people with bathing issues.

I knew Amanda was eager to go with me this morning, even though she'd just been to Edesa's church last week. I was surprised, however, when both Denny and Josh said they'd like to come too. Denny hates to miss any Sundays at Uptown. But he'd spent all day Saturday there, coordinating the crew of volunteers who came from suburban churches to participate in Uptown's outreach to the homeless, so I guess he figured he could be absent with a clear conscience. He'd been one of those "commuting" volunteers for eons till last year, when the Baxter family had moved into the wildly diverse Rogers Park neighborhood near the church—a move I was still trying to reconcile with the girl who grew up with picket fences around our all-white neighborhoods in Iowa.

At least Denny remembered some of his high-school Spanish. Maybe he could help me decipher the worship service at Iglesia del Espirito Santo.

When we got to the address Delores had given to me in one of the west Chicago neighborhoods, all I saw was a large industrial-type building with no sign. I was about to wonder out loud if we were at the right place when Amanda said, "This is it." She practically skipped inside, where Delores and Emerald and a few of the younger Enriques children were standing in the foyer, waiting to meet us.

I wanted to ask why there wasn't any sign, but several good-looking young men in black suits and classy ties stepped up to greet us—Denny and Josh had come in slacks and silk sport shirts, considered "summer dressy" at Uptown—and directed us into a large room with tweedy, blue carpet and matching chairs.

"Whoa," murmured Denny. "Bet this room could hold about a thousand folks." Whatever its former life, the factory had been transformed into a bright and pleasant sanctuary. I poked Denny and waved my hand in front of my face. *Ahh. Air conditioning.*

Delores stayed in the foyer to wait for any other Yada Yada visitors, but Emerald took Amanda by the hand and led us to the left side of the building. "They have English translation here," the youngster chirped, leaving us for a moment then returning with four headsets. "But just during the message—oh! There's José!" She motioned to him vigorously.

Emerald's older brother sheepishly made his way toward where we were sitting. I could hardly believe he was the same boy I'd last seen lying in a hospital bed last May, shot in the back. His dark hair was nicely combed, he had on a white dress shirt and tie, and a healthy color warmed his cheeks.

"*Buenos dias,* José." Amanda took charge like we were visiting *her* church. "I think you met my mom already, but this is my dad and my brother, Josh."

"*Hola.*" José stuck his hand out to Denny, then Josh. Josh towered over him by a good six inches. "Nice to meet you, but I gotta run." José flushed. "I'm on drums today."

I watched him head for the platform, where a truly amazing set of drums gleamed from behind a clear plastic soundboard. The instrumentalists were already warming up: a keyboard, electric guitar, and a small organ. The organist was obviously African-American, complete with cornrows that ended in tiny braids down to his shoulders—a fact that Florida didn't miss, as she scooted into the row beside me. "Look there. A brother. Now I know we gonna get some whoopin' and hollerin' today." She gave me a hug. "Hey, Jodi."

"Look. There's José," I whispered, tipping my chin toward the drums. I surely didn't want to thank God that José got shot, but I was suddenly overwhelmed with the realization that God had used that horrific event while we were at the Chicago Women's Conference to catapult our hodge-podge conference prayer group into the real thing.

"Uh-huh," murmured Florida. "And Amanda lookin' at him too."

I glared at her then dared to glance at my daughter—who was definitely watching the handsome teenager settling in behind the drums. I swallowed. *Oh God, I'm not ready for this!*

The seats all over the room were filling up. Delores and her brood ushered Avis and Stu into the comfy padded chairs in the English-translation section. Avis had picked up Florida but had gone to park the car; Stu came by herself. Edesa squeezed in beside Amanda and Emerald even though there were only two seats.

I thought that might be all from Yada Yada besides us Baxters, but just as the instruments brought everyone to their feet with the first worship song, accompanying a praise team of fifteen or so Latino men and women clapping enthusiastically, Ruth clambered over everybody in our row and dumped her things in the last free chair. She leaned across Florida. "Would Ben come?" she said loudly, barely audible over the pulsing music. "You'd think I'd asked him to eat pork. Suddenly he's Jewish." She rolled her eyes and leaned back. Florida and I tried to stuff it, but we couldn't help laughing.

Fortunately, the words to the songs were flashed on identical screens at both sides of the platform. Even though I didn't know Spanish, I tried to sing along.

> *El es el Rey de Reye*
> *El es Señor de Señores*
> *Su nombre es Christo . . .*

Josh leaned down to my ear. "Did ya catch it, Mom? 'He is the King of kings . . . Lord of lords . . . His name is Christ.'"

I nodded, wondering if I was too old to learn Spanish. My kids were showing me up and loving it.

The worship was similar to Nony's church—joyous, deeply felt, loud—but multiplied by five. The congregation was huge. By the time the pastor came onto the platform, the worship leader was glistening with sweat. The praise team sat down, but Pastor Rodriquez, a man with wiry black hair on the verge of gray, was still caught up in the spirit of worship. The musicians stayed right on his every word and gesture, providing background music as he spoke and launching immediately into this or that song—sometimes no more than a phrase or two—which he peppered throughout his message. His expressive face fascinated me. He smiled, grimaced, laughed, squeezed his eyes shut—and as far as I could tell, he hadn't even gotten to the sermon yet.

Was he speaking in Spanish? Or speaking in tongues? It was hard for me to tell until I noticed Amanda waving her headset at me from her seat on the other side of Denny. I put mine on; so did Florida and Ruth. Suddenly a woman's voice translating the pastor's words spoke clearly and passionately into my ears. "Brothers and sisters, yes it's a battle. But it's a battle that Jesus has already won. Hallelujah!"

Out of the corner of my eye, I saw Amanda looking up all the Scripture references in her new Spanish-English New Testament. *Okay, Lord, whatever it takes to get her into Your Word.*

The service went a good two-and-a-half hours, but the enthusiasm from both platform and congregation never abated. Several people gave testimonies: a man who was healed of cystic fibrosis after the church prayed for him; a woman who led her mother to the Lord; another who just babbled in tongues and cried and praised "Jesu" and I never did figure out what for. I wasn't sure how I felt about churches that majored in healing and tongues —but when the pastor gave an invitation to those who wanted salvation, the front was suddenly full. I squeezed my eyes shut. *Oh Lord, I'm so glad You're not limited by my own understanding. Whatever work You're doing here in the lives of these people, thank You.*

Finally we were back out in the foyer, getting introduced by Delores and Edesa to a steady stream of friendly faces that streamed past. I was curious. "Delores! Where's the sign for your church? If Amanda hadn't been with us, I'm not sure we would've found it."

Delores rolled her eyes. "*Sí*, I know. Taggers. Spray-painted all over the sign. It's down for a face-lift." Then her smile tightened, and she leaned close to me. "Please pray for Ricardo. He hasn't found a job yet, and he's yelling a lot and drinking—when he's home." Her smile dissolved. "Just . . . pray."

I gave her a hug, kissed Emerald, said good-bye to the other Yada Yada sisters—and then realized Amanda wasn't with us. Denny went to look for her and came back with Amanda and a twinkle in his eye.

Good grief. She'd probably been hanging out with José. I glared at Denny, my message clear: *Don't encourage this!*

WE TALKED ABOUT OUR EXPERIENCE at Iglesia all the way home in the Dodge Caravan and through our lunch of BLTs and corn on the cob. Then Amanda and Josh headed for the beach, while Denny and I took advantage of their absence and snuck in a "nap." Willie Wonka, knowing good and well that we were in the bedroom, scratched and whined on the other side of the door till we finally let him in.

"Voyeur," Denny muttered.

Later, when the kids had gone to youth group at Uptown, Denny and I walked to the Heartland Café, the neighborhood's classic throwback to the hippie sixties, and ordered iced coffees while we sat in the screened-in area on the sidewalk behind the Morse El stop. Our walks to the lake would have to wait till my leg felt stronger. Neither one of us mentioned the obvious: Adele had not shown up at Iglesia that morning.

Not a big deal in itself—neither had Chanda or Yo-Yo or Nony or Hoshi. But I called up our e-mail before heading for bed, just in case . . .

No answer to the e-mail I'd sent her either—and it had been three days.

10

I stood in the middle of my third-grade classroom the next morning. What a mess—boxes, stacks of curriculum and old papers, and dust everywhere. Where to start? Eight days till school opened. If nothing else, last year's experience had taught me one thing: I had to think "outside the box." It wouldn't be enough to arrange the desks in friendly clusters or make sure I had all the materials I'd need to teach the first quarter's subjects or do my Welcome Bulletin Board. I'd also need to stock up on extra notebook paper and pencils for kids who came with not one thing on the supply list; juice boxes and granola bars for the ones who came to school hungry; even a stash of socks, underpants, shoelaces, mittens, and ear muffs to cover accidents and lost (or nonexistent) items. Most of this had to come out of my own pocket, though the Salvation Army store was a gold mine. Avis was sympathetic, but no way could the school budget fund these items for the entire school.

As I leaned against my desk, I realized I had a new resource this year: Yada Yada. Last September I'd felt totally alone and in way over my head. I knew Avis slightly from Uptown Community Church and knew her professionally at school. But it wasn't till she invited me to the Chicago Women's Conference last spring, where God plunged us both into a prayer group of twelve women from all over the city, that I began "to know and be known"—or *yada,* as we discovered the word meant in Hebrew. The Yada Yada Prayer Group had hung with me through the darkest days of this past summer, when I didn't believe anybody, not even God, could love a sinner like me.

Surely they'd hang with me through teaching third graders who came to school with no socks.

I stared at the bulletin board. What could I do with the tired old thing that would make my new class feel welcome? The story I'd read about Jesus blessing the children popped into my mind. *Hmm.* A bulletin board with Jesus Loves You! in big, colorful, construction paper letters? *Oh, right.* Even Avis wouldn't be able to stop the school board from firing me. Yet *something* that would let the children know, "I'm important. I belong here. Somebody loves me."

It wouldn't be easy. Sentimental notions aside, not all of them were lovable.

Lovable. That's what Amanda's name meant in Spanish. And suddenly I had an idea.

By the time I'd finished for the day, I'd done an inventory of classroom materials, filled out my purchase orders to turn in to the office, made a list of learning games to watch out for at garage sales, and begun work on my idea for the Welcome Bulletin Board.

It occurred to me that Yada Yada had been teaching me something else I could use to start off the school year: praise and prayer. Mostly because people like Avis and Florida and Nony—well, all the sisters of color—thanked God first then looked at the facts. Ruth Garfield, lugging her Hebrew/English dictionary, had also discovered that *yadah*-spelled-with-an-h meant "to praise, to sing, to give thanks . . . to acknowledge the nature and work of God." Whew. We'd had no idea when we pulled "yada yada" out of the air, almost as a joke, as the name for our prayer group.

I peeked into the hallway to see if I could do this uninterrupted for a few minutes, then I took the printout of my incoming students and stopped by the first short desk. "Lord God, bless Ramón. Help me to love this boy like You love him." I moved to the next desk. "Thank You for LeTisha." *Hoo boy.* I was going out on a limb thanking God in advance for this one. I'd had a LeTisha in my class last year, and that little girl knew more cuss words at age eight than I even knew existed. "Bless Chanté . . . thank You for Hakim . . . bless D'Angelo . . . thank You for Savannah . . . Britny . . . Sherrie . . . Darien . . ."

By the time I flipped off the light, I'd blessed that room from corner to corner and all the little warm bodies that would soon fill it. Juggling my bulging tote bag, purchase orders, and a stack of readers to mend, I gave the classroom door a firm bump with my hip. "Aaaa-men!"

MY GOAL OF GETTING MY SEWING PROJECTS completed before school opened was severely challenged by two Professional Development days and a Teachers' Institute. I was bored out of my mind listening to speeches by a rep from the teachers' union, another from the superintendent's office, and the president of the parents' group. I caught myself thinking, *Yeah, yada-yada-yada*—and had to guzzle from my water bottle to drown my giggles.

On the second day, Project JAM and the Howard Street Community Center, both of which offered after-school programs, perked my interest, but I'm afraid I faded out again during the PowerPoint presentation of "Curriculum Alignment with State Goals."

The Institute day got down to business for Bethune Elementary. Avis—*Ms. Johnson,* I reminded myself—introduced the new staff, several of whom were student teachers. Poor kids. Fresh from college, doing their student teaching, their notebooks full of ideas, idealism dripping from every pore. I hated to see their idealism dry up when reality smacked them upside the head with the first kid who spit or cursed in their face.

I felt sorry for one student teacher who hadn't been pre-assigned to a classroom. Avis asked for volunteers to add her to their classroom, but no one spoke up. She began calling names. Clara Hutchens, the owl-eyed matriarch of first grade, sniffed, "Can't. Already got a teacher aide." Tom Davis, who taught second grade, just shrugged. "Sorry."

The student—a tall, slender girl with dark, curly hair framing almost milk-white skin and wearing a wedding ring on her left hand—kept a smile pasted on her face, but I could imagine how awful she felt. I raised my hand. "I'll take her." Avis gave a silent nod, but her eyes were smiling.

The young woman scurried to my side as we broke into teams. "Thanks. I'm Christy James." She pumped my hand. "I thought I'd be aiding kindergarten or first grade, so you'll have to clue me in."

"Jodi Baxter." I smiled, hoping I'd done the right thing. A student teacher could be a godsend—or just another headstrong "kid" who thought she knew more than you did—but the wedding ring had convinced me. It said something about her. "You'll be fine."

I MISSED CALLING HOSHI on her birthday, but I sent her a "happy birthday" e-card a couple of days later. I wondered how the visit was going. Was no news good news? I'd been so busy that week I hadn't really been praying for her. Needed to change that.

I took the Labor Day holiday literally and "labored" all weekend at the sewing machine and doing school prep. My "bright idea" for the Welcome Bulletin Board took longer than I expected, but at least it gave me an excuse not to join the wall scrapers in Amanda's room, prepping for that coat of yellow paint. What a mess! I told Amanda it was fine to paint her room this weekend, but everything had to be back in her room by the time Yada Yada arrived at our house Sunday evening.

Stu was at worship Sunday morning, and Avis, of course. Seemed like Stu had pretty much adopted Uptown as her church, even though she had to drive all the way from the West Side. Wouldn't be surprised if she signed up for Pastor Clark's membership class in the fall. So far, Ms. Perfect hadn't "taken over" the church as I'd feared, but what if—as Florida kept prodding her—she moved into the neighborhood?

As much as I'd enjoyed Iglesia del Espirito Santo last week, I was glad to be back at Uptown, where I knew the words to the songs and could hear the sermon in my own language without earphones. Yet it had opened my eyes. No wonder the Hispanics and Pakistanis and Cambodians who populated Rogers Park didn't flock to our church. Diversity among blacks and whites was challenging enough, but at least we spoke English—though even then I wasn't sure we always spoke the same language.

Like Adele. Denny and I might as well have been speaking Chinese in the phone messages and e-mail we'd left for her, for all the silence we'd gotten back in return. So you could've knocked me over with a pinfeather when Adele showed up for Yada Yada at our house that evening at five minutes past five, marching past me with a crisp nod and taking up residence on one of the dining-room chairs I'd brought into the front room.

Other people arrived about the same time, or I might have given her a piece of my mind. *If you're gonna come to Yada Yada at my house, Adele Skuggs, couldn't you have come a half-hour early so we could talk about what happened when MaDear went off her rocker? You know Denny and I want to talk!* But she had already folded her arms across her wide bosom like an impregnable stone wall. She obviously wasn't here for talking.

Not that it would've done any good anyway. Denny and Josh had gotten the bright idea to invite Yo-Yo's teenage half brothers to go with them to the Jazz Fest down at Grant Park, and they'd left right after lunch to pick them up. It was part of our scheme to "invite them first" before we had another incident, like the time Pete Spencer invited Josh and Amanda to a teen rave, which—unknown to us babes-in-the-city—was practically advertising the drug Ecstasy on the flyer.

Bottom line: Denny wasn't even home.

Amanda had wanted to go with the guys, but she got her period in church this morning and had been in bed with cramps all afternoon. Poor kid. I ought to take her to a doctor to see why it hits her so hard. She was camping out in our bedroom, because hers was still a mess from prepping the walls and the first coat of paint.

Ruth Garfield bustled in alone, sniffing at the new-paint smell—Yo-Yo got called last minute to work at the Bagel Bakery, she grumbled. Chanda was home with sick kids. Edesa and Delores wouldn't be making it either; Delores had to work the evening shift at the county hospital and Ricardo had taken off who-knows-where, so Edesa was baby-sitting the Enriques kids.

So that was four who couldn't make it. Would Hoshi show up with her mother? *That* would be interesting.

I was especially sorry that Edesa and Delores couldn't come. I wanted to bounce my Welcome Bulletin Board idea off them and get their help with my Latino students' names. As I tried to figure out who else might be coming, Avis pulled me into the hallway.

"Just wanted you to know that I phoned Adele this afternoon and encouraged her to come tonight—to not let her mom's confusion isolate her from the group. But don't push her about what happened at the shop. She still needs time."

"Why can't we talk about it?" I knew I sounded exasperated, but I couldn't help it. "It would help clear the air. It's no fun that MaDear thinks Denny's some redneck racist who killed her brother."

"I know." Avis's voice was soft, almost swallowed up by the doorbell. "Let's talk later, all right?"

I hustled to the front door, which was standing wide open so people could walk right in. Hoshi and Florida stood on the other side of the screen door. "My mother insisted we ring the bell," Hoshi apologized. Even through the wire mesh, she looked stunning in a tailored white pantsuit, her long black hair caught back in the simple ponytail at her neck. Florida said nothing, but her amused grin said everything. "Mother" was standing a good five feet behind them, clutching her handbag.

"We are so glad you have come!" I said, a bit too loudly, pushing open the screen door. "Come in, come in!"

In contrast to her tall, svelte daughter, Mrs. Takahashi looked like a prim ladybug in a red blazer, navy skirt, and walking shoes, her own dark hair coiled neatly into a bun at the back of her head. Hoshi led her mother around the room and introduced her to Avis . . . Ruth . . . Stu . . . Adele . . . Florida she'd already met . . . and Nony, of course. Everyone greeted her and shook her hand, as warm and courteous as Wal-Mart greeters, but Mrs. Takahashi looked like she hadn't defrosted from the Ice Age.

"Any word about Carla?" I whispered to Florida as I headed for the kitchen to get cold drinks, but her smile died and she shook her head. *What does that mean?* I wondered as I returned with a pitcher of sweet tea for the sisters who grew up down South, and a pitcher of ice water for those not yet accustomed to drinking tea-syrup. *Will they start Carla in school near her soon-to-be ex-foster parents? How dumb could that be!*

The typical banter that usually characterized the first fifteen minutes of Yada Yada had been replaced by polite conversation directed at Mrs. Takahashi: "Did you have a good flight?" "How do you like Chicago?" "You must be very proud of your daughter." Except Florida couldn't resist bugging Hoshi: "Girl, why'd you bring your mama on the El? Ain't that hustlin' her cultural exposure a bit too fast?" She was grinning as big as a toothpaste ad and wanting to laugh, I could tell.

Avis suggested we start our prayer time, and Mrs. Takahashi perched on the edge of one of the dining-room chairs as if the back might be a pincushion in disguise. Her Royal Uptightness put me on edge, too, but I tried to focus on the psalm Avis was reading.

"Give thanks to the Lord," she read, sounding like she was giving a call to worship at Uptown, "for he is good! His faithful love endures forever. Has the Lord redeemed you? Then speak out! Tell others he has saved you from your enemies. For he has gathered the exiles from many lands, from east and west, from north and south."

She looked around the room. "Psalm 107 seems written just for Yada Yada, especially tonight, when Mrs. Takahashi has joined us all the way from Japan."

Those who had Bibles hurriedly flipped to Psalm 107 in our various translations as Avis continued. "We represent many lands: South Africa, Jamaica, USA, Israel, Asia—even Mexico and Honduras, though Delores and Edesa couldn't be with us tonight."

Ding-dong.

The doorbell? I set my Bible down and headed for the foyer. Who had come late? The door was still standing open to catch any evening breeze, but I didn't recognize the person on the other side of the screen. "Yes?"

"I gots yo' Avon order."

"Avon? I didn't order any Avon." I tried to speak quietly, so as not to disturb Avis's devotion going on in the front room. But as my eyes adjusted to the dim daylight on the front porch, I wanted to burst out laughing. I'd never seen an "Avon lady" wearing wrap-around shades and a tight red bandana around her head. This one looked like she'd been poured into her jeans too.

I suppressed a smile. "Sorry. Maybe it's for my upstairs neighbor. What's the name on the order? I could give it to her." I opened the screen door, ready to take the brown paper bag she held in her hand.

The woman in the bandana jerked the screen door right out of my hand. "It's for *you!*" The paper bag dropped, and in its place she held a butcher knife, waving it in my face. "Git inside!" she hissed. "Git inside *now.*"

11

I nearly wet my pants. *I can't let this crazy woman come in!* Then the woman shoved the knife just inches from my throat. Like stop-frame photography, I noticed the tip was broken off. Yet the blade itself was ten inches long—long enough to go through my neck and out the other side.

I backed up.

"Turn around an' walk inta that room." The hiss was low, like a talking snake. "Don't mess wid me, an' nobody'll git hurt."

My mind felt detached from my frozen body. Would my feet even obey me? But I turned around and started—slowly—for the living room. The stranger crowded behind me, something—her hand? the knife?—pressing into the small of my back. *Oh God! Oh God! What should I do?* Within seconds I'd be bringing danger into a roomful of unsuspecting women—my sisters, my friends. *Yell! Run!* But the words stuck in my throat, and my feet kept walking.

I could hear Florida's voice, then Ruth. Nobody paid the least attention as I mechanically crossed the hall into the living room, my shadow close on my heels. Suddenly the "Avon lady" shoved me aside. "Dis is a stickup!" she yelled. "Don't nobody move!"

The shove nearly sent me to my knees. I caught the back of a chair and managed to remain standing, though my legs felt like rubber bands. Someone screamed. I didn't recognize the voice till I saw Mrs. Takahashi's mouth stretched into a big O. Everyone else sat like ice sculptures. Ruth's hand hung in the air—she usually talked with her hands—and Avis's finger still touched the open page of her Bible, like she was about to make a point.

Mrs. Takahashi was babbling gibberish or Japanese. I didn't know which.

"Shut up! *Shut up, you—!*" The bandana woman pointed the knife straight at Hoshi's mother, spouting a string of obscenities.

Hoshi flinched and put a hand over her mother's mouth, like she was shushing a toddler. "Shh, shh, *mama-san*. Please don't." Tears puddled in Hoshi's eyes then ran down her face.

Oh God. She's terrified.

The intruder strutted into the middle of the circle, still waving her knife. "Jist do as I say. Ain't nobody gonna git hurt." She stopped in front of Nony, who was wearing a necklace of multiple chains and chunky gold earrings. "The jools. Take 'em off. Rings too." Nony's hands trembled as she obeyed.

The woman stuffed Nony's jewelry into the pocket of her denim jacket then held out her free hand to Stu. Stu had to fiddle a long time with the row of little earrings that ran from her lobe to the top of each ear, then she practically slapped them into the intruder's outstretched hand. The stranger pushed her wraparound shades right up into Stu's face. "Don't mess wid me, snow bunny."

My own legs wobbled so much I finally sank into the chair. The woman whirled at my movement. "Don't *you* go nowhere." She peered beyond me to the hallway. "Who else be here?"

Amanda! My heart thudded so hard in my chest, I thought sure it could be heard clear across the room. *Oh God, oh Jesus, keep Amanda out of this.* The last I'd seen Amanda she was reading a book in bed, earphones clamped over her head. And Willie Wonka. For the first time in my life I was grateful the old dog was almost stone-deaf.

I shook my head. "Nobody," I lied.

The intruder stopped in front of Avis. "Gimme dat." She pointed at a pin Avis was wearing that fastened the long, bright-colored scarf she was wearing around her neck. "An' dat." The woman pointed to Avis's wedding ring.

Avis looked up into the woman's face. She was calm, but a thin film of sweat glistened on her forehead and upper lip. "Please. Don't take my wedding ring. It's the only thing I have left to remember my husband."

"What? He dead?" The woman stared at Avis for a moment then motioned with her free hand. "Okay, okay. Just gimme da pin. Hurry it up."

Florida narrowed her eyes when the stranger stopped in front of her. "What? Do I look like I got jewelry?" Florida's voice dripped sarcasm. "I know where you're comin' from, scrub. You're pumped off your head. You snootin' snow? Shootin' H? What?"

"Shut up! Mind yo' own bidness." She moved on.

I noticed the wiry intruder avoided Adele, who sat with her arms crossed in front of her, big and foreboding. I got no such clemency. "Yo' rings, fool." She danced around, keeping an eye on the circle of women, waving her knife, as I tried to wiggle my wedding ring set over my big knuckles. I wanted to throw it, scream at her, do *something*—but I numbly put it into her hand and watched it disappear into her jacket pocket.

When she got around to Hoshi and Mrs. Takahashi, the older Japanese woman pinched her mouth like it was stitched together and pulled her handbag close to her chest. The thief pointed the broken tip of the knife. "You. Gimme da money."

Mrs. Takahashi shook her head.

The stranger grabbed for her purse. "I *saw* you git money outta dat ATM, slit eyes!"

Ohmigosh. She'd followed them here!

Fire smoldered behind the pressed lips and almond eyes. Hoshi's mother held on tight to the handbag and swatted at the knife waving in her face—and suddenly a wail filled the room. A line of bright red blood appeared across Mrs. Takahashi's palm down to her wrist.

"You *grabbed* it, you blasted fool!" the intruder shrieked. She whirled around and looked at me. "Git her somethin' quick. No! Don' leave da room—whatchu got?"

Blood was running down Mrs. Takahashi's arm. *"Mama-san! Mama-san!"* Hoshi cried. Her shoulders were shaking.

Ruth Garfield whipped out a large white handkerchief—Ben's,

no doubt—stalked over to Mrs. Takahashi's chair, and wrapped it tightly around her hand. "Press here," she commanded Hoshi, indicating a vein on her mother's wrist. "Hold her hand up— high." She turned and glared at the stranger. *"Vilda chaya!"* she spit out and stalked back to her chair.

"Whatchu call me? Din't I tell you nobody git hurt if ya do what I say?" The woman behind the shades was practically screaming.

Adele rose up out of her chair, like a bear coming out of hibernation. "That's *it*. You've gone too far. Get out." She pointed toward the front door. *"Get out.* You got what you wanted. Get out!"

I would've run, if it'd been me. But the bandana-headed woman eyed the big ruby ring on Adele's right hand, and her eyes seemed to glitter. With a sudden movement she grabbed Mrs. Takahashi out of her chair and held the frightened lady, still clutching her handbag, in front of her in a one-arm grip.

"I tol' you. I don't wanna hurt nobody—but I *will* if ya don't siddown *now*, Big Mama."

Adele didn't move. "She needs medical help!" The handkerchief around Mrs. Takahashi's hand was staining bright red.

The knife moved slowly to Mrs. Takahashi's neck. *"Siddown!"*

Adele slowly sat.

The intruder kept a grip on Hoshi's mother, who was too terrified to scream or cry, and caught my eye. "You! Tie up Big Mama there."

Tie up Adele? I couldn't have been more shocked if she'd asked me to walk on the ceiling. "With what?" *Think, Jodi! Say you've got rope in the basement then call the police . . .*

The woman gestured with the knife toward the box fan in the front window. "Use th' estenshion cord. An' hurry up, you—" She peppered me with all the cuss words in her gutter vocabulary.

I took a deep breath, hoping my rubbery legs would hold me up, and stumbled toward the fan. The rest of the room was deathly silent, except for Hoshi's stifled sobs and the intruder's raspy breathing. I unplugged the cord and turned to face our adversary. Surely she wouldn't make me—

"You! Big Mama. Put yo' hands behind yo' chair." Then she pointed at me. "Now tie her to the chair."

This was a nightmare! I couldn't tie up *Adele*—of all people! But the crazy woman was glaring at me from behind Mrs. Takahashi's terrified face, so I walked in a daze behind Adele's chair, knelt down, and began to wrap the extension cord around her hands. "I'm sorry, Adele—so sorry," I whispered behind her back, but Adele gave no sign that she heard me.

"She tied up?" the intruder's voice demanded. "Now take 'at ruby ring off her han', an' be quick 'bout it."

With dread practically dripping from my pores, I wiggled the ring from Adele's thick finger. *Oh God, Oh God . . . send somebody . . . do something!* Finally the ring popped off into my hand and I stood up—and nearly stopped breathing. The stranger's back was to the hallway, but over her shoulder I saw Amanda standing behind her in the doorway.

I wanted to yell at my daughter to run. Instead I said loudly,

"Here's the rotten ring" and stepped forward—but not all the way, making our captor push Mrs. Takahashi back into her chair before reaching out to snatch it. When I looked again, Amanda had disappeared. *Thank You, Jesus, thank You, thank You*—

"An' tie that one too!" The knife pointed toward Stu. "I don't like Cinderella's attitude."

Before I could obey—did we even have another extension cord in the living room?—I suddenly heard the click of Willie Wonka's nails in the hallway. "Woof! Woof!" The chocolate Lab skidded to a stop in the hallway just outside the living room. Willie hardly ever barked; he wasn't much of a watchdog. Yet he knew something wasn't right.

The dog's bark freaked the bandana woman. She whirled on the dog, slashing her knife through the air.

"He won't hurt you!" I yelled.

"Then git him to shut up, or I'll hurt *him*," she snarled.

I knew Willie wouldn't leave voluntarily, so I grabbed his collar and dragged him over to the front window and made him lie down against the wall. Before I could straighten up, I heard a demanding male voice: "What's going on here?"

Denny! I looked up just in time to see the intruder whirl around to face my husband, pointing the knife at his throat. Where had he come from? Like actors in a tableau, Denny and the woman faced each other, motionless. My heart raced. But time seemed to stand still—half a second? half a minute? Then she lunged with the knife.

I screamed. *"Nooooooo!"*

12

It happened so fast, it was over in a blink. As the crazy woman lunged at Denny with the knife, he grabbed her wrist. The next moment she was on her back on the floor with Denny spread-eagle on top of her.

"Jodi!" he yelled. "Take the knife!"

My body parts suddenly came alive, and I scrambled toward the pair on the floor.

"Git off me, you—" The woman struggled beneath Denny's weight, letting loose a string of cuss words that made all the words she'd been throwing around for the last fifteen minutes sound like kindergarten babble.

"Take the knife!" he commanded again, trying to keep from getting kicked from behind by her flailing legs. The woman still held the handle of the butcher knife in her right hand—how in the world was I going to get it away from her? As Denny dug his nails into her wrist, she finally let go. I snatched it.

"Call the police!" he bellowed.

"I already did, Daddy." Amanda reappeared in the living-room doorway, barefoot, wearing only an oversized T-shirt, her brown eyes wide and her face chalk-white.

"An ambulance we need too." Ruth appeared at my side. "And take that horrid knife away, Jodi."

I stared at the ten-inch knife in my hand as though seeing it for the first time. A streak of Mrs. Takahashi's blood was smeared along the sharp edge. I had an overwhelming urge to throw it away from me, but instead I ran to the kitchen and dumped it into the sink. "Don't touch that!" I hissed at Amanda, who'd followed me. "And call 911 again for an ambulance." I ran back to the living room, just as I heard sirens screaming . . . coming closer . . . and screeching to a stop outside our house.

Stu was busy untying Adele. Nony, Ruth, and Avis huddled around Hoshi and Mrs. Takahashi, and Florida flung open the screen door for the police. The crazy woman was still cussing a blue streak on the floor.

Four big police officers—two black, two white—pounded into our living room. "Police! Don't anybody move!" One had his gun out of its holster. Taking in the scene at a glance, he pointed it straight at Denny's head. "Okay, buster, let 'er go. Put your hands behind your head."

"No!" I yelled. "Not him—*her!*"

Immediately the other women in the room started talking all at once, arguing with the police, pointing at the intruder on the floor, holding up Mrs. Takahashi's wounded hand.

"Quiet!" yelled the cop with the gun. He looked at me. "You. What's going on here?"

I couldn't believe this! "That . . . that woman on the floor came in here with a knife . . . and . . . and she robbed us . . . and cut Mrs. Takahashi's hand. And that's my husband—stop pointing that gun at him!"

"She's tellin' it," Florida declared. A murmur of assent rose from several others.

The intruder must have known it was all over, because she quit struggling.

"All right." A pause. The police officer holstered his gun. "We'll take her, sir. Get off easy, now. Fellas . . ."

The four police officers each took a wrist or ankle. Denny released his hold on the woman's wrists and scrambled to his feet. No sooner did the four men start to lift the bandana woman to her feet than she seemed to explode—kicking, scratching, cussing, and calling down all sorts of calamity upon their heads. The rest of us backed off, watching in disbelief. It took all four of them to finally get a pair of handcuffs on her, and still she kicked and screamed all the way to the paddy wagon, which was blinking its hazard lights in front of our house.

"Denny!" I ran to my husband, who was leaning over, hands on his knees. "Are you okay?"

He nodded mutely.

A few moments later, two of the officers came back in the house, brushing off their uniforms as if trying to regain their dignity. "Everybody sit down, please," said the one who seemed to be in charge. His cheeks were ruddy, giving him a boyish look even though his paunch suggested he was older—forty, maybe fifty. "I'm Sergeant Curry. We're going to need a statement from each one of you."

"But my mother!" Hoshi cried. "She's hurt! She needs a doctor!"

Denny jerked his head toward the sound of another siren that suddenly choked off in midwail directly in front of our house. "We called an ambulance."

"And that thief just walked out of here with our jewelry in her pocket!" Stu stormed.

"Yes!" Nony wailed. "My wedding ring—please get it back." Even as she spoke, we heard the paddy wagon pull out to make room for the ambulance. Nony began to weep quietly.

The sergeant punched his walkie-talkie. "We need some ETs here. Lunt Avenue. On the double." He sighed. "I'm sorry, ladies. We're going to have to keep everything she had on her person as evidence. We'll"—he cleared his throat nervously—"be sure to return everything to you."

For the next few minutes, the house was full of medics who tended to Mrs. Takahashi's hand then trundled her out to the waiting ambulance. Nony insisted on accompanying Hoshi, so the second police officer also went along to get their statements at the hospital. No sooner had they left than two more police officers arrived. The evidence technicians, I presumed.

Sergeant Curry turned to me. "Ma'am, you mentioned a knife. Where is it?"

"I . . ." For a moment I couldn't think. "Uh, I put it in the kitchen sink." I led one of the ETs to the kitchen, where he pulled on a pair of rubber gloves, retrieved the knife, and put it in an evidence bag. Good grief. *My* fingerprints were all over that knife too!

When we returned to the front of the house, everyone else was sitting down again except Denny and Amanda, who was sobbing quietly under her daddy's arm as he leaned against the arched doorway. The officer in charge pulled out a small notebook. "Who encountered the woman first?"

I lifted my hand.

"Okay, let's start with you. Tell me what happened."

Tell him what happened? I just wanted them to leave! I wanted to hold Denny and Amanda. I wanted to hug my Yada Yada sisters. I wanted to go to the hospital to see if Hoshi's mother was going to be all right. I wanted to ask Adele if I hurt her when I tied her hands. I wanted to . . . to have a good bawl!

No. I was not going to cry in front of these police officers. I drew a breath. "Okay. We"—I indicated the other women—"were having, uh, a prayer meeting. My husband was out; my daughter was in her bedroom. The doorbell rang, but we weren't expecting anybody else. A strange woman stood at the door, said she had my Avon order . . ."

Sergeant Curry was busily taking notes. "Describe her, for the record."

"Well, she was black, wearing a red bandana and wraparound shades—"

Florida snorted. "That wasn't no black woman."

Stu frowned. "Sure she was. Light-skinned, maybe."

"That girl was *white,*" muttered Adele.

I stared at Florida and Adele. From the moment I laid eyes on the "Avon lady," I thought she was black. The way she talked black or hip-hop or something. I looked at Avis for help.

Avis shrugged. "Hard to tell behind those shades, light-skinned as she was."

"Why'd you think she was *black?*" Adele was downright scornful. "Because she was whacked out on drugs? talked street jive? cussed you out?"

I looked helplessly at Denny. Could this get any worse?

The sergeant cleared his throat. "Ladies, it doesn't really matter. We've got the suspect in custody. Let's go on. What happened after she rang your doorbell?"

THE POLICE OFFICERS FINALLY LEFT after taking everybody's statements and making a list of the stolen jewelry. Adele started to follow the officers out the door, but Avis said, "Wait a minute, sisters. If ever we needed to spend time praying together, this is it. Ten minutes, tops. We've got some praising to do. Nobody got killed; everybody's going to be all right, even Hoshi's mother. We've also got some serious spiritual battle to do. That woman's drowning in darkness."

Reluctantly, Adele rejoined the group. Florida pulled Amanda and Denny into the circle, and we all held hands. I held on for dear life to Denny's hand on one side and Ruth's on the other. *Thank you, Avis! Yes, yes, let's pray. Otherwise I might just fall apart, right here and now.*

THE PRAYER WAS GOOD. It helped me calm down, let me focus on what we could thank God for in the midst of the trauma we'd just experienced. Nony called in the middle of the prayer, saying that Mrs. Takahashi had to have seventeen stitches in her hand but was going to be all right. Both Hoshi and her mother had been given a sedative by the emergency-room staff, and a police officer took them back to the Orrington Hotel. Now could someone come to St. Francis Hospital and pick her up? Nony's car was still at our house.

That's when I learned that Josh still had *our* car and was driving Pete and Jerry home. Which meant he'd dropped Denny off.

It had to be God.

So Stu went to pick up Nony at the hospital and brought her back to get her car. We hugged out on the sidewalk, and Nony shook her head, deeply concerned. "Pray without ceasing for Hoshi. Her parents are terribly upset."

Understandably. Stu's "great idea" for Hoshi to bring her mother to Yada Yada had turned out to be an utter disaster.

Can't go there, Jodi. It's not Stu's fault.

Finally everyone was gone. Josh came home and seemed rather

disappointed that he'd missed all the excitement. Amanda gave him a blow-by-blow account, puffing up her role a bit, I noticed, describing how she sneaked the cordless out of the house and dialed 911 from the backyard. Well, why not? She had behaved admirably under the circumstances.

At last Denny and I were alone in the living room—after I made sure our front and back doors were locked. "I'm starving," he announced. "Be back with a four-course dinner in two minutes." He turned at the doorway. "Turn on that fan, will you? It's hotter'n blazes in here."

I picked up the extension cord where it had dropped after someone—Stu, I think—had untied Adele's hands. I stared at the innocent-looking cord. Had I really tied up Adele Skuggs with this thing? Numbly, I connected the fan cord and the extension then plugged it into the socket. The cooling night air flowed into the room.

Denny returned with chips, salsa, leftover sweet tea, apple slices, and peanut butter. Not exactly the four-course meal he promised, but hey, he brought it out on a tray, and all I had to do was dig in. No complaint from me.

We sat on either end of the couch, our legs entwined, munching quietly for several minutes. Then Denny said, "God spoke to me."

I stopped eating. "What do you mean?"

"When that woman lunged at me with the knife. God told me, *'Grab her wrist. No one is going to get hurt.'* It was as if time slowed down, and everything happened in slow motion. She lunged. I

114

grabbed. I pulled her across and tripped her. Not even sure how I did it, but I wasn't afraid. I knew God was helping me."

I shuddered. "I was afraid."

He leaned forward and began to massage my leg, the one with the steel rod in it. "You've had a pretty rough summer, babe."

Wasn't *that* the truth! I could get a good pity party going if given half a chance. Yet if Avis could look for things to thank God for only moments after being grilled by a police officer, maybe I could put the pity party on hold.

"Adele came to Yada Yada, as you saw," I mused. "Didn't get to talk to her, though. She seemed pretty distant—even before we got robbed. Avis told me to give her some space."

Denny heaved a big sigh. "Yeah. What happened tonight won't make it any easier, will it?"

We sat quietly for a few moments, munching on our snacks and washing them down with sweet iced tea. Then Denny started to chuckle.

"What?" I dug an apple slice into the peanut butter.

He tried to wipe the grin off his face. "It's really not funny, but . . . while I had that woman pinned, I thought, *'Does this crazy person have a name?'* I mean, it wasn't so bad tackling a cutthroat druggie, but what if she has a name like . . . like Susie or Denise or Tammy? I tell you, my superhero status starts to slip if I had 'Susie' spread-eagle on my living-room floor."

"No!" I started to laugh too, which wasn't easy with peanut butter in my mouth. "She couldn't have a name like Susie. It's gotta be some street moniker. Like Krazy Kate or Maniac Mama."

Denny's chuckles gave way to belly laughs. "Maniac Mama! That's it! I pinned Maniac Mama to the floor till the police came!"

All the tension of the evening erupted into hysterical laughter. I laughed so hard I almost lost all the snacks I'd just eaten. Even Denny was holding his side. Josh came out of his room, looked at us, and shook his head. "You guys are nuts."

Yet in the middle of the night, when I got up to go to the bathroom, my half-awake brain was jolted by the thought: *Florida was once a crazy drug addict.* My first memory of her flooded back: a tattered woman banging on the hood of my car, begging for money. Years ago. Just a panhandler then. Now she was Florida, my sister, my friend. Who but God could've done *that?*

I had a hard time going back to sleep. What happened to our intruder once that paddy wagon drove off? She wasn't just a thief; she was a woman—like me. Did they put her in a cell at Cook County Jail? Was she getting any sleep? Did she have a family? Did they know where she was?

Does she have a name?

13

*B*ecky Wallace. That was her name. We found out when Denny called the Twenty-Fourth District Police Station on Clark Street the next day and asked to speak to Sergeant Curry. It was Labor Day; we thought he might have the day off. But he called back a couple of hours later. I quietly picked up the kitchen extension but motioned madly at Denny to do the talking.

Sergeant Curry said "the suspect in question" was already in detox at Cook County Jail—a process that usually took about three weeks. After that, if she was found guilty, she was looking at some serious jail time. "Your wife and the other women she robbed willing to testify at her trial?"

Denny motioned at me to answer, but I shook my head and pointed back at him.

"Uh . . . probably," he said, rolling his eyes for my benefit. "Do we have to press charges or something?"

"No. We've got your statements. That will be enough for an arraignment. The state's attorney's office will decide what charges to file and will contact you if there's a trial."

I waggled my left hand across the room at Denny, indicating my bare ring finger.

"What about my wife's wedding ring and the other jewelry?"

A brief pause. "I'm sorry, Mr. Baxter. As I told you, it'll be awhile. Evidence."

"Right." Denny turned his back, as though he didn't want to get any more sign language from me. "What did you say the woman's name is?"

"Uh, just a sec. Got it here somewhere." We heard papers shuffling. "Wallace. She gave her name as Becky Wallace."

I just stared at Denny after we hung up. Surely the police sergeant was pulling our leg. The crazy woman who'd come charging into our house waving a ten-inch butcher knife and cussing like a gangbanger couldn't be a *Becky*.

Denny must have been thinking the same thing as he gave me a sheepish grin. "Sure glad I didn't know that before I threw her down. What would the guys say if they knew I'd manhandled a girl named Becky?"

I snickered. But knowing her name did feel weird. I kinda wished we hadn't asked. It was easier thinking of her as "that drugged-out crazy woman."

The last of the paint went on in Amanda's room—thanks to Josh and Denny—that morning, then Josh and Amanda took advantage of their last free day before school started to hang out at the lakefront, the last day the city lifeguards would be on duty. Well, let 'em. Tomorrow they'd stagger home with backpacks full of books and homework. And Josh had been getting college information in the mail all summer; soon he'd have to sit down and fill out applications and plan campus visits.

Let 'em have one more carefree summer fling.

As for me, I thanked God at least once every half-hour that today was a holiday. If I'd had to face the first day of school at Bethune Elementary after what happened last night, my emotions would probably be scrambled for life. I was sure Avis was grateful too. Everybody, in fact. We all needed a day to calm down and get our wits about us before facing real life.

Except Hoshi didn't have that luxury. What was happening with her? Her poor mother got the worst of it, and Hoshi was probably still picking up the pieces.

I dialed Nony. "Have you heard from Hoshi? How's her mother doing?"

A big sigh greeted my inquiry. "God in heaven, have mercy. The Word says the bruised reed will not be broken, nor the dimly burning wick extinguished . . ."

I waited. Sometimes it was hard to tell whether Nony was talking or praying. "What?"

She sighed again. "I went over to the hotel today. Mr. Takahashi insisted that they were leaving immediately. He was too polite to raise his voice in my presence, but he spoke sternly to Hoshi in Japanese, and when she shook her head, he stalked out of the room."

"What?"

"I'm getting there, Jodi! When her mother went to the bathroom, Hoshi told me her father said, 'This is what happens when a disobedient daughter turns her back on her parents and her religion.'"

"Oh no." I groaned. "He can't blame Hoshi! I mean, good grief! They've got crime in Japan, don't they?"

"They're upset, Jodi. Her father wanted her to go home with them. Today. Hoshi said no . . . she wants to finish her education."

"Are they paying her tuition? Could they—?"

"No. She has a full scholarship. But in Japanese culture, defying your parents' wishes is a very serious thing."

I felt heartsick for Hoshi—but part of me sympathized with her parents. How would I feel if Josh jettisoned his Christian upbringing for Shintoism? I'd freak out too. I managed to ask, "So where is Hoshi now?"

"She went to the airport with them by cab. I told her to come back to my house afterward. She really shouldn't be alone right now, poor thing."

I hardly knew what to think after I hung up the phone. What a mess.

DENNY DECIDED TO RUN OFF some of his pent-up emotions with a good jog by the lake. With everyone else gone, Willie Wonka followed me from room to room, standing in the way when I tried to move around the kitchen, lying on my feet if I sat down. He was getting on my nerves. Once I yelled at him to leave me alone—a lot of good that did, since he couldn't hear—but he looked at me reproachfully.

I relented. "Come here, guy," I said, plopping into a chair in the dining room and inviting him closer. Willie Wonka immediately stuck his face in my lap. *Humph.* Give a dog an inch, and he'll take a whole city block. I took his sweet doggy face in my hands. "You're still upset by what happened last night, aren't you? Well, so am I."

It was true. I felt so . . . violated. Like being strip-searched in a crowded room. A stranger had pushed her way into my home and threatened my family, my friends. I shuddered at what *could* have happened.

Willie looked hopefully into my eyes. So patient. As if waiting for me to say, *It's okay, don't worry, everything's going to be all right.* Why were dogs so trusting? Didn't they know we humans usually didn't have a clue? Unlike us, dogs seemed to love with no strings attached.

I stroked Willie's silky brown ears, my thoughts tumbling. Why was it so hard to trust God when things didn't go right? Surely *God* had a clue. I mean, He's God! That's His job description! I knew God loved me—and all of us in that room last night. So couldn't I stop stewing about it and trust God to work it out?

Okay. I was going to stop stewing and start sewing. "That's it, Willie." I got up abruptly, ending our little tête-à-tête. I had a sewing project to finish and research still to do on my Welcome

Bulletin Board idea. The computer was free; maybe I'd do that first while everybody else was out.

While I was waiting for the computer to boot up, my own thoughts came around again. *God loves all of us who were in that room last night. Even—*

Whoa. Even Becky Wallace?

I WORKED FOR A WHILE ON THE COMPUTER, using a search engine to chase down the meanings of the names of the students who would be in my class. D'Angelo was easy: "from the angels." So was Jade ("jewel") and Cornell ("hornblower"). But I was excited to not only find Ramón ("mighty protector") and Chanté ("to sing"), but also LeTisha ("joy") and Kaya ("wise child").

Hmm. So LeTisha meant "joy." This was going to be interesting. Last year's LeTisha had been anything *but.* I was starting to get excited. How would the children react to learning the meaning of their names?

What about Jodi? I'd never thought about it before. Did my name—

The phone rang. I thought I'd heard Denny come back and hoped he'd answer it, but it kept ringing, so finally I tried to make a dash to the kitchen phone. My leg had stiffened up sitting so long, and I almost fell. The answering machine started to pick up by the time I got there.

"Hello? We're here! Sorry it took so long."

"Jodi." I recognized Florida's voice, but there was something in her voice . . . Was she crying?

"Florida? Is something wrong?"

"No. It's good. I'm just . . . Jodi, DCFS just called. They're bringing Carla home. Today." Florida's voice faded; she must have put the phone down. Somewhere in the background I could hear her crying and praising. "Oh, thank ya, Jesus. *Thank ya!*"

"Florida? Florida!" I called into the phone. This was incredible! Wonderful news. She'd been trying to get her daughter back even before I met her last spring. Even after Stu—our wannabe social worker—had located Carla, the red tape had been like hacking through a jungle. I could hardly imagine how Florida got through each day, not knowing for sure when or if she'd get her daughter back.

Florida finally came back on the phone.

"Florida, that's wonderful," I said.

"Yeah, I know." Florida blew her nose. "But you gotta get the sisters to pray for us; that's why I called. Because they didn't *tell* me in time to get her registered for school"—Florida's tone got testy—"so I gotta take off work tomorrow, and—"

"Of course, Florida. I'll send an e-mail to everybody."

"That's not all." I could hear the tug between pain and joy in Florida's voice. "The social worker said Carla's upset. She doesn't want to start a new school. Wants to stay with her foster . . ." I could hear her crying again, softly. "Jodi? Am I doin' the right thing?"

14

I had no idea how to answer Florida. The right thing? *The right thing, Florida, would've been not to get strung out on drugs and lose your kid in the first place!*

But I wasn't about to say that. After all, "the right thing" for *me* would've been not to have a stupid fight with my husband and end up driving angry behind the wheel of our car—which had had far worse consequences.

A spasm of regret made me feel sick to my stomach.

Florida was hurting and waiting for me to say something. I tried. "Flo, I don't know. Except . . . God's done some pretty big miracles in your life already, including DCFS returning Carla to you *today!* So she can start school! You're always saying God didn't bring you this far to leave you, and He's not going to leave you or Carla now either." I heard the words I was saying, desperately wanting to believe them.

We'd no sooner hung up than the phone rang again.

"Jodi!" It was Yo-Yo. "Heard I missed all the excitement last night! Had to work."

I was in no mood to joke about it. "Guess Ruth told you what happened."

"Yeah. Can't shut her up. She's beside herself about what that kook did to Hoshi's mama."

"Her name's Becky Wallace."

"Who?"

"The kook, as you called her." I was feeling testy, though I wasn't sure why exactly.

"Ha. She told you her *name?* Like, hey, my name's Becky Wallace. Pleased ta meetcha. Gimme all your jools." She laughed.

"No." My annoyance meter was rising. "Look, Yo-Yo. If you called for some reason . . ."

"Hey, sorry." Her tone sobered. "Must've been tough for you guys. *Really* sorry to hear what happened to Hoshi's mom. That perp musta been postal."

I was too tired to unscramble Yo-Yo's language. "Yeah."

"Uh, I really called to tell Josh and Denny thanks for taking my kid brothers to the Jazz Fest yesterday. They came home tanked— you know, all excited. Mostly 'cause somebody was payin' atten- tion to 'em I think, though you'd never get either of 'em to admit it. Ben and Ruth used to do that kind of stuff with them—did it a *lot* when I was in the joint—but Ben's getting kinda cranky with them these days. Can't blame him; they drive *me* over the edge. They're, you know, mouthy teenagers. Anyway, tell your man thanks. Josh too."

"Okay. Sure." My insides relaxed a little. "Know something, Yo-Yo? If Denny had driven the boys home first instead of letting Josh drop him off here last night, no telling what might have happened."

"Yeah." A pause. "Guess the Big Guy upstairs was lookin' out for ya."

I smiled in spite of myself. Yo-Yo could never be accused of "churchy" language.

Neither one of us spoke for a moment. Then, doing a mental U-turn, I found myself saying, "Yo-Yo, remember when we were introducing ourselves at the women's conference last spring? I stuck my foot in it and asked where you learned to cook?"

The phone crackled with Yo-Yo's laugh. "Yeah. Wish you could've seen your face when I said prison."

"Yeah, I know." Even now I could feel my face getting red, but I pushed on. "You said, 'I had my reasons'—you know, for committing forgery. Uh, can I ask . . . what reasons?"

"Huh. Nosy chick, ain't ya." But she didn't sound mad. "School clothes. School supplies. Didn't know no other way to get what Pete and Jerry needed. My mom was in the ozone; she sure as heck wasn't getting them ready for school. It wasn't that hard to forge all those checks with my mom's ID. 'Course there wasn't no money in the bank . . ."

Did the crime, served my time. It's behind me now." That's what Yo-Yo had said last spring. Like it was nothing. I couldn't imagine even eighteen months shut away with people like . . . like Bandana Woman, who spewed filthy words five times in one sentence.

"What was it like?"

"What? Prison?"

"Yeah."

"Man!" That's all Yo-Yo said for a moment or two.

What were you thinking, Jodi? She obviously doesn't want to talk about it! I was just about to say, "Forget it," when Yo-Yo said, "It's tough, Jodi. Ya gotta *be* tough to survive in prison. Learned that the first day at Cook County. Was sittin' there in the common room, smokin' a cigarette an' mindin' my own business, when this big black girl comes over and says, 'Gimme a cigarette. *Now.*'"

I wondered why Yo-Yo mentioned the girl's race. It wasn't supposed to matter, was it? Yet it probably *did* matter in prison. "Like" allied with "like." I could just see Yo-Yo slouched in a chair, legs stuck out, one arm over the back—but probably without the overalls she always wore. Didn't prisoners at Cook County wear orange jumpsuits or something? Her skin was pale, and she rarely wore makeup; but her spiky hair with blonde tips called attention to itself. Yo-Yo wasn't a big person; she just seemed that way to me because of her blunt talk.

"Knew if I gave it to her," Yo-Yo went on, "it'd be over for me. I'd end up being some big mama's sissy. So I cussed her out good, told her to get out of my face. She backed off."

My knees literally got the shakes, and I had to sit down. I couldn't even bring myself to think beneath the surface of Yo-Yo's words. I wasn't tough. I was a wimp. I'd never have survived one day in prison.

I heard Yo-Yo sigh on the other end of the phone. "Didn't

especially like the person I had to be inside the joint, but that's the way it was. Ruth had to soften me up a bit once I got out."

Soften? "Soft" was not a word I would associate with Yo-Yo.

"Say, what's with all the questions?" she asked. "You got acquitted, remember? Don't go lookin' backwards."

"I know. Thanks, Yo-Yo. Sorry for getting so personal."

"It's okay, but gotta run. The Bagel Bakery is *not* closed on Labor Day."

We hung up, but for some reason I felt all confused. Uneasy. Yo-Yo forged checks to get school clothes—school clothes!—for her kid brothers and spent eighteen months in jail. I killed a kid in a car accident and *didn't* go to jail.

Then along comes Bandana Woman—yeah, that handle fit her a lot better than her so-called name—who terrorizes Yada Yada and cuts Mrs. Takahashi's hand and, frankly, I'm hoping she's going down for a long, long time. *She's a tough cookie*, I tell myself. *Nobody's going to mess with her.* Then an afterthought, *But if they do, it serves her right.*

MY PARENTS CALLED just as we were getting ready to eat supper.

I heard the phone ring, but it seemed like the phone had been ringing all afternoon—first Florida, then Yo-Yo, then Chanda, who was practically hysterical, even though she hadn't even been here last night. Somebody must have told her. Adele? They went to the same church—Paul and Silas Apostolic—but otherwise didn't seem to interact much. It annoyed me no end that I had to calm *her* down when she hadn't even been here to get robbed. "Oh, sista Jodee," she moaned. "Such a terrible t'ing." Her Jamaican accent got thicker, till I could hardly understand her. "So bad. So bad."

By the time Denny and the kids got home from their last fling with summer, the most I could manage for a Labor Day "picnic" was grilling some chicken in the backyard. Correction: Denny did the grilling. He knows I don't have the patience to sit there baby-sitting the grill, so the meat ends up BBB—"Blackened Beyond Belief."

Denny had just yelled, "Five minutes!" and I was putting some corn on the cob and fruit salad on the small back-porch table when the phone rang *again.* I was all for letting the machine pick it up, but Amanda can't resist a ringing telephone any more than Willie Wonka can resist scratching a flea. I heard her say, "Hi, Grandma! Yeah, it's Amanda."

My mother's timing is always exquisite. Just as we're sitting down to dinner, or just as we're rushing out the door to school, or even just as Denny and I are climbing into bed for a marital "roll in the hay." Which probably means I should call my parents more often when I do have a free minute—or ten, or thirty.

I heard Amanda say, "Yeah, we had a lot of excitement here last night—" I snatched the phone before my dramatic daughter could give her grandmother a blow-by-blow account of the robbery. "Hi, Mom!" I said breezily, shooing Amanda out the back door. *"Go ahead and eat,"* I mouthed at Denny.

"Hi, sweetie," my mom said. "Excitement? What excitement? You doing all right?"

My mom would probably never forgive herself for not rushing to my side when I'd had the accident earlier that summer. Yet she'd had a bad chest cold at the time, verging on pneumonia, and the doctor had advised her not to travel—praise be to heaven. I loved my folks, really I did. They were good parents, solid, full of faith, a bit too serious perhaps—but whew! They would've gone into shock when I got charged with vehicular manslaughter, even though it later got dropped. And what if they'd found out we'd been fighting that day over Denny drinking beer with the guys? Denny would never hear the end of it. Never mind that *I* was the one "driving mad."

No. God had created three hundred miles between Chicago and Des Moines, Iowa, which made it easier to keep things simple: *"It was raining. I had a car accident. A boy was killed—so tragic. I broke my leg and several ribs and lost my spleen, but I'm better now."*

"Sure, Mom. I'm fine. We all start school tomorrow, you know. The kids are excited."

"I know. That's why I called. Don't you think handling a class-room so soon after surgery will be too much? Maybe they could assign a substitute for a few weeks."

"No, Mom, really. I'll be okay. It'd be much harder to start late. How's Dad? You guys decide to get that motor home?"

"Oh, I don't know. It's secondhand, you know. Still in good condition, though . . ."

I closed my eyes as my mom fussed about spending the money, feeling relieved that she didn't pick up on the "excitement" we had around here last night—and guilty that I wasn't sharing things straight up with my parents. Yet I knew they'd be terribly upset and start fussing about why we were living in the city. Right now I could hardly handle my own raw feelings, much less theirs. There were some things you just didn't want to tell your parents—

Sheesh. Listen to me! Did Josh and Amanda think like that? What weren't they telling *us?*

Hmm. Maybe I should tell my parents. But later. I'd tell them later.

". . . come to see you for your birthday? Josh's birthday is the week after—maybe we could come the weekend between and celebrate both."

That got my attention. "Uh . . . sure, Mom. Let me check the calendar." *Oh God, give me strength.* Sure I wanted my parents to visit; the kids hadn't seen their grandparents all summer. At that moment, though, I felt overwhelmed. School was starting tomorrow. The upset at Adele's beauty shop was still unresolved. We'd just been robbed and terrorized right in our own home . . .

Well, at least that weekend looked free, between two Yada Yada meetings. And it was three weeks away. "Sure, Mom. That'd be great. Let's talk more about it later. Denny and the kids are eating without me, so I'll call you in a couple of days, okay?"

TRYING TO GET THE KIDS TO BED EARLIER because it was suddenly a school night was like trying to get a cat to heel. Finally I had a few minutes to send an e-mail to the Yada Yada list about praying for Carla and her reentry into the Hickman family. There were a few incoming messages—one from Stu, saying she had nightmares last night and for the first time in her life felt anxious about living alone, and she would have a hard time waiting another two weeks to pray together.

Hmm. That was a different side of Leslie "Stu" Stuart than I'd seen before. Nothing ever seemed to faze her. Guess she was human like the rest of us.

Nony had sent out a brief e-mail, bringing the group up to speed about the Takahashis leaving abruptly for Japan and urging us to pray for Hoshi, who was quite distraught. We all knew she'd been anxious about telling her parents she'd become a Christian, but this was far worse than anything she'd imagined.

Poor Hoshi. Maybe we could invite her to dinner soon and give her some emotional support. If I had any to give, that is. I moved that idea into a corner of my mind labeled "to think about later."

The last e-mail was from Ruth.

To: Yada Yada
From: Yid-dish@online.net
Subject: Rosh Hashanah

If Yada Yada wants to visit my Messianic Jewish congregation, the best time would be during our "high holy days" this month. I meant to invite you all last night, but with a robbery in progress, I can be forgiven, yes? But it can't wait till next time because Rosh Hashanah

(Jewish New Year) services are this weekend: 7:30 p.m. Friday and Saturday 10:30 a.m.

Or it could be Yom Kippur ten days later. Depends on whether you want to celebrate the New Year and EAT, or confess your sins and FAST.

Whichever, why doesn't Yada Yada meet at my house next time (right before Yom Kippur), and I could explain it all better then, though I'll probably have to throw Ben out.

Celebrating and eating sounds good to me, I thought. Something to get our minds off the trauma of yesterday's Yada Yada meeting, though this coming weekend might be a little soon for another church visit. Yet like Ruth said, the Jewish holy days weren't going to rearrange themselves for our schedule. I moved my cursor to Reply All and typed: "Great idea! Either holiday is fine by me. Jodi."

"Jodi?"

I turned from the computer screen. Denny was leaning against the doorway of the dining room, stripped down to a pair of boxer shorts. I thought he was going to say, "Coming to bed?" but he didn't.

"Could we"—he shrugged, as if embarrassed—"uh, pray together before we go to bed? I'm . . . I dunno. Just feeling un-settled. The business last night, but also Adele taking off without saying a word to me about MaDear and what happened. Still hasn't told me how much I owe her for your hair and nails either." He shrugged again. "Don't know why that bothers me so much, but it does. I've been trying to pray about it, to put it to rest, but seems like I go around in circles."

I just looked at my husband a moment, trying to read his face. Denny didn't often admit to "going around in circles." Or ask to pray together at bedtime. Unsettled? Yeah. I felt the same way. Like our private fears were lurking in the shadows, just out of reach, refusing to come into the light.

Standing there in his boxers asking us to pray, Denny looked about as vulnerable as I'd ever seen him.

15

The next morning the typical Baxter hurry-scurry kicked in, but we all managed to get out of the house roughly on time. Denny drove Josh and Amanda to Lane Tech in the "new" used minivan for their first day, then he headed for West Rogers High. I stuck the books I'd mended, the last pieces of my Welcome Bulletin Board, and a pair of loafers into my tote bag and headed out for the twenty-minute walk to Bethune Elementary.

I actually found myself looking forward to the first day of school. *Hoo boy!* Now if that wasn't a miracle!

Must have been the prayer with Denny last night. We'd just held each other in the dark in the living room, pouring out all the confusion and upset we'd both been feeling, telling Jesus it had been a rotten summer. We didn't know what to do about MaDear. Getting robbed in our own home had been terrifying. We also thanked God for a lot of stuff. Like Josh and Amanda and the rest of Uptown's youth getting home safely from Mexico and having a great time building houses with Habitat for Humanity. For the strength our Yada Yada sisters had poured into both of us with their prayers and their presence during those awful days following the accident. That the charges against me got dropped, and I was healing fast. That Denny still had a job at the high school.

Once we started, it seemed like there were so many things to pray about: Carla coming home to her family and starting a new school, Hoshi and her distraught parents, and even MaDear and the painful memories that haunted her.

"Good thing God is God all by Himself!" I'd muttered after our final amen. Florida's favorite phrase. "I'd sure hate to sort out all the stuff we just dumped in God's lap." That set us off laughing—but oh, my mutilated abdomen still hurt when I laughed.

I felt free this morning. Sort of like that old hymn, "Take your burden to the Cross and leave it there" . . . or something like that. Hadn't thought about that one for ages. We didn't sing hymns too often at Uptown Community, not like we did in the little Bible church I grew up in. I wondered if I had a hymnal somewhere; I could look it up.

Walking to school and carrying my heavy tote bag turned out to be a bit optimistic for the first day, because my left leg ached something fierce by the time I got there. But I was early enough to take a couple of pain relievers and told myself I'd make it through the day okay.

My student teacher was already in our classroom, looking as cute as Betty Boop with her short, dark, curly hair and a simple pale-blue jersey dress bringing out the blue in her eyes. "Blue is definitely your color, Christy," I said, giving her a hug.

She seemed a little flustered by the hug but gave me a big smile. "I'm really nervous, Ms. Baxter." She nodded toward the bank of windows that looked out on the playground. "All those children . . ."

"Feel free to call me Jodi when the children aren't around," I started unloading my tote bag, "but get used to being called 'Ms. James' when they are."

She giggled. "That will be so weird."

We set to work putting the finishing touches to the bulletin board. Christy had cut out each child's name in colorful bubble letters. Below each name I stapled a construction-paper cloud with the meaning of the child's name written in black letters.

"That is so cool, Ms. Bax— . . . um, Jodi." Christy studied the board.

The hands of the clock nudged toward 8:40. "Grab that class roster," I told Christy, heading for the door with a square of laminated paper that read "3-A." We made it to the playground just as the lineup bell rang. I held up the "3-A" sign, hoping parents had told their children which classroom they were in. A passel of energetic boys got in line pushing and shoving, their oversized backpacks bumping about on their skinny rumps. Most of the girls held back, out of the way of the pushers. I smiled at the first boy in line: a handsome child with hazelnut skin, brown eyes so dark they were almost black, and a nearly shaved head. Hmm. Without the hair I couldn't be sure about ethnicity—could be African-American or Middle Eastern. "What's your name, young man?" I asked.

"Xavier!" He shouted it out almost defiantly. The boy behind him giggled. *Still could be almost anything.*

The final bell rang. *Okay, Lord, this is it. See this line? They're mine for the year. Correction. They're Yours for the year. I'd appreciate a little help. Make that a lot of help.* I led them through the metal detectors that had been installed after 9-11 and down the hall to 3-A. Then I stood in the doorway as they jostled into the room.

As soon as each student—thirty-one of them!—found the desk with his or her name taped on it, I introduced "Ms. James" as my "team teacher" and wrote both our names on the chalkboard. We ran through the usual classroom rules—Respect People, Respect Property, Respect Yourself—and added my own clarifications: "When the teacher is talking, you're listening. Raise your hand if you have a question or need to use the washroom. No punching or spitting on other people."

Immediately there were a lot of spitting noises. I groaned to myself. *Shouldn't have given them the idea.*

I moved to the Welcome Bulletin Board while Christy sent the first child to join me. "Can you find your name?" I said to the little girl with three fat ponytail braids wrapped on each end with colorful rubber-band balls. She pointed to her name in bubble letters: Jade. "Can you read what your name means underneath?"

She squinted. "Jewel?" She looked up at me.

"Yes." I smiled. "Jade is a special kind of jewel, a very rich green color." I leaned toward her and spoke in a loud stage whisper.

"Green is one of my favorite colors."

I was rewarded with a smile, and Christy tapped the next student, a pug-nosed kid sporting an army-style buzz cut. "Cornell," he announced, pointing to his name. He studied the cloud underneath his name. "Horn blower?" he scoffed. "What's a horn blower?"

The other children laughed, but I held up my hand with a warning look. "Someone who can play a trumpet or a trombone or maybe one of those big baritone horns." I raised a quizzical eyebrow. "Did you ever think about joining the school band?"

"I don't got no horn!"

"You might want to think about it," I said, "with a name like that."

Now several hands shot up in the air, but Christy continued alternating a girl, then a boy, from different areas of the room. When Britny read, "From England," under her name, she scowled. "I ain't from no England." She certainly wasn't; she was as African-American as they come.

"But that's what your name means. Maybe . . ." I thought fast. "Maybe you could learn some things about England and tell the rest of the class. And maybe . . ." I whispered in her ear. "Maybe someday you will travel to England and see the queen!"

"Okay," she said and practically skipped back to her desk.

Now hands were flying everywhere. Everybody—well, almost everybody—wanted to know what their name meant. I tried to make a positive comment for each one, shamelessly bending some of them toward positive classroom behavior.

Ramón—"Mighty Protector." "Ah! Ramón must be our class

protector. He's going to protect anybody from getting bullied by somebody else."

"Yeah," agreed Ramón. "Any of you guys bully a little kid, I'm gonna smack you in the face." Laughter erupted once more, and I had to make sure Ramón knew that was *not* what I meant.

Xavier—"Bright." "Do you know what 'bright' means, Xavier?"

"Yeah." He spread his fingers on either side of his face, like sun rays. "I glow in the dark!"

Now the class was laughing nonstop. I was losing them. Just then the door opened quietly, and Avis slipped into the room. *Oh no.* I forgot that each classroom got a visit from the principal on the first day. She couldn't have come at a worse time!

I held up one hand like a traffic cop and waited till the children quieted. Then I turned back to Xavier. "Yes, that's one meaning of bright, like a dazzling light. It also means smart—very smart." I tapped the side of my head. "I think you are going to show us this year just how smart you are, don't you?"

Xavier strutted back to his desk, and I introduced "Ms. Johnson, our principal," who gave a little pep talk to the children about being good citizens of our school community and the importance of respect, rules, and teamwork. As she slipped back out the door, she caught my eye and tipped her head toward the bulletin board. "Clever."

The knot in my stomach untied. *Oh God, thank You for Avis!*

We went back to the meaning of our names, but when Christy tapped one boy on the shoulder, he scowled and scooted deeper in his seat. "Don't wanna. It's stupid."

I walked to where I could see his name on his desk. "Hakim?" I was surprised at his reluctance, but didn't want to force it. Instead I went back to the bulletin board and found his name. "Hakim . . . 'wise healer.'" *Oh dear.* I had no idea how to apply that to an eight-year-old. "Maybe," I tried, "you will be a doctor some-day."

"Don't wanna be a doctor." The boy's tone was fierce. "They ain't no good anyway."

Okay. Better just leave it alone. We moved on to the few remain-ing students.

THE TWO-THIRTY BELL RANG. The class started a stampede for the door, and we had to sit everyone down again and start over. "Line up! Everybody got your backpack and take-home folders? If you didn't bring the items on the supply list your parents got in the mail, there's a copy of that list in your folder."

As Christy led the line out the door, Britny suddenly stepped out of line and stood in front of me. "How come your name and hers"—she pointed at Christy's back—"ain't on the board? What do your names mean?"

We weren't supposed to use our first names with the children, but to tell the truth, I hadn't had time to look them up. *Jodi . . . Christy . . .* That would be interesting. I gave Britny a quick hug. "I don't know. Good question. I'll have to look them up."

I was so tired and achy when I got home, I just wanted to soak in the tub and crawl into bed. Amanda came home upset because she didn't get the teacher she wanted for Spanish II, and for a while there was a lot of door slamming between her room and the bathroom. Josh was his usual minimalist self, offering "Okay" and "Not really" to my questions about his first day as a senior.

Humph. So much for good communication with my teenagers. I took some iced tea out on the back porch, intending to sulk. Instead, the same hymn I'd been humming on the way to school popped back into my head. "Take your burden to the Cross and leave it there . . ." No, that wasn't quite right. What was it?

I dragged myself back into the house, found the red hymnal we used back at our church in Downers Grove, and turned to the index. There it was on page 353: "Leave It There." Except the actual phrase was, "Take your burden to the *Lord* and leave it there."

I squinted at the author: Charles A. Tindley. Wrote both the words and the music. Who in the world was he? I'd heard of Charles Wesley and Fanny Crosby, but Tindley? Curious, I looked in the author index to see if he wrote anything else. Yep. "Nothing between my soul and the Savior . . ." *Hmm.* I knew that one too.

I heard the back door bang. "Denny? Who's Charles Tindley?"

Denny appeared in the archway to the living room where I was sprawled in the recliner with the hymnal, his gym bag slung over his shoulder. "Hi to you too. Am I supposed to know this guy? I'm starving. What's for supper?"

He had to be kidding. He sounded like an Archie Bunker rerun. "Leftovers," I snarled. "Or PB&Js. Or we could go out to Siam Pasta. I'm beat." We didn't often take the kids out to eat—

not with their hollow legs—but, hey, we had all survived our first day of school. Cause for celebration. And Siam Pasta passed the test for a five-star rating from the Baxters: good food, lots of it, cheap.

Denny shrugged. "Why not? Beats PB&Js."

It actually turned out to be a good idea, because once we got the kids trapped in a restaurant booth—no phone, no distractions, no place to go—we actually got more lowdown about their first day of school. As for Denny, he said things went okay on the first day, though he had a lot of ideas that could improve communication among the coaching staff. "Though I don't think the athletic director wants to hear them from me," he grumbled. "Maybe he'll retire, and I can apply for his job."

I got a laugh out of Josh when I told them about our "mighty protector" threatening to smack anybody who bullied another kid. "Got the idea of looking up the meaning of their names from you, Amanda," I said. "Well, from Delores, really, when she said your name means 'lovable' in Spanish."

Amanda glared. *"Mom!* You weren't supposed to tell anybody!"

Oh. Right. Yet already I could see that trying to take it back would be like trying to retrieve dandelion fuzz after blowing it off its stem. I was sure the cogs in Josh's brain were clicking away, devising ways to hold this interesting fact over his sister's head. "Well, then, I'll just have to make the same rule for the family I made for the kids in my class: You can't use the meaning of somebody's name to tease them." *Oh, sure.*

Revived somewhat by supper "out," my curiosity got the best of

145

me and I turned on the computer. No e-mail messages from Yada Yada—everybody was probably too busy recovering from the first day of school. I wondered how Carla Hickman's first day went. Did Florida get her registered? I decided not to call. The Hickman family needed space to adjust to this new wrinkle—a *miracle* wrinkle—in their lives.

Instead, I called up one of the name Web sites I'd been using to locate the kids' names and typed "Jodi" in the search box. I stared at the page that came up on-screen.

> Jodi—a derivative of Joan.
> Meaning: "God is gracious."

Maybe I was just tired. Maybe the long, difficult summer finally caught up with me. Maybe it was just a reminder of something God had been trying to tell me for weeks. But I put my head down on the computer keyboard . . . and wept.

16

od is gracious . . . God is gracious . . . I didn't tell anybody the meaning of my name right away. I wanted to tuck it into a private place in my mind and let it soak down deep. I'd looked up Christy's name too, just in case Britny asked again. All the variations of "Christine" meant "Christ follower." What would Christy think about that? Was she or wasn't she? We weren't supposed to talk about our personal religion in public school.

Not that we had much time for chitchat. The first week of school was like trying to stay one step ahead of a steamroller driven by thirty devious eight-year-olds. One misstep, and the kids would run right over me. In the back of my mind I worried about Hoshi and wondered how Florida's little girl was adjusting, but it was Thursday night before I got a chance to call either of them.

Wednesday night, I'd decided to go back to Bible study at Uptown with Denny—I hadn't been since I'd been in the hospital.

Pastor Clark was beginning a study of the book of James, which sounded promising. Good ol' James, a down-to-earth brother if there ever was one. Practical. Straight to the point. Unlike the apostle Paul, whose sentences rambled on and on like a sweater unraveling, with just as many knots to untangle.

I saw Avis at Bible study, but we didn't really get to talk except in passing, when she said she couldn't attend Rosh Hashanah at Ruth's church this Saturday, but she'd like to hear about it if I went. I told her Denny and I hadn't talked about it yet.

Thursday night things were quiet at the Baxter house. Josh was at Uptown, manning the soundboard for the praise-team practice; Amanda was baby-sitting the Reilly twins, nine-year-old sweeties whose mom sang on the praise team and dad played guitar. In the living room, Denny was watching videotapes of other soccer teams in the high-school league, trying to identify patterns and weak spots.

"Looks like it's just you and me, Willie," I said to the dog. "Whatcha wanna do?" Willie Wonka ignored me and waddled off to do some male bonding with Denny.

I took the cordless out to the back porch and called Nony. One of her boys answered. "Smith residence. To whom do you wish to speak?"

I nearly fell off the porch steps. He sounded like an English butler. Weren't Nony's boys only nine and eleven? "Um . . . this is Jodi Baxter. To whom am I speaking?" To *whom?* I hadn't been this correct since high-school English.

"This is Marcus. Hi, Mrs. Baxter. Do you want my mom?"

I wanted to hug him. He was going to be a heartbreaker some-day. He probably put his dirty clothes in the laundry too—unasked. "Actually, Marcus, I'm calling for Hoshi. Is she there?"

"I'll get her."

I waited for what seemed a long minute, then I heard Hoshi's quiet voice. "Yes? This is Hoshi."

"Hi, Hoshi. It's Jodi. I've been thinking about you all week. Nony told us your parents went home. Are you okay?"

"Yes, I'm okay." Her voice was only a few notches above a whisper.

"How is your mom?—her hand, I mean."

There was a moment's pause. "I don't know, Jodi. I haven't heard anything since they left last Monday. The Smiths let me call to Japan, but nobody answered." She started to cry.

"Oh, Hoshi." The poor girl was going through hell, and I just dragged it all up again. "I'm so sorry. I didn't mean to—"

"No, no, Jodi, it's all right. Wait . . ." I could hear her blowing her nose before she came back on. "I'm happy you called. Please pray for my parents. That's all I know what to do. Nony and Dr. Smith—they are very good to me."

"Do you . . . would you like to come to dinner sometime next week?" *Oh, you're rash, Jodi. You can barely scratch dinner together for your own family on weeknights.* "Or do your classes start next week?"

"No . . . I mean, yes, I would like to come. Classes don't start till the last week of September. It would be nice to share the table with your family."

We tentatively agreed on the following Tuesday, with Hoshi

149

coming by the El and then we'd take her home. After we hung up, I went inside to check it out with Denny, but he was taking intense notes while guys in blue-and-gold uniforms—probably the Sullivan Tigers—ran back and forth on the TV screen. I knew better than to interrupt that focused look.

I retreated to the back-porch steps again and dialed Florida. Another male voice, but this one was deep and brief. "Yeah?"

I took a stab. Had to be Florida's husband. "Uh, Carl?"

"Yeah."

"This is Jodi Baxter. Is Florida there?"

Carl Hickman didn't reply. He just yelled off to the side, "Flo! Phone for you."

This time it seemed like I waited two, maybe three minutes. Finally Florida picked up the phone. "Hey, Jodi. Whassup?"

"Whassup yourself. I called to see how it's going with Carla. You get her registered for school?"

We chatted for about five minutes. The social worker at Carla's new school had been very helpful, she said, even suggested some family sessions with a school counselor to help ease the transition at home as well as school. "'Course you know, Jodi, if Carl got hisself a *job*, that would be one big help. Then we could get a bigger apartment. Right now I got all three kids in that closet they call a second bedroom."

I remembered when Amanda and I had visited Florida's apartment—before the accident. All I'd seen in that little bedroom was a double mattress on the floor. Surely Carla and the boys weren't sleeping . . .

"Beds, Florida? You got beds for the kids?" I couldn't help it. Had to ask.

"Yes, thank ya, Jesus. Found a bunk bed at Salvation Army for the boys and an army-cot thing for Carla—actually, that's all we got space for till we get a bigger place. Sheets, though. We could use some twin bedsheets. And pillowcases."

"I'll see what I can rustle up." Amanda still had a birthday "coupon" for a new comforter for her bed. Maybe we should get new sheets, too, and pass on her old ones to—

I stopped myself. Why did I always think in terms of passing on the old ones? *Maybe you should get new sheets for Florida's kids, Jodi Baxter. Would you want someone else's old sheets for your kids?*

At least it sounded like things were coming along with Carla. Yet I still felt overwhelmed for her. What Florida said was true: they needed a bigger apartment, and Carl needed a job yesterday. Maybe I should ask Denny to talk to Pastor Clark about Carl.

The TV was still going in the living room when we hung up. Should I check up on anyone else? I'd talked this week to everybody who *hadn't* been at the robbery, and most everybody who had . . .

Except Adele.

Had anybody heard from her? Should I call? Just to see how she's doing after Sunday night? That would be reasonable, wouldn't it?

Instead, I headed back into the house, hung up the cordless, and pulled out my school bag. Really, I needed to review my lesson plans for Friday.

THE WEEKEND SLIPPED BY, and I never did call Adele.

When I got home from school on Friday, I was too bushed to even think about going to Rosh Hashanah services with Ruth that night. And when Denny got home, he'd immediately gone out to the garage to work on the car—"while I've still got some light"—so the car wasn't available anyway.

I did check e-mail to see if Ruth got any response to her invitation, but this weekend must have been too soon for most folks, because only Stu said she'd like to come, probably on Saturday. Why wasn't I surprised? Stu always seemed to be first up to the plate. Several other Yada Yadas said they'd try for Yom Kippur.

I had to admit I was curious about Ruth's Beth Yehudah Congregation. Did we have anything going Saturday? I'd never been to a Jewish service before, even though there were a lot of synagogues in Rogers Park. Of course, this would be a *Christian* celebration of the Jewish holiday. Would it be mostly like church? Or like going to synagogue?

Only one way to find out.

I printed out Ruth's invitation and went hunting for Denny. Found his legs sticking out from underneath the minivan. "Something wrong?" I asked.

"Nope," came a muffled voice. "Just changing the oil." He pulled himself out from under the car, oblivious to the little black smudges dotting his face. "What's up?" He stood up and leaned under the hood to change the oil filter.

"Um, wanna do something different tomorrow—you and me?"

"Sure. As long as it's cheap."

Can't get any cheaper, I thought, *unless they take an offering.* "Well, it's Rosh Hashanah, the Jewish New Year, and Ruth invited—"

"Ah. I get it. Another date sponsored by Yada Yada."

I couldn't see Denny's face under the hood. Was he having a problem with this?

"We don't have to go; it was just an idea. Or I could go alone." I knew that sounded whiny, but I *did* want to go, and I wanted Denny to go with me. "Unless you have a better idea."

"Not really." He appeared from under the hood and started wiping his hands on a rag. "Just feels like a lot. We visited Delores's church two weeks ago—which I enjoyed, don't get me wrong. Then Yada Yada meets at our house last week and turns into a three-ring circus. *Next* week it'll be Yada Yada again, and aren't your folks coming the weekend after that for your birthday?"

I didn't answer, just watched as he scrunched back under the car to cap the dripping oil. He was right; it did feel like a lot. On the other hand, if we didn't plan our Saturday, he'd end up in front of the TV watching a string of games—baseball, football—it didn't seem to matter who or where, as long as there were two teams fighting over a ball.

He reappeared, dragging out the container of old oil. "On the other hand—"

"Denny!" I shrieked. "That's the plastic pitcher I use to make iced tea!" I whacked him on the head with the rolled-up paper in my hand. "I can't believe you used that!"

"Oh." He grimaced. "Sorry. Couldn't find the old milk jug I usually use, and this was sitting on the back porch . . ."

I rolled my eyes. He looked really funny holding that iced-tea pitcher full of cruddy old oil, probably considering whether he could wash it out. I started to laugh.

He grinned—relieved, I'm sure. "Okay, let's go celebrate the Jewish New Year with dear ol' Ruth Garfield. On one condition: we go to the Bagel Bakery afterward and get some more of that lip-smacking lox and cream cheese. Just tell me what I'm supposed to wear. Unless"—he dipped a finger into the old oil and advanced toward me—"you'd like to go 'Goth': a black smudge here and there . . ."

"Don't you dare!" I flew out the door toward the house. Maybe Denny agreed to go because he felt guilty using the good plastic pitcher. Whatever. I gave him a chance to come up with a better idea, didn't I?

I'd better call Ruth. I had no idea where to go, what to wear, or what to expect.

17

*A*ssured by Ruth Garfield that anything we wore would be fine ("Just not jeans or shorts—or halter tops, *oy vey!*"), Denny and I left a note the next morning for Josh and Amanda, who hadn't yet appeared in the land of the living, and set out in the Dodge Caravan for Beth Yehudah, Ruth's congregation.

"We're looking for what?" Denny said when I read him the directions. "Lincolnwood Presbyterian? I thought this was a Messianic congregation."

"It is. Beth Yehudah meets in a Presbyterian church on Saturday, so there's no conflict."

As we drove west from Rogers Park into Lincolnwood—indistinguishable from Chicago proper, as were all the other towns rimming the Windy City's borders—we saw numerous Jewish families walking to their local synagogue. Most of the men and boys wore yarmulkes; a few Orthodox could be identified by their traditional black-brimmed hats, prayer-shawl fringes dangling beneath their suit coats, and corkscrew curls in front of their ears. Children held their parents' hands or skipped ahead. Definitely a holiday feel.

I felt nervous, like I was intruding on their Sabbath. What did I know about Rosh Hashanah? These were Jewish holy days. Yet we'd been invited, I reminded myself as Denny pulled into the parking lot of Lincolnwood Presbyterian—a modern A-frame structure with lots of colored-glass windows in odd shapes. And these were fellow Christians, albeit Jewish ones. Maybe it wouldn't be so different.

We didn't see Ruth when we first came in, but a friendly greeter pointed us to the large "Fellowship Room," where most of the people coming in seemed to be headed. Folding chairs were set in rows facing a small oak table at the front, on which stood a tall wooden something—like a polished oak chest, up on end—with doors. Both table and chest had the same Hebrew inscription.

Another greeter handed us a booklet—the order of service, I supposed—and I nudged Denny into a row of chairs just shy of the middle, so we could watch what other people did but be close enough to see what happened up front.

I looked around, trying to spy Ruth. It all looked very ordinary—just a typical church building, a typical multipurpose room in the basement, and even the requisite keyboard, drums, and guitars off to one side at the front. As I scanned the people who were already sitting in the folding chairs, I noticed a familiar blonde head a couple of rows ahead of us. *Sheesh.* Stu had twice as far to drive as we did, and she still got here early.

Just then the blonde hair swung around, and Stu caught my eye. Getting up, she moved back to join us, booklet in hand, long hair falling over one shoulder of her neatly tailored navy pantsuit. Suddenly I felt underdressed in my khaki culottes, knit top, and sandals. "Hi, Jodi . . . Denny," she said, bestowing a bright smile on us as she settled into the seat next to Denny. "Seen Ruth yet?"

I shook my head. But just then we heard Ruth's voice over all the other murmured conversations going on. *"There* you are! Outside I'm standing, looking for you. How did you get past me?"

I smirked at Denny—*yeah right, she just got here and waited outside for thirty seconds*—then gave Ruth a hug as she plopped into the folding chair next to me, her hands clutching a roomy leather bag, her Bible, and the booklet, all of which she unceremoniously dumped on the empty chair next to her.

"Ben coming?" Denny craned his neck and looked around hopefully.

"Ben, Schmen." Ruth practically rolled her eyes. "Gave up attending temple years ago, he did—except for the occasional holiday—but set foot inside Beth Yehudah? He acts like God might strike him dead. But"—she leaned across me and winked at Denny—"he weakened when I told him *you* were coming today, Denny. He likes you."

"Maybe we could call him after the service and meet at the Bagel Bakery for lunch or something." Denny grinned at Ruth so wide his dimples showed. If it were anybody but frowzy Ruth, I'd swear he was flirting. But more likely he was thinking about that lox-and-cream-cheese bagel he had the last time we were there.

Now Ruth did roll her eyes. *"Goyim."* She lowered her voice. "It's *Shabbat*, Denny. It won't open till sundown."

I stifled a giggle, glad it was Denny who stuck his foot in his mouth, since I, too, had totally forgotten that the Bagel Bakery was closed on Saturday. Too bad. That would've been fun.

Several men and women were picking up instruments and testing microphones, and a middle-aged man wearing a gray suit with a white, fringed prayer shawl draped around his shoulders set up a portable lectern. Looked like things were about to get started. "What do the words on the table say?" I whispered to Ruth.

"'Holy to the Lord'—same as on the ark."

Ark? I peered closer at the upright chest thing. It didn't look like the ark of the covenant pictured in my Sunday-school pictures as a child, which always lay horizontal, like an old-fashioned hope chest.

A sudden long blast of a horn from the back of the room made me jump. I turned and stared. A tall young man with a dark beard was blowing a long, curved ram's horn—the "shofar" I'd heard about. Again and again he blew the horn, as if he were standing on a hillside, summoning all within the sound of the horn. Goose bumps popped out all along my arms.

As if on cue, the man at the front in a prayer shawl raised his arms and called out, "Wake up! Yeshua, our God and King, is coming soon! Wake up!" The sound of the horn died away, along with my goose bumps. "The Lord has given us these days for joy and thanksgiving—a new year! The blowing of the shofar also calls us to a season of repentance, a time to examine our hearts and confess our sins that we might be prepared for His return. Let us give thanks." The leader held up the booklet. "Please turn to page 53 and read responsively."

I fumbled for the booklet I'd been given and opened to the first page. Page 192? Then I heard Ruth hiss, "The back—it reads back to front."

Oh. I turned the book over. Sure enough, the back cover said, "Mahzor for High Holy Days." By the time I flipped to page 53, the leader had already started to read: "Give thanks to the Lord, for He is good."

Then the congregation chimed in: "His mercy endures forever."

"To Him alone who does great wonders."

"His mercy endures forever . . ."

After the responsive reading, an African-American woman, her head wrapped in an African-print cloth, stood up and began to sing—in Hebrew, I supposed, since the words were not English—accompanied by a tambourine, guitar, and piano. A Christian Jewish African-American? I had supposed that all Messianic Jews were probably Jewish first, but what did I know? I closed my eyes and let the unknown words sink in. The tune had a distinctly Israeli flavor, and I could almost imagine an Israeli folk dance. Then the Hebrew words flowed into English: "Blessed are those who know the sound of shofar, who walk in the light of Your presence, Oh Lord."

After the song, people stood and turned sideways, facing the wall. *What in the world?* "East, toward Jerusalem," came the whisper in my ear. The Hebrew words rolled easily off the tongues of people around us:

She-ma Yis-ra-el: A-do-nai e-lo-heinu, A-do-nai e-chad!
Ba-ruch shem ke-vod mal-chu-to le-o-lam va-ed!

And then the leader boomed out in English:

Hear, O Israel: The Lord our God, the Lord is One.
Blessed be his glorious name whose kingdom is forever and ever.

This declaration—the "Shema," Ruth informed me—was followed by a prayer from the leader, and then the instrumentalists started up again. The beat was decidedly bouncy. A young woman kept brisk time with the tambourine, and everyone began to sing: "Oh come, let us sing! Let us rejoice! Messiah has come! And He brought joy!"

I grinned at Denny. Celebrating that "Messiah has come!" was no doubt a Messianic addition to the traditional Rosh Hashanah service.

As the song continued, a few people at the front grabbed hands and began a line dance around the room. More people popped up and joined them—a mix of young and old, skipping feet, and bobbing yarmulkes of all different colors. When the line passed by the middle aisle, someone reached out to Stu, who was sitting on the aisle seat, and she joined them, her long hair flying as she quickly picked up the steps.

It looked like fun! I was tempted to join them, too, but dancing so soon after getting off my crutches was not a good idea. I'd probably fall down and make a fool of myself. And then it was over, and Stu collapsed, laughing, back in her seat. Lucky her.

A few more songs, and then the congregation was invited to turn to the "Avinu Malkenu" in the *mahzor*. I noticed that on the right-hand pages, everything was printed in Hebrew script; the English translation was printed on the left. First the leader sang the Hebrew in a sing-song chant, and the congregation responded, also in Hebrew. I could hear even children's voices saying the Hebrew words and shook my head in amazement. Were they actually reading those exquisite squiggles and dots? I could imagine learning French or Spanish or any other language that had a similar alphabet to English—but Hebrew? Whew.

The Hebrew song-chant was followed by the English, simply spoken: "Our Father, our King, forgive and pardon our iniquities . . ."

After the Avinu Malkenu, two young men wearing prayer shawls strode toward the wooden chest sitting on the table. As if on signal, the congregation stood. They opened the box and reverently took out the Torah, dressed in a silk purple sheath with golden tassels, a brass plate hanging by a chain on the front—an "ephod," I guessed, like the priests used to wear in my old Sunday-school pictures—and topped with a crown. Everyone in the room seemed to hold their breath in a collective hush as the two young men removed the crown, then the ephod and the purple silken cloth, so the scroll could be unrolled.

"The Torah is read with great respect every Shabbat," Ruth murmured, almost causing me to miss the leader saying, *"Ba-ruch Adonai ham-vo-rach . . .* Blessed are You, Lord our God, King of the Universe, who has chosen us from all the peoples and has given us Your Torah."

One of the young men began to read in Hebrew from the huge scroll in a sing-song chant. Then the leader read the words in English from his Bible: "On the first day of the seventh month hold a sacred assembly and do no regular work. It is a day for you to sound the trumpets . . ." I noticed Ruth had her Bible open to Numbers 29. Other scriptures were read, then the Torah was re-dressed, and the two young men began to parade it slowly around the room and up the middle aisle. As they did so, people leaned out of their seats to touch it as it passed.

Ruth's breath brushed my ear. "The Jewish people hold the Torah in high reverence."

I couldn't imagine parading the Bible around Uptown Community. In fact, half the congregation didn't even *bring* their Bibles to church, much to Pastor Clark's dismay. Yet as I watched the Torah being carried about the room, I felt wrapped in awe. How little I really knew about the roots of my own Christian faith or my spiritual ancestors, even though I'd been raised on Old Testament stories along with the New.

When the Torah had been safely shut once more within the "ark," the leader began his sermon. I saw Denny hunch forward, elbows on his knees, chin on his hands, listening intently as the man in the prayer shawl began to explain the meaning of the various Jewish feasts and how each one prophetically pointed toward the coming of the Messiah.

Passover—the Lamb whose blood saved the people. Day of First Fruits—the resurrection. *Shavuoth*, or Pentecost (which traditionally celebrated the giving of the Ten Commandments)—the coming of the Holy Spirit, who now writes God's law on our hearts. Rosh Hashanah—yet to be fulfilled in Yeshua's second coming. And finally, Yom Kippur—when the Book of Life will be opened and read.

I was fascinated. I knew Jesus had broken the bread and passed the wine at Passover, saying, "This is My body. This is My blood." But I'd never really given any thought to the other Old Testament festivals as having anything to do with me.

"The days between now and Yom Kippur, the Day of Atonement," Beth Yehudah's leader continued, "represent the time we have been given to intercede for our people, that their names would be written in the Book of Life. Just as the prophets of old, we too must identify with the sins of our people—the sins of Israel and the sins of the church—and repent, calling on God for His mercy and forgiveness."

I felt Denny jerk upright beside me. I tried to catch his eye. Was something wrong? He seemed distracted, distant.

After the sermon, the instruments came out once more, thrumming a rhythmic song that reminded me of a slow dance in heavy boots: "Come back people . . . children of Abraham . . . open your eyes, your redemption is nigh." I closed my eyes, wondering what it meant to be part of a people by shared history and faith, rather than the American version of Christianity I grew up with: "just me and God." How presumptuous was *that?*

At the end of the service, the shofar blew again as we opened our *mahzors* and read the "Tekiah" (one long blast on the shofar) . . . the "Shevarim" (three short blasts) . . . and the "Teruah" (a string of staccato blasts that left the horn blower gasping).

After the service, people stood and chatted in little groups, while kids darted here and there. *"L'Shanah Tova,* Jodi," Ruth said, giving me a hug. "Happy New Year!" Stu squeezed past Denny's knees and claimed her hug from Ruth's plump arms. *"L'Shanah Tova,* Stu." Ruth beamed at us both. "Thank you so much for coming! You have no idea how much it means—"

Ruth stopped midsentence and peered behind me at Denny, who was still sitting in his chair like a brooding sculpture. The Thinker, with clothes on. "Denny? School's out—you can get up now." She frowned. "You okay?

Denny looked up and blinked. "What? Oh. Sorry. Just thinking." He rose hastily and gave Ruth a hug. "Forgive my manners. Thanks for inviting us—well, for inviting Yada Yada." He jerked a thumb at Stu and me. "Hope you don't mind me tagging along."

I smirked at him. *That's okay, Denny. You don't have to admit I dragged you here.*

"Well, come on," Ruth ordered, heading toward a table in the back. "You can't leave till you've had some apples dipped in honey—traditional, you know."

APPLES DIPPED IN HONEY might be traditional, but it didn't make it as "lunch." Denny and I were famished. We splurged on huge burgers at a new Steak 'n Shake on Howard Street, so it was almost two o'clock by the time we got home. I tried asking Denny what he'd been thinking so hard about after the sermon, but all he said was, "Oh, all that stuff about 'repenting for the sins of the people.' Don't know what I think about it."

Didn't know what I thought of it either. Seemed one thing for Old Testament prophets to pray "on behalf of the people," but nobody else could repent of my sins, could they? Didn't I have to repent my own self? Wasn't that what "personal salvation" was all about?

Willie Wonka dashed past us as we came in the back screen door, as if he'd been waiting a long time for somebody to let him out. The back door was standing open—had the kids gone out and left the house unlocked?

Then I noticed the In Use button on the kitchen answering machine was blinking and the cradle was empty—somebody was talking on the phone somewhere. "Helloooo?" I called, dumping my tote bag on the dining-room table. "Amanda? Josh?" Then I saw a note in Josh's scrawl on the table. "Getting a haircut. Back by supper.—J"

A haircut? Denny usually cut Josh's hair with his old electric clippers. But if Josh wanted to use his own money to get his hair cut, more power to him. So it must be Amanda on the—

"Uh, hi Mom. Hey, Dad." Amanda appeared in the doorway between the hall and dining room with the cordless in her hand. "You guys went to church on *Saturday?*"

"Uh-huh." Denny waggled his eyebrows. "Yada Yada let me tag along."

"Oh, stop," I said. "It was interesting, Amanda. You would have enjoyed it." I tipped my head toward the phone in her hand. "Who's on the line?"

"Oh . . . nobody. Just talking to a friend. They hung up." She scuttled into the kitchen, replaced the phone in the wall cradle, and then turned to me. "Can you take me shopping for a comforter today, Mom? It's been two weeks since my birthday and you promised."

Oh, yes. The birthday coupon. I sighed. "I guess. Just give me fifteen minutes before I have to get in the car again." Well, there went the rest of my Saturday. I'd been thinking about a good nap.

As I checked out the refrigerator, which looked pretty much like Mother Hubbard's cupboard, I felt slightly annoyed. Why didn't Amanda just say who she'd been talking to?

18

Amanda and I actually found something she liked for a decent price at Target—or "Tar-*zhay*" as the kids called it, bestowing a phony French accent on the name of the discount store. Of course, *I* would have preferred the comforter with big yellow sunflowers, but Amanda didn't give it a second glance and went for the yellow-and-black geometric shapes. I couldn't look at it too long or I started feeling dizzy.

While wandering the aisles of household items, I remembered Florida said Carla and the boys needed sheets. I stuck two sets of Spiderman twin sheets and one set with rainbows into our shopping cart.

"Uh . . . Mom?" Amanda curled her lip at the juvenile sheets. "No way!"

"Not for you. Florida's kids."

"Oh. Cool."

No complaint about needing new sheets herself. I wanted to

hug her. Amanda's soft spot for kids did indeed make her "lovable," but a hug right in the middle of Tar-*zhay* would *not* be cool.

After we got home I called Florida to see when I could deliver the sheets. "Don't go makin' no trip," she said. "I'll get them tomorrow."

"What do you mean? Yada Yada doesn't meet this week." Or did it? Wasn't the robbery just last Sunday?

"Nah. I mean I'm bringin' the kids to Uptown tomorrow. Gotta start goin' to church somewhere reg'lar as a family."

"Carl too?"

"Huh. Now wouldn't *that* be a miracle."

A door slammed, and I turned to see Josh coming in the back door. Florida's voice chattered on in my ear, but I didn't hear a word she said as I stared at my son's head.

"Hi, Mom," he said, avoiding my eyes while strutting past me, through the dining room, and disappearing down the hall toward his bedroom.

Josh's head had been shaved completely bald—except for a small ponytail high on the back of his head. A bright *orange* ponytail.

LORD, HAVE MERCY. Why didn't somebody tell me raising teenagers was like trying to herd cats, I muttered to myself as I struggled up the stairs to Uptown Community's second-floor meeting room the next morning, lugging the heavy bag of sheets in one hand and a chicken-and-rice casserole for Second Sunday Potluck in the other. I quickly ducked into the kitchen off to the left, both to deposit my casserole and to avoid people's dropped mouths when they first caught sight of my son's bald head.

"Why, Josh?" I'd wailed. *"You had such nice hair!"*

He'd shrugged. *"What's the big deal? Look at Michael Jordan."*

Humph. Michael Jordan, aging superstar, was one thing. Joshua James Baxter—my son—was another. Amanda, of course, said, "Cool!" I don't think Denny liked it, but he did pull me aside and suggested we basically ignore it. *Oh, right.* Ignore your son's head looking like a light bulb with an orange pull-chain on top.

I put on a smile and greeted Brenda Gage, who was sorting food by main dish, salad, or dessert. "I love the curtains you made for the baby's room, Jodi," she said warmly. "Main dish?"

"Uh-huh." Remembering the fiasco the last time I'd brought this dish—I forgot to *cook* it, much to the amusement of Stu, who was visiting Uptown for the first time—I stuck it in the big oven in the church kitchen and turned it on to 300 degrees. *There. Take that.*

As I came out of the kitchen, sure enough, Florida and her crew were coming up the stairs. She had eight-year-old Carla by the hand, followed rather glumly by Cedric and Chris, eleven and thirteen. "Got a ride from Stu," Florida huffed. "She's parkin' the car."

I handed the bag of sheets to Florida and lightly punched both boys on the shoulder. "Hey, guys. Good to see you." I got a mumble and a half-smile in return.

Then I knelt down on my good knee at Carla's eye level. "Hi, Carla. Remember me? You came to my house a couple of months ago . . . the first time you visited your mom."

169

Carla, her hair neatly combed into several fat ponytails tied top and bottom with colorful glass beads, looked questioningly up at her mother. Florida prompted, "The lady with the crutches—remember?"

Carla stared back at me. "Oh. You the same lady had the big ol' black eye?" She looked me up and down, like a kid expecting a magician to reveal how he'd done that latest trick.

I was saved by Avis's voice up front giving the call to worship, and we hustled to find seats. "Great Sunday to bring the kids," I whispered to Florida as we crowded into a row behind Denny and Amanda. "We're having a potluck after service." I craned my neck, looking for my son's bald head. Ah, good. He was manning the soundboard at the back of the room. At least I didn't have to look at it—or people's stares—all through service.

"Girl, I didn't bring no food for no potluck," Florida whispered back.

The praise team had launched into an enthusiastic version of "Shine, Jesus, shine! Fill this land with the Father's glory! . . ."

"Don't worry about it. There's always plenty."

She smirked at me. "Well, that ain't no pot*luck,* then. More like a pot *blessing,* I'd say."

Most everyone was standing in response to the stirring music. I closed my eyes, trying to get focused on worship. Pastor Clark often said we should come to the service "in an attitude of worship," but just getting everybody up, showered, fed, and out the door in time to make the 9:30 service rarely left me in an attitude of worship—*especially* not on potluck Sundays, when I had to throw together something edible to take with us.

At the end of the first song, Rick Reilly—the twins' father—gave up his guitar for a set of bongos as the praise team launched into "Hail, Jesus, You're my King! Your life frees me to sing! . . ." I noticed Chris and Cedric perk up and begin to clap along with the strong percussive beat.

I clapped too—it was almost impossible not to!—and sang, "Hail, Jesus, You're my Lord! . . ." That was one thing I liked about Uptown Community: we sang about Jesus a lot. No one who visited even one Sunday would go away thinking we preached a watered-down gospel about a generic God. Yet it occurred to me that at Beth Yehudah, "Jesus" was always translated as "Yeshua"—the Hebrew form of Jesus. And something else: in the *mahzor,* the names "God" and "Lord" were always printed as "G-d" and "L-rd." At first I thought it was a typo, but it happened again and again. I'd meant to ask Ruth about that but forgot.

We didn't have many traditions or liturgy at Uptown—a fact that appealed to people who were kind of burned out on church. Appealed to *me,* frankly. I'd grown up in a small, nondenominational Bible church, and liturgical worship felt kind of perfunctory whenever we went to church with Denny's family. But the Rosh Hashanah service had felt so . . . rich, somehow. It was easy to imagine Jewish people in hundreds of nations using a similar liturgy on this traditional feast day—though Beth Yehudah obviously expanded the meaning of the service to celebrate Yeshua as the Messiah.

After the last worship song, two of the men brought out a

small table covered with a white cloth that had figures representing children around the world embroidered along its edge. Communion today? It was usually the first Sunday. Must've been moved because of the Labor Day holiday last week when a lot of people were missing. Pastor Clark removed the cloth, revealing a round loaf of bread, a ceramic pitcher, and two ceramic goblets. I smiled to myself. I liked the way Uptown celebrated communion —literally "breaking the bread" and "passing the cup." Guess we had our own rituals, after all.

Pastor Clark, wearing a brown Mister Rogers cardigan and a truly awful green tie, read the familiar scriptures about Jesus saying, "This is My body" and "This is My blood." Then he added, "As we partake of these elements today, let us meditate on what the apostle Paul said about Christ's death: 'God demonstrates his own love for us in this: While we were still sinners, Christ died for us.'" Then he broke the loaf of bread in two and handed the pieces to the first two people who came forward. After they'd broken off a bit of bread, they each passed their hunks of bread to the next person, followed by the cup of wine.

I got up from my chair when the line wasn't very long. I could hear the murmured voices as I moved forward: "The body of Christ, broken for you . . . The blood of Christ, shed for you . . ." And then the hunk of homemade bread was put into my hands.

As I started to break off a small piece, Pastor Clark's admonition replayed itself in my ears: *"While we were yet sinners, Christ died for us."* Oh . . . my. Suddenly I remembered the prayers yesterday at the Rosh Hashanah service, "repenting for the sins of the people." That had struck both Denny and me as a bit strange—to identify with the sins of others as if they were our own and ask God's forgiveness. Fact was, it felt challenging enough to identify my own sins and ask God to forgive *me*. I still struggled to feel forgiven for the accident that killed Jamal Wilkins.

But Jesus . . . whew! What Jesus did took that a *lot* further—identifying with the sins of others to the point of taking their punishment. That was the whole point of salvation, of course: Jesus died for *our* sins, not His own. But did the concept of "repenting for others" or "taking somebody else's punishment" have any application in our own day-to-day—

I felt a poke in my back. "Jodi!" Florida stage-whispered in my ear. "Ya gonna pass that bread on or what?"

Good grief. How long had I been standing there? Pushing my thoughts to the back of my mind, I put the bit of bread in my mouth, turned, and handed the larger piece to Florida. "The body of Christ, broken for you, Florida," I said—and wondered, *Would I be willing to take the responsibility for your sins, Flo?*

I couldn't imagine it.

19

What with Rosh Hashanah, Florida coming to Uptown on Sunday, and my son looking like a Hare Krishna, I almost forgot I'd invited Hoshi to dinner on Tuesday, except she called the night before to ask what time she should come. Minor panic threatened to consume my entire Monday evening. Should I cook Chinese? Bad idea. I didn't have a clue, beyond the sweet-and-sour pork roast my mom used to make, or stir-fry where we throw in whatever fresh veggies we happened to have on hand along with some beef or chicken.

Maybe Japanese people didn't eat Chinese anyway.

I polled my family. To a man—and girl—they told me not to make it a big deal. "Just cook one of your favorites, Mom," Josh said, banging the back screen door behind him as he took Willie Wonka out for his nightly constitutional.

It's annoying when your family is right so much of the time.

So I decided on pasta with a Gorgonzola cheese sauce, salad, and garlic bread. Simple, yummy—those two magic words—and I had all the ingredients, even a hunk of Gorgonzola in the freezer. I was good to go.

The second week of school was going pretty well so far, except some of the kids in my class were way below grade level. Kaya, my supposedly "wise child," didn't have a clue how to write a two- to three-sentence summary of a *Scholastic* article I'd assigned over the weekend, even though she'd raised her hand when I asked who had read it. I sent Christy to work with her awhile, but later she told me Kaya couldn't even read the title of the article, which was "Teamwork." *That* was discouraging. We'd talked about the article in class just that morning, even referring to the title several times. Christy persevered, covering up part of the word, showing how it was really made up of two words. Still no recognition from Kaya. Finally, when Christy broke it down even further, to just letters and sounds, Kaya laboriously sounded out the word.

My student teacher came to me in frustration. "Ms. Baxter, *what* is this child doing in third grade?" My thought exactly.

However, with a few exceptions, most of the children were getting into the rhythm of the school day, needing some reminders about the rules, but otherwise muddling along in good spirits.

Except Hakim. He wasn't rowdy or a troublemaker. But he didn't like to be called on and stubbornly refused to answer. I didn't want to force him and make a big scene; on the other hand, it would be all too easy to skip over him and pick on one of the madly waving hands, letting him slide into a black hole.

I was thinking about Kaya and Hakim while stirring the

Gorgonzola sauce Tuesday evening. *Okay, Jesus, You said let the children come . . . but what if they don't want to?* I didn't want to leave Kaya or Hakim behind, but I had to keep moving forward with the other children.

Grabbing a Post-it note from the counter beneath the wall telephone, I wrote, "HAKIM . . . KAYA . . . JESUS, HELP!" and stuck it to the hood above the stove just as the doorbell rang.

"Denny!" No answer. "Josh? Amanda?" Where *was* everybody? Somewhere in the back of the house I heard music coming from behind a closed bedroom door. Turning the flame to low, I ran for the front door—it'd be quicker to answer it myself.

Hoshi, dressed neatly in beige slacks and cotton sweater set, held out a bouquet of daisies as I opened the door. "Am I too much early?"

"No, no, right on time." I took the flowers and gave her a hug. "You didn't have to do this!"

She smiled—a bit sadly, I thought. "My mother would say, don't arrive at host's house with empty hand!"

"Well, come on—oh, help! My sauce!" I ran for the kitchen, hoping Hoshi would follow.

The Gorgonzola sauce had only begun to brown slightly on the bottom. *Major* save. I quickly poured it into another saucepan, dumped a box of linguini into the big pot of water boiling on the stove, and hunted for a vase for the flowers. As I cut off their stems and ran water into the vase, I craned my neck to look into the dining room but couldn't see Hoshi.

"Hoshi?" No answer. I retraced my steps and found her

standing in the archway of the living room, seemingly lost in thought. "Hoshi, are you all right?"

She turned quickly, as if I had startled her. "Oh. Yes, I am all right. Just . . . seeing this room makes me think about that terrible woman. How could she do that?—hurt my mother? We do not treat guests to our country that way."

I wanted to slap myself upside the head. It had never occurred to me how coming to our house—the scene of so much trauma the last time she was here—might make Hoshi feel.

"She hurt me too," Hoshi murmured. "More than if she had cut me with that awful knife. She cut me off from my family."

"Oh, Hoshi. I am so sorry." I felt so helpless. The cut on Mrs. Takahashi's hand would heal long before the cut in Hoshi's heart.

The corners of her mouth turned upward politely. "It is not your fault, Jodi. You are kind to invite me to dinner. Can I help?"

It was Amanda's turn to set the table, but I let Hoshi carry out the plates and utensils to give her something to do. I did drag Amanda out of her bedroom, though, and sent her out to the garage to fetch her father and brother, who were still tinkering with our "lightly used" minivan. Finally everyone was corralled in the dining room.

Hoshi, bless her, smiled like a saint at Josh, light bulb and all. We held hands around the table, and I marveled how long and smooth Hoshi's fingers were as Denny prayed. "Lord God, bless this food, bless the hands that prepared it, bless our sister Hoshi, and we also ask Your blessing on her family in Japan. Amen." Denny was not long-winded when it came to mealtime prayers.

Hoshi looked up. "Thank you, Mr. Baxter."

"Just Denny, please. Hey, this looks great, Jodi." Denny passed the pasta dish to Hoshi, followed by the salad bowl and garlic bread. I was glad to see Hoshi fill her plate. The kids had been right to keep it simple.

Amanda, of course, asked Hoshi what meals were like in Japan. Hoshi laughed. "Fish. Lots of fish. And rice. Japan is an island, you know. So fish is one of our main sources of food."

"Like sushi?" Amanda wrinkled up her nose.

"Well, yes, but we eat much fish, many kinds. Lots of shrimp, scallops, oysters. Also *ika-yaki*—grilled squid. And *hanpen,* a steamed fish cake. Also seaweed salad, called *kaisou.*"

I wanted to laugh. Josh and Denny were practically drooling, while Amanda looked like she'd just gagged on a fly. Yet I had to give her credit for not spewing the usual, *"Eewww. Gross."*

"Maybe you could fix us some Japanese food sometime." Josh was nothing if not direct.

Hoshi beamed. "Yes! I only wish I could cook like my mother. Now, she is good Japanese cook."

At the mention of Hoshi's mother, the table got quiet and the smile drained from Hoshi's face. I was tempted to cover up the silence with my usual blather, but instead I let it sit a moment. Then I said, "I wish we had gotten to know your mother, Hoshi— your father too. I am sure they are wonderful people."

She lowered her eyes and blinked rapidly. "Yes. Yes, I wish this too." Then to my surprise, she abruptly changed the subject. "Tell me, Jodi, about your school."

I was impressed. Hoshi obviously felt deeply about her parents, but she also seemed eager to move forward. So I launched into the saga of my first week of school, including Ramón's threat to "smack" anybody who bullied other kids, and Britny matter-of-factly accepting my suggestion to visit England someday, since that was the meaning of her name. That brought a smile to Hoshi's face. When I talked about Hakim and the shell he seemed to carry around him, her expression grew thoughtful.

"I wonder," she said, "if he is sad about something. Sad children do not volunteer to do things."

"Oh. Oh my." That was a thought. I laid down my fork. "Like what?"

"Maybe his mother and father just got separated or divorced," Amanda chimed in. "That would make *me* sad."

I caught Denny's eye. Did Amanda ever worry about that? We'd never given her cause—had we?

But Hakim, now. "That could be . . ." I murmured. Hakim had been the only one who didn't want to find his name on the Welcome Bulletin Board that first day. "I wanted to encourage him, so I told him his name meant 'wise healer.' Even suggested he might be a doctor someday. But he almost got angry. Said, 'Don't want to be a doctor. They ain't no good anyway.'"

"Hmm," said Denny. "Maybe his mom is sick or in the hospital."

"Or maybe his family lost someone they know in the 9-11 tragedy," Josh suggested. "It's the first anniversary this week, you know."

I nodded. What Hoshi said made so much sense. Whatever

was making Hakim sad, I hoped I could show him I cared and that our classroom was a safe place to come out of his shell.

HOSHI'S COMMENT stayed with me the rest of the week as I observed Hakim. He didn't react in any special way to the moment of silence our school observed the next morning in memory of the 9-11 victims. He didn't seem motivated at all, though when he did apply himself to his work—with constant nudging from me or Christy—he was bright enough. He balked when it was his turn to read in reading group, but he would read aloud if Christy sat with him one-on-one. "He knows most of the words," she reported. "Just doesn't seem to care what they say. If I ask him questions about meaning, he just shrugs."

I knew it. There was a smart kid underneath all that stubbornness. We were going to dig him out, I told Christy, inch by inch, like archaeologists carefully exposing rare bones with a toothbrush. And as the weekend finally arrived, I decided to ask Yada Yada to put Hakim on their regular prayer list.

I was glad Yada Yada was scheduled to meet this Sunday evening—the first time since Bandana Woman had terrorized us. We needed to get together (not at my house, though, thank goodness!) to catch up with each other and pray. Hoshi needed some healing, for sure. All of us did, for that matter.

Today was Saturday . . . what else was happening this weekend? I jolted my mind awake with a cup of hot coffee and checked the kitchen calendar. *Whoa.* It said, *"Jodi PT 11 a.m."* I had totally forgotten I had a physical-therapy appointment this morning—and Denny was out in the alley washing the car. I mentally rearranged my morning as I studied the calendar. Today was the fourteenth—almost two weeks since Bandana Woman had been arrested.

Was Saturday different than any other day at Cook County Jail? The sergeant had said B. W. was in detox, but had she been arraigned yet? My arraignment had been two weeks and one day after the accident—but then, I'd been in the hospital. How soon would her trial date be set? Soon, I hoped. I wanted my wedding ring back!

I refilled my coffee mug and wandered out to the alley, where Denny was hosing down the minivan behind our garage. "Hey, Denny. Forgot to tell you. I've got an eleven o'clock at the physical therapist. Will the car be done?"

"Guess so. I was gonna wax it, but I guess I'll do that next time."

I watched as he took a soapy brush to the front grill. "Um . . . would you be willing to call Sergeant Curry this morning and ask if a trial date has been set for Bandana Woman?"

He snorted. "Bandana Woman? Is that what you call her?"

Did I really say that out loud? "Well . . . yeah."

"Smarty. Same initials as her real name, huh?" he grunted, moving the bucket to the side and starting in on the wheels.

I frowned. Bandana Woman. Becky Wallace. B. W. *Sheesh.* It had never occurred to me. "Whatever. Will you call?"

"They said they'd call *us*, Jodi."

"I know, but . . . Yada Yada meets tomorrow night, and I'm sure people will want to know—especially if they're going to be called to testify." I picked up the hose and rinsed the still-soapy grill.

Denny sighed. "All right. I'll try."

"Great." I let the hose fall and headed toward the house.

"Or you could do it!" he called after me. I pretended I hadn't heard him.

THE THERAPIST put me through a bunch of range-of-motion exercises with my left leg, which I did pretty well except for a leg lift lying on my side, which nearly killed me. "That's the one you need to be working on," she said, jotting some notes for me. "One more session. Two weeks okay?"

I wanted an excuse to put it off. Only two weeks? I'd never be able to do that leg lift in such a short time. Yet I couldn't use my birthday and my folks coming as an excuse, since that was this coming week. I sighed and accepted the appointment card.

A thunderstorm rolled through our neighborhood that afternoon, watering our pathetic patch of straw-colored grass and leaving the air smelling like it'd just come out of the wash. Denny asked if I was up for a walk to the lake after supper. "We could stop at the Heartland Café on the way back," he tempted.

On the way to the lake, cars full of young Latinos passed us, honking and waving and flying huge Mexican flags from their windows—a sure sign Mexican Independence Day celebrations had started. I did okay on the walk to the lake, but I was glad to collapse at one of the Heartland's sidewalk tables on the way back. We ordered their homemade salsa and chips to split between us. The café was full, a buzz of conversation and laughter going on all around us. I sipped my ice water and watched people strolling by, enjoying the last weekend of summer with their babies or dogs or just their own selves before fall officially arrived next week.

"I called Sergeant Curry," Denny said.

"Huh?" I turned back to my husband. Our chips and salsa had arrived and I hadn't even noticed. "Oh . . . great! What did he say?"

To my surprise, Denny didn't answer right away.

"Denny? Did a trial date get set?"

He shook his head. "There isn't going to be a trial."

I couldn't have been more startled if he'd thrown his glass of ice water in my face. *"What?"*

20

I must have screeched, because several heads turned in our direction. I shrank down into my chair. Denny let out an exasperated sigh. "There's not going to be a trial, Jodi, because she pled guilty at the arraignment yesterday and she's gone. They took her to the women's prison in Lincoln today."

"Oh. I thought you meant they were going to let her go." I thought about what he'd said. "Doesn't everybody get a trial? You know, America and all that."

Denny shrugged. "Why waste time and money on a trial if a person pleads guilty? Guess the judge sentenced her right then and there."

"But we didn't even testify! How does the judge know what sentence to give if he hasn't heard the evidence?"

"The police took our statements, you know."

A big mad was building inside of me. Not good enough. I wanted a judge to hear firsthand how B. W. had barged into my home and terrorized all my friends. Hear Hoshi describe her frightened mother and that wicked knife, how the long-awaited visit had been cut short. Wanted Bandana Woman to have to listen too. Now she'd pled guilty and denied us the privilege.

All I knew was, she better get more than Yo-Yo's eighteen months.

I sucked in my breath. "So. Did Sergeant Curry say what her sentence was?"

"Yeah. Ten years for assault."

I took a sip of water to steady my nerves. "What does that mean? That she'll be out on parole in a measly five years?"

Denny shook his head. "Dunno. They've got 'truth in sentencing' now. Not sure when her parole could come up."

The waiter refilled our glasses of ice water, and we munched on the chips and salsa for a while in silence. So Bandana Woman got a short ride to prison. Wasn't that good news? Why did I feel so disturbed?

Denny and I held hands as we walked down Lunt Avenue toward our house, past the houses hunched between the newer apartment buildings. Had to admit he'd been pretty tolerant with my reaction to the news. I wondered what the sisters in Yada Yada would think. Should I e-mail them tonight or just tell them tomorrow? *Guess tomorrow is soon enough.*

As we reached our front walk, I stopped short. "Wait a minute. If Bandana Woman has gone to prison already, does that mean we can get our jewelry back?"

Denny shrugged. "Probably." He saw me open my mouth again

and beat me to the punch. "No, *you* can call Sergeant Curry and ask him."

AMANDA WAS WAITING FOR US when we came in, nervously bouncing in her socks. "Hi, Mom. Hi, Dad. Can I go to Iglesia tomorrow for church?"

I tried to catch Denny's eye, but he chose that moment to squat down and greet Willie Wonka, who assumed we were all standing in the hall for his benefit. Okay, if Denny wasn't going to deal with this, I would. "Honey, you were there two weeks in a row in August. A visit now and then is fine, but we need to be faithful at our own—"

"I've *been* at Uptown the last two Sundays!" she wailed. "Besides, the Mexican Independence Day parade is tomorrow— maybe Edesa would take me and Emerald after church." I'm sure she sensed that Denny and I were wavering, because she moved in to nail the deal. "We get extra points in Spanish for cultural activities, you know."

How Amanda talked us into letting her take the el to Iglesia del Espirito Santo by herself, I'm not sure—especially since she had to transfer. But she did the good-grief-I'm-not-a-baby-any-more bit and promised, "I'll take the cell and call you when I get there, okay?"

She must have gotten on the phone with Edesa because a short while later she popped her head into our bedroom and said, "All set!"

YADA YADA took Ruth up on her invitation and met at her house Sunday evening. I didn't want to leave before Amanda got home from the parade, but she called around four-thirty just as she was transferring to the Red Line, so Josh met her at the Morse Street station, and they walked from there to Uptown Community for youth group. Denny and I would have to hear all about the parade later.

Denny got the bright idea to drive me to the Garfields' and get Ben out of the house. *For a drink?* I wondered. Ben Garfield certainly liked his beer, and it wouldn't be the first time if he asked Denny to join him. But I needed to let Denny handle that. I'd gotten myself in enough trouble nagging Denny about it and jumping to conclusions.

The Lincolnwood area where Ruth lived wasn't easy to reach by public transportation, so everybody got a ride with somebody. Chanda called us at the last minute saying she needed a ride, so Denny and I swung by her apartment building in Juneway Terrace, a depressing concrete jungle that straddled south Evanston and Rogers Park.

"Ooo, that Ruth got herself a real cute house!" Chanda gushed as we parked in front of the Garfields' twenty minutes later. I glanced at the small brick bungalows lined up along the street like square Monopoly pieces. Frankly, they pretty much looked alike to me: Three concrete steps up to the front door, a tidy bay window on the right, one window on the left. The only variations were the curtains in the windows and what flowers or shrubs flanked the steps. Ruth obviously had a green thumb, because a profusion of black-eyed Susans, decorative grasses, and fall mums brightened up the front of her house.

Ruth's husband—number three—opened the door when we rang the doorbell. Ben Garfield's silver hair was brushed back from his broad forehead in a wave reminiscent of Itzhak Perlman. "Where all of you women are going to sit in this shoebox is beyond me," he grumbled, waving us into the small living room behind the bay window, "but that's your problem. Denny, here, has taken pity on an old man, and we leave you to your prayers."

"Oh, take yourself out of here, Ben Garfield," Ruth fussed. "Thank you, Denny." She pecked Denny on the cheek. "Now shoo, both of you." Ruth shut the door behind them and rolled her eyes. "Men."

"Humph. Should be t'ankin' God you *got* a mon," Chanda pouted, plopping down in a big easy chair.

We chattered for about ten minutes, emptying the bag of day-old *rugelach* Yo-Yo had brought from the Bagel Bakery while waiting for the latecomers. Chanda downed at least six pieces of the rich Jewish pastry as the others straggled in.

"Hey, Jodi. How ya feel?" Florida gave me a quick hug in passing as she and Avis shed their coats. We hadn't had much time to talk that morning at worship—she'd brought the kids again—and I wondered how her second week had gone with Carla at home. Figured I'd find out soon enough.

Stu arrived last with her carload; they'd been delayed by Mexican Independence Day traffic. Somehow we all found places to sit in the small living room. It felt odd to be together again after the robbery two weeks ago. We hadn't talked about it much online or even by phone. But it was comforting too. Hoshi got a lot of hugs and seemed a little overwhelmed by the attention. "I think everyone's here," Avis said finally.

"'Cept Adele," Chanda said with her mouth full. "She not comin'."

I'd pretty much guessed as much when Chanda called us for a ride. My feelings were mixed—again. With Adele not here, at least I could relax about that whole mess. On the other hand, wondering why she didn't come left me feeling annoyed. Like *we'd* done something to *her.*

"We should get started then," Avis said. "Does anyone have a song of praise to start us off?"

For some reason the hymn that had been bouncing around in my head the last two weeks popped out of my mouth. "Does anyone know, 'Take your burden to the Lord and leave it there'?"

"Oh, sure." Avis hummed a few bars. "One of Charles Tindley's hymns."

"Wait a minute. You know who Charles Tindley is?"

"Of course. Famous African-American preacher from Philadelphia. He wrote hundreds of hymns."

"My mama used to sing Tindley hymns when we was comin' up," Florida chimed in. "She was so proud of that man. She'd tell us the story—born a slave, taught himself to read, ended up the preacher of a huge church in Philly. My mama said they called him the Prince of Preachers. Ain't you never heard of him, girl?"

I shook my head.

"Huh. Well, I ain't surprised. White folks ain't been givin' black folks any credit if they can help it."

That stung. Yet I couldn't argue with her. We'd sung his songs, all right—at least the two in our red hymnal. Maybe more. But no one had ever bothered to mention that the songwriter was black or tell his story when they told stories about other famous hymn writers like Charles Wesley and Fanny Crosby.

"I'm sure Tindley wrote his hymns for everyone," Avis said, saving me from having to respond to Florida. "Whoever knows it, join in." Without further ado, she began to sing the words to the first verse, which I didn't know by heart, but I joined in with several others on the chorus:

Leave it there . . . leave it there . . .
Take your burden to the Lord and leave it there;
If you trust and never doubt, He will surely bring you out
Take your burden to the Lord and leave it there.

In gospel fashion, we ended up singing the chorus a couple more times before Avis led out with an impassioned prayer that we'd take the words of this hymn to heart "and bring our burdens to You, Jesus, and leave them there rather than dragging them around, letting Satan beat us down, all hangdog and discouraged." She could've been an old Baptist preacher herself, for she sailed right back into the last two phrases of the chorus: *"Mmmm-mmm . . .* If you trust and never doubt, He will surely bring you out . . . Take your burden to the Lord and leave it there . . . *mmmm-mmm."*

I stifled a grin. What would the teachers at Bethune Elementary think if they could see *this* side of their cool-headed principal? God must have prompted me to suggest that song because singing "Leave it there" with my sisters calmed the anxious spirit I brought to the meeting, though I wasn't exactly sure why I felt so unsettled. Too much unfinished business, I guess.

"These last two weeks been one thing after another, know what I'm sayin'?" Florida piped up after the prayer. "Ain't had no time to think about that robbery, though I get hot as pepper sauce when I do. But can't afford to be mad, 'cause I got a little girl who's mad enough at the world and especially me right now 'cause I took her away from her foster mama. Though it ain't all bad," she hastened to say. "We doin' all right. She out with her daddy and brothers tonight eating pizza."

Nony reached over and laid a hand on Florida's knee. "Please let us know what we can do."

"Probably what you doin' now—prayin'. Got sheets, thanks to Jodi. Now anybody who's got some sassy girl clothes to pass along, could use some of them. But you ain't no help in that department, Nony." A grin softened Florida's worry lines. "All you got is those two handsome boys."

"I've got girls," said Delores. "They wear out their clothes pretty bad, but I'll see what we can come up with."

Chanda's pout deepened. "Mi still hain't heard what happened at sista Jodee's house. Start at da' beginning."

Avis quickly discouraged simply rehashing the details. "We need to help each other move beyond the trauma to a place of faith."

"Uh-huh." Ruth considered that. "So spiritual, I'm not. Exactly how do you do that?"

Stu snickered. "You sound like Yo-Yo."

Yo-Yo, sitting cross-legged on the floor and cleaning her fingernails with a pocketknife, just grinned.

Avis took the question seriously. "By confessing the Word—"

"Avis! Plain English!" This time Yo-Yo did speak up.

"All right, plain English. But it's an important concept, so I'm going to break it down. *Confessing*—it literally means 'to tell, to make known.' *The Word*, of course, is what God says in the Bible. So we can either go around *confessing*, 'Oh, wasn't that awful' or, 'I'm so scared' or, 'I'm so angry about what happened.' Or we can *confess* the *Word:* 'I'm created in the image of God.' 'God knows and cares when even a sparrow falls to the ground; how much more He cares about me!' 'All things work together for good for those who love Him and are called according to His purpose'—to name just a few. That's what I call 'confessing the Word.'"

I knew I needed that kind of encouragement, to actually *speak* the Word. Say it out loud. Remind myself what *God* said about stuff that happens when my feelings are flying off in every direction. I certainly didn't do that last night when Denny told me that Bandana Woman had pled guilty and skipped a trial. On the other hand, that seemed like asking a lot of somebody who'd just suffered a trauma—especially Hoshi, who was suffering a lot more than the rest of us as a result of the robbery. Still, I was a little shocked when Stu put my thoughts into actual words.

"Avis, isn't that expecting people to deny their feelings?" Stu's voice got sarcastic. "I just got robbed at knifepoint—well, praise the Lord! Hoshi's family has disowned her—but all things work together for good!" Stu's chin went up. "I mean, maybe praise and thanksgiving are *your* first reactions when something bad happens, but I'll bet most of us would like somebody to say, 'Gee, that's tough,' or 'You have a right to be upset!'"

It suddenly felt like all the air had just been sucked out of the room. No one spoke. I didn't know where to look, so I stared at the curlicues in the carpet. Even Yo-Yo quit cleaning her fingernails. I felt defensive for Avis. Stu had just rejected everything she'd just said. At the same time, I'd been thinking pretty much the same thing—maybe others had too.

Finally Avis spoke. "Stu, I don't mean to deny anyone's feelings. We all have natural feelings—including me. Yes, I felt angry. Yes, I was upset. I don't think one day has gone by that I haven't cried about Hoshi's pain, and I don't know how God is going to work that together for her good. It looks pretty bad. But I do know that if I stay there in the natural, focusing on all my feelings, Satan gets a foothold in my heart. I begin to doubt God's love. My trust slips—is God really in control? All I'm saying is, what I need to do is confess the promises of God, and I need to do it right away. 'Satan, you're a liar!' 'God, Your ways are above my ways, so I trust You!'—even if I don't feel like it. Because that's the only way I can keep my feet on solid ground and my heart from giving in to fear."

Fear . . . had to admit that was usually my first reaction. Not just physical fear, but fear I'd look stupid or make the wrong decision. I glanced sideways at Stu. Avis had won that round in my book, but would Stu come out swinging?

It was Hoshi who spoke. "Thank you. It is what I needed, Avis. My heart is shaking. It is hard to trust God. I am new Christian and don't know all that God says. All I know is, I can't go back. God has been good to me, and what happened at Jodi's house— that was not God. Satan wants me to go back to my old religion, but I will not go back. Please, show me what God says to make me strong and not so afraid."

The carpet blurred beneath my wet eyes. I understood what Stu had been saying. To be honest, I felt that way too. But this— *this* was moving us toward faith.

21

elores Enriques spoke up. "Fear dogs my footsteps every day, especially for José. He's a good boy, but . . . what if those gangbangers come after him, to make sure he won't talk? I have to keep telling myself, 'God hath not given us a spirit of fear but of power, and of love, and of a sound mind.'"

Good verse, I thought, *if you can get past ye ole King James English.* It still surprised me when Delores and some of the others in Yada Yada quoted the old KJV with all its "haths" and "cometh." Nobody at Uptown Community used King James. Well, maybe Avis. And Florida. None of the WASPs, anyway.

Soon Bible promises were popping like popcorn from others, not just for Hoshi, but for all of us struggling with anger and fear after the robbery. "Fear not, for I have redeemed you; I have called you by your name; you are Mine" . . . "I know the plans I have for you, declares the Lord, plans to prosper you and not to harm you, plans to give you hope and a future" . . .

I was scribbling references down as fast as I could so I could look them up later—and almost missed Florida's question.

"I wanna axe you all somethin'. What about this woman—the one who robbed us? She ain't that different from me five years ago, you know, 'cept I faint dead away at the sight of blood, so you know I ain't never gonna take up no knife."

The thought of Florida fainting dead away over blood stirred up some chuckles. "You didn't faint when Hoshi's mama was bleeding," I kidded.

"Too scared. *Couldn't* fall out."

Now we did laugh, and the atmosphere lightened up, like someone had opened a window. "Yes," Nony seconded, "I wonder about her too. How do we find out what's happening?" She held up her left hand with its bare ring finger. "And I want my wedding ring back."

I sucked in my breath. "Well, I've got an update. Denny called Sergeant Curry yesterday to ask if a trial date had been set"—I left out the part about me bugging him to death—"and guess what? The woman pled guilty at her arraignment on Friday and *bam!* She's already down at Lincoln serving a ten-year sentence."

Everybody looked at me like I was making it up. "Honest. That's what he said."

"Humph. Don't blame her," Yo-Yo muttered.

I frowned. "What do you mean?"

Yo-Yo hugged one denim knee to her chest. "Prison ain't no picnic, but it's a heck of a lot better than bein' stuck for months at

Cook County Jail. What's-her-name—Becky, right?—probably got put right off in the wing with other violent offenders. If I was her, caught in the act and knew I was goin' down for sure? I'd plead guilty, too, just to get outta Cook County, 'stead of waitin' months for a trial date."

Now everybody stared at Yo-Yo.

"How do you know her name?" Hoshi said, her voice barely above a whisper.

Yo-Yo looked up at me. "Didn't you tell me her name was Becky Something?"

Was Yo-Yo really the only person I told? And she hadn't even been there that night. I nodded, feeling guilty that I'd sat on it. "Yeah. Becky Wallace. That's what Sergeant Curry said her name was." *Bandana Woman . . . B. W. . . . whatever.*

Stu made a face. "Feels funny to know what her name is."

"Humph." Ruth folded her arms across her bosom. "A disgrace to such a pretty name, she is."

Yo-Yo snorted. "In case you guys never thought about it, everybody in prison has a name. Maybe you guys—" She checked herself. "Maybe *we* are s'posed to, you know, pray for her. Or visit her. You know, like Ruth did for me."

"Oh, who's sounding 'spiritual' now?" I snapped. "Ruth wasn't your *victim*. And all you did was forge a couple of checks." I shut my mouth, afraid of the sudden anger that heated my words.

Yo-Yo just shrugged, unperturbed. "All I'm sayin' is, this *is* the Yada Yada *Prayer* Group, ain't it? So . . . pray."

Where did she get off getting so holy all of a sudden? Yo-Yo hadn't been a Christian more than a few months, didn't even go to church yet. What did *she* know?

She knows what it's like on the other side.

The thought was so loud in my head I looked around the room to see if somebody had spoken it aloud. But no one was looking my direction.

"Well, now, the way I see it is . . ." Florida jabbed her finger at no one in particular. "I don't like this woman. Wouldn't mind if I never saw her again all my born days. Same time, I didn't like myself five, ten years ago either. And God still saw fit to give me another chance. So I say, maybe some of us *should* go visit this woman, this Becky whoever. And 'cause I been where she is—not in prison, thank ya, Jesus!—but drugged out and desperate, I might go visit her if some of you all would come with me."

No one else spoke for a long moment. Then Yo-Yo said, "Well, I been where she is, too—not drugged out, 'thank ya, Jesus!'"—she smirked at Florida—"but stuck in prison for long enough. Some people don't have nobody to visit 'em."

"*Mmm.* Lord have mercy," Avis murmured. Her lips continued to move, like she was praying in tongues or something.

Hoshi put her face in her hands and started to cry. "No, no. I couldn't . . . couldn't."

Nony put an arm around her. "Shh, shh. No one's asking you to, Hoshi. It's all right."

"Besides," Yo-Yo went on, "you can't just show up at Lincoln to visit somebody. They gotta put you on their visitors' list."

My ears perked up. "What do you mean?"

"Somebody has to write and tell what's-her-face that we want to come visit her, and she'd have to put our names on a list."

Oh! Relief surged through me. *No way would Bandana Woman put any of our names on her visitors' list!* That would be bizarre beyond belief. I felt let off the hook.

But my relief was short-lived.

"Maybe Jodi could write and axe her to put our names on the list—she's good at that sort of thing." Florida talked like I wasn't even there, but when I glared at her she just grinned back at me.

"I don't know," I mumbled. "I don't think . . ."

"Won't hurt to ask. All she can do is say no." Yo-Yo's logic was maddening.

Avis broke in. "I don't think we ought to decide anything for sure right this moment. This might be the right thing to do—or not. Let's pray about it and see what God says. If she's already been sent to Lincoln, she's not going anywhere soon. We have time to pray."

I flashed Avis a grateful look then bowed my head, all ready to tell God privately that this wasn't such a hot idea, didn't He agree? But Ruth said, "Um, before we pray . . . could I say something? Jodi and Denny and Stu came to the Rosh Hashanah service at Beth Yehudah last weekend, which I appreciated, can't begin to tell you. Tomorrow is Yom Kippur—some of you are coming, yes?" A few heads nodded around the room. "I want to explain about the Ten Days of Awe—the period between Rosh Hashanah and Yom Kippur. Because, to tell the truth, I think it applies to what we've been talking about here."

There was an awkward pause. This certainly sent the flow of the meeting on a detour, but Nony graciously said, "Of course. I would like to hear. Mark and I and the boys are coming tomorrow."

I felt impatient to get on with our prayer time but settled back reluctantly, hoping Ruth wouldn't go into a long description of everything we'd already heard at the Rosh Hashanah service.

"Rosh Hashanah, the New Year, begins a time of introspection, looking back at the mistakes of the past year and planning the changes to make in the coming year—a spiritual inventory, as it were." Ruth's face took on a flush of excitement, like a babushka showing her grandchildren around the ancestral farm. "Although it's not spelled out in the Torah, most Jews consider the blowing of the shofar during Rosh Hashanah to be a call to repentance."

"Yes, I remember that from the sermon that your rabbi gave at Rosh Hashanah," Stu put in.

Ruth gave her a look, just like the one my mother used to give me and my brothers that meant, *I'm doing the talking here. Zip your lip.* "Pastor," she said impatiently. "Beth Yehudah's got a pastor like everybody else. He's not a Jewish rabbi."

I wanted to snicker. *Sorry, God.* But I did love it when Stu got put in her place.

"Messianic Jews," Ruth went on, "believe *all* the Jewish festivals and holy days are not only a remembrance, but a foreshadowing of Messiah Yeshua. During the Ten Days of Awe, we are preparing our hearts for His return."

"This is so interesting." Avis leaned forward. "All the years I was coming up in the African-American church, we identified strongly with the Old Testament stories and the history of the Jewish people. Now that I think about it, a lot got focused on God's deliverance of His people from Egypt and the meaning of Passover—not the meaning of the others feasts and festivals."

"Uh-huh. 'Go down, Moses!' and 'Let My people go!'" Chanda rolled her eyes. "Rev'rend Miles at Paul and Silas Apostolic? He preachin' on that two, maybe t'ree times a month!"

Nony tossed her head, setting her newest 'do of curls dancing behind a bright-colored head wrap. "A lot of white Christians presume we're stuck there too. Mark and I were invited to a gospel concert at a big North Shore church, and the choir mostly sang spirituals from slavery times, as if that was the sum total of black contribution to gospel music. Why is that?"

Florida snorted. "'Cause ya sing spirituals slow, and white church folks can't sing fast and step and clap at the same time."

That got a laugh, even from us "white folks." Except Ruth. She was giving Avis "the look" for getting us offtrack again.

"Sorry," Avis said, trying to hide her smile. "Go on, Ruth."

"Where was I?" Ruth frowned, hands on her knees.

"The Ten Days of Awe."

"So I was. During the Ten Days of Awe, we not only confess our own sins, but we intercede on behalf of our people. Not just asking God to bless us, but asking God to forgive the sins of our people. For Messianic Jews, that means the sins of our fellow Christians as well. All of which culminates in a time of fasting and prayer at Yom Kippur."

203

Ruth sat back in her chair. The room was silent till Yo-Yo said, "That's it?"

"Well, no, there's lots more, but that's mainly what I wanted to say."

"So . . . how does that relate to what we were talking about?" I didn't mean to make that sound so challenging—or maybe I did.

"I think I know," Stu offered. "We can 'intercede' for our thief—uh, Becky, did you say?—because she's probably not at a place she can do that herself. Like European-Americans needing to take responsibility for how our ancestors treated the Native-American people—or ask forgiveness from African-Americans for the terrors of slavery."

Oh, thanks, Stu. I didn't ask you. Sounded like a lot of "politically correct" stuff from the current crop of social activists.

Florida muttered, "That would be the day." Ruth just nodded.

We finally got to our prayer time, though it seemed shorter than usual. I heard the front door open while Delores was praying for "the Becky woman" in prison and whether we ought to visit her. Then I heard Ben's voice mutter, "They're still at it," and the door closed again. Finally we ended with some good old-fashioned praise, did a lot more hugging, and got ready to go.

Just as I was trying to catch Chanda's eye to say Denny was waiting for us outside, Delores pulled me aside. She hadn't said anything about Ricardo tonight—I wondered if things had gotten worse. I looked at her expectantly.

"You know Amanda came to Iglesia this morning, *si?*"

"Well . . . sure. She said she wanted to go to the parade with

Edesa and Emerald afterward." *Oh dear. Guess I should have called Delores and checked it out with her, since it involved Emerald. Is she upset?*

Delores seemed embarrassed. "I wondered about that . . . but thought you should know. Amanda called the house last night and asked José to take her to the parade."

22

*I*t drove me nuts that we had to give Chanda a ride home, so I couldn't talk to Denny about Delores's revelation the whole way. The moment Chanda got safely inside the front door of her apartment building, I exploded. "I'm going to strangle that girl!"

Denny looked at me as if I was crazy. "Who? Chanda? *What* are you talking about, Jodi?"

I told him what Delores had said. "Amanda never called Edesa about going to the parade! She lied to us, Denny!"

"Hmm." Denny frowned as he turned off Clark Street at the Rogers Park Fruit Market to do the "square dance" around the one-way streets to get to our house. "Sure sounds like it."

"Sounds like it! She said she was going to call Edesa, but Delores said she called *their* house and asked *José* to take her! If that's not a lie, I don't know what is."

"I know. Just . . . let's not go off half-cocked till we hear what Amanda has to say."

Half-cocked, my foot. I was ready to go into the house with both barrels blazing. What was Amanda thinking, anyway? Why didn't she just say she wanted to go to the parade with José? *Oh, right, Jodi—like you would have said yes. She's no fool.*

I was, though. I should've obeyed my instincts and said no to the whole crazy scheme in the first place.

Denny drove the Caravan into the garage and turned off the motor. "You ready to go in the house, or do you want to calm down first?"

"Don't patronize me, Denny," I snapped. "Why shouldn't I be upset? Why shouldn't Amanda *know* we're upset?"

He didn't answer, just made no move to get out of the car. I sighed. He was probably right. I needed to calm down before we confronted Amanda. But what was with that? Seemed like parents used to tell their kids what's what and didn't stress so much about their kids' feelings.

After a minute, Denny spoke. "What are you most upset about, Jodi? That Amanda told us a lie? Or that she went to the parade with José? What if she had asked us if she could go with José—would we have let her?"

I opened my mouth to say, *"That she lied, of course!"* but I shut it again. Yes, I was upset by the lie, but if I was really honest, I was more upset about her going with José.

Denny waited. Finally I worked up courage to voice my thoughts. "Okay, both. I mean, I like José—he seems like a nice boy, what little we know about him. But I like him mostly because I care about Delores, and I know she tries her best with those kids.

They all seem sweet. Yet . . . cultures are different. Expectations are different. I don't know."

"We've got to think about this, Jodi. If there's a problem, we've got to address the real problem, not a bunch of vague fears and prejudices."

Oh, thanks, Denny. Play the prejudice card.

"There *are* real concerns, Denny. For one thing, José's only fifteen—too young to be responsible for Amanda in a rowdy crowd like that parade. I thought she was with Edesa, an adult. You *know* forty or fifty people usually get arrested for disorderly conduct whenever there's a big parade in one of the Chicago neighborhoods. Edesa would be wise enough to take the girls out of harm's way. But José—he's just a kid himself! And Delores said she worries some gangbangers will go after him someday to keep him from testifying against the guys who shot him." I hit my forehead. "Sheesh! A big Latino parade like that? Probably crawling with Latin Kings and Spanish Cobras. Didn't even *think* about that when we said she could go."

Denny gave me a hard look. "Did anybody ever get arrested for shooting José that day in the park?"

I shook my head. "Don't think so—not that I've heard. José didn't see who did the shooting, though I suppose he could identify the Spanish Cobras he talked to just before it happened."

"José had asked them to leave so the little kids could play, right?"

"That's the story."

Denny blew out a sharp breath. "Does sound dangerous. Guess

it's a good thing we found out. But Jodi, *not* because of José. He's not to blame here. It wasn't a wise situation, and Amanda was wrong to deceive us. *That's* what's wrong here. We agreed on that?"

My eyes felt hot, like I wanted to cry, and it was hard to swallow past the lump in my throat. *Oh God, I don't want to have to deal with this. It's too big, too complicated. I just want to raise my kids someplace safe . . . and normal . . . and . . .*

I finally nodded. "Agreed."

AMANDA gave us a deer-in-the-headlights look when we appeared in her bedroom doorway. I could practically see her thoughts: *"Busted!"* She had to know we'd find out, since I'd just spent the last couple of hours with Edesa and Delores. Amanda protested that she *had* gone to church at Iglesia and thought maybe everybody—Edesa and the whole Enriques family—would go to the parade afterward, and she'd just go along with them.

"Amanda, *stop.*" Denny nipped that bit of nonsense in the bud. "You let us think you called Edesa and that it was 'All set,' when in reality you called José and planned all along to go with him. That's deception. That's a lie."

Amanda hung her head and wiped her nose with the sleeve of her sweatshirt.

"And *did* you go to the parade with 'everybody'? Or just José?"

She started to cry. "Just José," she whimpered. "We didn't do anything wrong, Dad, honest! I just . . . " She wiped her nose on her sleeve again. "José was telling me about the parade and it sounded like fun, but I *knew* you guys wouldn't let me go if I said José asked me."

"And why is that?" Denny put it right back in her lap.

Amanda pulled a pout. "'Cause you guys get all weird if a boy asks me to do *anything*. And"—she lifted her chin defiantly— "'cause the parade was in Little Village. Not exactly your comfort zone, Mom."

A few choice words would have put Miss Sassy in her place, but I pinched my lips together. I didn't like it, but what she said was true.

"Don't forget," Denny said, "we *did* let you go when we thought you'd be with Edesa, an adult we trust—or even if the rest of the Enriques family had been with you too. But big crowds can be dangerous for a young girl in an unfamiliar place, even with José."

Humph. *Especially* with José, I wanted to say, if some Spanish Cobras out there wanted to silence him for good, but again I held my tongue. Maybe Denny didn't go there for a reason.

Amanda was grounded to the house for the rest of September —a little over two weeks—no phone, no TV, no new baby-sitting jobs, no outside activities except school and church. Frankly, I wished we could've come up with some other consequence, like doing the dishes for the rest of her natural life or something. I hated grounding, because we ended up with a glum teenager kicking around the house 24-7. But what else can you do when they're fifteen?

I said as much to Delores when I called later to let her know the story from our end. "*Si*, I know what you mean," she said. "Too big to spank; too young to kick out of the house."

Denny got on the phone to make it clear that as far as we knew, the fault was Amanda's alone. José might have asked Amanda to go to the parade, but it was Amanda who chose to deceive us. "Please make it clear we are not angry with him, Delores—only that Amanda lied to us."

We heard Delores sigh on the other end of the phone. "*Si. Gracias*. But I don't know . . . you think they are sweet on each other?"

DELORES'S QUESTION was still dogging my heels when I walked into my third-grade classroom on Monday morning. Was it *that* obvious that Amanda and José were "sweet" on each other? What was going on that I hadn't noticed? Lots of phone calls, obviously. But why did Delores sound so concerned? I thought she liked Amanda! Did *she* worry about the cultural and racial differences?

That gave me pause. It never occurred to me that anybody would have concerns if their child wanted to date one of *my* kids. I mean, Delores should feel darn lucky if José was sweet on Amanda—

Just listen to yourself, Jodi Baxter! You're about as two-faced as a smiling thief.

Ouch. *Okay, God, You really gotta help me out. I admit it—I'm*

*uncomfortable with this cross-racial dating, especially when it's my kid.
. . . Aren't there some real concerns here?*

I had to shelve my thoughts and get on with the day before my
students realized I wasn't paying attention. While I was taking
attendance, I noticed Hakim turning around in his seat and
snatching things off the desk behind him. Something inside me
cautioned, *Don't single him out; don't give him attention for misbe-
havior.* So as I asked for volunteers to go to the board and solve the
math problems I had written there, I casually walked around that
side of the room and laid a firm hand on his shoulder for one full
second without even looking down, then walked on. Out of the
corner of my eye I saw Hakim glare at me. Then he turned back to
his own desk and put his head down on his arms.

I sighed. Didn't know which was worse: Hakim acting up or
Hakim slumped inside his shell. *Darn. Forgot to ask Yada Yada to
put Hakim on their prayer list.* Well, I'd send it around by e-mail
tonight. Hakim and I needed prayer *now*—we couldn't wait two
weeks.

When I got home from school, the house was empty except for
Willie Wonka, who needed to go outside. Amanda was supposed
to come "straight home" from school—but what did that mean
when she had to catch a city bus from Lane Tech? Traffic . . . a
missed bus . . . a full bus went by the stop—there were plenty of
realities she could use as excuses for being late. We better pin that
one down.

I sat down at the computer to send out the prayer request about
Hakim—then remembered that I promised to let the group know

how we could get our stolen jewelry back. So I reached for the phone book, looked up the number for the Twenty-Fourth District Police Station, and dialed.

Sergeant Curry wasn't in, so I asked if someone else could help me retrieve my stolen property. I gave our case number to the officer who came on the phone then had to wait for several minutes while he looked up the file. I walked around the kitchen with the cordless cradled in the crook of my neck, pulled some chicken pieces out of the freezer, popped them into the microwave to thaw, then started loading the breakfast dishes into the dishwasher—

"Mrs. Baxter?" The man's gravelly voice came back on so suddenly I nearly dropped a glass. "That property will be released later this week. Call back Wednesday or Thursday. You can probably pick it up this weekend."

"Where? At the police station?"

"Normally, all recovered stolen property is sent to Twenty-Sixth and California for trial." My heart started to sink. Twenty-sixth and California was the address for the Cook County Courthouse, way on the south side. But the officer continued. "However, in this case the perp pled guilty before we had time to send it down there. So you can pick up your property here. Do you know where we are? Clark and Schreiber."

"That's great. Thank you! But, sir? . . . Sir?" I thought he was going to hang up. "I have another question. Can I pick up *all* the stolen property? It was all taken from my house, but it doesn't all belong to me. We were robbed while I had guests at my—"

"Sorry, ma'am. Can't do that." The officer's voice sounded

extremely impatient, like I'd gone over my limit of questions. "The statements taken the night of the incident described what was stolen from each victim, so each of those individuals will have to come down to the station and claim their own property."

"Oh. All right. Thanks." I hung up. *Bummer.* Seemed like a lot of unnecessary trips. But at least we could all get our jewelry back. I tried to think who'd had stuff stolen: Nony's ring and necklace . . . Avis's pin, though not her wedding ring—that was *so weird* that Bandana Woman didn't take it . . . my wedding ring set . . . Stu's earrings. Nothing from Florida 'cause she didn't have anything, and not even Mrs. Takahashi's money. I had to smile, remembering the grip Hoshi's mom had kept on her purse. Anybody else?

Adele. Bandana Woman had made me take off Adele's big ring myself.

I stood in the middle of the dining room, looking back and forth between the computer and the telephone. Adele needed to know that the thief had been sentenced already, and we could get our jewelry back. Should I just send out that information to everybody in an e-mail, including Adele . . . or should I tell her myself by phone?

It made a darn good excuse to speak to Adele person to person, and I was tired of this little game we were playing.

I picked up the phone.

23

As the phone rang, I chastised myself. This was dumb, calling the shop. Adele was certain to be busy, and a message from me would just make her wary. I was about to do a quick hang-up when someone answered the phone. "Adele's Hair and Nails."

Adele's voice.

"Oh. Hi, Adele. It's Jodi. Sorry to bother you at work. If this isn't—"

"It's all right. What's up?"

What's up?! Like we haven't left a zillion messages in the last four weeks. "I wanted to let you know about your stolen ring." *That'll keep her on the line.*

"What about it?"

"Well, Sergeant Curry, the officer who took our statements that night—"

"I *know* who Sergeant Curry is."

Easy, Jodi, that's just Adele's way. Don't get jelly-knees over it.

"Well, Sergeant Curry told us that . . . that . . ." *Becky Wallace? Bandana Woman?* ". . . uh, the woman who robbed us pled guilty, and she's already been sentenced to ten years at Lincoln Correctional Center."

"What about my ring?"

"That's just it. Since there isn't going to be a trial, they're releasing our stolen jewelry. No evidence needed. You can pick it up at the Twenty-Fourth District Police Station on Clark—not too far from your shop."

"So I gotta go pick it up?"

"That's what they said."

"All right. Thanks, Jodi—"

"Wait. Adele, do you have another minute? I really need to talk to you about what happened the day you gave me the makeover for my anniversary."

For a moment only silence answered me from the other end.

"Adele?"

I heard a sigh. I could well imagine Adele's large chest heaving in exasperation, and I was glad we weren't actually face to face. "Just a minute" was all she said, then her voice moved away from the phone yelling, "Corey! Can you keep an eye on the desk? An' answer the phone if it rings—line two. My four-thirty's late. If she comes in, tell her to wait."

I couldn't hear what Corey said in reply, but it must have been in the affirmative, because I could hear Adele walking—a soft *shush, shush, shush*—then a door closed.

"All right. You wanna talk."

Ohmigosh. My mind was suddenly blank. Where should I start? "Yes. Uh . . . first of all, how is MaDear?"

Another big Adele sigh. "She's hangin'. Has some good days an' some bad days. Nights are worst. Nightmares, screaming . . ."

"Oh, Adele." My heart sank. "I'm so sorry." I paused, but Adele didn't offer any more. "Avis told us why MaDear screamed at Denny that day—I mean, who she thought he was . . . and what happened when she was a girl."

Silence.

"Adele, Denny and I had no idea she had suffered such a terrible tragedy. I wish there was a way we could communicate to her how sorry we are."

"Wouldn't help. Would just set her off. Just . . . leave it be."

I tried to gather my courage. "That's hard, Adele. It really hurts Denny to think your mother thinks *he's* the guy who . . . who murdered her brother. That's like . . . like a false accusation!"

"Look." I heard Adele suck in her breath, and her tone got hard. "Don't go telling *me* MaDear's making a 'false accusation.' She's got dementia or Alzheimer's—whatever. Don't take it personal, but as long as she thinks that way, do me a favor and just stay out of her life, okay?"

I winced. Adele's words were hard, unsympathetic. But I pushed on. "Okay, but why are you staying out of our life?"

"Whaddya mean?"

"You know. Not returning our phone calls, staying away from Yada Yada. I feel like you're blaming us for something we didn't do." There. It was out. I held my breath.

The silence was long and heavy on the other end. Finally Adele spoke, her words measured and tight. "Look. Right now, I can't really be worried about how you and Denny are feeling. What happened that day . . . *get over it.* It's not a big deal for you; just a misunderstanding by a senile old lady. But it is a big deal for me. It is a big deal for my mother, who wakes up at night terrified, and it's two, sometimes three hours before I can get her back to sleep."

I heard the front door slam. Usually Amanda called out, *"I'm home!"* but all I heard was something being dumped on the floor—backpack, probably—and footsteps stalking down the hall. I caught a glimpse of my daughter as she stomped past the dining room doorway and into the bathroom. Another slammed door.

I stifled a groan. It was going to be a long two weeks.

"And to be honest?" Adele continued in my ear. "It's brought up a lot of old feelings I thought I'd dealt with. My uncle was murdered—*murdered,* Jodi—by a bunch of white racists for who-knows-what stupid offense. Acting like a human being, no doubt. That was before my time, and my sister and me, we always rolled our eyes at the old stories. We pretended everything was different now, even when we got chased out of stores just for lookin' and when Daddy got stopped by the cops just for 'drivin' black.' But seeing how that lynchin' still terrifies my mother . . . yeah. I got some feelings. And I'm sorry if that's steppin' on your toes."

I had no idea what to say, so I didn't say anything, just sat slumped over the table with the phone at my ear. I half-expected Adele to slam down the phone, but Adele was on a roll.

"As for what happened at your house a couple of weeks ago?

That was just the last straw. I talked myself into coming to Yada Yada that night. *Big* mistake. I know, it was traumatic for everybody. Wasn't your fault—wasn't nobody's fault. But with MaDear half off her rocker 'cause of what white folks did when she was a kid—not to mention everything my family has put up with from ignorant bigots all the years I was comin' up—the last thing I needed was some doped-up white floozy messin' with *me*. Tie me up? Steal my grandmother's ring? If I think on it too long, I'll get crazy myself, probably do something I regret." She blew out a breath. "So. You asked. That's my answer. I'm takin' a break from Yada Yada, and from white folks in general if I can help it. And don't come crying to me about how bad you feel. What you feel ain't *nothin'* compared to what I'm dealing with right now, and I don't have time to worry about your hurt feelings. Get over it, Jodi—that's all I can say."

A dozen backlashes sprang to my tongue, but I knew I wouldn't say them. I wanted to yell, I wanted to cry—but mostly I wanted to get off the phone before I did either. "All right, Adele." My voice came out in a croak. "You made yourself plain. I'm sorry. That's all I know to say." And I hung up.

I was so mad and so hurt, I wanted to throw pots and pans or break a window or something—anything. Instead I just clenched my fists and sputtered, *"Arrrrrggghhhh!"* at the top of my lungs. I paced back and forth between the kitchen and dining room, holding a hundred angry dialogues with Adele in my head, telling her *she's* the one who needs to "get over it" instead of taking it out on friends who never did anything to her—not just me and Denny, but all the Yada Yada sisters.

221

I got out a pot, dumped it into the sink, and filled it with water for chicken noodle soup. I banged it onto the stove, slopping some of the water and putting out the gas flame. By the time Denny and Josh walked in the door, the soup was almost done, the kitchen was a mess, Amanda was holed up in her room, and I was in no mood to be social. "Dish up some soup when you get hungry," I grumbled. "I'm taking Willie Wonka for a walk."

WILLIE WONKA lasted about twenty minutes—long enough for us to make it to Touhy Park, which normally took five minutes— but I hadn't figured on Willie stopping to sniff every tree, leaving his "mark" to let the next dog know who'd passed by. By the time we got to the park, he was huffing. I found a bench and sat down so Willie could rest up for the walk home.

The conversation with Adele kept replaying in my mind. *"Don't come crying to me about how bad you feel . . . ain't nothin' compared to what I'm dealing with . . . get over it, Jodi . . . don't have time to worry about your hurt feelings . . . I'm taking a break from Yada Yada and white folks in general . . ."*

But rehashing it only fed my festering anger. I sighed. *Okay, God. What am I supposed to do now? You tell me—'cause I don't have a clue.*

It was starting to get dark by the time I dragged Willie into the front door forty-five minutes later. Denny and Josh were in the living room flipping channels and watching sports news, empty soup bowls cluttering up the coffee table. Amanda, no doubt, was still sulking in her room.

Denny glanced up. "Good. You're back." His tone was reproachful, like, *"Okay, you're mad, but don't make me worry about you."* I stood in the doorway a minute, wishing he'd jump up and say, *"You upset about something, honey? Wanna talk?"* But I knew it wouldn't happen. When Denny's feelers pick up that I'm working on a mad, he usually backs off and leaves me alone till I cool off.

Grow up, Jodi. He probably thinks you're mad at him *for who-knows-what.* I unsnapped Willie Wonka's leash and straightened. "Yeah. Sorry I went off like that. I had an upsetting phone call with Adele. Had to blow off steam before I was ready to talk about it."

That got Denny's attention. He even got up off the couch and followed me to the kitchen, leaning against the doorway while I dished up a bowl of chicken noodle soup. "Wanna tell me about it?"

I nodded, and we sat at the dining-room table while I recounted the conversation as best I could between spoonfuls of soup. The hot, salty liquid felt good going down, like a hot water bottle soothing my ruffled feelings. Denny was hearing the conversation for the first time, and by the end he was pacing around the room, rubbing the back of his head.

Finally he threw up his hands. "Well, that's it. I don't know what else to do. Maybe Adele's right. Just get over it." He practically threw himself down on a chair.

"Yeah. Except . . . it's hard to 'just get over it' when she's dropping out of Yada Yada too. All the sisters are gonna feel hurt."

I pushed away my empty soup bowl, and we both sat silently at the table, hugging our own thoughts. It suddenly occurred to me I was still thinking mostly about me. In the quiet of the dining room, with only the TV providing distant background noise, I rehearsed our conversation once more, but this time paying more attention to what Adele was feeling . . .

"It is a big deal for me . . . my uncle was murdered, Jodi—by a bunch of white racists . . . my mother wakes up at night terrified, and it's two, sometimes three hours before I can get her back to sleep again . . . my sister and me got chased out of stores just for lookin' . . . Daddy got stopped by the cops for 'drivin' black' . . . everything my family has put up with from ignorant bigots . . ."

I looked up at Denny, who was still slumped in one of the dining-room chairs. "I know what we can do."

"What?"

"Pray for Adele and MaDear."

He cocked an eyebrow at me. "O-kaaay. Sounds, uh, virtuous."

I giggled. "I know. But I'm serious. How many times do I actually pray for my so-called enemies—or even someone who makes me upset? I stew . . . I fret . . . I try to work it out. But Adele's right about one thing—I wanted to talk to her to make *me* feel better."

Denny sighed. "Yeah. Me too. Okay, let's pray for Adele and MaDear. But there's something else I gotta do."

"What?"

He got up and grabbed the checkbook we kept in the computer desk. "Pay Adele something for your anniversary makeover. Don't want that to come back to bite me."

224

24

$\mathcal{I}$ called Avis the next evening to get her best "guess-timate" at what my hair and nails would cost at Adele's Hair and Nails, and I ended up telling her about the phone call. I felt slightly guilty blurting it all out—was I gossiping about Adele? But I decided that at least Avis should know what was going on. We'd asked her to be the leader of our prayer group, and Adele's decision to drop out definitely affected everybody. I needed to be careful, though. It would be tempting to "let others know" in subtle ways that made Adele the Bad Guy and us the Poor Innocent Bystanders.

"Uh . . . Avis. Maybe I'll let you figure out what to say to Yada Yada about Adele's absence. Florida and Stu may figure out it has something to do with what happened at the shop, but nobody else knows what happened that day. Are you okay with handling this?" There. That made me accountable to Avis. As well as let me off the hook.

"All right. Guess that's best. The Lord is going to have to give me the right things to say . . . but I don't think we should say too much. Nothing is written in stone—not since the Ten Commandments anyway. Let's give the Holy Spirit some room to work."

Room to work? Please! Take all the room You need, God! Then—I swear—a voice in the back of my head said, *Then you need to get out of the way, Jodi.*

I was so startled that I almost missed Avis's next words. ". . . any thoughts since Sunday about writing a letter to Becky Wallace?"

It took me a moment to reorient my brain. "Letter?"

"Right. Yo-Yo's suggestion that some of us go visit her at the prison."

"Uh . . ." My thoughts scrambled. I had put the whole idea out of my head the moment I walked out of Ruth's front door. "I thought you said we weren't going to make a decision about that yet—that we were going to pray about it."

"True. I was just wondering if you'd been praying about it and what God had been saying to you."

Whoa. Why was this all coming back on me? I decided to be honest. "Sorry, Avis. Haven't thought about it. Haven't prayed about it. What has God been saying to *you?*"

"Mmm. Not sure I have any wisdom about what's best, but in my prayer time, I was impressed that a couple of the sisters— Florida and Yo-Yo, at least—are willing to visit her. So the Holy Spirit seemed to say, 'If Becky Wallace is willing to have visitors, then God has opened a door.' We won't know unless we write, will we?"

"Um . . . okay, I'll think about it."

"Pray about it, Jodi."

"Right."

Denny poked his head around the door as I hung up. "Did she say how much?"

I must have looked at him blankly, because he waved the check-book.

"Oh. She suggested sixty for hair and nails."

He considered. "I'm gonna add ten more. I'd rather err on the plus side at this point. Okay with you?"

I waved him away. *Whatever.* I didn't want to think about Adele . . . or Becky Wallace . . . or any of that mess right now. Didn't want to pray about it either. I just wanted to go to bed.

I WOKE UP THE NEXT MORNING before the alarm, fighting off a familiar anxiety dream: I was back in college, facing my final biology exam—but I hadn't been to class all semester! *Humph.* Wasn't hard to put my finger on the causes of my anxiety . . .

Adele.

Letter to Bandana Woman—or not.

And my parents were arriving tomorrow. For my birthday.

At least it wasn't the nightmare again. I pushed that thought up to "thankful" category and padded to the back door to let Willie Wonka out. I glanced at the kitchen clock—fifteen minutes before I normally got up on a school day. Good. I could—

You could pray, Jodi.

I sighed. *Right. Said I was going to pray for Adele and MaDear. And I practically promised Avis I'd pray about writing that letter to Bandana Woman. Guess I can pray about my parents' visit while I'm at it.*

I left Willie Wonka out in the backyard, realizing the sun hadn't even come up yet. Did I dare put on some music? Something quiet . . . meditative. I picked up the new Clint Brown CD Denny had picked up for me while I was laid up after surgery and scanned the back. There. The song, "You Are" was quiet and meditative.

I turned on the light long enough to stick the CD into the player, punched in the number of the selection, then flopped on the couch and soaked in the words.

You are . . . the hope that I cling to . . . You are my everything . . .

Willie Wonka barked at the back door, and the alarm was going off in our bedroom, but the words to the song kept me rooted to the couch.

. . . couldn't take one step without You . . . don't have the strength to make it on my own . . .

Didn't exactly get much praying done, but maybe this was like "pre-op"—necessary preparation for the kind of "surgical prayers" I needed to do. Surgery on my attitude, frankly.

I DON'T REMEMBER PRAYING ACTUAL PRAYERS that morning, but by the time I got home from school on Wednesday, I felt like God and I had been "doing business" on the side all day, and we'd struck a deal: why *not* write that letter to Bandana Woman? She wasn't likely to want any of us to visit her—how weird was that?—but if she did, wasn't God big enough to handle it?

Yet how in the world would I get a letter to her? Didn't I need her prison ID number or something?

Amanda came in the door in what passed for "straight home" from school, and for some strange reason, I told her what Yada Yada was thinking about doing and my problem about how to get a letter to a prisoner. To my surprise, her face perked up.

"Google it, Mom. They've got everything on the Web."

"What do you mean?"

Dumping her backpack on the floor, Amanda booted up the computer and then called up the Internet. She typed "Lincoln Correctional Center" into the Google search engine and began following the various prompts: "Visitation Rules" . . . "Inmate Search" . . .

"What's her last name, Mom?"

"Um . . . Wallace. Becky Wallace."

A list of Wallaces in the Illinois Department of Corrections came up, and there she was: name, prison ID, everything. *Sheesh. Hanging out on the Web for all the world to see. So much for privacy.* Amanda clicked on the name in the list, and a new page appeared.

Somebody named Becky Wallace stared back at us from the screen, a front and side view. All her vitals were listed—weight, height, race . . . I squinted at the tiny print: "Race: White." *Huh.* Guess I was wrong about *that.* Under sentencing information, it read: "Armed robbery. Sentence: ten years. Projected parole date: 2006."

Amanda let out a breath. "Wow. That's her? She looks different."

She did look different without the wraparound sunglasses and bandana. An actual face looked back at me—short dark hair, dark eyes—but it was the same woman, all right. Her mouth was hard, and I could almost hear the obscenities she'd spewed around our house that night, like a sewer that had backed up and overflowed.

I grabbed a notepad and wrote down her ID number and the address to send inmate mail. "Thanks, Amanda." I glanced at the clock. Denny and Josh would be home soon—better get supper going. It was Bible study night at Uptown, but I was going to make a case for staying home, since we had to get the house ready for my parents' arrival the next day. I'd write the letter later.

DENNY DISAPPEARED AFTER SUPPER, saying he had to run an errand. I washed towels and sheets so I'd be sure to have clean linens for my parents, hid the two bottles of wine—one half-empty—that we had sitting on top of the refrigerator, and gave Amanda and Josh a choice: run the vacuum, sweep the hallway and dining room, or clean the bathroom.

They chose vacuuming and sweeping, so I ended up scrubbing the tub. Rats.

Lathering hand cream on my water-wrinkled fingers after finishing the bathroom, I sat down at the computer and started drafting a letter to the woman who had robbed us—and immediately ran into problems. How did I address her? "Dear Ms. Wallace? Dear Becky?" One sounded too respectful for the likes of B. W., and the other sounded too friendly. So I finally settled on "Dear Becky Wallace."

No sooner had I stated the purpose of my letter and wrote the names of the two women who wanted to visit her than I realized we had another big problem. Neither Florida nor Yo-Yo had a car. How in the world were they supposed to get to Lincoln, which was at least two to three hours away by car?

The back screen door banged, and in a second or two I smelled Denny's aftershave and felt his lips on the back of my neck. "Whatcha doing?" He leaned over my shoulder. "What's this? A letter to *Becky Wallace?*" He pulled over a dining-room chair.

I told him what Yada Yada had talked about at Ruth's house— a little detail that had gotten lost in the revelation that Amanda had lied to us and gone to the Mexican parade with José—and how Avis suggested testing the waters to see if she would respond. "But if—big *if*—she says okay, how in the world would they get down there?"

Denny was quiet a long time. He leaned forward, elbows on his knees, chin resting on his clasped hands—like he did after the Rosh Hashanah service. Finally he leaned back. "I'll drive them."

"Really?" His offer surprised me. I had to be careful about Yada Yada making decisions that implicated him. He was already borderline resentful of our twice-monthly meetings, the extra phone calls, the church visits. "You don't have to make this your problem, Denny."

He snorted. "Becky Wallace robbed *my* house, frightened *my* family, terrorized *our* guests, and pointed her butcher knife at *me*. I'd say it's already my problem."

I swatted him on the shoulder. "You know what I mean."

The smile vanished. "If anybody's going to go, maybe it should be you and me, Jodi. After all, she did barge into our house, and I was the one who wrestled her to the floor. We've got a lot of feelings too. Maybe it would be good to face her. Maybe it would be good for her to face *us.*"

I rolled my eyes. "She's *not* going to put us on her visitors' list."

But in the end, I typed all four names into the letter: Florida Hickman . . . Yolanda Spencer . . . Denny and Jodi Baxter.

25

EEEEEEEEEEEEEEEEEEEE! I bolted upright in the bed. What was that? . . . The fire alarm! Throwing off the quilt, I vaulted out of bed as quickly as my morning-stiff leg would allow and grabbed for my robe in the dark. Just as I stuck my arm in the sleeve, the obnoxious racket stopped as abruptly as it had started, and two seconds later Denny poked his head into the bedroom door.

"Sorry. It backfired on me."

By this time I was totally awake and robed. "What backfired on you?" I followed him out into the hall, where a bleary-eyed, bald-headed Josh was standing in the doorway of his bedroom, looking totally confused. A plaintive wail rose from Amanda's bedroom: "Da-ad! Is there a fire? Or can I go back to sleep?"

"Sleep!" Denny called. "For fifteen more minutes!"

Josh sighed and disappeared behind his own door.

I stopped at the archway to the dining room where shadows

and glowing lights danced all over the walls. Whichever way I looked, candles in all shapes and sizes flickered warmly in the dining room . . . kitchen . . . living room . . . even the bathroom.

Denny stood in the middle of the dining room in his T-shirt and sweat shorts, holding the dismantled fire alarm. A sheep couldn't have looked more sheepish. "Uh, sorry, babe. I wanted to start off your birthday special—didn't know all these candles would set off the alarm."

I started to laugh. "Oh, this is *special,* all right. I'll never forget it—and I'm never going to let *you* forget it either!" I headed for the candlelit living room. "You can make it up to me by bringing me a *big* mug of coffee, because I am going to sit in the recliner and reign like a queen for at least fifteen minutes."

"Yeah, well," he called after me, "if you're going to be queen, you better check your royal robe—you've got it on inside out!"

BIRTHDAY OR NO BIRTHDAY, we all had to be at school at our regular time. With just minutes to catch the city bus to Lane Tech, Amanda was fishing in the desk drawer in the dining room. "Mom! Don't we have any more stamps? I need a stamp!"

I couldn't remember the last time Amanda actually wrote a letter. "I think so—somewhere in there. Do you need it now?"

"Yes, I need it *now!* . . . Never mind. I found one." Her tone by now was decidedly cranky, and she slammed the front door behind her.

Who was Amanda writing to? We'd said no phone calls; we didn't think about letters. Couldn't be any of her friends at school—she saw them during the day.

I sighed. *Probably José.*

I tried not to let Amanda's surly mood and my parents' impending arrival distract me from my lesson plans for that day, but I wished I felt better prepared emotionally. How would Dad react to Josh's light-bulb head? Mom would silently disapprove, but Dad would definitely say something. *I should have warned them,* I scolded myself, as I set up a balance scale for today's lesson on "Find the missing addend." *Given them some time to get used to the idea.* After all, it had taken me awhile to get used to it—no, take that back. I *wasn't* used to it, didn't like it, and would be very glad when he let it grow back in again. Or at least shaved off that orange topknot!

My students had fun with the balance scale. I wrote "2 + ? = 5" on the chalkboard and let "helpers" place two counters on one side of the scale and five on the other. I explained that they had to place the correct number of missing counters on the "addend" side of the scale in order to make it balance with the "sum."

Kaya carefully added one at a time to the two already on the scale—one . . . two . . . three—and beamed happily as the scale balanced with the sum of five. I wrote a second problem on the board: "5 + ? = 7." Cornell dumped a whole handful of counters on the addend side and took some off one by one till it balanced with the other side—but then he didn't know how many he had "added." Well, try again. "Who'd like to be next?"

Hakim's hand shot up. "Me! Let me do it, Miz B."

I was so surprised, I ignored his calling me 'Miz B.' Hakim's math papers so far had been pathetic. Trying to act matter-of-fact, I wrote another problem on the board: "3 + ? = 10," and put the known number of counters on both sides of the scale. Frowning, Hakim studied the scales a moment, then picked up seven counters and piled them next to the three already on the scale. When the scale balanced with the ten, a wide smile broke his face.

"Hakim, how did you know how many counters to put on the scale?"

He looked at me scornfully. "See those three there? An' ten there? Just counted backwards three times—ten, nine, eight. Seven to go. Didn't you know that?"

Christy and I both rewarded him with big grins. "I did indeed, Hakim. But you are smart to figure out that you have to *subtract* to find the missing addend. Why don't you show the rest of the class how it's done?" I put two more problems on the board then wrote them again as subtraction problems to get the same answer after Hakim figured out the missing addends in his head and balanced the scale both times. Now more hands shot up wanting to find the missing addend "in my head."

I was so elated by Hakim's participation and success that I was still grinning inside when the dismissal bell rang. Gathering up my stuff quickly, I determined to get home before my parents arrived who-knew-when. But as I made a beeline for the front doors of the school, the school secretary stepped into the hall and waved me down. "Ms. Baxter? Ms. Johnson wants to see you for a minute."

For a second I felt like a kid being called to the principal's office. What had I done now? *Don't be stupid, Jodi. This is Avis, remember?*

As I peeked into her inner office, Avis Johnson was on the phone, but she waved me in, motioning for me to shut the door. Shut the door? Maybe it was something serious.

Avis hung up the phone and smiled. "Hi, Jodi. How was your day?"

I relaxed. Couldn't be too serious if we were doing first names. "Good. Real good." *Should I tell her about Hakim's little breakthrough?* I decided not—at least until I found out what this meeting was about.

"Wonderful." Avis opened one of her desk drawers, pulled out a glittery gold gift bag with tissue paper and an envelope sticking out of the top, and handed it to me with a smile. "Happy birthday."

"Oh, Avis!" I was so startled I just stood there like a carved duck. "You didn't need to—"

"Jodi." Avis leveled her eyes at me. "Just take it. And enjoy!"

I dropped my tote bags on the floor. "Thanks, Avis. Can I open it now?" This was too much—a birthday gift from my principal! I opened the card first. A Mahogany card about "A friend who is like a sister to me . . ." I could hardly speak. I took out a small square box from the bag and opened it: a scented candle. Green apple.

That made me laugh. "Oh, Avis, if you only knew! I gotta tell you how my day started this morning!"

BEFORE I LEFT THE SCHOOL OFFICE, I remembered to ask Avis if she got the copy of the "Becky Wallace letter" I'd sent to her by e-mail attachment last night. I'd also sent copies to Ruth (for Yo-Yo) and Florida. "Any feedback?"

She arched an eyebrow. "I noticed you added yours and Denny's names to the visitors' list. That's good. I stand in agreement with you. Now . . . we pray."

Well, yes, I thought a few minutes later, walking fast to make up for lost time. *But am I praying that B. W. will or won't put us on her visitors' list?* After one block at a good clip, I realized I better slow down to a steady pace so I'd make it still in one piece. Didn't want to have a relapse the minute my parents walked in.

A familiar light-blue Buick sedan was double-parked in front of our house, the trunk lid up. *Help! How long had they been waiting?* "Mom! Dad! Here I am!" I hustled the last half-block as my father, still wearing the old tweedy English driving cap he'd had for years, threaded his way between two parked cars and set suitcases on the sidewalk.

Sidney Jennings was not a large man—maybe five-ten, thin, almost wiry, a testament to his farm heritage. He straightened, a wide smile creasing his face as I dropped my tote bags on the walk by the suitcases.

"Here's the birthday girl!" My father held his arms wide and enveloped me in a bear hug. Old Spice aftershave tickled my nose. "How's that for timing?" he said, letting me go. "We just drove up. Couldn't find a parking place, though. Clara? Clara! Come on, get out of the car. Jodi's here now."

I hustled up the porch steps to unlock the front door as my dad helped my mother out of the car. My left leg and abdomen were aching from my effort to get home quickly, but their backs were turned so they probably didn't notice as I pulled myself up the steps by the railing. By the time I got the door open and had dumped my bags on the floor of the entryway, my mom—hair graying, no makeup, but cheeks pink and eyes twinkling—was coming in the door. *Oh Jesus, I am glad to see her,* I thought, giving her a big squeeze. I looked over her shoulder and yelled, "Dad! Drive around to the alley. I'll open the garage so you can park there!"

By the time I got my parents and their bags settled in our bedroom—no way would it work to put them on the foldout in the living room since they usually went to bed at nine—Amanda had come in from school, forgetting her poor-me pout long enough to give her grandparents a big squeal of welcome. Both kids had had to downsize to small bedrooms and single beds when we moved from Downers Grove, but at least they didn't have to give up their rooms now when the grandparents came. That fell to Denny and me—a fact that Denny grumbled about last night, but he finally agreed it was the only thing we could do under the circumstances.

Amanda gave my parents a quick tour of our first-floor apartment in the two-flat, including a peek at our postage-stamp backyard and a trip to the basement, while I filled the teakettle and hunted for cookies. I could hear their voices in Amanda's room. "Painted it myself," Amanda bragged.

Oh, right. With a little help. I finally found the package of lemon crèmes, my dad's favorites.

"That yellow paint sure brightens up this small room." My mom's voice had that find-something-nice-to-comment-on quality that irritated me, because it barely masked a veiled comment. *Small room.*

The tour over, they came back to the dining room. "Now don't go fixing your own birthday supper," my dad chided as I poured hot tea and passed the plate of cookies. "We're taking you out." He chucked Amanda under the chin. "Oh, all right; I guess we'll take you, too, princess."

My father may be the only person alive who could treat Amanda like a little girl and get away with it. But going out was fine with me. I'd be thrilled not to cook my own birthday supper.

I knew Josh had a soccer game and wouldn't drag in till close to seven. As we chatted over our tea at the dining-room table, my mother suddenly peered at me closely as if she had x-ray vision. "Are you all right, Jodi? After the accident, I mean."

"Of course she's all right!" My dad waved a lemon crème in my direction. "She looks great!"

Thanks, Dad. I really can talk for myself.

He leaned toward me and talked behind his hand, pretending my mom couldn't hear. "Your mother simply can't forgive herself for not being here for you, Jodi. I told her you'd mend better without us."

What did he mean? Because Mom had been sick herself? Or did he suspect I hadn't wanted them around? "Oh, Mom. I know you wanted to come, but you just couldn't." *Much to my relief at the time,* but I didn't say it. "Please don't worry about it. In fact, I could ask you the same thing: how are *you* doing since that terrible bronchitis?"

My dad butted in with a rundown of my mother's illness that had kept them in Des Moines last June. I only half-listened, annoyed at his habit of answering for others. I was concerned about my mom. She looked . . . older. More frail than I remembered. What was she: seventy-one? seventy-two? Not very old. It occurred to me that my parents would not be around forever.

I suddenly felt incredibly selfish. We needed to make sure we saw them more regularly. Des Moines wasn't *that* far. Maybe we could go visit them for Thanksgiving or during the Christmas break.

I glanced at the clock: 6:45. Denny and Josh ought to straggle in any minute. Amanda was in the middle of telling her grandparents about the Uptown youth group's mission trip to Mexico, when I saw my mom glance at something behind me, eyes widening; her hand went to her mouth. I turned to see Josh in the kitchen doorway, school backpack slung over one shoulder, his sport bag over the other.

Rats. I totally forgot to warn my parents about Josh's bald head.

26

rankly, I told Denny later, it went better than I expected. "Hi, Gramps!" Josh had said with a wave. "Hi, Gram."

He went to his grandmother and gave her an awkward hug from his six-feet-on-the-hoof down to her five-four perched on one of the dining-room chairs.

"Your . . . head!" my mother said, blinking rapidly. Couldn't blame her; I'd had exactly the same reaction.

"Oh, that." Josh casually ran his hand over his smooth dome. "Just trying to imitate Gramps here." He leaned over and patted my dad's rapidly receding hairline.

My dad frowned, eyeing the orange tuft on the back of Josh's head. "At least the hair I've got is a natural color," he growled.

"Hey. Had to be sure people could tell us apart." Josh grinned.

Oh, Josh, you're good, I thought.

My son looked around at the tea things and lack of supper activity in the kitchen. "Isn't it Mom's birthday tonight? What's happening?"

243

At least he remembered. I told him Gramps was taking us out and we better get ready so we could leave when Dad got home with the minivan. With only one bathroom, it took a bit of shuffling for everybody to "use the facilities," as my mother insisted on calling it, but we were more or less ready when Denny came in the front door. "There's a monster in the garage with Iowa plates!" he said in mock horror. "Flee! Flee!"

"Oh, Daddy." Amanda rolled her eyes. My father guffawed. He liked Denny's sense of humor, even if he was slightly suspicious of his son-in-law's New York, mainline-church upbringing. I caught my husband's eye as he hugged my parents, hoping he could read my mind: *Garage okay?* We hadn't talked about it, but I didn't want to risk parking my parents' car out on the street, even if it had been bought several years ago—"in the last century," Josh liked to point out.

Denny went back out to retrieve the Dodge Caravan, which he'd had to park in the next block, and we all piled in for the short trip to Bakers Square, Rogers Park's best bet for decent Americana food, really good pie, and a tab that would be easy on my dad's wallet. Over thick burgers dripping with avocado, bacon, and sprouts (Josh, Amanda, and me), honey-mustard chicken with rice pilaf (Denny and Dad), and a grilled chicken salad (Mom), our conversation bounced from the Chicago Bears' poor start—*again*—to Hakim popping out of his shell long enough to show the third-grade class how to "subtract in your head," to Josh's soccer game tomorrow night. "Wanna come, Gramps?"

My dad seemed pleased. He turned to Amanda. "What about

you, princess? You want to keep Gramps company at your brother's game?"

Uh-oh. We hadn't talked about how to handle Amanda's grounding while her grandparents were visiting. "Sure!" Amanda smiled sweetly at her grandfather, ignoring the warning look I sent her. I kicked Denny under the corner booth that accommodated the six of us, but he just gave a short nod that meant, *"Later."*

We were all too full to eat dessert right away, so we bought a triple-berry pie to take home. As we climbed into the minivan, I noticed that my dad had cornered Josh out of earshot in the parking lot. *Hmm. What's that about?*

Back home, Denny made decaf coffee and warmed up the pie while I opened presents: large wind chimes from my parents that looked like organ pipes, a pair of silver drop earrings from Josh and Amanda, and a slinky black dress from Denny.

"Try it on, Mom," Josh urged. Denny just grinned.

I hustled into the bedroom and slid on the dress. *Mmm, yummy.* I gave a quick brush through my hair, which was back to its old basic style, stuck my bare feet into a pair of low heels—I could stand it for a minute—and sashayed out into the dining room.

Denny whistled. My dad clapped. Mom smiled sweetly. Who knew what she *really* thought? But I didn't care. Even the kids nodded approval. "Next time we go somewhere fancy," Denny said, "you won't have to borrow a dress."

"So there's going to be a next time?" I fluttered my eyelashes shamelessly.

"Well, yeah. Our fiftieth anniversary is coming up in another thirty years."

My father thought that was knee-slapping funny. Then he stood up abruptly. "Well, it's off to bed for us. Happy birthday, sweetheart." He gave me a peck on the cheek. "Come along, Clara."

My mother obediently got up and trailed Dad toward our bedroom. I dashed ahead of them to grab the clothes I'd just taken off and a few other necessities we'd forgotten. The door shut behind me.

Well, one day down; three to go.

I made up the foldout in the living room while Denny cleaned the dessert dishes. On my way to the bathroom, I knocked quietly on Josh's bedroom door. "Yeah?" came the muffled reply. I poked my head in. Josh was sprawled on his bed doing homework, earphones to his CD player cradling his ears.

I shut the door behind me. "Just curious. What were you and Grandpa talking about in the parking lot at Bakers Square—or dare I ask?"

Josh slid off the earphones. "He wanted to know why I left the little tuft of hair when I shaved my head. Said it made me look like somebody into Eastern religion."

Humph. I'd wanted to say that very thing to Josh myself.

"Told him I *wasn't* into Eastern religion, and Jesus said people shouldn't judge other people based on how they look, and that oughta include hair."

Okay. Josh had a good point. Brave of him to challenge my dad. "What'd he say to that?"

"He agreed, sorta, but he said how people dress is often a statement of who they identify with. Asked me to think about it."

"What'd you say?"

Josh shrugged again. "Said I'd think about it." He put the earphones on again. Conversation over.

ON FRIDAY, my parents decided to visit the Museum of Science and Industry since the rest of us would be at school all day. If they got back by three o'clock, I hinted, they could stop at Bethune Elementary to see my classroom. "You'll miss rush-hour traffic that way," I added.

Sure enough, I saw my dad peeking in the window of my classroom door just as the dismissal bell rang. Hoping they wouldn't get run down by the herd of eight-year-olds stampeding for their hard-earned weekend, I called them in, introduced them to my student teacher, and showed them around the now-empty classroom.

My dad stopped by the stove-size, foil-covered box I used as a lost-and-found. "What's a 'Darn Lucky Box'?" I explained that if kids left their things lying around, into the box they went, and the kids were "darn lucky" to get them back—*if* they paid a twenty-five-cents fine.

My mother frowned. "But did you have to say 'darn'?"

I decided to let that one go and hustled them out of the classroom. "Someone I want you to meet." I hoped Avis was still in her office.

She was. I ushered my parents in and closed the door. "Ms. Johnson, these are my parents, Sid and Clara Jennings. Mom and Dad, this is the principal of our school—Avis Johnson."

Avis, as usual, made a good first impression: professional and attractive. She shook my parents' hands warmly. "Jodi is a great addition to our staff," she said graciously. My parents beamed.

"Avis is also the worship leader at our church, and we're in the same prayer group."

My parents hardly knew what to say to that. I'm sure it wasn't what they expected of a public-school principal. Or maybe they were surprised that an African-American was the worship leader at their daughter's church. Or was it that she was a *woman* leading worship? I couldn't tell.

My dad recovered first. "Well. I am so glad to see that God is still allowed in the public school. Praise the Lord!"

Yikes. Had my dad's voice carried to the outer office?

A smile tickled the corners of Avis's mouth. "Praise the Lord, indeed," she said, lowering her voice to a conspiratorial whisper. "Though we aren't supposed to shout about it in a public school."

"Nice lady," my dad commented as we walked toward their Buick in the school parking lot. At least I got a ride home.

Amanda was grumpy that she had to come all the way home from school if we were just going back to watch the Lane Tech soccer team play Wheaton North at five o'clock. Pulling her out of earshot of my parents, I told her she was welcome to stay home with her grandmother, who was tired out from walking around the museum and electing to stay home and rest. Or she could quit grumbling and count her blessings that we were letting her out of the house to go to Josh's game. She heaved a persecuted sigh and followed my father and me to the garage.

Once at the game, however, she forgot she was sulking and yelled, screamed, jumped up and down, and otherwise cheered the Lane Tech Indians, even though they trailed behind all the way and lost to Wheaton North's Falcons. She also managed to talk to a lot of school friends who came by, I noticed. *Oh well.* At least she stayed in our general vicinity.

After the game, Josh clomped over to us in his soccer cleats and muddy green-and-gold uniform. "You *don't* want to hug me!" he warned, but he seemed pleased that the three of us had come to the game in spite of the loss. By the time we waited around for Josh to change, I knew supper was going to be very late. At least I'd remembered to bring the cell.

I got Denny on the third ring. "Just got home myself," he said. "Don't worry about it, Jodi. I'll order a couple of pizzas."

After polishing off two medium pan pizzas from Gulliver's, we played table games—well, not Josh. He excused himself to go play pool at a friend's house. Amanda went head to head with her grandmother for the highest Scrabble score. My mom won by two points—a feat that put pink splotches of pleasure into her cheeks.

Later, after my parents had gone to bed, Denny and I lay on the foldout watching the news. "Kinda nice that Amanda's grounded," I murmured during a commercial. "She's hanging around her grandparents more than she would normally."

"Shh. I wanna hear this." Denny turned up the volume as the news came back on.

I pulled the blanket over my head. Two days down; two to go.

Even though it was Saturday morning and I could sleep a little longer, I woke up at the usual time. *Ah, a few moments to myself.* I let Willie Wonka out into the backyard, started a pot of coffee, and booted up the computer. Hadn't checked e-mail for a couple of days. Hadn't thought much about the Becky Wallace letter either. Still time to chicken out.

But there were e-mails from both Florida and Ruth with "Re: Letter to Becky Wallace" in the subject lines.

"You write a good letter, girl!" wrote Florida. "See? I knew you were the one. Glad you and Denny deciding to come too."

Ruth's was even shorter. "Yo-Yo says fine. Send it."

Then I saw one from Nony, dated late last night. I clicked it open.

> To: Yada Yada
> From: BlessedRU@online.net
> Subject: Urgent prayer

> Dear sisters,
> I just got word from my brother in Pietermaritzburg,
> SA. My mother had a stroke. My brother says not to

come; she will recover most faculties in time. But it is terribly difficult to be so far away from my family at such a time. I want to take the boys to see their grand-mother while she still knows who they are. Mark does not think I should take them out of school. Please pray that we will have wisdom—and agree on what to do.

Love, Nony

Oh wow, that's tough. I clicked on Reply and sent back a quick message: "Praying for you big-time." *Huh. Easy to say, Jodi. Better do it.*

By the time I printed out the Becky Wallace letter, hunted up an envelope and a stamp, and spent some time praying for Nony and her family, I could hear Denny folding up the couch in the liv-ing room and my father's footsteps shuffling toward the bathroom. Better start breakfast. It wasn't too warm for oatmeal, was it?

"Ah! My favorite breakfast!" my father said, coming into the kitchen ten minutes later. "What's on the docket today, princess?"

Grr. When was my dad going to figure out I wasn't his "little princess" anymore? But I put on a smile. *"Somebody's* got to hang that monster mobile you gave me for my birthday."

"Watch out!" He rubbed his hands together gleefully. "Once I get my hands on a hammer and nails, no telling what's going to get nailed down."

Amanda wandered into the dining room as the four of us— Denny and me, Mom and Dad—were starting in on our oatmeal. "Got enough for me?" She plopped down in an empty chair.

My mother leaned over and patted me on the hand. "Glad to see that the kids eat a good breakfast, at least."

It was all I could do to keep from yelling. *Okay, Mom. So they've had burgers and pizza the last two nights. It hasn't exactly been a normal two days. Sheesh.*

I started to pull my hand away, but my mother suddenly held on, staring at it. Then she looked up at me accusingly. "Where is your wedding ring, Jodi?"

27

y wedding ring! I mentally raced through possibilities. *"It's getting cleaned"* . . . *"It got too tight"* . . . "What? Didn't Mom tell you?" Amanda piled brown sugar and raisins on her oatmeal. "Her ring got stolen when that crazy robber—"

"Stolen!" Both my mom and dad yelped like Willie Wonka with his tail caught in a door.

"Wait! Wait! Calm down." I waved them back into their chairs. "I'm getting it back. In fact, I'm picking it up today."

"Picking it up?" my mother croaked. "Where?"

"Uh, the police station. It's not far."

"You mean to say," my father said slowly, "they caught the burglar, and he still had your ring? How . . . ?"

"Wasn't like that," Amanda piped up. *"Dad* caught the—"

"Amanda!" Denny's gruff voice stopped her midsentence. "We'll do the telling." He turned to my parents. "The thief was caught in the process. We called the police, the thief pled guilty and is now in prison, and they said we can pick up our jewelry." He shrugged. "That's pretty much it."

Amanda rolled her eyes. "'Scuse *me.*" She headed for the bathroom, locking the door behind her.

"She gets a little dramatic." I put on a lame smile.

My father was still frowning. "Why didn't you tell us?"

"I'm sorry, Dad. We didn't want you to worry." That was certainly the truth. "The thief was caught right away, and I'm getting my ring back—it didn't seem necessary."

The four of us sat in awkward silence for a long half-minute. I didn't think I was fooling my father; he still looked troubled. But my mother patted my hand again. "Well. At least it's not, you know, you and Denny—"

I jerked my hand away. *"Mom!* Is that what you thought? That Denny and I are having marital problems, and I took off my *ring?"* I must have looked so horrified that Denny started to laugh. My mother smiled tentatively; even my father chuckled. I gave up and laughed too.

MY FATHER hung the wind chimes on the back porch, practically giving *me* a heart attack as he climbed up on a rickety stepladder from the garage. Asking him to do this was a bad idea, but he whistled as he worked, came down the ladder in one piece, and gazed proudly at the result. A small breeze cooperated by moving the chimes, which gave off a melodic *ding-a-ling-dong.*

Nice in the daytime, I thought. Not sure how I was going to feel about those chimes on a windy night with my bedroom window mere feet away.

We needed groceries, and I'd planned to sneak in a trip to the police station to pick up my ring while I was out. Now that my stolen wedding ring was common knowledge, I asked my parents if they wanted to run errands with me "and see the neighborhood."

"Oh, you go on." My mother settled in the recliner with her bag of knitting. "I had enough walking yesterday."

My dad, though, pulled on his windbreaker and tweedy driving cap, ready to go. We took my folks' sedan so Denny could have our minivan. A group of suburban volunteers were coming to Uptown today for orientation to the church's outreach ministry, and Denny was going to give them a tour of the Rogers Park area.

Dad and I hit the new Dominick's on Howard first, and he patiently wheeled my cart up and down the aisles. Then we pulled into the Rogers Park Fruit Market on Clark Street, where ten bucks went a long way. As usual, the Greek owner was omnipresent, greeting customers by name, helping to bag groceries, talking to delivery drivers. "Hey, Nick!" a dark-haired man yelled in the owner's direction. "You got any African yams?"

As we pulled out of our parking space ten minutes later, I told Dad to go around the block and get back on Clark. "I think I can find the police station—it's on Clark Street, not too far from here." I wasn't sure how far, but I remembered the modern two-story brick building, looking out of place on this long strip of storefronts, laundries, and ethnic eateries. Sure enough, a couple of blocks south of Pratt I saw the dusky brown bricks spelling out the word POLICE in a huge half-moon, standing out in stark relief along the front side.

Dad drove around to the parking lot in the back. As we got out of the Buick, I saw a policeman assisting a teenage girl—jeans, sweatshirt, athletic shoes, long brown hair—into the back seat of a squad car. *Giving her a lift home or something?* Then I noticed that the girl's hands were handcuffed in front of her. My heart felt like it lurched upward into my throat. *Oh God. She's just a kid!*

My knees suddenly felt rubbery. I didn't want to go inside. I'd had more involvement with the police in the past few months— interrogating José Enriques in the hospital after he got caught in gang crossfire, getting charged with reckless homicide after the terrible car accident that killed Jamal Wilkins, and having my house full of police and evidence technicians after the robbery— than I'd had in my entire life. None of which I'd told my parents about.

Trust your parents more, Jodi.

"Jodi? You all right?"

I didn't realize I'd stopped right in the middle of the parking lot till my dad spoke. "Uh, sure, Dad."

The police station bent like an L around a small plaza on the corner of Clark Street and Schreiber, which boasted a couple of benches and a modern sculpture of who-knows-what rusty beams. We headed for the revolving door set into a long bank of floor-to-ceiling windows, hesitating long enough for the person pushing through from the inside to come out before we made our move.

As the woman exited, charging out in a steamy huff, my eyes

bugged. Close-cropped reddish 'fro, chunky gold earrings, substantial bulk inside her long coat—

"Adele!"

Adele Skuggs stopped short and looked at me, then at my father, then back at me as if she needed to process who I was. "Jodi."

"Uh, Dad, this is Adele Skuggs—another woman in my prayer group." *Or was.* I blundered on. "Adele, this is my father, Sid Jennings."

Adele gave a distracted nod in my father's direction. "If you're here to pick up your jewelry, don't bother. Man told me I had to go down to Twenty-Sixth and California to pick it up. Like I got *time.*"

"What? The man I talked to—"

Adele snorted. "Maybe so. But just now, the man's telling me I gotta take off from work, go all the way down to the south side, just to get my own property back. Humph." She started to leave.

"Adele, wait! I'm *sure* the officer on the phone told me we could pick up our stolen property here. Let me see what I can find out." I headed into the revolving door, not even waiting to see if my dad was following.

Two white officers sat behind the long desk that cut kitty-corner across the airy foyer. Signs that said, "Do not enter beyond this point" stood at either end of the long slab, prohibiting access to the rest of the building without authorization. One officer was talking to a young couple filing an accident report. The other one looked up. "You being helped?"

"Not yet." I stepped up to the counter, gave my name, and stated my business. I was aware that my father had come in and was standing beside me.

The man nodded sympathetically. "I'm sorry, ma'am. You'll have to pick up your stolen property at Twenty-Sixth and California. That's where they keep evidence till after a trial—"

"I know." Stubbornness gave me courage to plunge ahead. "But there was no trial. The perpetrator pled guilty and was sentenced inside of two weeks. I was told the stolen property hadn't left this station, and we could pick it up here."

The officer frowned. "Do you have the case number?"

I dug in my purse and pulled out a scrap of paper. "Here."

The man scribbled the case number on a piece of paper and left the room. I turned to see if Adele was still waiting and realized she had come back into the station and was standing a few feet away, watching. I gave her what I hoped was an encouraging smile.

A month ago, I probably would have gone over to chat with Adele while we waited. Though after what she said when I called earlier this week, I didn't think she felt like "chatting" with me. I kept my eyes forward and waited for the officer to return.

The man eventually came back with a metal box. "You are?"

"Jodi Baxter."

"ID?"

I dug out my wallet.

The officer consulted a list, opened the box, and handed me a stiff plastic Ziploc bag. "Here you go."

I smiled. My wedding ring. Safe and sound.

Then I remembered Adele. "Sir? My . . . friend had her property stolen at the same time." I motioned to Adele. "Adele Skuggs. She's on that list."

"ID?"

Wordlessly, Adele handed over her driver's license, her eyes smoldering.

The man fished through the plastic bags in the box and handed one to Adele. "Will you both sign this release that you have picked up your property?" He handed a form to each of us.

Adele scrawled her name with one of the cheap pens lying on the desk and threw it back down. Then she jabbed a forefinger at the officer behind the desk. "You wouldn't listen to *me*, would you? How come I couldn't get my property till these white folks show up? Huh?"

Adele did not wait for an answer. She whirled around and made for the revolving door, pausing only long enough to nod at my father and say, "Nice to meet you, Mr. Jennings." And then she was gone.

I was so startled I barely remember walking back to our parked car. Once inside, however, my father did not turn on the ignition. Instead he looked at me. "Jodi? I think there's a lot more to this than you've let on. What's going on?"

The voice in the back of my head nudged me again. *Trust your parents more, Jodi.* I hesitated. Where in the world would I begin? It was all so . . . so complicated, with the Yada Yada Prayer Group getting robbed at my house, including Adele, and how frightening it was, and feeling so violated. But even before that, the day at the beauty shop when MaDear accused Denny—on top of all the trauma surrounding the accident that had killed Jamal Wilkins, the haunting nightmare that still plagued my sleep . . .

I took a deep breath and opened my mouth, but instead of words, an involuntary sob escaped from my throat. And then tears. Suddenly I was sobbing in my father's arms. Weeks of pain and loss, fear and frustration, guilt and remorse came spewing out like the discharge hose of my washing machine, spraying water everywhere through the wire mesh lint trap left too long, full of crud.

28

I watched my parents' Buick head up our one-way street, hoping they'd find their way out of the city without any traffic tie-ups. Never could tell, even on a Sunday. They'd decided to leave right after church, not even taking time for lunch, so they could get to Des Moines before dark. "Call us when you get home. Promise?" I'd said, sounding—good grief!—just like my mother.

Denny and the kids headed back inside, but I stood out on the sidewalk until their car disappeared. *This is good. We have the rest of the day for some downtime, to get ready for next week.* I lingered on the porch steps. All in all, it had been a good visit. I was glad they had come. I'd wondered how they'd react to worship at Uptown Community, which was pretty tame compared to the churches I'd visited with Yada Yada but probably still a stretch for my parents, who'd been in the same church, singing the same hymns, accompanied by the same upright piano for the past forty years.

My dad seemed to hit it off with Pastor Clark—they were about the same age—and my mom kept making a fuss over Florida's kids. Too much fuss, if you asked me. Like she was trying too hard. "I just love how they do little black girls' hair, don't you, Jodi?" she'd said while I mentally willed the ground to open and swallow me. Or her. Momentarily, anyway.

But lots of Uptown people greeted them after the service, giving me a chance to grab Florida for half a minute. "Flo! How's Carla doing?"

Florida shrugged. "We hangin'. She visited her foster parents yesterday—part of the deal set up by DCFS. When they brought her back—oh, Lord. What a scene! Was afraid the neighbors would think we were beatin' the life outta her, she screamed so." She pressed her lips into a tight line. "Just keep prayin' for us. We gonna make it, though."

Now I sank down on the front porch steps, remembering my own crying jag in my dad's car outside the police station yesterday. To my surprise, he had pretty much just listened as I dumped everything into his lap. "Guess you can tell Mom too," I'd snuffled, finally blowing my nose, knowing my face was probably red and blotchy. I knew I couldn't do it again. As it was, I felt like I'd just turned my insides out inside that car.

I'd expected my dad to give me some fatherly advice or tell me we'd bitten off more than we could chew by moving into Chicago, but to my surprise he said no more about our "talk" till they were ready to leave. Mom was already in the car when he pulled me aside. *Uh-oh,* I thought. *Here it comes.*

"Jodi, your mom and I worry about you—and what you told me yesterday tells me we have good reason to worry! But this morning I was reading in Philippians." He pulled out his little pocket New Testament, which had print so tiny I was surprised he could still read it. "Chapter four, verse six. 'Be anxious for nothing, but in everything by prayer and supplication, with thanksgiving, let your requests be made known to God . . .'"

My father stopped midsentence, and he got a funny look on his face. I was familiar with these verses and could probably have finished quoting them myself, but I waited. And when he started reading again, his voice was husky. ". . . and the peace of God, which surpasses all understanding, will guard your hearts and minds through Christ Jesus.'" He stuck the Testament back in his pocket and pulled on his driving cap. The funny look had settled into a rueful grin. "Hmm. I was reading that for your benefit, but maybe that verse is supposed to be for your mother and me."

And then they were gone.

I got up from the front steps and made my way back into the house. Josh was sitting on a stool in the kitchen, and Denny was in the process of shaving off the little lock of orange hair with the hair clippers.

"Josh!" I couldn't believe this. "Why didn't you cut it off while your grandparents were still here? They'd have been delighted!"

My son just gave me a knowing smile beneath the purr of the clippers.

Kids. Honestly!

JOSH, NOW LOOKING LIKE A HIP-HOP Mr. Clean instead of a light bulb, drove Amanda to youth group—hallelujah! The caged animal was out of the house, so Denny and I took a walk to the Heartland Café, where I finally got a chance to tell him what happened when we ran into Adele at the police station. Denny shook his head. "Didn't she even say thank you for helping her out?"

"No. I think she was too upset about getting the runaround until we 'white folks' showed up."

"Man." He threw up his hands. "Can't win with Adele. Damned if we do; damned if we don't."

"Maybe." I shrugged. After getting all the frustration off my chest with that good cry in my dad's car, it was easier to see what happened from Adele's point of view. If I'd been in her shoes, it would've been embarrassing for me too. Like getting treated like a child. Not worth the bother for them to go check.

And as I headed for Bethune Elementary the next day, I determined not to let all the unfinished business with Adele get me down. After all, we'd survived one week of Amanda's grounding; only one week to go. (Frankly, I wasn't sure who got punished more by a grounding—the kid or the parents who had to put up with her! Still, I was pretty sure Amanda would think twice before lying to us again.) After Hakim's unexpected participation last week, I felt hopeful as I walked into my third-grade classroom. Maybe we had turned a corner with one kid, at least.

My high hopes were short-lived. I gave the same math problems we'd done with the balance scale on a quiz, and Hakim missed every one. What was *that* about? And twice that week I had to break up schoolyard fights between Hakim and D'Angelo. Neither boy would tell me what the first fight was about, but when it happened again, Britny tattled that D'Angelo had been bragging, saying *his* big brother could lick anybody else's brother.

That's a twist, I thought wryly. *Didn't it used to be, "My dad can lick your dad"?*

Yet we had to nip this little rivalry in the bud. I told both boys that if it happened again—and I didn't care who started it—they'd both get sent to the principal's office and face suspension. Fighting would not be tolerated in this school. We had parent open house coming up on Friday evening. It would be good to meet Hakim's parents, maybe get some clues how best to get through to him.

Josh's birthday snuck up on me again—ours were just a week apart. Eighteen! "Be nice to me," he said at breakfast that Thursday, reaching for the milk to pour on his heaping bowl of corn flakes. "I'm old enough to drop out of school and join the military."

I snatched the milk out of his reach. "Josh! That's not funny." Since 9-11, more and more U.S. soldiers were getting deployed to the Middle East, and now it looked like we were headed for another war with Iraq. This was no time to drop out of high school. *"Promise* me."

"Okay."

I handed him the milk.

"How about dropping my curfew instead?"

"Nice try," Denny said. "When you've got a diploma."

Josh *was* pleased by the extra set of car keys Denny gave him when he opened his gifts after supper. "Hey, could I drive the car to Great America on Saturday, take a couple of friends? Maybe Yo-Yo's brother would like to go too."

It happened every fall. Chicagoland's huge amusement park beckoned on weekends, one last day of thrills before shutting down for the winter. I checked the calendar. *"Jodi PT 10 a.m."* it said. "I've got physical therapy at ten, but I oughta be back by eleven or so. My last appointment. Yea!"

"So you wanna come with us, do a few roller coasters?" Josh knew he was safe with *that* invitation.

"Oh, right. I'd have to start physical therapy all over again. You go. Have fun. Happy birthday."

"Everybody's having fun except *meee!*" Amanda wailed.

Josh knuckled the top of Amanda's head. "Wasn't going to take you even if you *weren't* grounded, shrimp."

THE PARENT OPEN HOUSE on Friday evening was a bit nerve-wracking—like getting inspected by the Big Brass at army basic training. We left the Welcome Bulletin Board up so that parents could enjoy the meaning of their kids' names and gave a demonstration of the balance-scale activity. That's when I realized neither Hakim nor his parents had shown up. Disappointment mingled with my irritation.

Figured.

When I got back from my doctor's appointment on Saturday,

clutching a list of exercises I was supposed to do and one bag of groceries I'd picked up at the fruit market, Josh was waiting impatiently for me. I started to hand him my keys, but with a gleeful grin he dangled his own set in my face and took off in the Dodge Caravan to pick up Pete Spencer and two other friends. I vaguely wondered how Pete could afford the pricey one-day pass but figured Josh—or Denny—was handling it.

I brought in the mail, sat down with a sandwich, and rifled through today's offerings: vitamin catalog, two pizza ads, coupon booklet, gas bill, and a long envelope addressed in unfamiliar handwriting. Pencil. I squinted at the return address—and nearly dropped the envelope.

Becky Wallace, LCC, Lincoln, Illinois.

I hardly knew what to think. Avis had encouraged us to "test the waters" by going ahead with the letter, and we'd know what God wanted us to do if Bandana Woman wrote back. Now that her letter was staring at us in the face . . . well, Yada Yada was meeting at Avis's apartment Sunday night, and we could decide what to do then.

JOSH DROPPED ME OFF at Avis's apartment on Pratt Avenue— good thing; it didn't look like there were any empty parking spaces in the whole block—then he and Amanda went on to youth group at Uptown. I was supposed to hitch a ride home with somebody.

By the time five-thirty rolled around, Avis had a full apartment.

Everybody had shown up, puffing and complaining about the climb to the third floor, then *oohing* and *ahhing* over the polished hardwood floors, shelves of books and pictures, and plants hanging in the windows. Everybody except . . .

"Where's Adele at?" Florida asked. "She ain't been to Yada Yada since the robbery. What's goin' on?"

"Longer than that," Stu said. "She came the night of the robbery, but she hasn't come to anything else since MaDear went off on Denny back in August. Taking it a bit too far, if you ask me."

"Whaddya mean, MaDear went off on Denny?" Yo-Yo looked around the group. "Did I miss somethin'?"

Avis came to the rescue. "Let's get started, have some prayer, and then we can fill you in on why Adele isn't here. We've got some major prayer concerns this week—and decisions too. Oh, Father!" Avis moved right into her prayer. "We need Your presence now more than ever in our lives . . ."

We spent the next five minutes, not praying for any requests, just praising God and remembering promises. Finally Avis said, "Amen."

All eyes fixed on Avis. *Oh God, I'm so glad she agreed to do this!* I was feeling pretty tongue-tied even *thinking* about talking about Adele.

Avis gave a brief rundown of what had happened at Adele's Hair and Nails back in August when Denny had brought me for an anniversary makeover. "Since then," Avis continued, "MaDear has been going through a difficult time with painful memories, and Adele is stressed. At my urging she tried coming to Yada

Yada on Labor Day weekend, but . . . well, we all know what happened at *that* meeting. Right or wrong, it was 'the last straw' for Adele. She's trying to simplify what she's dealing with, and unfortunately, that means pulling back from Yada Yada."

"Just for now, right?" Delores's eyebrows rose hopefully.

Avis shook her head. "Honestly? I don't know. She needs space, which we need to respect. But maybe down the road . . ."

Chanda pulled a pout, looking for all the world like a ten-year-old. "You mean ta say that Jodi, Avis, Florida, and Stu all knew 'bout dis ting what happened a whole month ago, but you jus' now tellin' us?"

Well, I would have liked to tell Yada Yada weeks ago—but I didn't say it.

Edesa spoke. "Jodi. How's Denny?"

Bless you, Edesa! Somebody around here realizes it's been tough being the target of MaDear's misplaced anger. I opened my mouth, but just then Stu snickered. "MaDear didn't throw the hairbrush *that* hard, Edesa! He's fine—right, Jodi?"

I stifled an urge to smack her. "No, he's not fine. Physically, sure, but emotionally, it's been really hard knowing MaDear thinks he's some kind of racist murderer." I blinked rapidly, hoping I wouldn't start blubbering. "Especially since Adele won't talk to us about it."

There. It was out.

"Well, stuff like that sure did happen back then," Florida muttered. "Don't really blame Adele. Hard to deal with if it happened in *your* family."

Avis cut in. "The point is, we need to be praying for Adele and MaDear—*and* Jodi and Denny. Sometimes we need to learn how to wait. And this seems to be one of those times."

The group prayed then, and the prayers were comforting. Once again, Avis had reminded us that we need to stand with each sister in Yada Yada, even when it seemed that our life experiences put us on opposite sides of the problem.

At the end of that prayer, Avis said, "Nony? You have something to share."

I tried to catch Avis's eye, pulling a corner of the letter from Lincoln Correctional Center out of my tote bag. She glanced my way and nodded, but she turned her attention to Nony.

Nony sighed. "You know my mother had a stroke last week. I want to take the boys to see their grandmother before it is too late, but Mark . . ." Tears puddled in Nony's large eyes. "He doesn't want the boys to go. Not till Christmas, when school is out. Then, he says, we can all go to South Africa together."

"But your Mama is sick now!" Florida pointed out.

"Humph." Chanda fanned a paper in front of her face. "No mon be tellin' *me* I canna go see my mama if she sick, even if it be on da' *moon.*"

Nony waved her hand. "No, no, don't misunderstand. Mark says of course *I* can go now to see my mother, but about the boys . . . we do not see eye to eye."

Avis looked thoughtful. "How do you want us to pray, Nony?"

The large eyes flashed. "To change Mark's mind! I *must* take the boys."

Several heads nodded around the circle. "Keep your own bank account, I always say," Ruth muttered.

Avis gently pressed. "I think we should ask God to show you *and* Mark what is best for all of you and to give you one mind and heart. And for you, Nony, to trust God for the outcome."

Nony nodded slowly, and Yada Yada prayed once more, clustering around our sister, so far from her family, her country. We prayed for Nony's "mother heart" that yearned for her sons to know their heritage; her "daughter heart" that yearned for her mother to know her grandsons. We prayed that God would knit the hearts of this family together and that Nony and Mark would trust God in each other.

But I missed Nony's own prayers, the way she "prayed Scripture" into whatever we were praying about. Tonight she was quiet, her eyes closed and lashes wet, letting the prayers rain down on her head.

We finally resumed our seats and Avis raised an eyebrow in my direction. Finally! I pulled out the letter and read the return address.

"You've *got* to be kidding!" Stu's mouth dropped and her eyes bugged, making her look like one of those thin, pale fish that stare at you through the glass at the Shedd Aquarium. "That woman had the nerve to write back?"

"Apparently." Ruth tapped her knee. "Jodi. Read."

I unfolded the single sheet of notebook paper. "She doesn't say much. No salutation . . ."

Chanda snickered. "You mean, she don't say, 'Dear sistahs' . . . ?"

Ruth glared at Chanda. "Just read the letter, Jodi."

"She just says, 'I put your names on the list. Sincerely, Becky Wallace.'"

Silence reigned in the room for at least five seconds. I noticed that Hoshi was staring at the floor.

"That's it? 'I put your names on the list'?" Stu was still incredulous.

"Rather a miracle, don't you think?" Avis said.

"*Si!*" Delores shook her head. "I can hardly believe it."

"So now what?" Yo-Yo hunched her shoulders inside her overalls. "Florida said she'd go, and me. And Jodi and Denny's names are on that list too. So . . . when we gonna go?"

29

We agreed to go the following Saturday, the first weekend in October, depending on whether we could get Yo-Yo back in time to work Saturday evening and if Denny's coaching schedule was clear. Personally, I wasn't sure why it had to be so soon. Sometime in January would've been soon enough for me. Good grief, let Bandana Woman get oriented to prison life first, clean up her mouth, have some time to think about her sins, finish detox. Whatever.

Nony and Hoshi dropped me off after Yada Yada, and Denny met me at the front door. "Was that Nony?" Something in his voice . . .

"Uh-huh. Anything wrong?"

He shrugged and followed me back toward the kitchen, where I put on the teakettle. "Mark called while you were at Yada Yada."

"Nony's husband?" Now *I* was curious.

"Yeah." Denny leaned against the refrigerator. "He was pretty sure Nony would ask Yada Yada to pray about taking the boys to visit her mother in South Africa." Denny lifted an eyebrow at me, waiting for confirmation.

"Well, yeah, she did."

Denny sighed. "He's scared, Jodi. Scared she won't bring them back."

"What?" I nearly dropped the mug I was getting out of the cupboard. "Why wouldn't she bring the boys back?"

Another shrug from Denny. "He thinks . . . to pressure him. To move the family to South Africa. She knows he's not going to lose his family."

Well, of course not! True, Nony often talked about her desire to move back to South Africa—her heart's longing, for sure—but from everything I could tell, she and Mark had a stable, loving marriage. No way would they split over this.

The teakettle whistled frantically. I turned off the burner. "Whew." This was huge. Hard to believe, though. "What did you say to Mark?"

"Mostly listened. He . . . asked me to pray for him." Denny's mouth twisted in a half-grin. "Not sure I've ever prayed with another guy on the phone before—though I know you Yada Yada sisters do it all the time. Uh, could I have a mug of whatever you're making there?"

"Oh. Sure." I'd totally forgotten about the tea water. I grabbed some herbal tea bags and another mug.

"And," Denny added, "I told him to trust his wife—and the Spirit of God within her."

I smiled as I poured the hot water. Now that was a good answer.

THE FOLLOWING SATURDAY found all four of us—Denny, me, Florida, and Yo-Yo—sailing south on route I-55 toward Lincoln, Illinois, but it took a lot of juggling. Yo-Yo had spent the night at our house, along with Pete and Jerry—Yo-Yo on the foldout; the boys camping out in Josh's room—so we could get an early start. It wasn't easy dragging Amanda out of bed at 6:00 a.m. so we could drop her off at Edesa's for the day, leaving Willie Wonka in charge of the three boys. On the way to Edesa's, we picked up Florida in the Edgewater neighborhood, dropped off Amanda on the Near West Side—never mind my uneasy realization she would be spending the day only a mile or two from José Enriques—and finally made it out onto the interstate.

I'd brought two thermoses of hot coffee, four travel mugs, some sticky pecan buns I picked up at Dominick's in-store bakery, and a bunch of bananas to pass around for breakfast on the road. "Now this is nice," Florida said, pouring a refill into her travel mug. "No kids all day, fancy breakfast food. Almost like a vacation."

I twisted around in the front passenger seat. "I can think of a *lot* of places I'd rather spend a vacation day than going to a prison, Florida."

"Yeah. Me too," Yo-Yo said glumly. "Didn't think I'd be going back voluntarily."

Denny chuckled from behind the wheel. "Better voluntarily than *not.*"

Yo-Yo guffawed. "Ha! Ya got that right."

"What are Carla and the boys doing today, Flo?" I asked.

Florida sighed. "Carla goin' to her foster family again today—s'posed to be the first and third Saturdays every month for a while. I know they care about her, but don't see how these visits help *us* none." She was silent a moment. "Still, it'd be harder to make this trip if she was home. So maybe just as well . . . say! I usually have a cig with my morning coffee—mind if I light up? Just *kidding,* Jodi! But we'll be stoppin' along the way, right?"

Denny glanced in his rearview mirror. "Just say the word, Flo."

"Hey, those trees are real pretty," Yo-Yo said. A cold snap the preceding week had turned the usually boring countryside along the interstate into a kaleidoscope of color. Golden elms and maples, rusty brown oaks, crimson sumac bushes, and the occasional brilliant red maple flashed by, resembling a colorful afghan tossed on a large, flat bed. "Wish Pete and Jerry coulda come. Don't think they ever been out in the country."

"My babies neither," said Florida.

I twisted in my seat again. "You mean . . . they've never been outside Chicago?"

Florida and Yo-Yo answered like a chorus. "Nope."

I was flabbergasted into silence. We'd always taken *some* kind of vacation when I was a kid, even if it was just visiting my grand-parents on the farm. And then there was that memorable car trip West one summer, to see the Grand Canyon splitting the earth like a gigantic gash to the bone, then heading north to gawk at Old Faithful and the bears at Yellowstone National Park. I could still remember the rotten-egg smell of the sulfur hot springs and the amazing mud pots going *blop, blop, blop*—marred only by my brothers' incessant teasing that they were going to push me in.

I couldn't imagine never setting foot outside Chicago in my whole life. *Oh Jesus. If you ever plop a million dollars into my lap, I'm gonna buy a huge bus, hire a driver, and take Florida and Yo-Yo and Chanda and all their kids and whoever else wants to come and see the whole country . . .*

The other half of my brain put on the brakes. *Oh, right, Jodi. All those kids? Sounds like a recipe for disaster.* Well, it wasn't like I was going to actually *get* a million dollars—though for half a second I felt tempted for the first time in my life to play the lottery.

We stopped twice at roadside rest stops to stretch our legs and get some cold drinks. It took a little longer than usual, because Florida and Yo-Yo sat out on a picnic table for a cigarette break both times. So it was almost eleven o'clock by the time we drove up to the gate of the Lincoln Correctional Center. We had to state our business, open the back of the minivan, and get out while a security guard did a cursory check of the car. Then we were permitted to drive into the parking lot.

Chain-link fences and rolls of razor wire stretched out on all sides of us as far as I could see. Beyond the wire, off in the distance, lay a typical Midwest town nestled among the colorful trees, church steeples sticking into the blue October sky. So close, yet so far. I swallowed. Is this where I'd be if the charge against me of vehicular manslaughter had stuck? My knees felt rubbery as the four of us walked toward the main entrance.

A lot of visitors were checking in at the main desk, but finally it was our turn. We immediately ran into trouble. Each of us was asked, among other things, if we had ever been convicted of a crime or incarcerated. Now it was Yo-Yo's turn to gulp as the truth came out.

"We can't let you visit an inmate without special permission of the chief administrative officer," the freckle-faced security officer at the desk said flatly.

We all looked at each other.

"Sir, we've driven all the way from Chicago." Denny was exceedingly polite. "Would it be possible to get that permission, uh, today?" He turned to Yo-Yo. "Ms. Spencer was a former inmate here at Lincoln—her records must be available. Given the nonviolent charges against her and her clean prison history, I'm sure you will see that she does not present a risk."

Florida kept her mouth shut, but *"You tell him, Denny!"* was plastered all over her face. I wasn't so sure Denny's charm was going to work with this buster, though. The man gave us an impassive stare, excused himself, and left us waiting.

It took another hour to get clearance for Yo-Yo, but somehow it happened. "Thank ya, Jesus!" Florida crowed, which earned her a funny look from the freckle-faced guy. We were then ushered into security areas—this way for women, that way for men—to be searched. Florida, Yo-Yo, and I had to take off our shoes, which were shaken and examined before we were allowed to put them back on. We were each assigned a locker for our purses, jackets, and personal items. Then we were patted down by a female guard and made to walk through a metal detector. *Sure glad I wore a pair of jeans*, I thought. I could hardly bear to think about being patted down under a skirt.

We met Denny outside the visitors' room and walked in together. The room was devoid of any color or decoration—just gray walls, beige floor tile, gray plastic tables, and gray plastic chairs. At most of the tables, a female inmate wearing street clothes—mostly jeans, sweatpants, and T-shirts—was surrounded by mothers or sisters and kids of all ages. At two of the tables, a man—boyfriend or husband—held hands with a woman across the gray plastic tabletop. Not a DOC uniform in sight.

The four of us sat at an empty table, pulling over another chair so we'd have five. And waited.

I hardly recognized Becky Wallace when a guard let her in the room. In fact, I didn't realize who she was until I saw the guard point toward us. A wiry woman wearing a shapeless T-shirt and baggy sweats walked slowly in our direction. Instinctively, all four of us stood up.

Florida thrust out her hand. "You Becky Wallace?"

The woman nodded, her dark eyes darting from one person to the next. Her dull brown hair was cut short; her skin was sallow, devoid of makeup or natural color. She looked tired, like an old woman who wasn't getting enough sleep.

Except she was young—not more than twenty-five. Her birth date must've been on that file I'd pulled up on the computer, but somehow her age hadn't registered.

"Well, I'm Flo Hickman. This here's Yo-Yo Spencer. And them two is Jodi and Denny Baxter."

We each shook her hand, which she extended reluctantly, and we all sat down. For a moment no one spoke. *Oh God,* I moaned inwardly, *this is so awkward.*

Finally Becky spoke. "You all at that house the night I got busted?"

Denny nodded. "Except Yo-Yo. She had to work that night."

The woman's eyes narrowed in Yo-Yo's direction. "Why you here then?"

Yo-Yo stuck her hands behind the bib of her overalls and slid down the chair into her customary pose—feet straight out, fanny and back resting at two points on the chair. "Wasn't there that night," she said, "but I been *here* and came out better'n I went in. I'm thinkin' the same about you."

The woman's lip curled. "Why should you care?"

Yo-Yo didn't blink. "'Cause somebody cared about me. Made a difference."

I was still tongue-tied. My emotions bounced around like little pinballs. Why *did* we come anyway? Wasn't she going to apologize for terrorizing us that evening?

Becky looked Denny up and down. "You the guy that pinned me down?"

Denny nodded. I could see a little twitch at the corner of his eye. Ha! Denny was nervous too. "I . . . hope I didn't hurt you."

"Nah. Ya did whatcha had to do."

The silence stretched out long again. It didn't seem the right time for small talk. Finally Florida spoke. "You finish detox?"

Becky's eyes dropped. "Huh! Got out of Cook County 'fore my three weeks' detox was up. Hit withdrawal big-time when I got here." She cussed under her breath. "Worse pain ever had in my life." She eyed Florida. "You?"

"Uh-huh. Writhin' all over the floor, screamin' for somethin', anything. Sure been there."

"You clean now?"

Florida grinned. "Yes, thank ya, *Jesus!* Five years saved and five years sober!"

The woman's lip curled again. "You all religious types?"

"Yep! That's what we was doin' when you came in the door— havin' a prayer meetin'." Florida nodded at Denny and me. "At their house."

Becky Wallace squirmed in her chair. "Guess I gave y'all some- thin' to pray about, huh."

That's it? That's all she's going to say about what happened that night? I swallowed the sharp retort that rode the tip of my tongue. "Yes. We did too. Pray for you that night, I mean. And ever since."

Becky's mouth twitched. "Don't bother," she muttered. "Ain't worth it. Save your prayers for that lady what got her hand cut."

I noticed she didn't say, ". . . *for that lady whose hand I cut.*"

"Oh, we prayin' for her too," said Florida. "And her daughter. They was all shook up."

Becky shot us a wary glance. I could practically read her thoughts: *Knew it! Knew you guys are just itchin' to tell me how what I done made you feel.*

But nobody said anything more. Finally she seemed to slump

inside her ill-fitting clothes. "Didn't mean ta cut that lady," she mumbled, staring at the table. "Didn't want ta hurt nobody. Jus' . . . jus' needed money for a fix."

"I know," Florida said. "We all know that."

We asked if she had family. She shrugged. "Somewhere. Ain't heard from 'em in a long time." We asked if she had kids. Her eyes twitched. She gave a short nod. "Lil' boy. Don't know where he be, though. His daddy took 'im away from me. Said I wasn't fit." Did she need anything? She shook her head. "Nah. What's ta need? I ain't goin' nowhere."

The clock on the wall inched its way toward 1:00. My stomach was rumbling. Maybe Becky Wallace had missed lunch too. But if Avis were here, no way would she miss an opportunity to pray. Why not? I had absolutely no other idea how to end this awkward visit. "Could we . . . uh, pray for you before we go?"

That seemed to unnerve her. She stood up. "Ya can pray all ya want after ya get on outta here. I gotta go." She started to leave, then she turned back. "Don't know why y'all come on down here, but I . . . I 'preciate it." Without waiting for a reply, she strode quickly across the room, motioning to the guard to let her out the locked door.

And then she was gone.

30

None of us said much as we left the prison and climbed back into the car. I felt irritated that my mental image of Bandana Woman didn't stand up to the dull-eyed, pathetic creature we'd just left. But I didn't want to feel sorry for her. *Isn't some anger appropriate, God? After all, Hoshi's relationship with her parents is a wreck now, thanks to B. W. If we're going to actually relate to this woman, she needs to face that somehow.* With a twinge of satisfaction, I felt my level of anger—righteous anger, of course—nudge back up a notch.

She was so young, though . . .

"How old do you think she is?" I said to no one in particular.

"Dunno," Yo-Yo said. "Maybe 'bout my age."

"Which is?"

"Uh . . ." She paused, like she had to think about it. "Gonna be twenty-three in a week or so. Say, we gonna eat? I'm hungry."

We found a McDonald's in the town of Lincoln and got milkshakes to go with the sandwiches and apples I'd brought along. Got the coffee thermoses filled up again too.

Florida eyed the wheat bread suspiciously as she took a sandwich. "You got somethin' against white bread, Jodi?"

I stifled a snort. She probably meant that cheap spongy stuff in long "family-size" loaves that passed for bread in the grocery store. Might be good for *something*—like maybe caulking leaky windows in an emergency. I smiled apologetically. "Sorry, Flo. Just used what I had on hand."

We munched in silence for a while before I noticed that Denny had not gotten back on the interstate. "Taking the back roads home?"

He shrugged. "Thought we might find a roadside stand that sold pumpkins."

"They sell 'em at the *store*, Denny," Florida said, her mouth full of sandwich.

Denny grinned. "I know, but it's kinda fun to buy them right off the farm."

"Josh and Amanda still carve pumpkins? Them big kids?"

"Sure," I piped up. "We do it every year." Or was it Denny and me who carved the pumpkins now?

Sure enough, we saw a hand-painted sign boasting "Pumpkins, Apples, Squash." Denny pulled into the farm driveway. "Pick out a pumpkin for Carla and the boys, Flo. My treat." He eyed Yo-Yo. "You want a pumpkin? Take your pick."

Yo-Yo got out of the car, taking in the rows and rows of pumpkins lined up on the ground like so many Munchkins from the

Land of Oz with big orange heads and little green hat-handles, sorted by size behind signs that said, "Large $5, Medium $4, Small $3." She jammed her hands in the low pockets of her overalls. "Never had an honest-to-God *real* pumpkin before."

I stared at her. "Never?"

Yo-Yo shrugged. "My mom wasn't big on holidays. Maybe Christmas now and then—if she was sober."

"What about birthdays? She made a cake, that kind of thing, right?"

Yo-Yo shook her head. "Nah, but it's okay, ya know. I try to do somethin' for Pete and Jerry when it's their birthday. But we never had a pumpkin." She moved over to the rows of "Small" pumpkins. "If I get one, would one of ya tell me how ta, y'know, make it glow?"

I laughed, but I felt like crying. *"My mom wasn't big on holidays ..."* How much I took for granted! Never thought that some families—families I rubbed shoulders with—didn't even do *birthdays.* "Sure. Maybe we should have a pumpkin-carving party. You wanna, Florida?"

"Cool. I'll bring Carla. Chris and Cedric gonna think they too big. Can I have this big 'un here, Denny?"

"Yeah. They gotta be big for carving. You guys pick out three big ones. I'll go pay." Denny headed for the outdoor counter.

"Pay for four, Denny!" I yelled after him. "I'm gonna get one for Chanda's kids too."

As we pulled back on the road, Yo-Yo stared at the field next to the roadside stand, where pumpkins dotted the ground, still clinging to their sprawling wilted vines. "Huh. So that's how they grow." It was a statement of wonder, like the way I felt watching Neil Armstrong set foot on the moon on my TV screen.

We finally got back on I-55. Denny didn't ask me to drive, and I didn't offer. One of these days I needed to muster up the courage to drive at highway speeds again. But not today. Nobody talked much about our visit to Becky Wallace on the way home. Maybe we all needed to digest the experience for a while.

I stuck in a *Songs4Worship Gospel* CD and glanced back into the second seat as the Colorado Mass Choir filled the car with "Let everything that has breath praise Him!" I turned the volume down a notch. Florida was sleeping in spite of all that coffee; Yo-Yo just stared out the side window of the minivan, nursing her own thoughts.

An idea began to percolate in my head . . .

AS FAR AS I COULD TELL, our kids had handled the day pretty well. Amanda volunteered that she and Edesa had gone over to the Enriqueses' house to make "real" tortillas with Delores and Emerald. *And to see José,* I guessed. Yet did it really matter, if the whole family was together? What harm was there in that? Josh and Yo-Yo's brothers played video games, ate the two frozen pizzas I had in the freezer, cleaned us out of ice cream, and left all their dishes in the sink. So what else did I expect? Though I was a little rattled by the cigarette butts I found out by the garage. Who'd been smoking—Pete? Well, so did his sister-guardian. Not much I could do about that.

At Uptown Community the next morning, Florida got up during the testimony time and shared briefly about our visit to Lincoln Correctional, mentioning the robbery that had preceded it "at the Baxters' house." I saw heads swivel as people looked at us, no doubt surprised that they were just now hearing about this. "That girl needs some serious prayer," Florida said. "So I'm askin' the church to keep her covered. God saved me, so I know He can save her too. Pastor?" She handed the mic to Pastor Clark and started to sit down, but Pastor Clark motioned her to stay up front and asked Avis and Stu and the Baxter family to join her and be included in his prayer.

Funny. I hadn't really thought about asking Uptown to pray about stuff related to Yada Yada. For one thing, Yada Yada was women from a bunch of different churches—not really an Uptown thing. And prayer requests shared in the group were confidential. Yet maybe Florida was right. This was bigger than any of us, bigger than Yada Yada. My eyes misted as Pastor Clark prayed for protection, for healing of the experience, for Becky Wallace's salvation.

Well sure, let's pray for her salvation. *Just don't turn her back out on the street, God,* I added as we sat down again.

Once back into the school week, though, I didn't have time to think much about Becky Wallace. On Monday I congratulated myself that my third-grade class was starting to gel. On Tuesday, Terrell tripped Darian as they came into the classroom, and the day seemed to unravel from there. Chanel was absent for three days, and we had to send a note home to all the parents that said, "A case of lice has been reported in your child's class, so please take the following precautions . . ." When Chanel returned with her head wrapped in a blue scarf, all the kids knew who the "case of lice" was, and I had to keep her in the classroom during lunch to prevent the inevitable meanness, in spite of the lecture I'd given the class on respecting others' feelings.

The week wasn't a total loss, though. I turned Christy James loose to plan our reading segment for the next couple of weeks, since that seemed to be of special interest to my student teacher. She started reading the story of Johnny Appleseed to the class, then she encouraged the students to write a poem using the letters of his name as an acrostic. The results weren't terribly creative, but some were pretty cute. Most of the kids seemed proud of their "poems," decorating their papers with round red blobs that were supposed to be apples.

Hakim, however, just sat and looked at his paper, as if he didn't have a clue. My heart constricted. Why was written work so hard for him? He was obviously very bright—the balance-scale episode proved that. I motioned him to a table at the back of the room. He came reluctantly, like he might get yelled at. "It's okay," I said. "Look, let's do it this way." I covered up all the letters of the acrostic except for the J and asked him to make up a sentence beginning with that letter. "You tell me what you want to say, and I'll write it down," I said. That seemed to make a difference. Working this way he finished the acrostic poem.

J—Just the other day
O—On my way to the store, I
H—Hollered to the old man
N—Next-door . . .

Not bad. It actually rhymed. "It's the written work that trips him up," I murmured to Christy as we tacked the papers up on the bulletin board after school. "I wonder if he's ever been tested?"

On Friday, Christy brought a couple of bags of apples to class, a big plastic bowl, and a roll of paper towels and let the kids "bob for apples" as the last activity of the day. I should have advised against it, but I didn't want to squelch her ideas. The kids were already squirrelly, given that it was late in the school day just before the weekend, but it might have gone all right if Cornell hadn't started acting smart by rocking the bowl. Before we could stop him, the bowl tipped over, and we had water all over the floor—which meant a trip to the janitor's closet for a mop and bucket and a dozen disappointed kids who hadn't gotten to bob for apples yet. Ramón yelled at Cornell for ruining their turn, Cornell slugged Ramón, and we ended up having to send both boys to the office.

"Sorry, Ms. Baxter," Christy said sheepishly as she gathered up the remaining apples and the bowl. (The paper towels had paid the ultimate sacrifice mopping up the floor instead of kids' faces.)

"Don't be sorry, Christy. It was a great idea. Next time we'll just nail down the bowl." For a second there, I think she thought I was joking.

ON MY WAY OUT OF SCHOOL that Friday, I caught Avis on the fly and told her Yo-Yo would be twenty-three "in a week or so" but had never had a birthday party. "What do you think of celebrating her birthday Sunday night at Yada Yada? She'd really be surprised."

"*This* Sunday?" Avis frowned. "Well, okay . . . but Natasha's coming home from college this weekend—her high-school homecoming, I think—and Charette is coming up from Cincinnati with the twins. We're all going to the South Side to see Rochelle and the baby. I won't have time to plan anything. Not even sure I'll be at Uptown on Sunday. Might go to church with Rochelle."

"That's okay. I'll—"

"Where would we meet?"

"Meet? I thought we agreed on Nony's at the last meeting. Haven't been there since August."

"Yes, but Nony called me last night and said she and the boys are leaving for South Africa on Sunday. Not sure how long she'll be gone—several weeks anyway."

Nony *and* the boys? I hadn't said anything to Avis about Mark's phone call to Denny. "Well, good for Mark." Avis looked at me funny. *Oops! Did I say that out loud?* "I mean, good that our prayers were answered—you know, that they came to an agreement," I amended hastily. I made a mental note to give Nony a call before she left.

But where to meet? Only about half the group was able to host a Yada Yada meeting. Stu lived too far away; Delores had too many kids . . . I shrugged. "Guess I'm next on the list, if it's not too soon after the . . . you know."

Avis raised an eyebrow. "We're not going to let Satan rob us of anything, Jodi—not our joy, not where we meet for Yada Yada." She looked at her watch. "Look, I've got to run. Let me know if you want me to bring something. I'll be there."

"Just a card for Yo-Yo!" I called after her as she flew out the door. By the time I crossed the parking lot to head home, her car was gone. Must be anxious to see her grandkids.

SURE ENOUGH, Nony had plane tickets for Sunday afternoon for herself, Marcus, and Michael. "I'm so sorry, Jodi, not to tell you sooner," she said when I called, "but it's been so hectic, getting passports for the boys, getting their schoolwork so I can home-school while we're gone. I don't know why Mark changed his mind, but God's name be praised! Will you let the rest of the sisters know? And give them my love."

Indeed. Just don't stay too long, Nony.

I sent out an e-mail Friday night to Yada Yada, telling them about the change in location for Sunday's meeting and Nony's news. And since I knew Yo-Yo didn't have e-mail, I broadcast my idea for a birthday surprise. "Just bring cards," I suggested. "I'll make a cake."

When I went to the store on Saturday to get a card for Yo-Yo, I couldn't find anything that seemed appropriate. What could I say to encourage a young woman who'd once said about her name, *"Oh, right. Yo-Yo—a spinning toy going nowhere."*

That actually gave me an idea. Back home I got on the computer, called up the Web site where I'd found the meanings of names for my Welcome Bulletin Board at the school, and typed "Yolanda" into the search. I blinked when the meaning came up on the screen.

"Yolanda. From the Greek: 'Violet Flower.'"

Wow. If I were going to hang a flower on Yo-Yo's name, I'd choose something hardy, sturdy enough to weather all sorts of conditions. Like marigolds or mums. But in the Bible, names had significant meaning. Maybe there was a meaning for Yo-Yo here that wasn't that obvious.

I was just about to shut down the name site, when a curious thought popped into my head. *What did Becky Wallace's name mean?* Immediately followed by: *Why should I care?* But I was curious enough to type "Becky" into the search bar and waited while that name page came up.

I stared. Was this possible?

"Becky. A familiar form of Rebecca. From the Hebrew: 'Bound, tied.'"

Oh God.

31

I was so focused on trying to pull off Yo-Yo's birthday surprise that Amanda's request after church on Sunday almost didn't register. "Invite who to youth group tonight?" I said absently, studying my recipe for red-velvet cake, wondering if I'd have to run out to Dominick's for two bottles of red food coloring.

"*José*. Mo-om! Aren't you listening?"

Well, she had my attention *now*. I leaned back against the kitchen counter and looked at my daughter. Okay. Should've seen it coming. After all, her two-week grounding had been for lying to us, not for being friends with José Enriques per se. However, I'd been hoping that the budding romance would wither on the vine for lack of attention—ignoring, of course, that "absence makes the heart grow fonder."

I sighed. "Don't they have a youth program at Iglesia?" *Oh brother. That was lame.*

She shrugged. "Sure. Some weeknight—Thursday, I think. What's your point?"

Watch it, young lady. I took a breath. What *was* my point? "I . . . is something special happening at Uptown tonight?"

"Kinda. The Reillys are gonna be talking about the music teens listen to—I thought José might be interested. They told us to bring friends. And our CDs."

"That's a long way to come—"

"Mom! Mrs. Enriques is coming to Yada Yada tonight, right? Here at our house? José could come with his mom, and we'll take him to youth group." She zeroed in for the kill. "Besides, isn't that what you and the other Yada Yada women do? Visit each other's churches?"

I hated it when my kids pointed the finger back at me to get what they wanted. The next item in her bag of tricks would be to remind me we'd told her that if she wanted to see José, to invite him up here.

I tried to back out gracefully. "Sure. Good idea." Amanda disappeared with the phone before I even got the mixer out.

As it turned out, the idea spread, and Josh called Ruth Garfield to ask if she'd bring Yo-Yo's brothers, ". . . since you and Yo-Yo are coming anyway." Chris Hickman came with Florida too. We didn't have that many high schoolers at Uptown, so the "youth group" started at eighth grade. It was a bit hectic at first, with Yada Yada arriving and teenagers leaving, but eventually we got everybody sorted out. Denny decided to go with the kids and "learn something about teen music." Poor guy.

I was glad to see Hoshi made it, since Nony was probably somewhere over the Atlantic by now. I made a mental note to take Hoshi back to campus after Yada Yada so she wouldn't have to ride the el alone after dark.

By mutual agreement, nobody said anything about Yo-Yo's birthday when we first started. Right after our beginning prayer and praise time, Avis asked for a report of the visit to Becky Wallace. *Oh, help.* I didn't know what to say. Admit I was still hanging on to my mental mad, even after meeting B. W. face to face and seeing her as a real person?

Florida saved the day. "I know what happened here that night was bad news. But that girl—why she's only a day or two older'n Yo-Yo here. Just a baby. Why, she—"

Yo-Yo loudly cleared her throat. "Just a baby, huh?" We all laughed.

"Oh, girl, ya know what I mean. She's got her whole life in front of her, and if somebody don't do somethin', it's gonna be messed up big-time."

"Messy, schmessy," Ruth huffed. "Seems like she's already done a good job of that. What are we, the local rehab?"

Exactly what I was thinking.

Stu frowned. "Why would you say that, Ruth? You befriended Yo-Yo in prison, looked after her brothers, got her a job . . ."

Chanda wagged her head. "If dat what you tinkin', don't look at *me.* I canna give no reference to mi ladies on de North Shore. You wants ta go in dey houses, you gots ta be squeaky clean. No drugs, no rap sheet, no nothin'."

I noticed Hoshi sat stiffly on her chair, twisting and untwisting a handkerchief with lacy edging.

Avis steered us back to center. "It's rather a miracle that Becky Wallace agreed to let some of us come visit. One step at a time. Right now, the most important thing to do is keep praying, but before we do that . . . Yo-Yo? Or Jodi? Anything you want to share from the visit to Lincoln?"

Yo-Yo shook her head. "Glad I went, though. Reminded me I don't wanna go back. Inside, I mean."

My turn. "To be honest? Don't know if I'm glad I went or not. I mean, it was probably the right thing to do, but . . . it's kinda hard to give up my feelings about what she did, barging in here and terrorizing everybody and hurting Hoshi's mother." Out of the corner of my eye, I saw Hoshi stop twisting the handkerchief and just stare at the floor. "Yet she didn't seem like a monster when we visited her in prison. Just someone sad and pathetic and lonely. Which is hard for me to accept, because I don't want to feel sorry for her. She really hurt us—all of us."

Hoshi spoke, her voice low and intense. "Yes. I don't want to feel sorry for her. Maybe that is not good, but that is how I feel."

I was glad Hoshi had the courage to say that. It wouldn't be fair to her if we were more concerned for the perp than for the victim. But even as I entertained those thoughts, I realized an unsettling truth: Visiting B. W. *had* taken away the sting of that night. I no longer felt the same fear when I thought of her. And maybe that was a good thing?

Tentatively I voiced this new realization.

Avis nodded. "When we hold on to our anger, we allow the person who hurt us to keep hurting us again and again, every time we think about what happened. That gives Satan way too much power! That's why the 'Jesus way' points us to reconciliation and forgiveness. But"—she held up her hand like a stop sign—"maybe that's something for us to think and pray about. God understands we need time. Why don't we pray for Hoshi and her mom and all of us still struggling with the after-effects of the robbery? And pray for Becky Wallace too."

Everyone seemed willing to get into the prayer time, also remembering to pray for Nony and her boys making their way to South Africa that very moment . . . for Mark Smith, home alone without his wife and children for several weeks . . . for all our teenagers at Uptown this evening. Edesa, bless her, prayed for Delores's husband, still without a job, still drinking too much to drown his discouragement.

During a short lull, I said, "And, Jesus, I want to pray for Adele . . ." Yet I had no idea what to pray *for*, so I just left it hanging there. Others filled in the gap with "Yes, Jesus!" and "You said You'd never leave her or forsake her!"

When it seemed like Avis was wrapping up the prayer time, I slipped out to the kitchen to light the candles on Yo-Yo's cake, smothered in whipped-cream frosting. I was realizing that twenty-three was a *lot* of candles when Stu slipped into the kitchen too. "Here, you need help with that." She struck a match and started in on the other side. *Humph.* Not *"Can I help you with that?"* Just *"You need help with that."* Which was true, but still.

297

We got all the candles lit, and Stu picked up the cake plate. "You go first and start them singing 'Happy Birthday.' I'll follow with the cake." She stood aside for me to go ahead of her.

Now I really was annoyed. Good grief! *I* made the cake, and *I* wanted to carry it in.

"Is that for Yo-Yo?" Stu nodded at the gift sitting on the counter, loosely tied up in lavender tissue paper and white ribbon. Darn if she wasn't right. I couldn't carry both the gift and the cake, even if I wanted to. I picked up the gift and started for the living room. *Okay, God, I know this is no time to get all hot and bothered by Stu's bossiness. Just keep me from smashing that cake in her face.*

We made it to the doorway just as Avis pronounced the final, "In the name of Jesus!" Perfect! As people's eyes popped open, I started singing, "Happy Birthday," and everyone joined in—even Yo-Yo, looking around as if trying to figure out who we were celebrating. When we all sang, " . . . dear Yo-Yo," Stu carried the flaming cake across the room and stood in front of her. "Happy birthday to you."

Yo-Yo's mouth dropped open, then her eyes darted this way and that. "Me?" she finally said. Man! Why didn't I remember my camera? The look on her face was priceless.

By now everyone was clapping and hollering. "Hey! Happy birthday, Yo-Yo!" "Blow out the candles! They're gonna drip all over the cake!" and "Make a wish first!"

"But it's not my birthday."

"When is it?" Ruth demanded.

"Uh . . . Tuesday."

"So? What's two days? Blow!"

Firelight from the shrinking candles danced on the blonde tips of Yo-Yo's short, spiky hair. "Okay, okay," she said and blew—spraying wax all over the frosting. But who cared. We all cheered.

Stu started to hand off the cake platter to me, but I held up the gift in my hands. "Oh. Could you cut the cake, Stu?" I asked sweetly. "But don't go yet. Got another presentation here."

"Hey, hey! Quiet, everybody," Ruth ordered.

I sat down on the floor in front of Yo-Yo's chair. She hunched forward, elbows on her denim knees, chin in her hands, staring at the toes of her sneakers. "Do you remember," I started, "when we were talking about what 'Yada Yada' means, and Avis or Nony—somebody!—said God calls us by our name? Well, I looked up the meaning of Yo-Yo's name—Yolanda, actually—and here it is." I held out the tissue-wrapped gift.

Yo-Yo stared cautiously at the lumpy gift. "Bite you, it won't," Ruth grumbled, waving her hand at her. "Open it!"

Yo-Yo let me place the gift in her hands. Hesitantly, she untied the white ribbon and the tissue paper fell away, revealing a large African violet with small clusters of bright purple flowers. Yo-Yo looked up. "I don't get it."

I smiled. "That's what your name means: 'Violet flower.'"

"Now dat nice," Chanda murmured.

Yo-Yo nodded. "Oh. Thanks. It's nice. Though . . . don't think that describes *me* very well." Leaving the plant on her lap, she held her arms wide, as though reminding us of her shapeless, same-old denim overalls.

299

I gave her a hug. "Oh, I don't know about that. My mom raised African violets all the time. And they'd just sit there growing leaves for months, then we'd get up one morning, and those gorgeous flowers seemed to have burst out overnight. Personally? I think there's a lot of beauty inside you that *you* might not see, but the rest of us do."

"You got that right," Florida crowed. And the clapping and cheering started all over again.

"Me tinks it be time to *party!*" Chanda jumped up, waving a CD she'd brought with her. "Go! Go! Cut dat cake," she said to Stu, who was still holding the cake platter, waving her away toward the dining room. "Jodi! How dis player work?"

In moments, Chanda had popped in the CD, turned up the volume, and was pushing furniture out of the way. The words to "Shout Hallelujah!" filled the house, while a tidal wave of drums, keyboards, and electric bass rumbled from the speakers.

> Come on and shout! hallelujah
> It's the highest praise!
> Dance! the devil is defeated
> He's under my feet! . . .

It was impossible *not* to dance to that music. Chanda pulled Yo-Yo to her feet, and pretty soon the two of them were doing a step-shuffle-and-shake number in sync. Avis and Florida were each "gettin' down" too. Ruth, Delores, and Edesa joined in, with results that looked a cross between a Jewish line dance and the

Macarena. Me—I didn't really know how to dance, but I tried to copy Chanda and Yo-Yo's steps. The results were pretty sloppy, but nobody seemed to care. Even Hoshi clapped along from the sidelines, a smile cheering up her face.

Shout! . . . Dance! . . . Clap! . . .

The CD was full of good "dance" songs, but it didn't take long for my left leg to start aching. Feeling guilty that Stu was off cutting the cake, I slipped down the hall to the dining room and took the cake knife from her. "Go on, I'll finish up. Go dance." I smiled at her and actually meant it.

We ate cake, gave Yo-Yo our cards, laughed, played music, and danced till the kids and Denny came back. They stood in a ragged line in the living-room doorway—Chris, Jerry, Pete, Josh, Amanda, and José—staring at their mothers and friends like a freak show. "C'mon, c'mon," Chanda waved at them. "Show us!" She put on the "Shout Hallelujah!" song again.

With a sly grin, José took up her challenge, and Pete followed—though how he could dance in those baggy crotch-around-his-knees pants, I'll never know. Feet flying, shoulders shrugging, the two young men did a hip-hop something to the pulsing praise music, while Chanda and Yo-Yo copied their moves. Everyone clapped and whooped. Encouraged, the rest of the kids joined them—even Josh and Amanda. *Hmm.* Where did they learn to move like that?

The living room was definitely crowded now, so most of Yada Yada faded back and let the young folks dance, while we cheered them on.

Not sure how I heard the doorbell, but I saw Denny go to answer it. *Good,* I thought. *If it's another Bandana Woman selling Avon,* he *can handle it.* But he came back and motioned to me.

"Upstairs neighbor," he said in my ear. "Complaining about the noise."

Oh, brother. It wasn't like we had a party every weekend—or even *once* since we'd moved here! I glanced at the clock. Good grief. It was only nine o'clock! And tomorrow was Columbus Day—a school holiday, anyway. But I turned down the volume on the CD player.

DENNY, BLESS HIS HEART, took Chanda and Hoshi home, and Stu somehow squeezed Delores, José, Edesa, Florida, and Chris into her two-door silver Celica. *Hope she doesn't get stopped by a cop,* I worried. As Ruth and Yo-Yo's brothers headed out to Ruth's car, Yo-Yo gave me a hug. "Thanks for the party, Jodi. And the African violet. Never had a birthday party before, you know."

I hugged her back. "I know."

Even after everyone was gone, the house seemed to ring with music and dance. *("Shout! . . . Dance! . . . Clap! . . .")* I sat down at the dining-room table with my school bag and pulled out my lesson-plan book, just to get an idea how much I needed to do tomorrow. A Post-it note stared at me from the cover. *"Send a note to Hakim's parents, suggest he be tested."*

Hmm. Should have asked Avis about that. Well, I'd write the note and check with her on Tuesday before sending it.

32

I managed to talk to Avis about three minutes on Tuesday, but she thought the testing could be arranged if Hakim's parents agreed. Satisfied, I sat down at my desk while Christy was reading *Ramona the Pest* to the class and pulled out the envelope with the note I'd written to his parents. I'd written the note in a friendly tone, even signed it "Ms. B" in quotes, which Hakim insisted on calling me. Only one problem: since neither his father nor his mother had come to the parent open house in September, I had no idea whether I should address it to "Mr. and Mrs. Porter," or just "Ms. Porter."

"To whom it may concern" didn't seem like an option.

I finally addressed it to "Ms. Porter" as the safest bet and asked Hakim to take it home to his mom. He eyed it suspiciously. "You gettin' me in trouble? I didn't fight nobody."

I smiled encouragingly. "Nothing like that. You've been fine. I just want to talk to your mom about how to make school better for you."

He frowned, like I'd just spoken gobbledegook, but he took the note and stuck it in the pocket of his sweatshirt. "Don't forget to give it to her," I called after him as he disappeared out the classroom door.

To my surprise, he brought the note back the next morning, with "Ms. Porter" on the envelope crossed out and "Ms. B" written in a strong, bold hand beneath it. Well, good for him. At least he remembered to give it to his mom. I didn't have time to read it at the moment, so I stuck it into the pocket of my corduroy skirt, intending to wait till lunchtime. Then I got so busy setting up our science experiment about ecosystems and the greenhouse effect that my student teacher was lining up the kids to come back in from the gym before I remembered the note.

Pulling the envelope out of my pocket, I opened the same sheet of paper I'd sent home with Hakim. The word *testing* had been circled in red ink, and at the bottom of the page was a note scrawled in the same bold handwriting: "Ms. B—Hakim is a smart kid. He does not need to be 'tested.' Testing is a cover-up for poor teaching. Just do your job." It was signed, "Geraldine Porter."

My whole face stung, like I'd just been slapped. *Poor teaching?!* The nerve of that woman!

I was so upset, I asked Christy to take over the class while I went to the teachers' restroom to pull myself together. I couldn't get rid of the accusing words ringing in my head: *"poor teaching . . . just do your job."* After ten minutes of pacing back and forth between the electric hand dryer and the overflowing trash can by the door, scorching my brain cells as I indulged in a one-side mental tirade at the lady, I decided to go see Avis.

A quick peek through the window in the classroom door satisfied me that Christy would survive another five or ten minutes without me, and I headed for Avis's office. She was on the telephone, but she motioned me inside. I shut the door.

She finally put down the handset. "Are you all right, Jodi?"

"No!" I handed her the note and pinched my lips while she read it.

"I see." Avis was quiet a moment. "Tell you what. I will do an informal evaluation of Hakim, just to assess the situation for myself. We better not do more than that, especially since we've asked and the mother has said no. Then, possibly I can contact the mother if we feel we need to pursue this further."

The principal contacting the mother sounded good to me. *Real* good. My steam level began to dissipate. "Hakim is bright, I agree. He shines when we do hands-on stuff. But put a sheet of paper in front of him, and he seems to freeze. Plus, he does have some troubling behavior problems. Either sulking and keeping to himself—or lashing out."

"Well, let's pursue it quietly for a while longer." Avis eyed me critically over the top of her reading glasses. "Don't let it get you down, Jodi. Leave it to God." Then she smiled, almost a tease. "And just do your job—like you've been doing."

LEAVE IT TO GOD ... *Leave it to God* ...

Avis's admonition followed me the rest of the week. Actually, it helped. I knew I was doing a good job—not perfect, but pretty darn good—teaching those third graders, and if I wasn't, I'd hear about it during staff evaluations. Like Avis said, I just needed to keep doing my job. And, I tried to tell myself, if Hakim's mother didn't want him to get tested, that was her problem.

No! I couldn't accept that. Because even though Hakim was bright, he *was* falling behind. And that wasn't fair to him.

Yet I had a whole classroom of kids to worry about. I couldn't tutor Hakim all day—unfortunately. Still, I determined to look for ways to give him more individual attention, especially with written work and reading. And parent-teacher conferences were coming up in a few weeks along with report-card pickup. Maybe that would provide a natural time to talk to Hakim's mom. If she showed up.

The weekend arrived before I noticed that the pumpkins we'd bought on the way back from Lincoln Correctional were still sitting in the garage. Yo-Yo and Florida had elected to leave theirs at our house since we'd talked about having a pumpkin-carving party with their kids. And I'd totally forgotten to say anything to Chanda.

But, hey, why not? It could be fun. I hadn't met Chanda's kids yet—this might be a good time. So I got on the phone with Florida, Yo-Yo, and Chanda, and we lined it up for the next Saturday. That gave a few days to enjoy the jack-o'-lanterns before Halloween, but not enough time for them to rot.

Since the Bagel Bakery was closed Saturday for the Sabbath, Yo-Yo didn't have to be at work till they opened at sundown. She didn't think she could drag either of her brothers, though. I laughed. "That's okay. You gotta hit twenty before you realize how much fun it is being a kid. Just bring yourself."

Fortunately, the weather cooperated—one of those treasure days of late October, when summer made one last attempt to return. Josh and Denny had soccer games on Saturday, but they both got rides, so I offered to go pick up Chanda and her kids.

"Why didn't you invite Emerald Enriques?" Amanda demanded, following me around as I hunted for my car keys. *Right. And José would have to come along to escort his sister on the el, I suppose.* I spied my keys on the stove—the stove?—and snatched them up before Amanda made a comment about me having a "senior moment."

"Next time." I smiled sweetly and pecked my daughter on the cheek. "Tell you what. You can either clean your room as usual or make some sugar cookies for our little party—pumpkins, with orange frosting or something."

I backed the minivan out of the garage, feeling smug about my little deal with Amanda. Of course, she might get huffy and not do either—you never could tell with fifteen-year-olds.

There was no quick way to Juneway Terrace on a Saturday afternoon, even though it wasn't that far. I mentally tossed a coin and headed for Sheridan Road. "So, God," I muttered as I waited at a red light on the busy north-south street. "What should we do about Amanda and José? Let them date? Figure it's puppy love and it will go away? What?"

The light changed to green and the line of cars crept forward, but the light turned red again just as I got to the intersection. Why didn't they widen this road? It was only two lanes, with parked cars crowding both sides. Drumming my fingers on the door rest, a man with dreadlocks and walnut-colored skin crossing the intersection in front of the minivan caught my eye. I half-expected him to be wearing an embroidered tunic over wide cotton pants, but the dreadlocks were pulled back into a ponytail, and he was wearing a tan sport coat, open-necked shirt, jeans, and carrying a briefcase. Then, for some strange reason, he turned beside my right front headlight and made his way between the Caravan's passenger door and the car parked along the curb.

Instinctively, I glanced at my door locks. *Not locked.* I pushed the button at my fingertips. The locks snapped into place with a loud *click.*

The man paused, slowly bent down, and caught my eye through the passenger side window. "That's right," he said loudly through the glass. "Lock your doors! But you really should keep them locked all the time, lady."

Ohmigosh. He heard me lock the doors! To my chagrin, the man pulled out a set of keys, unlocked the door of the four-door sedan parked along the curb, and got in.

Sheesh, Jodi. He was only getting into his parked car. I was so embarrassed that I didn't even notice the light had turned green until horns started to honk behind me. *Oh, God, he probably thinks I locked the doors because he's black and male and wearing dreads.* I pulled forward, but I wanted to go back. I wanted to say, *"I'm so sorry, sir. You're right. I should keep my doors locked all the time. I didn't mean to offend you.*" But a glance in my rearview mirror showed the sedan pulling around the corner and disappearing down the cross street.

For some reason, the incident rattled me. *Look,* I told myself as I double-parked in front of Chanda's apartment building and honked the horn. *You locked the doors because a man was coming close to your car door and you didn't know why. Not because he was black.* Or . . . did I?

Chanda and her three children trooped out of the apartment building door dressed like they were going to a party. The boy even had a bow tie! The kids piled into the backseats while Chanda climbed into the front. I tried to push the incident out of my mind.

"Dat big one in the back, he Thomas," Chanda announced. She pronounced it To-*mas.* "He eleven. Then Cheree. She seven. And Dia. She five. Say hello to Miz Baxter," she ordered over her shoulder.

A chorus of hellos echoed from behind us.

"Hi, kids." None of the kids looked alike. Made me wonder. "This car is kinda funny: it won't move until all seat belts have been fastened."

Chanda's eyes widened. "That true?" She wagged her head. "Cars too smart for dey britches now." She pulled her seat belt across her chest and clicked it.

Yo-Yo, Florida, and Carla were already in the backyard spreading newspapers on a couple of card tables when we pulled into the garage. Carla hid behind her mama while Chanda introduced her kids, but by the time I brought out black markers to draw faces on the pumpkins and serrated steak knives to cut them out, Carla, Cheree, and Dia were already giggling behind their hands.

"So glad Carla could come," I whispered to Florida. "This isn't the weekend she visits . . .?"

A shake of her head. No coppery ringlets or beaded braids today. Just pinned back with a few bobby pins. "Uh-uh. Just first and third weekends. But I tell you one thing—it ain't gonna be that way for long." Florida pinched her lips into a determined line.

Cleaning out those big pumpkins of their seeds and stringy matter proved to be a big job. Yet Thomas played the man, rolled up his sleeves, and dug out the gooey mess from two of the pumpkins, and Yo-Yo and I did the other two. The faces that got carved into the orange shells were rather lopsided. "But they'll look great with a candle inside when it's dark," I promised.

Amanda—will wonders never cease?—brought cutout sugar cookies, still warm from the oven, and a bowl of orange frosting. This was a big hit, as the girls dug in with table knives and blobbed frosting on the cookies. Thomas was content just to eat them, which he did in rather alarming numbers. But Chanda didn't stop him, so I didn't either.

That girl is really good with kids, I mused, watching Amanda hugging Carla and teasing Chanda's kids. Even Thomas warmed up to her. She made a game of stuffing the dirty newspapers and pumpkin innards into a trash bag, and the only fight the kids had was who was going to take it out to the trash can.

Yo-Yo left her pumpkin at our house and asked me to bring it when I came to Yada Yada tomorrow night at Ruth's house. Yet by the time I dropped off Florida and Carla at the Morse El station and took Chanda and her kids home, I was bushed. Not even sure I wanted to go to Yada Yada the next night.

Did I dare tell Yada Yada what happened today with that man? Made me look like a dork, for sure. Or revealed my prejudices beneath my smug exterior. Part of me wanted to tell them—or tell Avis, or somebody. Somebody African-American, who would affirm my motives. *"Of course you should've locked your doors! I would've! The man's just got a problem."*

On one level it didn't matter what my real motives were. The *man* obviously experienced it as just one more white woman protecting herself from a black man. And there was no way I could go back and fix it.

33

Denny let us out in front of Uptown's storefront the next morning as usual then drove off to find a parking place. A stiff, cold wind chased bits of trash down Morse Avenue. Yesterday must have been summer's last gasp.

Funny, I thought. *No lights on.* I pulled on the door handle. Locked.

"Hurry up, Mom!" Amanda whined. "I'm cold."

I shrugged. "It's not open." I checked my watch—almost nine-thirty. Should be open. Unless the Rapture had taken all the Christians during the night and the entire Baxter family had been "left behind." Or maybe Pastor Clark changed the time of service and we weren't paying attention. Or—

"Uh-oh." Realization dawned. "It's the last weekend of October. Daylight Savings Time ended last night. It's only"—my kids were going to kill me!—"eight-thirty."

Amanda's jaw dropped like I'd just announced the end of civilization as we know it. "Mo-om! We could've slept in another hour, and you got us up at the old time?" Josh gave me a dark look that said, *"Bad, bad mother"* and hunched his shoulders against the wind.

Denny came trotting up the sidewalk, trying not to be late, but he looked confused when he saw us still standing at the front door. When I told him we'd *all* forgotten to turn the clocks back—no way were they going to pin this on just me—he immediately moved into his okay-let's-fix-it mode. "So we've got an extra fifty minutes? Let's go eat! I'm still hungry."

We nixed going for the car—it would take too much time to drive anywhere—and opted for a neighborhood grill that advertised, "One egg, grits, bacon or sausage, toast, and coffee" for $2.99. The regulars—an assortment of men who all needed a shave and looked like they lived in a single-room-only hotel—stared at us kinda funny as we walked in and dropped into the chairs by a window table.

"Hey! There's Florida!" Amanda jumped out of her seat, pulled open the door, and waved them in. Florida looked confused, but she came in, followed by Carla, Cedric, and Chris, looking like chilly penguins. Her kids had the same reaction when they found out she'd dragged them out of the house an hour early, but now it was getting funny. At least we weren't the only ones who forgot the time change.

By the time we got to church—ten minutes earlier than our usual mad dash up the stairs to the worship space—Carla was hanging onto Amanda, Cedric was saying, "Hey, Ma. Let's forget to set our clocks next year and have breakfast again!" and Chris and Josh were still arguing about who was the best R&B singer on WCRX radio.

Stu waved at us from the second row. "Thought about calling

you guys and reminding you about the time change, but I see you remembered." She smiled approvingly.

I didn't dare look at Florida, or I'd bust out laughing. I felt her deliberately step on my toes, and I got the message: *"I won't tell if you won't."*

FLORIDA AND HER KIDS came home with us and spent the afternoon till it was time for Yada Yada. The kids seemed content with tomato soup out of the can and toasted cheese sandwiches, followed by popcorn and a heated game of Monopoly. Carla lost interest in the game, so I set her up on the floor with paper, markers, scissors, and tape. She immediately dumped out the markers and began to draw, saying something I didn't quite catch.

"What's that, Carla?"

Her head remained bent over the paper. "My other mommy gave me stuff like this too."

"My other mommy . . ." I looked up quickly to see if Florida had heard, but her spot on the couch, where she'd been watching the Monopoly game, was empty.

I found her out on the front porch "having a cig." I grabbed my coat from the front hall and joined her outside. She acknowledged me but returned to staring at the trees lining our street. "You okay, Flo?"

She didn't answer for a long minute, dragging on the cigarette and blowing smoke into the nippy air. Finally she stubbed it out and leaned against the porch pillar, hands in her pockets. "Don't know if me and Carl gonna make it, Jodi."

Oh God, not this. "What's wrong, Flo? Did something happen?"

She shrugged. "Nothin' in particular 'happened.' It's just . . . things ain't fallin' together for us." She was quiet for a few moments, and I just waited. "It's hard on a man when he don't have no job, know what I mean? He gets ugly—takes it out on me and the kids."

"Not . . .?" I couldn't say it.

"Hit us? Not me or Carla, anyway. But he whup those boys sometimes. Not that I don't think they need a good whack from time to time, but he yells—a lot. Makes the kids cry. Chris—he's just getting mad."

My heart was sinking. "Oh, Florida. You guys just got Carla back!" *Oh God. What would a bust-up in that family do to that little girl?*

Florida nodded. "I know. And if anything good in Carl's life, it's getting his baby back. She's his angel, but . . ." She didn't finish, just leaned on the post and shook her head.

I couldn't help it. I pulled Florida's hands out of her pockets and started to pray—out loud. Her usual *"Thank ya!"* was absent—just a muted "Oh Jesus" now and then. At the end of the prayer she squeezed my hands and said, "Thanks, Jodi. Just keep prayin'. That's all I know to do right now. Pray."

WELL, DENNY'S NOT HERE *to rescue Ben Garfield tonight,* I thought as we piled out of Avis's car in front of Ruth's house a couple of hours later. Denny had offered to drive Florida's kids home if we could get a ride with somebody. Yo-Yo showed up with another bag of day-old Jewish pastries from the Bagel Bakery, which we demolished in record time—some of us still had our mouths full when Avis called us to prayer. The prayer-and-praise time was a little muted till everyone had swallowed and got their voices back, then it was "praise as usual"—at least as usual for Yada Yada. Everyone talking to God at once, some clapping, some phrases sung from favorite praise songs, punctuated with "Glory!" and "You're a good God!" And we hadn't even shared our prayer needs yet.

Yet something was missing. Then I realized what it was: I missed Nony's rich voice praying Scripture verses, translating them in midprayer to make them personal. Where was Nony right now? How was her mother? Did she say when she was coming back?

"Did anyone hear from Nony?" I asked when the praise time was over and we had scrunched together on Ruth's small flowered couch, a couple of overstuffed chairs, and a bunch of folding chairs. "How about you, Hoshi?"

Hoshi, her willowy body almost swallowed up in Ruth's fat easy chair with the little lace doilies pinned to the back and arms, shook her head. "Nony has not contacted me. I did speak to Dr. Smith after class on Thursday, but he just said it would be awhile." She shrugged her shoulders, encased in a soft, baby-blue sweater set that set off her silky black hair. Her dark eyes shone with moisture. "I miss her," she added.

I could've kicked myself. Had I called Hoshi? Checked up on her since Nony left? *How hard would that be, Jodi?* Nony and the

Smiths were the closest thing to family Hoshi had in the States—but she couldn't very well go over to the Smiths' home with Nony and the kids out of the country and Mark home alone.

I made a mental note to call Hoshi at least once a week, maybe twice—but knowing me, a mental note wouldn't do it. I fished in my tote bag for a pen and some paper to make a to-do list, almost missing Hoshi's quiet voice as she continued.

" . . . have been thinking about what Jodi said about talking to the woman in jail, face to face . . ."

My head jerked up. Said? What had I said?

" . . . that the fear was gone after talking to the woman as a person—a person with a name." Hoshi tilted her chin up. "I'm thinking it would be good for me to go to the prison with you next time—if there is a next time."

"Alabanza Jesús!" Delores breathed. "Oh, Hoshi, that is . . . is . . ." She seemed to be searching for the right word. *". . . valiente. Si, muy valiente."*

"Very brave," Edesa translated, smiling at Hoshi.

Ruth shook her head. "Brave, maybe. But necessary? Why must she go? Three Yada Yadas already visited that Becky person in prison—like the Bible says we should do. Represent us, they did. *Everybody* doesn't need to go."

"That's right, Ruth," Avis said gently. "Everybody *doesn't* need to go, but if the Holy Spirit is prompting Hoshi to go, it may be an important step in the healing God wants to do. As she said, facing her fear. Because fear is not of God. Also"—she began thumbing through her big Bible—"it might prepare the ground for forgiveness." Avis found what she was looking for. "From the Lord's Prayer, the model Jesus gave us to pray: 'Forgive us our sins, *as we forgive those who sin against us.*'"

The living room was quiet, except for the sound of a TV from somewhere in the back of the house. *As we forgive* . . . Yeah. That was one of those sticky little things Jesus said which we piously recited as part of the Lord's Prayer, but when you came right down to it was hard to swallow. Almost sounded like a contract: "God will treat our sins in the same way we treat other people's sins." Ouch.

The silence was broken by a little laugh from Hoshi. "Do not talk me out of it—I will accept any and all excuses not to go!" But she leaned in my direction. "Jodi, will you write another letter to . . . to the woman, and ask if she will put my name on her visitors' list?"

Well, yeah, but that means you need a ride down there, so either Denny and I need to go again, or somebody else with a car needs their name on the list. I tried the back-door approach. "Sure, I'll write the letter. Anybody else want their name on the visitors' list?" I was hoping someone with a car would speak up, like Stu or Avis, or even Ruth—not likely—but no one volunteered. *Great. Just great.*

Avis moved on, collecting other prayer concerns. Florida didn't say much, just, "Pray for the Hickmans. Lot goin' on, not all of it good." We put Nony on the prayer list, and Avis volunteered to call Mark Smith to find out when she was coming back.

Chanda piped up. "Mi not get even t'ree words out of Adele at church dis mornin', but someone say it be her birthday week from tomorrow—four November. Yada Yada didn't visit nobody's church all month. Why don't ever'body come to Paul and Silas Apostolic next Sunday? Be a *big* surprise for Adele's birthday."

"Ahh . . . maybe too big a surprise, Chanda," Stu said diplomatically. "I think it would be very awkward. Avis said to give her space, remember?"

Heads nodded around the room, including Avis.

Yo-Yo spoke up from the floor, squeezed between Ruth's chair and a corner of the flowered couch. "But showing Adele we haven't forgotten her—that'd be good. Maybe we could all send her birthday cards."

"A good idea, that is!" Ruth beamed. "Kill her with kindness."

Stu groaned. "We're not trying to kill her, Ruth."

Humph, I thought. *It'd take a lot more than kindness to kill Adele anyway.*

34

*A*vis dropped me off after Yada Yada, and I let myself in the front door, dumping my tote bag and hanging up my jacket. *Hope Denny has changed all the clocks by now.* I kicked off my shoes and headed toward the light in the dining room. *No way do I want to show up at school tomorrow an hour early.*

Josh was at the computer, surfing the Net for college info. So much for writing that letter to Becky Wallace—not that I minded putting it off. With a hint of glee I noticed that Josh's head sported a brown shadow, like a thin mat of Astroturf. He was probably getting tired of having to shave it every two to three days. "Where's your dad?"

Josh grunted. "Living room, I think." He resumed clicking the mouse, intent on the computer screen.

The living room? It was dark when I came in. I headed to the front of the house. "Denny?"

"Yeah. In here." His voice came from the recliner near the bay windows.

"What are you doing sitting in the dark?" I shuffled in my sock feet toward the recliner, illumined only by the pale streetlights outside, and almost tripped over Willie Wonka, who was snoring right in my path.

Denny held out a hand and pulled me down onto the arm of the chair. "Just thinking."

Yuck. He smelled like cigarette smoke. I almost said something but caught myself, hoping he'd let me in on whatever he was pondering. Besides, we might argue over his occasional beer, but I *knew* he wasn't lighting up on the side. Not the way he jumped all over his student athletes if he caught them smoking.

"Florida get home okay?" he asked.

My perch on the arm of the chair was a little precarious, but I snuggled closer, in spite of how he smelled. "Yeah. She got a ride with Stu, who was taking Edesa and Delores home. Not really on the way, but you know Stu. Have car, will travel." *Listen to yourself, Jodi!* Even though Stu got on my nerves with her "instant solution" to everything, I had to admit she was generous to a fault, picking people up, taking people home, giving of her time to make Yada Yada happen.

"I met Carl."

"You met—oh! When you took Florida's kids home?"

"Yeah. Carla fell asleep in the backseat, so I carried her inside. Carl buzzed us in, but I'm sure he was expecting the kids to come up by themselves—at least he just stared at me when he opened the door and saw me standing there with Carla over my shoulder. I said, 'Hi, I'm Denny Baxter. Where should I put her?' And once inside . . . I dunno. Figured this was my chance to meet Florida's husband beyond just hi and good-bye."

"Ah. That explains why you smell like an ashtray." I sniffed pointedly.

"That bad, huh." He chuckled. "Well, yeah, he seemed pretty nervous. Must've smoked half a pack while I was there."

"Half a pack! How long did you stay? Did you guys actually, you know, talk?" *Oh, wow, God.* And I hadn't said anything yet to Denny about what Florida told me out on the porch.

"Yeah. Well . . . as much as guys talk who are sizing each other up like tomcats in an alley. Mostly we talked about his kids—I figured that was safe territory. Told him how much I enjoyed getting to know them; thanked him for sharing them with us. He seemed kinda surprised by that. We talked about Carla too—that opened him up a little. His face lit up talking about Carla."

"Did he say anything about needing a job?"

"Nope. I think that's kinda touchy. But I did invite him to church. Told him to come with Florida and the kids, that I'd be really glad to see him."

"And?"

Denny shrugged. "He said, oh yeah, yeah, he would. But who knows. Still, now that we've talked a bit, maybe I'll invite him to our next men's breakfast at Uptown."

Now I was sure this meeting was God-inspired. I told Denny what Florida had said on the porch that afternoon. "Maybe knowing some guys who care will make a difference."

"Maybe."

I rolled off the arm of the recliner and pulled up the frayed ottoman. *Ahh, much better.* Somehow I wasn't as flexible with a steel rod in my leg. "So why are you sitting here in the dark? I thought something was wrong." By now my eyes had gotten used to the dim light of the streetlights, and I could see Denny's face, puckered in a frown.

He sighed. "I don't know. Just started thinking on the way home. Thinking about a lot of things, stuff that's happened. I've been involved in Uptown's outreach for the last ten years, but that's nothing compared to the stuff we've confronted since Yada Yada walked in our door. You'd think I'd know something by now, but you know what?" He smacked the arm of the chair so hard, even Willie Wonka jumped. "I feel pretty darn helpless to make a difference! Carl Hickman? It's tempting to tell him to shape up and support his family, but what do *I* know about what he's had to face in his life? And Becky Wallace . . . what does God expect of us in that situation? I still get mad when I think about all the danger my wife and daughter and our friends were in that night."

He fell silent again. I laid a hand on his knee, but he didn't seem to notice. "Know what, Jodi? Want to know what bothers me the most?" His voice broke a little. "Adele. Adele and MaDear. Why did God let that happen? I'm not the man MaDear thinks I am—but it still rips me up that she thinks I am."

He pulled out a handkerchief and blew his nose. When he spoke again, I knew it'd been a cover for the tears he was fighting back. "Heck. I don't have a clue why we moved into Chicago. Thought I could make a difference. Ha."

I DIDN'T THINK OUR CONVERSATION in the dark was the best time to bring up the fact that Hoshi wanted—maybe needed—to visit Becky Wallace and face her fears, which obviously implicated Denny, since he and I were the only people with a car on B. W.'s visitors' list so far. Unless I drove.

Not sure I'm ready for that.

I put off writing to Becky Wallace for a few days, caught up in a school week that included Halloween, TV specials about ghosts and ghouls, and an entire classroom that would be high on sugar the next day. Not the best week to see what Hakim could do with some one-on-one attention, but between Christy and me, we managed to spend at least twenty minutes a day working with him verbally or hands-on in different subjects. Working that way, he seemed to catch on quickly, came up with clever answers, and beamed when he solved problems. Once, to test him a little, I waited half an hour then gave him the same comprehension questions we'd just discussed written out on paper. He got angry, drew a big X over the paper, and refused to cooperate the rest of the day.

"I think he has a learning disability," I told my student teacher. "Makes me so mad his mom won't get him tested."

"Maybe we can talk to her at parent-teacher conferences in a couple of weeks."

"We?" I pulled a face. "I was going to let *you* do that conference."

Christy's eyes widened under her cap of dark curls. "Ms. Baxter! You wouldn't!"

Wouldn't I? "Just kidding. Don't worry. Got any ideas for something fun we can do on Halloween—*besides* bobbing for apples?"

She grinned sheepishly. "We could let them 'wrap the mummy.' All we'd need is five or six rolls of toilet paper."

So on Thursday, Christy and I used the last half-hour of class time to divide into teams and let the kids "wrap a mummy." It was loud and chaotic, but most of the noise was laughter and squeals of excitement—except for the moment when Ramón pushed over his team's "mummy" because she wouldn't stand still. We sent the winning team out the door with red apples and gave yellow apples to all the runners-up. My feeble antidote to the usual candy frenzy.

Uptown Community sponsored a "Hallelujah Fest" at the church as a Halloween alternative—ghoulish costumes strongly discouraged—and Denny, Josh, and Amanda were shanghaied along with the rest of the youth group to help with games, eats, and a costume parade. I stayed home to answer the door for neighborhood trick-or-treaters, though I'd been told by Uptowners that "kids don't trick-or-treat in Rogers Park—it's too dangerous." Last year—our first in Chicago city limits—we'd gotten a few in our neighborhood, which still boasted a lot of houses, so I decided to have treats on hand "just in case."

At the last minute I remembered to light the jack-o'-lantern in the front window as daylight faded. Ugh, it was starting to rot. "Hang in there for a few more hours, buddy," I told the pumpkin, propping it up on the windowsill. "Then you can rot to your heart's content out in the garbage can."

The doorbell rang a few times, but the bowl of Tootsie Roll

Pops and bubble gum pretty much stayed untouched. So I figured this was as good a time as any to write Becky Wallace. Redeeming the time, so to speak. As I called up our e-mail, my heart did a leap as a new message joined the clutter in our Inbox: a note from Nony! I could hardly click it open fast enough.

To: Yada Yada
From: BlessedRU@online.net
Re: Hello from Kwazulu-Natal!

Dear Yada sisters,

Please forgive me for not writing sooner. Mark says, "Please e-mail Yada Yada! They keep calling to ask if I have any news about you!" I feel glad for your concern. My brother finally helped me access my e-mail online at his office, so now I can let you know how things are with us in South Africa.

What a joy to see my mother! She is still in hospital, but she improves a little bit each day. However, visits tire her, so we are limited to only one hour. I am not sure when she will be able to come home. I would like to stay until she is released from hospital, to help make arrangements for her care and see that she is settled.

Hmm, I thought. *Wonder how Mark feels about that? Her return date sounds rather vague.*

In the meantime, I am getting reacquainted with my country. Kwazulu-Natal is called "The Garden Province" with good reason! The summer season has just begun, so everything is in bloom. Lilies everywhere! African lilies, bugle lilies, lion's tail . . . the flowers must enjoy the humidity (though I confess, I don't). My mother is in hospital in Pietermaritzburg, but I am hoping to take the boys to visit their cousins who live along the coast and maybe even take a "safari" into the savannah—like real American tourists!

But, dear sisters, my heart is also heavy. It is one thing to read statistics about the AIDS pandemic in Africa. It is quite another to learn that my old school chum's teenage daughter was raped by her uncle, because he thought he could be cured of the disease by having sex with a virgin. Now she is HIV. Myths and ignorance abound! Proverbs 13:16 is so true: "Every prudent man acts with knowledge, but a fool exposes his folly." My brother, Nyack Sisulu, who does social research for the KZN Department of Health, told me that half of all fifteen-year-olds in South Africa and Zimbabwe will eventually die of AIDS. It is so hard to see the suffering and do nothing!

The doorbell rang again—*Okay, this is it,* I decided—and I dispensed candy to a Harry Potter look-alike and a ghost in a pillowcase with eyeholes. "Cute!" I said, waving to an adult standing out on the sidewalk. The ghost stood on my porch, pawing through his—her?—sack of goodies, trying to see what I put in there. "Go on, honey," I urged, casting an anxious eye down the block. I wanted to get the porch light turned off and the pumpkin blown out before any late trick-or-treaters took it personally.

After darkening the front of the house, I hustled back to the computer wondering just what Nony planned to "do" about the AIDS crisis. I scanned the page on my screen trying to find my place. Ah.

> As elsewhere, the poorest people pay more for less. Food prices are soaring in the Eastern Cape—a direct result of the political chaos in Zimbabwe, which used to provide one of our food staples: maize. Without their export, the price of maize has skyrocketed. And for South Africa's poor, maize is the primary food that they buy. Can you imagine spending over 50 percent of your income just on food?

No, I couldn't. Yet right now I was more concerned about Nony. Was Mark right to be worried that Nony's heart would find reason to stay in South Africa? I read on.

> But as always there is hope. This week the Sunday *Times* told a story about schoolchildren right here in Pietermaritzburg who collected 240 rand, or about thirty-three dollars, to help feed the Eastern Cape's

starving children. One boy gave his taxi money, which meant he had to walk forty-five minutes to get home. Another gave his birthday money. Many come from indigent families themselves. The children saw a need, set themselves a goal, and made personal sacrifices. These children are my heroes! And they give me reason to hope.

Love to all. I do so miss the Yada Yada prayer meetings.

Nonyameko

P.S. Marcus and Michael have their own new hero— Makhaya Ntini, a star player on South Africa's cricket team! SA is playing a series of tests against Bangladesh here in Kwasulu-Natal, and everyone is as excited as if the Chicago Cubs were playing in the World Series. Not sure the boys are going to want to come home.

Ha! Denny and Josh would get a kick out of that. The Chicago Cubs in the World Series. *Don't we wish.*

And then I read her last sentence again.

35

*J*called up New Message, wrote "Got Nony's e-mail. How do we pray???" and sent it to Avis. Nony had sent her e-mail to the entire prayer group, so it wasn't like telling tales. But it was a whole week till the next Yada Yada meeting, and I felt an urgency to be praying for Nony and Mark and their boys. I also felt perplexed. Maybe taking Marcus and Michael to South Africa was a mistake. I mean, a visit was great, but the boys couldn't help picking up on their mother's strong desire to return to South Africa to live.

I was still at the computer working on the letter to B. W. when Denny and the kids got back from the Hallelujah Fest. I handed Denny a printout of Nony's e-mail. "Maybe you should call Mark; see how he's doing."

He read the note, nodded, then leaned close to my ear. "Guess who showed up to play keyboard for the Hallelujah Fest?"

Keyboard? Who played keyboard? One of Yo-Yo's brothers? Florida's Chris? Or . . . *Duh. Of course.* "José." I sighed.

Denny waggled his eyebrows.

"Denny! You think this little romance is cute!"

He grinned. "Well, yeah, kinda. José is a neat kid."

"But, it's"—how did I say this without sounding narrow-minded?—"complicated."

He shrugged. "Love is always complicated."

I sucked back a sharp answer. *Huh.* This wasn't love. This was a teenage crush. I mentally rehearsed all the good reasons we should discourage this infatuation, wanting Denny to stand with me in a united front, but I knew that just before heading for bed was no time for an argument. Maybe I'd have to enlist Delores's support.

I FINALLY GOT THE LETTER to Becky Wallace in Saturday's mail, along with a birthday card for Adele I'd found at Osco Drugs. I'd vaguely wondered if I could do something with the meaning of her name, like I'd done for Yo-Yo, but the name Web site came up with: "Adele—a familiar form of Adelaide. Meaning: 'noble, kind.'" Noble? Kind? Not the first words that came to mind when I thought of Adele. So much for name meanings.

So I'd stood in the card aisle at the drugstore for the better part of thirty minutes, wondering what kind of card you sent a person who'd basically shut you out of her life. I passed over "To a Special Friend" and "Funny, You Don't *Look* Over the Hill," and finally settled on a card with a Maya Angelou quote: "Women should be tough and tender, laugh as much as possible, and live long lives."

"Yada Yada should've sent a card 'From the Whole Gang' and been done with it," I muttered as I stood at the mailbox. Even signing it had been a problem. *"Love, Jodi"?* Didn't think so. *"Your friend"?* Assumed too much. *"Praying for you"?* Too pompous. I'd finally settled for *"Wishing you God's best on your birthday—Jodi."*

Okay, God, You do the rest. I pulled open the yawning mailbox mouth, which gobbled both envelopes and practically smacked its lips.

It was the first Saturday of November, and hopefully parents were signing up for the midmonth parent-teacher conferences and report-card pickup at Bethune Elementary—first come, first served. Teachers didn't have to be at signups; too often, parents wanted to start talking right then. Call-ins had to take whatever slots were left. I was tempted to phone all thirty of my kids' parents and give them a lecture on the importance of parent-teacher conferences. After all, barely half of them had shown up for parents' night in September. Made me so mad! How could the school do its job without support on the home front?

When I got to school on Monday and checked the sign-up lists, I was pleased to see twenty-plus time slots filled. I ran my finger down the list, sometimes having to check the "Student's Name" column to figure out who was who, because last names didn't always match. *Ramón's father—good. Ebony . . . Kaya . . . Hakim . . .* Hey! Hakim's mother signed up. There it was: Geraldine Porter. Hallelujah! But on second glance the signature looked kind of funny. I squinted closer. The cursive was obviously juvenile—not the bold signature Geraldine Porter had scrawled on her note.

I paused by Hakim's desk while the class was doing silent reading. The third-grade reader sat closed on his desk, and he slouched in his seat. Like he was waiting.

"I see your mother signed up for the parent-teacher conferences, Hakim." I smiled encouragingly. "Did your mother come in, or did someone else sign up for her?"

The dark eyes got wary. "She works Saturday. Sent my cousin."

"Your cousin? How old is your cousin?"

Hakim squirmed. "She's fourteen. They said it was okay."

"It is! I'm just glad your mother is coming. I'm looking forward to meeting her." *Oh, right, Jodi. Like a toothache.* I touched the reader. "Would you like me to read with you awhile?"

He shrugged, his eyes still wary. "You gonna tell my mama I'm doing bad?"

I wanted to hug him. "On the contrary, Hakim. I'm going to tell her how smart you are when Ms. James and I let you work the way you do best." I tapped my head . . . and nearly fell over.

Because Hakim smiled at me.

HAKIM'S SMILE lifted me off my feet all day. Maybe I did like teaching at Mary McLeod Bethune Elementary. Maybe I could make a difference with some of these kids. Not to mention that Hakim's shuttered features—which usually kept you at a distance, like a barbed-wire fence around his soul—had been transformed by that smile. Today . . . the child radiated beauty.

I felt so upbeat that I made chicken cacciatore over fettuccini for supper, even dug out the half-full bottle of Chablis we'd hidden under the sink when my parents came to visit and added some to the sauce. Still some left—unchilled, but too bad—so I got out two wine glasses for Denny and me then gathered a bunch of candles, all different sizes, and lit them as a flaming centerpiece.

"We got company?" Josh asked when I called for supper, lifting the lid of the serving dish. "Yum."

Denny arched a questioning eyebrow. I could see him sorting through the possibilities in his mind. *"Not our anniversary—we did that. Birthday? Did that too."* "Okay, I give. What are we celebrating?"

I laughed, ready to say *"Monday,"* when out of the blue I remembered. "It's Adele Skuggs's birthday!" I laughed even harder at the look on his face.

"Oh. Adele's birthday. Balloons. Good cheer and all that." He sounded very much like a two-legged Eyeore.

By now even the kids thought it was a hoot. We joined hands for the dinner blessing, which Amanda offered. "Thanks for the food, God, and whatever got into Mom to make her celebrate a birthday for somebody who's not even here. Amen."

When all our plates had been served, Denny lifted his wine glass to make a toast. "To Adele. May she . . ." He paused, searching for words. "May she 'be anxious for nothing,' 'give thanks in all things,' and experience a 'peace that passes all understanding.' And . . . I do mean that."

We clinked glasses. Then I raised my glass again. "To Adele—noble and kind."

Denny's glass paused in midair. "Noble. And kind." His expression begged for an explanation.

"That's what the name Adele means: noble and kind."

He grunted. "I think she missed her calling."

"Or maybe that's how God thinks of her," Amanda said. Denny and I stared at our daughter as she nonchalantly shoveled in another mouthful of cacciatore.

Out of the mouths of teenagers, Lord . . .

I checked e-mail after supper while Denny and Josh did the dishes, which, I pointed out, shouldn't be a big deal since I'd already washed the cooking pots. (Big brownie points for Mom.) I scrolled through the pileup in our Inbox. Squeezed in among a bunch of spam and a dozen messages for Josh or Amanda were two messages to Yada Yada. "Denny!" I called into the kitchen. "We really do need to set up individual e-mail addresses for the kids!"

"Yeah, Dad," Josh echoed. "Ever heard about privacy?" Denny's only response was a noncommittal grunt.

The first message was from Stu: "Did everybody remember to send birthday cards to Adele?" I rolled my eyes at the screen before hitting Delete. *Yeah, yeah, we're all grownups, Leslie Stuart.*

The second was from Avis with "Re: Prayer for Nony" in the subject line: "Sisters, remember: we're not God. We may think we know 'what is best' for Nony and her family, but let's not get in the way of the Holy Spirit. We can certainly pray for unity of heart and mind for Nony and Mark, for safety for Nony and the boys, and that God will use this trip to further His purpose in the Smith and Sisulu families." Then: "P. S. Next Yada Yada is at my apartment, right? Just checking—don't want to clean house for nothing. Smiles."

I snorted. Frankly, I doubted if a speck of dust would have the courage to settle on one of Avis's spotless surfaces. As for the prayer focus, guess I needed to scrap the one I'd been praying: *"God, get Nony home quick!"*

I LOVED MEETING at Avis's apartment. Just being there seemed to gather up all the loose ends flying around in my rather scattered spirit, knitting them for the moment into a warm, comforting shawl for the soul. Why Avis had that effect on me, I wasn't sure, because at the same time the striking art prints on her walls, brimming bookshelves, stacks of Bibles and devotionals, and framed photos of her deceased husband and beaming grandbabies also seemed like a crossroads where past and present, the exotic and the familiar, work and worship, her world and my world met. And it was all good.

Not everybody made it to our first November meeting that second Sunday. Chanda's kids were sick, and Delores had to work at the hospital. *Rats. I wanted to talk to her about Amanda and José.* But I was able to tell Yada Yada that I had written to Becky Wallace about adding Hoshi to her visitors' list, and Avis once again prayed that Becky's answer would be our answer. Carl had not come to Uptown with Florida the last two Sundays, even though Denny had invited him, and Florida didn't even want to pray about it. "We pray about it, I go getting my expectations up," she groused. "If God wants to get Carl to church, He can just surprise me."

I wondered out loud whether anyone had heard from Adele. Did she receive our cards? "Yes," Stu said, looking perfectly positioned for *House Beautiful* on Avis's beige-and-black furniture. "I called her last Monday on her birthday. She said she'd received several cards from Yada Yada and to tell you all she appreciates it."

I waited, but Stu was done. I'd been hoping that all of us remembering Adele's birthday would break down the wall she had built around herself, and she'd say she was coming back to Yada Yada. But . . . Guess it was still good that we sent the cards.

We spent a lot of our prayer time praying for Nony, with Avis praying a long time "in the Spirit." Frankly, it seemed appropriate to pray in an unknown tongue and let God figure it out, since we didn't really know how to pray for Nony right now. We also gathered up other concerns, so I threw the upcoming parent-teacher conferences in the pot, being careful not to make Avis-the-Principal think Jodi-the-Teacher was too stressed out about them.

Yet I was. Last year's fall parent-teacher conferences—my first at Bethune Elementary—had been grueling. For one thing, I'd felt very self-conscious, like a glaring white crayon among a sea of hues in a box of sixty-four Crayolas. Admittedly, most of the parents who showed seemed genuinely concerned about their children and expressed appreciation for anything that smacked of improvement.

But I'd had three doozies: one father who showed up an hour late reeking of alcohol and got angry that I wouldn't see him *now;* a Pakistani mother who couldn't speak a word of English, so we ended up just nodding and smiling at each other and saying, "Good, good"; and another mother who kept complaining about "the neighborhood," as if I was personally responsible.

I determined not to approach these parent-teacher conferences like the "old Jodi." After all, my name meant "God is gracious," and I had a new weapon: praise. So for the next few days, I kept the gospel and praise CDs going before and after school, focused on praying for each of my students by name as I walked to and from school, and as Wednesday dawned, even thanked God for whatever He brought my way that day.

Conferences started at noon, since we went till eight that evening. This was Christy James's first experience as a student teacher with parent-teacher conferences, and she was a trooper. She even ducked out a couple of times to bring back fresh coffee and Krispy Kremes from the convenience store a block away, leaving the carrot sticks and apples I'd brought from home languishing in my tote bag.

No one had signed up for the 6:45 slot, which was strange since that was "prime time" for working parents, but I still had four more parents to go: LeTisha's . . . Hakim's . . . Chanté's . . . and D'Angelo's. Well, okay. All four had positive reports, as well as "areas that need improvement." Since I had a breather, I ducked out into the hall to see if I could catch Avis. It might be helpful if she sat in on my conference with Hakim's mother so I wouldn't be the only one encouraging some testing. But Avis wasn't in the office or in the hallways—she must be meeting with another teacher and student.

Shoot. I should have arranged this ahead of time. *Okay, Jesus, guess it's just You and me.*

Both of LeTisha's parents came to the conference, *with* LeTisha, which sent their approval rating on the Jodi Baxter Parent Scale right up to the top. I even told them LeTisha was living up to her name in the classroom: "joy." The mother teared up at that and told me they'd almost lost LeTisha to a heart defect when she was a baby. "Baby, look at you now," the father teased, chucking the embarrassed eight-year-old under the chin.

I was still smiling as they left. "You can send the next parent in!" I called after them.

Christy took LeTisha's folder from me and handed me the next folder: Hakim Porter. I barely had time to glance at my notes when I heard a boyish voice: "Hi, Miz B. Me an' my mama came."

I looked up to give Hakim a welcoming smile—and froze.

Standing before me was a woman I'd seen once before. In a courtroom at the Second District Courthouse. A woman who'd wanted to see me in jail.

Every inch of my body wanted to scream: *How can this be?* Because standing in my classroom was the mother of Jamal Wilkins, the boy I'd struck and killed with the Baxter car.

Recognition dawned on the other woman's face at the same time. Her dark eyes narrowed. Her mouth drew tight, leaving room to spit out only one word: *"You!"*

36

$\mathcal{I}$ groped for the desk behind me, trying to steady myself. *Oh Jesus . . . Jesus! Help me!* Hakim and Jamal—*brothers?* But the names! Porter . . . Wilkins . . .

"You!" The woman spat again, slicing into my jumbled thoughts with her sharp, piercing eyes. Hakim's eyes pooled into confusion, swimming back and forth between us. His mother suddenly seemed to realize he was standing there and spun him around. "Go back into the hallway, Hakim!"

"But, Ma—"

"Now!" The woman thrust her finger toward the classroom door.

Out of the corner of my eye, I noticed Christy quietly lead Hakim out into the hallway, easing the door shut behind her. *Oh please, Christy, go get Avis Johnson! Hurry!*

As the door closed with a soft wheeze, Geraldine Porter swung her accusing finger into my face. "What kind of diabolical joke is this?" Her fury slashed at me, like barbed wire whipping in the wind. "You . . . you kill my son! You walk away scot-free! Now here you are, acting like nothing happened, messing in my family's life, hiding behind a clever smokescreen—'Miz B' or whatever you call yourself." The barbs melded into a sneer.

I gulped for air. "No, no! Ms. . . . Ms. Porter, believe me! I had no idea Hakim was—"

"Well, I won't have it, do you understand me?" Geraldine Porter trampled my protest. "I . . . will . . . not . . . let . . . you . . . teach . . . my . . . son!" Each word hit me like a shotgun pellet.

Suddenly she whirled, her eyes sweeping the room. "Where's Hakim's desk?" She marched up and down the rows, glaring at the names taped carefully to each one. "Don't just stand there—show me where my son sits!"

Barely trusting my legs to hold me up, I made it to Hakim's desk then watched helplessly as she pulled out dog-eared pocket folders, pencils, a knit cap. "Ms. Porter, *please*, can we talk? Hakim is so bright, but he needs some special help. And I want to help him." My words tumbled out, almost falling over each other in my urgency to salvage something from this disaster. "If he could be tested—"

"Tested!" She slammed the top of the desk down. "Oh, yes, I know about this *testing*. It starts now, doesn't it—tracking kids into dumb and dumber, prettying it up under fancy titles like 'special needs.'" She was shouting at me. "Well, get this straight, Ms. Baxter. You don't have to worry about testing Hakim, because I am going to transfer him out of this classroom! Out of this school! Jesus!" Suddenly her features crumpled and her words descended into a moan. "Jesus! How much can one person bear?"

Instinctively, I reached out to her, but she jerked back, pulling her moment of vulnerability behind her flashing eyes. She straightened, and once again I saw the woman, hardened in her grief, who had faced me down in the courtroom after the charges against me had been dropped "for lack of evidence."

"Goodbye, Ms. Baxter. You won't—"

The door of the classroom opened. We both jumped. I caught a glimpse of royal blue as Avis Johnson came into the room and made her way quickly to where we were standing by Hakim's desk.

"Ms. Porter," she said, her composed, authoritative voice spreading calm like foam over a wildfire. She extended her hand to Hakim's mother. "I am Avis Johnson, principal here at Bethune Elementary. I don't believe I've had the pleasure."

The woman seemed taken off guard. "Wilkins-Porter," she corrected. "Geraldine Wilkins-Porter." She lifted a determined chin. "I would like to have my son transferred out of this class-room immediately."

Oh God! My spirit sank. *She really is going to take Hakim out.* I didn't know whether to try to explain to Avis, but by now I was fighting back tears. Did she recognize the woman? Avis had come to the hearing and sat in the back of the courtroom—to pray, she'd said. This woman had been there too. But if Avis knew what this was about, all she said now was, "Why don't we go to my office, and we can discuss it."

Hakim's mother tossed her head. "There is nothing to discuss.

Hakim will not be back in school until the necessary arrangements have been made. I will call you." She pressed the collection of items from Hakim's desk against the front buttons of her trim, navy-blue suit and strode resolutely toward the classroom door.

Out in the hall I heard Hakim wail, "Why we goin' home, Mama?" and a sharp, "Because—that's why!" before the door closed again.

Avis and I just stared at each other. Finally, Avis broke the fragile silence. "That was . . . Jamal Wilkins's mother?"

I nodded, not trusting myself to speak. The tears I'd been fighting back slid over the edges and ran down my cheeks.

"Lord, have mercy!" Avis sucked in her breath as though gathering her wits about her. "How many more parent conferences do you have, Jodi?"

I held up two shaky fingers.

"Christy can do them—I'll sit in with her. You go to the teachers' lounge and pull yourself together. But don't leave until we talk, all right?"

I was so grateful, I wanted to throw my arms around Avis or fall down and kiss her feet. Nodding mutely, I found the box of tissues on my desk, blew my nose, and moved numbly toward the door.

HOW I MADE IT THROUGH the teeming hallway without running into a distracted parent or an open door, I'll never know.

Mercifully, the teachers' lounge was empty, and I collapsed on the lone, saggy couch just as the dam of frustration and humiliation burst in a flood of tears. *Oh God, Oh God, Oh God, Oh God* . . . For some reason my desperate prayer got no further, and I let the silent sobs take over till they shook my whole body.

Finally I mopped my face, blew my nose, and tried to corral my wildly bucking thoughts. *What did she mean, 'hiding behind a smokescreen'? I'd only signed that note 'Ms. B' because that's what Hakim called me. My full name had been on room assignments mailed to each student's family, hadn't it? Surely she remembered my name from the hearing—probably kept it pinned to her wall and threw darts at it. Hadn't I tried to reach out to her that day, tell her how terribly sorry I was?* The helpless feeling washed over me once more. *Oh God, what more can I do?* I'd give anything if I could change what happened that dreadful day! But—

"But you can't, can you?" That's what Jamal Wilkins's mother had said to me after the hearing.

I felt cornered. What good was God's forgiveness if the person most affected by the accident that snuffed the life from her son wouldn't—couldn't—forgive me?

The door to the lounge opened and shut. I barely looked up but saw Avis's blue suit move toward me. I knew my eyes were puffy, my mascara probably smudged, my skin red and blotchy. I didn't care. Avis had seen me worse in the hospital.

Bethune Elementary's principal sat down beside me on the couch; I caught a whiff of silky perfume. Avis's presence, her smell, her voice usually filled me with a quiet joy, as though the Spirit of

God within her filled the space wherever she went. Today, the sweet scent seemed dissonant, like rose petals wafting through a garbage-strewn alley. *Ha!* Even Avis couldn't fix *this* mess. How many other parents and teachers had heard Hakim's mother yelling at me? What were they thinking right now? Would this cause a scandal for Bethune Elementary?

Geraldine Wilkins-Porter was right about one thing: it was some kind of sick joke.

I started to laugh—harsh, unhappy laughter. My shoulders shook again, and I threw my head back against the couch and howled.

"Jodi, stop."

I couldn't. *Jamal Wilkins . . . Hakim Porter—who could've known? I killed one. I was teaching the other.* It was hysterical when you thought about it. I shrieked. I let it all come out. I didn't care who heard me.

"Stop."

I stopped. It was the slap that did it. Avis Johnson slapped me.

"AVIS . . . SLAPPED YOU?" Denny drew back and stared at me as I told him the whole sordid story an hour later.

I nodded sheepishly. "I know what you're thinking. *Very* unprofessional. Except we weren't 'Ms. Johnson' and 'Ms. Baxter' at that moment—just Avis and Jodi. I deserved it, I'm afraid. I was getting out of control."

When I'd finally gotten home from school about nine o'clock, I pulled Denny away from *Law and Order* on TV—high-school conferences had been the previous week—and said I really, really needed to talk. Now we were sitting on our bed, backs propped against as many pillows as I could find, door shut against all intruders—except Willie Wonka, that is, who scratched and whined at the door till we let him in. Now the chocolate Lab sat with his white-whiskered chin resting on the side of the bed, brow wrinkled like tire treads, knowing in that peculiar way of dogs that something was wrong.

"Frankly, I'm mad, Denny—*really* mad at God, because I *prayed* about these conferences, prayed for all my students, and . . . and I feel *tricked*. How could God let this happen?" Avis had just listened to me rant and cry for a while, and so did Denny. I finally blew my nose. "Then she hugged me and said we'd talk later and sort it out somehow. And she promised to call Hakim's mother" —*Jamal's mother!* a voice in my head accused—"to talk about the situation."

Denny nodded. "You've got to let Avis handle it, Jodi. It's out of your hands. There's nothing you can do."

He reached out and pulled me against him, and I tried to relax in the curve of his arm, but my emotions still bounced around like ping-pong balls. Was that true? It was out of my hands? There was nothing I could do?

Denny's just trying to comfort you, Jodi, trying to help you let go.

But, my mind argued, hadn't I started something with Hakim? Something good? Why wouldn't God let me finish what I'd started?

Hadn't I been learning about His grace? Even my name: *God is gracious.* Yet maybe grace wasn't enough—

"—not if she won't forgive me!" My loud voice in the dark quiet startled me. *Good grief, I said that aloud.*

Then I heard Denny's whisper muffled against my hair: "Yeah. Goes for me too."

37

had the nightmare again during the night, except the face lit up in my headlights kept shifting: *Jamal's eyes, wide with sudden terror . . . Geraldine Wilkins's face, an ice sculpture of fierce anger . . . then Hakim, looking straight at me, betrayed, accusing.* I made myself wake up and go to the bathroom, even chugged a whole glass of water. Yet the moment I laid down again, the three faces recycled behind my closed eyelids like a PowerPoint loop.

I was exhausted when the alarm went off. Still, I put my body on autopilot, let Willie Wonka outside, started the coffee . . . and suddenly realized what Denny had meant last night when he said, *"Yeah. Goes for me too."* He meant MaDear and Adele. The three of them, trapped in a tragic dance. Forgiveness would be so freeing, but . . . whom to forgive?

When I got to school, the halls were empty. Good. I'd deliberately left home twenty minutes early so I wouldn't run into any of the other teachers and have to explain what happened last night. I collapsed at my desk and tried to pray, but all I could do was mumble over and over, "Oh God, help. Please help me—"

"Jodi?"

Startled, I looked up at Avis's voice. I hadn't heard the door open. The royal-blue suit had given way to a casual pair of black slacks and mocha sweater set. She pulled up a chair beside my desk. "Good. I'm glad you came early. I wanted to talk to you a minute before the school day started."

I just looked at her, too worn-out to use up extra words.

"You said last night that you're mad at God," she began. I didn't need reminding. I was still mad. "But can you handle the truth, Jodi? God has promised that He is working *all* things together for the good of those who love Him, who are called according to His purpose. *His* purpose, Jodi. His purpose for *you.*"

I recognized the scripture she was quoting: Romans 8:28. *Oh sure.* One of the bedrock verses I'd memorized as a kid, convenient to haul out whenever anything went south. But I wasn't sure I really believed it at that moment.

Avis rested a hand on mine, which were clenched together in front of me on the desk. "Be encouraged, Jodi. I know it's hard to see right now, but if you have a minute before the kids come in, read Isaiah 55." She stood to go then turned back at the door and smiled. "Frankly, I think God is doing something big—very big."

She was gone, although I could still feel the touch of her hand on mine. I didn't move for a few moments, thinking about what she'd said. Then I glanced at the clock—five minutes till the bell rang.

Christy would be here any moment. Curious, I dug into my tote bag and pulled out the small Bible I'd started to carry around, even at school, and flipped pages until I found Isaiah 55.

I skimmed the passage and landed on verse eight. *"For my thoughts are not your thoughts, neither are your ways my ways,' declares the Lord . . ."* I almost snorted. *Guess not! Wouldn't mind if God checked with me before putting me through a meat grinder, though.* I kept reading. *"So is my word that goes out from my mouth: It will not return to me empty, but will accomplish what I desire and achieve the purpose for which I sent it.'"*

Hmm. That's what Avis just said—that God was going to accomplish *His* purpose. It'd sure be nice if He gave me a clue now and then what that was.

I heard voices in the hallway and was just about to shut the Bible when my eyes caught the next verse: *"You will go out in joy and be led forth in peace . . ."*

The door opened, and Christy rushed in. "Sorry I'm late, Jodi. I'll go out and bring the kids in." My young student teacher, cheeks pink from the nippy air outside, looked at me kindly. "Are you okay after—you know, last night?"

I nodded. Even smiled. Yes, I was going to be okay . . . *I think.*

HAKIM WAS NOT IN SCHOOL that day or the next, and then it was the weekend. I tried to put him out of my mind and focus on the other children in my classroom, but they were all safe, just being their same squirrelly selves. But Hakim . . . what had his mother told him? Did he think I was some kind of monster? That I didn't care about him anymore? What was he doing today? Did she really put him in another school? Or was he just sitting at home, watching TV, pulling back into his shell?

My heart ached. Was this how the shepherd in Jesus's parable felt about the one lost sheep when He left the ninety-nine others safely corralled in the sheepfold and went looking for it?

I also read and reread the scriptures Avis had given to me that morning in my classroom until I thought the pages might fall out. On Saturday, after Denny left early to pick up Carl Hickman for the men's breakfast at Uptown Community—we were both surprised he had agreed to go—I turned the verses into my version of a "Nony prayer" and wrote it in my prayer journal:

"Okay, God. I'm going to trust that You are working all this mess together for something good, according to Your purpose—which, I admit, looks pretty foggy to me. Yet You made one thing clear: Your ways are not my ways. So I'm choosing to believe that 'Your Word' will accomplish Your desire and achieve Your purpose. Not just for my good, Jesus, but Hakim's too." I reread my prayer, then wrote: *"And for Hakim's mother too."*

By the time Denny got back around eleven, I wouldn't say I'd gotten all the way to "joy," but I was starting to feel some of that peace Isaiah talked about—not because I had any answers, but because I decided to start trusting God to figure it all out.

"Kids up yet?" Denny asked, opening the refrigerator door.

I shook my head. "Still zonked. Haven't heard a peep." A weird thought crossed my mind. Both kids could've snuck out in the wee hours, and I'd probably never know it, because I never checked on them once they were in for the night.

Stop it, Jodi! They're teenagers—they're just sleeping till high noon. I left Denny still rummaging in the refrigerator and did a quick room check. Two familiar lumps of covers in the dim bedrooms. *See, Jodi? Don't borrow trouble.* I headed back for the kitchen. "Didn't you guys just eat breakfast?"

Denny was forking cold leftover spaghetti straight from the Tupperware. "Two hours ago." His fork paused in midair. "Guess what? Mark Smith came too."

"Carl Hickman *and* Mark Smith?" Now there you had polar opposites. But if their wives—Florida Never-Been-Out-of-Chicago Hickman and Nonyameko World-Traveler Sisulu-Smith—could be sisters in the same prayer group, why not their husbands? I stared at my own husband with interest.

Denny set down the empty plastic container and belched. "Asked Mark Smith to come for Thanksgiving—hope that's okay."

"Thanksgiving! Don't you think Nony will be home by then?" Thanksgiving was less than two weeks away, and she'd been gone five weeks already. Still, if she wasn't . . .

Denny shrugged. "I don't think Mark knows yet. Said he would, unless his family comes home."

Thanksgiving. I hadn't given it a smidgeon of thought—except that we wouldn't be going to Iowa, since my folks had decided to drive to Denver to spend Thanksgiving with my oldest brother, Jim, and his family. Jim and Jeff . . . hadn't seen either one of my brothers

353

for a while. I felt a small pang. It was so easy for families to drift apart.

Or fall apart. "Maybe we ought to invite Hoshi too," I said suddenly. "If Nony's not back, she won't have any place to go either." I sat down to make a list. Who else in Yada Yada might be alone? Not Avis—she'd be with her daughters and grandbabies on the South Side. Most of the others probably had family in the Chicago area. Anybody else? Stu?

I suddenly realized I knew nothing about Stu's family. She was single, she lived alone in Oak Park, she worked as a real-estate agent, and she'd latched onto Yada Yada and adopted Uptown Community as her church—that was all I knew. She had never offered information about any family, and I had never asked. Well, okay, I'd ask. Yada Yada was supposed to meet at my house the last Sunday of the month, just before Thanksgiving. If Mark and Hoshi were coming, I might as well invite a few more.

AVIS CALLED ME AT HOME that Saturday afternoon while Amanda was running the vacuum cleaner. "I had a meeting with Hakim's mother after school Friday."

"Just a minute—I can hardly hear you." I headed for my bedroom and shut the door, then took several deep breaths till my insides calmed down. "Okay."

"I met with Hakim's mother yesterday afternoon. She is adamant about removing Hakim from Bethune Elementary. However, school transfers are not that automatic, and I made it quite clear to her that further absence would be truancy. So we came to a compromise."

"What compromise?"

"Hakim will return to school on Monday but will be placed in the other third-grade classroom while she pursues a transfer. And, Jodi . . ."

"What?" That came out more snappish than I intended, but there it was.

"I agreed that you would not try to talk to Hakim, interact with him on the playground, or create any activities that would bring Hakim under your supervision."

"Avis!" How could she betray me like that? "He's going to think I don't care about him anymore! That *hurts,* Avis. Really hurts."

"Mmm. I'm sure it does. But I want you to know that I didn't promise that *I* wouldn't talk to Hakim. Actually, it didn't come up"—I could almost hear her stretching into a smile—"and I fully intend to talk to Hakim on Monday, maybe even check in with him daily. We don't know yet how he is reacting to all of this, but I will let Hakim know that you *do* care about him."

I let out a long sigh, paying out the head of steam I'd been building. "Thanks, Avis. Really. Don't know if this is good news or bad news. It'll be hard to see him in the school and not say anything."

"I know. Smile and wave—from a distance."

My thoughts scrambled. "Did you figure out why she had no clue that I was Hakim's teacher? I mean, my name should've rung a bell. And"—this question had been bugging me for days—"the two boys with her in the courtroom . . . does Hakim have more brothers?" I'd guessed their ages at the time as about ten and maybe sixteen. If so, why wasn't the ten-year-old a fifth grader at Bethune Elementary?

"Mmm, not sure. She didn't mention any other sons. Might've been cousins. From what I gathered, Geraldine had been living with her sister looking for a place to live in this area when the, uh, accident happened last June. Finally found a place in September— probably explains why she didn't pay too much attention to school notices. Also, she works as a night-duty LPN, so Hakim spends a lot of time at his aunt's house."

"Okay. It's just . . . so weird." *"A diabolical joke,"* the woman had said. I quickly shook off the thought. Couldn't go there. If I chose to believe that, I might as well give it all up right now. After I got off the phone, I dug out my journal and reread the prayer I'd written that morning. Then read it aloud to drown out the accusing laughter in my head.

I DECIDED NOT TO HIDE THIS MESS from Yada Yada—not like the incident with MaDear, where I kept waiting for someone else who'd been at the beauty shop to bring it up. I didn't even check with Avis, just wrote a long e-mail spelling out what had happened at the parent-teacher conferences, the scriptures I was hanging on to, and the focus I was trying to keep—that God would work this out not only for my good, but for Hakim and his mother too. ". . . even though," I admitted, "nothing can bring Jamal back. I know that. It's a reality I live with every day. So please, help me pray."

The responses I got from different Yada Yada sisters reinforced the impression I had when "Prayer Group 26" first met at the women's conference last spring—that drawer full of crazy-colored, mismatched socks. It didn't matter; just knowing my sisters cared kept me going that whole awkward week, catching glimpses of Hakim, trying to send him a smile and wave from a distance but only getting a head down in return. For solace, I kept the Scripture reading and prayers going and checked my e-mails each evening.

"*Si!* Of course I will pray!" Delores wrote. "I consider it a privilege to pray for you, my sister—a small payment on the debt I owe for all the prayers Yada Yada has spent on the Enriques family."

Ruth's note made me laugh out loud: "Go shopping. Forget about your troubles for two hours and buy a new hat." Hadn't she noticed yet that I never wore hats? Still, it was actually tempting. A wild, crazy hat. What would Denny think of *that?*

Hoshi's note was brief: "Praying for you as you requested. Did you get an answer yet from the woman who cut my mother?" *Sheesh*. Hoshi had her own demons to fight. I hit Reply and typed, "Not yet. Will let you know." Then I hit Send.

Even Stu responded. "I am so sorry, Jodi. I wonder if Hakim's mother has gotten any counseling to help her deal with the loss of Jamal. It sounds like she's a ticking time bomb." *Okay, Stu, I'll let you suggest it.*

Florida didn't bother with e-mail but called me up. "Girl! You attract sticky situations like that nasty ol' flypaper! But don't you worry none. God's got your back. Say, that man of yours around? Wanna thank him for taking Carl to that guy breakfast last Saturday. He say much to you about it?"

"Who? Denny? Not really. Mark Smith came too." Had to admit I'd been kind of distracted and hadn't really pressed Denny for details. "What did Carl say?"

"Not much—Carl ain't a big talker. But he did say Pastor Clark got the guys shootin' off their mouths about what they think a 'real man' is. Guess it was some list." She laughed. "I think Pastor gave each man a Bible verse to look up, maybe to compare God's design with their own bright ideas, 'cause my Bible went missin' for a day or two then showed up again."

"That's great, Florida. Are things any better—at home, I mean?"

She snorted. "Ain't seen any miracles yet, but maybe it's a chink in the wall. Say . . . Yada Yada is meetin' at your house next Sunday, right?"

Which was true. And Chanda—who didn't have e-mail, so she didn't get my long version of what happened when Hakim's mother showed up—fussed at me up and down when Sunday evening rolled around and she discovered she was the only one at Yada Yada who didn't know what happened.

"I'm sorry, Chanda. I should have called," I said, even though I knew I couldn't have gone over the whole thing again on the phone. Now that Adele—who used to share e-mails with Chanda—was off the loop, Chanda did seem to get left out a lot from the online "chatter" between Yada Yada meetings.

We spent a long time that night praying for "the Hakim situation" and also for Nony and her boys. As far as we knew, there was still no word about when she planned to bring the boys home. I felt surrounded by the prayers of my sisters, like a wall of protection, and I wondered . . . did Nony sense our prayers halfway around the world? Feel that protection?

I did have one "answer" to prayer: a second letter from Lincoln Correctional Center. "Just arrived yesterday," I said, waving it in the air.

That got everyone's attention, especially Hoshi's. "Read it please, Jodi," she said, sitting straight, hands folded in her lap. Her eyes flickered, like Christmas lights ambivalent about whether they were going to burn bright or go out.

I unfolded the single sheet of paper. "Dear Mrs. Baxter," I read. "Don't know why Miss Takahashi want to be on my visitors' list, but can't feel any worse about what happened than I already do. Guess any visitors are better than no visitors. Sincerely, Becky Wallace. P. S. Last time you all was here you asked if I need anything. Could sure use some hand cream or the like. I'm working in the kitchen and my hands red all the time. But you can't bring it. Has to come straight from the store."

No one spoke for several moments while I refolded the letter. Hoshi looked down at her own hands, long and smooth. "Yes, I will go."

Guess that means Denny and I are driving to Lincoln one of these Saturdays.

"What dat she need?" Chanda piped up. "Maybe we chip in and buy her two or t'ree t'ings—hand cream or fancy bath stuff. You know, be a Christmas present."

Edesa nodded. "*Sí.* I will contribute, but it would be easiest to send it with Hoshi and whoever goes to visit her, wouldn't it?"

Yo-Yo leaned back in her chair and stuck a leg out. "Can't. Security reasons. Any gifts gotta come straight from the store or get ordered on the Internet or something. An' forget the fancy bath stuff. Gang showers ain't conducive to beauty baths."

Ruth groaned. "Now *that's* a reason not to get yourself arrested."

"Well, I'll be glad to order something and get it sent," Stu jumped in, "but I'll need her address. Just give me that envelope, Jodi." She held out her hand for the letter but shook her head when several people reached for their purses. "Later, okay? I'll buy something then figure out how much everybody owes. If we all chip in, should only be a few dollars each."

I handed over the envelope and remembered: I was going to ask Stu if she'd like to come for Thanksgiving. *Humph!* Maybe she'd like to organize the whole meal?

38

Stu arrived at one o'clock sharp on Thanksgiving Day, her silver Celica loaded with a veggie tray, a big bag of chips, two kinds of dip, homemade cranberry bread, small paper plates with a Thanksgiving motif, and a tin of mixed nuts. "Hey. Real food," Josh salivated, helping her carry the goodies into the living room. He had the bag of chips opened and a handful into his mouth before I even got the front door closed.

"You didn't have to do that, Stu," I said, watching her dump the chips into a basket she'd brought along and arrange the snacks artfully on our beat-up coffee table. "Didn't I tell you to just bring yourself?"

"I know, but you can always use munchies on Thanksgiving Day—right, Josh?" She beamed at my eighteen-year-old Hollow Leg, who was now sampling the tin of mixed nuts.

Not if you want your kids to actually eat dinner at two, I grumbled to myself. Yet I had to admit the cranberry bread looked tempting.

I got a cutting board and bread knife from the kitchen and cut a thin slice. *Oh my, to die for.* "Thanks, Stu. Yummy. I've got mulled cider. Want some?"

By the time Amanda and I got back with mugs of steaming cider—Amanda had insisted on garnishing each mug with a cinnamon stick, which of course didn't want to be found—Stu had curled up in the recliner by the front windows with a paper plate of veggies and dip. "Mark and Hoshi not here yet?" she asked, taking a mug from Amanda.

"Not yet. I told them one o'clock, so they should be here any minute."

As it turned out, Denny had finished grilling the turkey outside, stuck it into the oven to keep warm, and the hands on the clock were nudging up toward two o'clock before the doorbell finally rang.

"Sorry we're late, Jodi," Mark Smith said, ushering Hoshi inside then thrusting a large bouquet of mixed mums into my arms—eye-popping yellows and oranges and rust against a bed of leather leaf and delicate baby's breath. "Hope we didn't hold anything up." He helped Hoshi take off her long coat, adding it to the pile on the coat tree in our entryway.

"Mark! They're beautiful!" I said, taking the flowers. "You aren't that late . . . though we were starting to worry that maybe something had happened." I headed for the kitchen to hunt up a vase, passing Amanda in the hall carrying a tray with two mugs of cider on it. I gave her a thumbs-up. "Help yourselves to some snacks in the living room," I called back over my shoulder. "Denny! Mark's here!"

362

It took me a good five minutes to cut all the stems and get the mums arranged into a vase, but it certainly dressed up our dining-room table. I needed to remember that little nicety: bring a hostess gift when invited to dinner. At Uptown Community, we tended to pooh-pooh that mentality, opting for just-come-on-over-and-bring-yourselves simplicity. But the flowers were nice. Thoughtful. Gallant.

When I got back to the living room, Hoshi was saying, " . . . stopped by a policeman and made to get out of the car. I was worried for Dr. Smith."

"What's this?" Denny sat forward on the couch.

Mark quickly shook his head. "Nothing. Just one of those things." He smiled at me—a little forced, I thought. "Are you call-ing us to dinner, Jodi?"

"Well, yes. Everything's ready. Might as well eat." But I defi-nitely wanted to hear more about what happened. *Sheesh*. That's all Hoshi needed was another scare.

Stu, Denny, and Amanda helped me put the food on the table: grilled turkey (Denny's big idea, of course), candied yams, stuffing that hadn't been "stuffed" in the turkey, fresh green beans with almonds, store-bought dinner rolls, mashed potatoes, and gravy. I had to cheat on the gravy, though, because I didn't have any turkey drippings this year. After everyone had found a seat, I lit the candles, and we joined hands around the table to sing the Doxology: "Praise God from whom all blessings flow . . ." I grinned to myself as Hoshi's sweet soprano, Stu's alto, and Mark Smith's deep baritone added to the Baxter bash of voices. We actually sounded decent.

After the "Amen," I opened my mouth to give passing instructions, when Mark said, "Would you all like to sing the African-American version of the Doxology? Same words."

"Cool." Amanda grinned.

And so we sang it again, but this time Mark started low and slow: "Praise . . . God . . . from . . . whom . . . a-all . . . ble-essings . . . flow . . ." The rest of us chimed in as we caught on until the last phrase swelled to a stately crescendo. We all sat there after the "Amen," still holding hands, awed at the fresh power of the old words. The same way I felt when I heard Mahalia Jackson slow down "Amazing Grace," savoring each word, each truth.

"Sweet," Josh said. "Let's eat." Everybody laughed and started passing platters and bowls.

"What? No macaroni and cheese?" Mark said, filling his plate and winking at Amanda.

"Macaroni and cheese? At Thanksgiving?" Amanda asked.

"Hey. Thanksgiving wasn't Thanksgiving without mac 'n' cheese as I was coming up." He grinned, spreading his thin moustache, which dipped down on either side of his mouth and outlined his chin in a faint goatee. "Turkey and ham and mac 'n' cheese and two kinds of sweet potatoes, and greens—not to mention sweet-potato pie at the end of the food chain. Add two dozen relatives dropping in all day long to graze at my grandma's table, bringing all kinds of baked things and mysterious things dripping in sauce."

My mouth was probably hanging open. I had imagined Mark Smith growing up in a wealthy upper-class home, sort of like *The Cosby Show.*

"Sounds scrumptious," Stu said. "Did you grow up in the South?"

Mark turned out to be a wonderful storyteller about growing up in small-town Georgia. Amanda and Josh hung on every word as he described the "go-carts" he and his friends built out of baby carriage wheels and orange boxes, racing them down red-dirt hills and smashing them—and themselves—into trees that got in the way. "Shouldn't even be alive today," he laughed.

From what I gathered, he and a younger brother were mostly raised by his grandmother and a great aunt. He didn't offer what happened to his mother, and we didn't ask.

"You've come a long way, Mark—small-town Georgia to a major university," Stu said.

Mark grinned wryly. "You could say that. First person in my family to go to college, much less get a Ph.D. Grandma and Auntie Bell told me once a day, if not twice, that God put a gift in me, and it'd be a sin not to be the 'somebody' I was created to be. I'll probably never know what they sacrificed to get me there, but you should've seen those two when I got my doctorate. Jumping up and down, weeping and carrying on—though Grandma made it very clear I still had to wipe my feet at the front door and say 'Yes, ma'am' at *her* house."

That got a chuckle from the rest of us. But even as we laughed, I noticed a small frown gather on Mark's face, and he pushed his potatoes around absently. "Then there are days I realize we haven't come very far, after all," he said softly.

The table got very quiet. What did he mean? Civil rights?

Progress for blacks? Of course we'd come a long way . . . hadn't we?

"I think," Hoshi said in her quiet voice, "Dr. Smith refers to what happened today with the police."

"Tell us what happened, Mark," Denny said. "It's important for us to know."

Nony's husband laid down his fork and sighed. "Just one of those things, really." He half-laughed and shook his head. "Shouldn't be surprised, but I was. Since our dinner date wasn't until one o'clock, I decided to run up to Highland Park Hospital to see a colleague of mine who is recovering from surgery. Hoshi asked if she could ride along instead of picking her up later, since this man is one of her professors too. I was glad for the company and decided to drive up Sheridan Road—you know, to gawk at all the big mansions along the North Shore, show Hoshi how the upper crust *really* lives. I actually forgot about 'driving black' in an all-white area—stupid me. Next thing I knew lights were pulling me over. Cops made me get out, patted me down, ran my license plate . . . and got very vague when I asked why I'd been stopped."

Tiny beads of sweat gathered on Mark Smith's face, and his jaw muscles tensed. "They even asked Hoshi if she was 'all right.' Bless her—she got indignant and said, 'Of course I am all right. We are going to the hospital to visit a sick friend!'" He quoted her in that "correct English" way of hers with a brief smile. "But I admit to a moment of panic. If they'd kept asking questions and discovered she was a student and I was her teacher . . ." He threw his hands open. "Well, there you have it. They let us go with a warning to 'drive careful, now.'"

Denny was incredulous. "What did they think—that you'd stolen the car or something?"

"Dr. Smith," Amanda said, her brow creased with confusion, "why didn't you just tell them you're a professor at Northwestern? They probably got you confused with somebody else."

He grimaced. "Unfortunately, you're right about that, Amanda. Once I step away from Northwestern's campus, I'm just another black man. Whatever those particular cops think about blacks in general, well, that's what they see." He clapped his hands. "Enough about that! I think I need some more of those sweet potatoes. Almost as good as my grandma's, Jodi. Not quite, but almost." His teasing grin was back.

I swallowed my mouthful of candied yams with difficulty. *Just another black man . . .* That was what the man who'd heard me lock my car doors had probably been thinking: *"All she sees is just another black man."*

AFTER DINNER, Amanda snared Stu, Hoshi, and Josh into a game of King's Cribbage that she'd gotten from the grandparents last Christmas. To my surprise, Mark joined Denny and me in the kitchen, rolling up his sleeves and scrubbing pots while I put away food and Denny loaded the dishwasher. I don't know why, but suddenly I blurted out my whole awkward encounter with the man getting into his parked car.

"To be honest, Mark," I said, standing in the middle of our

not-too-big kitchen with a box of plastic wrap in one hand and the remains of the green beans in the other, "I waver between feeling badly about how I made him feel . . . and feeling like he was judging me too. I go over it again and again in my mind, imagining that the man is white or Asian or Italian or from Mars, and I *still* think I would have locked my car doors."

I don't know what I expected Mark to say, but he was quiet for a minute—a *long* minute—while he gave particular attention to a sticky baking dish in the sudsy water. He seemed about to say something when the phone rang. "Josh? Amanda?" I yelled into the living room. "Get that, will you? . . . Sorry, Mark."

He finally turned around, leaning back against the sink. "Unfortunately, Jodi, both blacks and whites in this country, no matter how well-meaning—and I do believe you didn't mean to humiliate him—end up living with the sins of the past. That means some racist cop will assume I'm up to no good if I show up in the wrong community until I prove otherwise, and it means that brother will assume you're just like all the bigoted white folks he's had to deal with in one way or another all his life until you prove different. We're all involved in an anxious dance, like the Jets and the Sharks in *West Side Story,* trying to survive on the same streets, in the same society, but not sure what's going to happen if we step over the line."

"Dad? Mom?" Amanda stuck her head in the doorway. "Um . . . José wants to know if he can come up to see us. You know, hang out. Play games or something."

"See us" my foot. I glanced at Denny. He gave a brief nod.

"Okay," I said impatiently. "Next time excuse yourself. We were talking." But Amanda had already disappeared.

I turned back to Mark, frowning, mulling over his "anxious dance" comment. "So, how do we tango instead of . . . you know, tap-dancing on eggs like boxers waiting for the knockout?"

Denny laughed out loud; even Mark grinned. I hadn't meant to be funny, but even I had to laugh when I realized I was still standing in the middle of the room waving around the plastic wrap and leftover green beans.

39

José Enriques showed up about five o'clock, handing me a tin with some kind of sugary cookies. *"Pan de polvo,"* he said, nodding politely. "Mama made it for you, *Senora* Baxter." He flashed a grin in the direction of my shoulder, and I wondered briefly if the boy had trouble looking adults in the eye—then realized the dazzling smile was directed at Amanda, who stood slightly behind me. I tried not to roll my eyes. *Oh Lord, give me strength.*

King's Cribbage gave way to a two-pack card game of Slap Jack that José taught us that soon had my head spinning. Mark Smith seemed to hit it off with José and caught on fast to the game. The rest of us lost all our cards one by one, and a fierce competition developed between Stu, Mark, and José. Amanda parked herself close to José, murmuring encouragement. In the spirit of fairness, Josh—his hair grown out to an astonishing half-inch—blatantly cheered every time Mark Smith won a hand.

Finally out of cards, Stu threw up her hands. "Can't keep up with those two. Just as well. Time to get home. I've got three real-estate showings tomorrow. I'm in the wrong business when it comes to holidays—but *that's* going to change." Hoshi and I walked her to the front door after she said her good-byes to the crew in the living room. Stu gave me a buss on the cheek. "Thanks for the invite, Jodi. Best Thanksgiving I've had in years."

I wanted to ask about her family—didn't she ever see them at holidays?—but she abruptly changed the subject, looking at Hoshi curiously. "Did you guys settle on a date for your prison visit?"

Both of us shook our heads. But before Hoshi left that evening, we decided this coming Saturday, before Hoshi's semester exams, was maybe the best time to make the trip to Lincoln Correctional Center. Denny agreed. "December weekends get awful busy with Christmas stuff."

"*Holiday* stuff," Mark teased, helping Hoshi into her coat. "You teach in a public school, remember?" Then a cloud crossed his face, like a remembered pain. "Thanks for getting me through *this* holiday. It's . . . tough without Nony and the boys. Pray for us, okay?"

Denny frowned. "Still no return date?"

Mark shook his head. "Guess this is something she needs to do." Then he laughed, but it was hollow. "Last thing she said? Oprah Winfrey is coming to South Africa next week to film a Christmas special highlighting the plight of AIDS orphans, and they need local volunteers at each of her stops. Nony thinks it would be an awesome experience for Marcus and Michael." He shrugged, but the pain had not left his eyes. "It would . . . if it didn't keep us on opposite sides of the world."

JOSÉ STAYED until nine o'clock then shrugged off an offer for Josh to run him home. "I can get home by El—*no problema.* See you Saturday."

I shut the door behind him and turned to Amanda. "Saturday? What's this about Saturday? Aren't you supposed to *ask* before you—"

"Mo-om! It wasn't even me. Ask Josh! Good grief!" She flounced off to her room.

I stared at Josh. "What?"

"Parental unit on overload. Begin cool-down cycle." Josh headed for the living room, where his father had turned on the TV to catch highlights of Thanksgiving Day football. "Youth group, Mom," he said over his shoulder—a tad too smug, in my opinion. "Service project, remember? We're going down to Jesus People USA on Saturday night to help serve dinner to the homeless. José heard us talk about it and said he'd like to come. I might ask Yo-Yo's brothers too. They'd fit right in at JPUSA." He grinned. "Can I have the car? I volunteered to drive."

I followed Josh into the living room, somewhat mollified that it was a youth-group activity. "No, I don't remember—and the car's a problem. Dad and I are taking Hoshi to visit Becky Wallace on Saturday. Downstate."

"But Mom! I said I could drive! And if Yo-Yo's brothers go, I have to pick them up."

So what's wrong with public transportation? I groused to myself—even though I knew when it came to my own kids, I'd much rather they get a ride. "Talk to your dad," I said, heading for the kitchen to clean up the remains of the apple crisp I'd made for dessert. *Let Denny figure it out.*

AS IT TURNED OUT, Denny didn't think it'd be a problem. "We'll leave early, be back by four. Then Josh can have the car." Amanda had dance practice at Uptown Saturday morning for this Sunday's Advent candle lighting—could the Christmas season be upon us already?—so we ended up leaving both kids at home. Had to admit it was a lot easier than the juggling act we pulled off the last time to get Amanda to Edesa's for the day. I took the cell and told her to call us if she made any other plans.

At the last minute Florida got wind that we were going to the prison this weekend and called to see if she could go along. "Carla's foster parents got her this weekend, and I'm about to go crazy if I stay here. I'm still on the visitors' list, right? Do you mind picking me up?"

So once again we hit Route I-55 heading for Lincoln, Illinois, on an early Saturday morning with our thermoses of coffee, some fruit and sweet rolls, and what was left of Delores's *pan de polvo*. The sky was overcast, like it was thinking about snow. "Sure hope that weather holds off till we get home," Denny muttered to no one in particular.

Right away Florida piped up from the second seat of the van. "All right now, Jesus. You heard the man's prayer. We're askin' for good weather all the way to the prison and back again, and we thank ya in advance for whatcha gonna do."

Denny and I exchanged grins. *Yes, God, make my prayers as natural as breathing . . . or talking.* I turned back to the passing landscape, stripped of the brilliant colors we'd enjoyed on our last trip. Now bony tree-fingers jabbed the sky and blankets of tired, yellowed grass lay crumpled everywhere, waiting . . . waiting for winter.

Hoshi didn't have much to say on the trip downstate. She was probably apprehensive. At least the three of us were along to help her sort it out if she wanted. Pawing through the CDs that were starting to collect in the van, I picked up one of Integrity Music's *iWorship* albums and stuck it in the player. The first track nearly blasted the car off the road till I frantically turned down the volume. "Sorry about that," I muttered. "Josh must've driven the van last."

Now that we could hear the words, the song seemed to speak to the raw feelings we all had after that awful night when Becky Wallace broke into our Yada Yada meeting: "I'm trading my sorrows . . . I'm laying them down for the joy of the Lord . . ."

"I like that," Hoshi said. "Can you play it again?"

I hit the Repeat button, and the last line was still going through my mind when we pulled up to the security gate at Lincoln Correctional Center at eleven o'clock. *"Though the sorrow may last for the night, His joy comes with the morning."* I took Hoshi's arm as we entered the door of the stark, gray building and headed for the visitors' desk. Had to admit it was as much for my own comfort as to comfort Hoshi. Even though this was my second visit, I was nervous. Again. I mean, how weird was it to visit the thief who'd terrorized us all with a knife? *We could all use some of that morning joy, Jesus.*

Hoshi's lip trembled when a female guard patted her down and made her leave her belongings in the locker. Didn't blame her. Getting searched made *me* feel like a criminal. But without Yo-Yo's prison history to delay us this time, we were soon shown into the visiting room and found an empty table.

And then we waited. Ten minutes . . . fifteen. "Maybe she changed her mind and does not want to see us," Hoshi said. She didn't seem to know what to do with her hands and kept fidgeting with an opal ring on her right hand.

Denny got up and spoke to a guard stationed at the door that let prisoners in and out, and the guard mumbled something into his walkie-talkie. Finally Becky Wallace stepped into the room. Not the same Becky Wallace. Healthier, fresher. She also looked incredibly young in a tank top, tight jeans, and jean jacket. She seemed to take a big breath then headed for our table.

"Hi." Her dark eyes were wary, but she sat down and greeted us each in turn. "Mr. Baxter . . . Miz Baxter . . . an' Miz Hickman, right?" Then she looked at Hoshi. "An' you must be Miss Tak—" She stumbled. "Takahashi."

Hoshi nodded but said nothing, like she had stage fright.

"First names are all right," Denny said. "May we call you Becky?"

"You lookin' better, girl," Florida blurted. She did too. The dull brown hair had grown an inch or two, even had a little wave and some shine. The dark circles around her eyes were gone, her face fuller. I noticed she even had on a hint of blush and mascara.

Good grief. She's almost pretty. I hardly knew what to do with the revelation.

Becky's lips twitched . . . not quite a smile. "Yeah. Been clean for two months. I'm sleepin' better. Food ain't so hot, but at least it's three squares a day."

Stillness settled around us like an invisible cocoon, muffling the hum of conversation at the other gray plastic tables. We just looked at each other or down at our hands, wondering what to say next.

Florida broke the silence. "What 'bout your kid? Heard anything?"

Becky nodded, but she swallowed several times before speaking. "Got word that DCFS put 'im in foster care." She shrugged and looked away, blinking rapidly. "Prob'ly best. Jus' . . . dunno if I'm ever gonna see my boy agin."

Florida reached out and gripped Becky's wrist. "Girl, I been there. But God gave me my baby back. Tell you what. We gonna track down your kid and make sure they send you word regular. We got just the friend to sic on DCFS!" Florida grinned at Denny and me and actually laughed.

Oh, Stu is going to love this, I thought.

"Really? You'd do that? After what I done ta . . ." Becky stopped and glanced at Hoshi. "Told these guys last time, but I . . . I didn't mean ta hurt yo' mama. Hope she's okay."

It wasn't exactly an apology, but the words seemed to electrify Hoshi. She sat up in her chair, looking lovely even in those drab surroundings. She quit fingering her ring and looked into Becky's face across the table. "Yes. She will be all right. I . . ." She stopped. We waited. The unspoken sentence hung in the air. Becky had no way of knowing that the cut that hurt the deepest was not her mother's hand. Would Hoshi say something?

To my surprise, Hoshi held out her hand, her long, tapered fingers with the perfect white moons reaching for the nail-bitten hand of Becky Wallace. "It is not easy to say, but . . . I forgive you. God forgives you too."

Their hands touched. Then Becky pulled back. "Nah. God ain't about ta forgive *me*. Y'all don't know the stuff I done."

"God forgave me—why not you?" I was startled to hear my own voice.

Becky looked me up and down with nothing short of a leer. "You? What do *you* know 'bout needin' forgiveness? You had a bad thought? Snitched cookies when yo' mama said not to? Huh!"

"No. I . . . killed somebody. A boy."

Becky's eyes widened, and we just stared at each other. For some reason, the meaning of her name resonated in my head: *"Bound."* And in the next breath, the meaning of my own: *"God is gracious."* And for a jumbled moment, the two names and the two meanings merged in my understanding. *I was bound . . . but God is gracious and set me free.*

Becky's eyes darted at Denny. "For real? She kill somebody?" She clearly did not believe me.

"Yes." Denny's eyes begged my permission before he continued. I nodded, then closed my eyes while he told the short, sad story of our stupid fight, me driving angry in a storm, a boy trying to get out of the rain, the terrible crash, a life snuffed out.

"But it be an accident, right?"

I opened my eyes. She was looking straight at me. "I didn't hit him on purpose, if that's what you mean. And the charges against me were dropped, but his mother can't forgive me, just the same. Yet God has forgiven me. That's what gives me courage to go on." *Say it, Jodi, say it! It's true—even though you don't always believe it. Becky Wallace needs to hear it!* "You already have Hoshi's forgiveness, Becky, and God will forgive you too. Just . . . ask Him."

Becky looked from Denny to me, then to Florida and Hoshi, testing the story with her eyes. "Man! You guys are a trip!" She slowly stood and looked toward the "inmate" door then, like she'd forgotten something, turned back and shook each of our hands. "Thanks for comin' ta see me. You guys all right."

She walked across the room and was gone.

The four of us just looked at each other. Finally Denny scratched his head. "Well, it wasn't exactly the Four Spiritual Laws, but"—he smiled big, making his dimples cave in—"I think something important just happened for our 'Bandana Woman.'"

40

We left the prison parking lot in silence, a little afraid to break the spell. At least, I was wondering what Becky Wallace was thinking right about now. What had Hoshi's words, "I forgive you," meant to her? Especially since B. W. hadn't actually come out and said, "I'm sorry."

Huh. Not that you've ever fuzzed the edges of an apology, Jodi Baxter. Well, okay, so it was a lot easier to say, *"I didn't mean to"* or, *"Guess I messed up."* Saying "I'm sorry" was downright admitting that a wrong had been done, a wrong that needed forgiving. And to be honest, I wasn't very quick on the forgiving end either. Didn't want to let the person who wronged me off the hook *that* easy.

But I told Jamal's mother I was really sorry—hadn't I? Or had I? Sorry about what? That the accident had happened? That she'd lost her son? Or sorry that I'd been driving angry, distracted from my driving, responsible for—

"I am glad I came." Hoshi's quiet voice from the backseat broke into my tumbling thoughts. "My only memory of that woman since that night was her screaming at us, waving that knife around, looking like a wild woman. Every time I thought about her, I felt afraid all over again."

I turned my head so I could see Hoshi, staring out the window behind Denny. "Yeah, know what you mean. Except whenever I thought about her, I just felt angry. Kinda resented finding out she was a real person."

Hoshi kept her head turned toward the window, as if talking to her own reflection. "I could not imagine saying, 'I forgive you,' but when I saw her today . . . it wasn't so hard. Not after she said, 'I'm sorry.'"

I started to say, *"But she didn't, really"*—then realized that Hoshi had given Becky the benefit of the doubt; she had listened beyond her words to her heart.

"Uh-huh," Florida muttered. "It's when they *don't* say 'sorry' that forgivin' gets hard. Still, sometimes ya gotta do it for your own sanity. Maybe that's why Jesus told us to forgive our enemies— more for our sake than theirs."

I twisted further in my seatbelt so I could see Florida behind me. "What do you mean, Flo?"

"Girl, it's just like Avis said a couple of weeks ago. If Hoshi didn't forgive Becky Wallace, she be lettin' that woman hurt her all over again every time she thinks 'bout what happened. But you watch. A little forgiveness goes a long way. Gonna take the sting out."

As I straightened around in my seat, I saw Hoshi turn from the window and take Florida's hand, a teary smile on her face. *Huh,* I thought, watching the bleak landscape slide past my own passenger side window. *Never thought about it like that.* I'd always thought "love your enemies" and "do good to those who persecute you" was kind of a be-holy-like-I-am-holy test. Never sounded fair—or even possible!—though of course a good Christian girl from Des Moines, Iowa, would never actually say so. Maybe Florida was right, though: maybe God wanted us to forgive people for our own good too. Even people who didn't say "sorry."

"For my own good," I whispered, watching my warm breath spread a misty cloud on the cold window.

THE SNOW HELD OFF till late that night, and then it was mostly lake-effect snow, whipped up by a chilly wind, laying down an inch or two, but not serious enough to even get out the snow shovel.

"Lucky you," I told Josh as he drove us to Uptown Community Church the next morning. "This was only a teaser. Wait till January. You'll have to set your alarm two hours earlier to shovel us out before school."

"That's why we need a snow blower," Josh countered. "Then Amanda can do it."

"Ha!" Amanda swatted the back of his head with a glove. "Just drive, muscle man. I need to get to church early, remember?"

Denny, riding shotgun in the front seat, didn't bother to tell

Josh that our short sidewalks—front and back—could practically be measured in inches, so forget a snow blower. In fact, Denny had been unusually quiet on the way home from the prison yesterday. Didn't even ask many questions about the youth group's service project at Jesus People USA last night, though both Josh and Amanda had said it was "cool." Whether they meant serving a couple hundred meals to homeless men and women and scrubbing pots and pans afterward, or just hanging out with a bunch of "Jesus people" who all looked like they'd just been roped in off the streets, I wasn't sure. By the time they got home from taking Pete and Jerry back to Yo-Yo's house after dropping José off in Little Village, Denny and I were heading for bed.

Not exactly the kind of youth-group activities I was weaned on, I thought as we headed up the stairs at Uptown Community, leaving Josh to go park the minivan. *Bible sword drills . . . Youth for Christ rallies . . . an occasional roller-skating party—the "sanctified" substitute for dancing.* I felt a pang. Nostalgia for a simpler time? Or realizing just how unprepared I'd been for how complicated and untidy the Christian life felt at the moment. Ever since the Yada Yada Prayer Group dropped into my life, frankly.

Amanda disappeared to get ready for the Advent candle dance, and Denny and I had our choice of seats for a change. Even beat Stu getting to church—now *that* was a first. She came in a few minutes later, sat down behind us, and leaned forward. "How did the visit to the prison go yesterday?"

"Good," I said. "Tell you more later, okay?"

I wanted to be quiet for a moment, to focus on the upcoming

worship service. An Advent wreath was suspended from the ceiling by purpoe ribbons; four fat candles representing each Advent Sunday nestled among the fake greenery. Advent . . . the beginning of the Christmas season. Communion Sunday, too, by the looks of the small table off to the side, covered with the cloth embroidered with "children of the world" figures.

The upstairs room filled. The lights dimmed. Three recorders began the familiar Advent hymn, and we all joined in on the words: "O come, O come, Emanuel . . . And ransom captive Israel . . ." Josh slipped into the seat beside Denny. *Sheesh. He must've had to park six blocks away.* And then someone else sat down. I leaned forward.

José Enriques. *Oh Lord, he must've come to see Amanda dance!* This was getting serious.

I was so distracted for a moment I almost missed Amanda and two other teenage girls coming down the aisle like bridesmaids at a wedding, bearing lighted candles—though the black skirts, white socks, and white tops kind of spoiled the "bridesmaid" image. As the music swelled—"That mourns in lonely exile here . . . Until the Son of God appears"—the three girls fanned out gracefully across the front, causing their tiny lights to flicker and dance in the darkened sanctuary.

"Rejoice! Rejoice!" we sang. My eyes were glued to Amanda's face as she lifted her candle heavenward. Her own eyes glowed in the candlelight as she lifted her face, following the light. And then, "Emmanuel . . . Shall come to thee, O Israel." Amanda and the other two girls turned and dipped their tapers toward the wick of the first candle in the Advent wreath. The room seemed to hold its collective breath until the fat candle glowed, the dancers blew out their tapers, and the candle wreath shone with the first promise of Advent.

Beautiful. I glanced at Denny. His eyes were swimming.

The lights came on, and I expected Avis to get up and launch us into some spirited praise and worship. Instead Pastor Clark came to the front—*Somebody's got to tell him to lose that awful green tie*—and said we were going to do things a bit different today. I swept my eyes around the room. Where was Avis, anyway? And then I saw her, sitting toward the back. And there was someone with her—a man. An older man, maybe late fifties, with graying hair at his temples. An African-American man at that.

I faced forward once again, my spine tingling. Avis with a man? *Calm down, Jodi. Maybe it's her brother or cousin or uncle, here for Thanksgiving.* I grinned to myself. *Yeah, right.*

" . . . not only the first Sunday of Advent," Pastor Clark was saying, "but the first Sunday of the month, when we celebrate the Lord's Supper." And the two celebrations, he said, have a great deal to do with each other. "During Advent, we celebrate God's promise to send the Messiah and 'ransom captive Israel.' Because not only Israel, but all of us are stuck—stuck in our sins. But in breaking the bread and sharing the cup of the Lord's Supper, we celebrate the purpose for which the Messiah came: to sacrifice His own life, taking on Himself the penalty for *our* sin. He suffered whips, humiliation, crucifixion, and finally death—none of which He deserved. That was *our* punishment. For our sins, our mistakes, our oversights, our weaknesses, our failings."

He paused for a long moment, lost in his own thoughts, almost as if he'd forgotten about the rest of us. And then he said simply, "So that we might live. Forever."

I forgot about Avis and the mystery man. I forgot about José. I almost forgot to stand when it was my turn to go up to receive the bread and wine. For some reason Pastor Clark's powerful words echoed something Mark Smith had said at Thanksgiving: *"Both blacks and whites in this country end up living with the sins of the past."*

Stuck. That's exactly how I'd felt when Mark said that. Stuck with the legacy of sin hanging over our heads. If Jesus was our example, though, the way out was *repentance . . . forgiveness . . . ransom . . . sacrifice.* I felt on the verge of something incredibly important—but for the life of me, I wasn't sure what it was.

I put the piece of bread in my mouth. *Christ's body, broken for me.* I took a sip of wine from the ceramic goblet. *Christ's blood, shed for me.* I turned, and passed both bread and wine to Denny. "Christ's body, broken for you," I whispered.

I'll never forget the look in his eyes.

WHEN WE GOT HOME AFTER CHURCH, the answering machine light on the kitchen phone was blinking. I pressed the Play button while I unwound my long neck scarf and unbuttoned my coat, still thinking about meeting Avis's "old friend" from Philadelphia. "Jodi, this is Peter Douglass," she'd said. "An old friend of Conrad's." I had tried to give her a meaningful look, which she totally ignored. But she wasn't going to get away that easy.

"Denny or Jodi. It's Mark." The answering machine sprang to life. "Nony's mother has taken a turn for the worse. Nony called last night, asking me to come . . ."

"Denny!" I yelled. "It's Mark! Come listen!"

" . . . bit of a mess, with term papers and exams coming up," Mark's message continued as Denny appeared in the doorway between the dining room and kitchen, "but I think I need to go. So, as soon as I can make arrangements with my department, I'm leaving. Jodi, will you ask Yada Yada to pray? For Nony and"—I almost didn't catch his next words—"for me."

The machine clicked off. "Wow. Wonder what that means? It's good, I think. Don't you, Denny?"

Denny nodded. "Uh-huh." He seemed deep in thought— thoughts he'd been carrying for days, it seemed, like Frodo Baggins, intent on getting that ring to Mount Doom in spite of all the obstacles . . . slowly, but surely. I gathered up my coat and scarf. *Guess he'll tell me when he's ready.*

I started for the front hall to hang them up, but Denny stopped me. "Jodi, how long does Adele's Hair and Nails stay open on weeknights like tomorrow?"

41

*M*onday. Back to school after the Thanksgiving holiday. Christy James's last week as my student teacher. Back to kids already revved up for Christmas . . . and Hanukkah, and Kwanzaa, and the TV-commercial glut otherwise known as "the holidays." Back to seeing Hakim from a distance, lining up with the other third-grade teacher, hardly daring to wonder what he must think of me now. The lady who'd killed his brother.

"Okay, God, I know it's not just about me," I muttered out loud as I hustled to school with my tote bags, trying to keep warm. The rod attached to my left femur ached in the cold. "So please give Hakim what he needs in the other classroom. Finish what You started in him, okay?"

Denny hadn't told me what he had in mind for tonight, just asked if I would go with him if he went to see Adele and MaDear at the shop. *"But why?"* I'd argued. *"Adele made it clear we would only upset MaDear."*

He had stood hunched in the middle of the dining room, one hand in his pants pocket, the other rubbing the back of his head. *"I just know it's time. And today during Communion, God gave me peace that it's going to be all right."*

I pulled open the double door of Bethune Elementary and headed into the welcome warmth of the hallway. *Problem is, "our time" and "Adele's time" might be light-years apart.* I peeked into the office to see if Avis was there. I was dying to know more about the "old friend" from Philadelphia—he didn't look so old to *me*—but the inner office was empty. Oh well. I'd get her later.

I realized how much I was going to miss Christy when I sent her out to bring in the kids from the playground while I set up the day's lessons. The kids trooped in noisily, shedding coats, mittens, and scarves to a cacophony of, "Hi, Miz Baxter!" "That's *my* hook." "Stop steppin' on my scarf!" "See my new mittens?" Thank heavens the snow had fizzled. At least we didn't have to deal with a pile of boots as well.

I was helping Kaya and Chanel stick their mittens in their coat sleeves when I heard Avis's voice behind me. "Mrs. Baxter? Could I see you a moment? Hi, Britny. Yes, I see your new mittens. So sparkly!"

I motioned to Christy to take over the mitten situation and hastened to the door, which Avis was holding slightly ajar. Sounded like "business"—guess I'd have to ask her about Mr. Philadelphia later. She motioned me out into the hall.

A child, still bundled in a brown-and-black padded winter jacket, its hood up and tied with a long, red knit scarf, was sitting in the chair that stood outside the classroom door, swinging boy-ish athletic shoes against the chair legs. *Thump. Thump. Thump.* I peered around the hood to see who Avis had brought. A new student?

Familiar dark eyes peered out at me. "Hakim!" Startled, I looked at Avis.

Avis smiled pleasantly, as if this was really not a big deal. "Hakim is coming back to your classroom. Is his desk still avail-able?"

My heart was thumping so hard I could hardly get my breath. "Uh . . . yes! Absolutely!" I beamed at Hakim. "It's been waiting for you."

Hakim jumped off the chair and took my hand. "Tol' Miz Johnson no other kid better be sittin' in my desk."

My head was spinning. What had brought about this miracle? I let Hakim lead me back into the classroom, but not before I jabbed a finger at Avis and mouthed, *"You wait right here! I'll be back in a sec!"*

I handed Hakim over to Christy to deal with the jacket-scarf-mittens routine, ignoring her dropped jaw, then poked my head back out into the hallway. "What in the world?" I asked.

Avis was leaning against the wall, perfectly calm in her two-piece gold-and-black dress. "It was Hakim. He kept telling his mother he wanted to go back to 'Miz B's class.' Made such a fuss—'raised holy hell' was the way she put it—she finally let him come back. Plus, he was acting out big-time in Ms. Towers's class. Ms. Towers came to me last week looking a bit frazzled and

highly recommended he be placed back 'in his own classroom.'"
Avis was grinning big-time now.

"But you didn't say anything to me!"

She shrugged. "Didn't know anything for sure, but Hakim
showed up this morning with the aunt and a note from his mother.
I don't think she's happy about it, but at least she's considering
what's best for Hakim." Avis pushed off from the wall and headed
down the hall with a wave. "Have a great day, Jodi."

WOULD WONDERS NEVER CEASE? I was so happy to have
Hakim back in my class that the whole day felt like a Christmas
gift from God, wrapped in gold ribbon. Hakim seemed happy too.
Even asked for me to read with him one on one while Christy led
group-reading time.

Couldn't wait to tell Denny, but only Willie Wonka was there
to greet me when I got home. "Guess what, Wonka?" I said, taking the dog's face in my hands and kissing his soft brown forehead.
"God is gracious! God is soooooo gracious!" Willie Wonka had
natural urges on his mind and wiggled free, heading for the back
door. I let him out into the backyard but felt like I wanted to
dance, so I hunted around till I found the *iWorship* CD we'd been
listening to lately and put on the first track by Darrell Evans.

> I'm trading my sorrows
> I'm trading my shame

I'm laying them down
For the joy of the Lord

I was right in the middle of hopping around the living room to the
spunky vamp—"Yes, Lord, yes, Lord, yes, yes, Lord!"—for about
the umpteenth time when the Baxter crew all showed up, raiding
the kitchen and giving me looks that said, *"Mom's gone off again."* I
just laughed at them, turned down the music, and told them about
my miracle.

"That's great, Mom." Amanda actually gave me a hug.
"When's supper?"

Denny wrapped his arms around me and held me for a few
moments. "I'm glad, Jodi. Really glad," he murmured into my hair.
Then he pulled back, but I could see he was frowning slightly. "Uh
. . . what time did you say Adele's shop closed?"

Good grief. I'd completely forgotten about promising to go
with Denny to Adele's Hair and Nails. "Seven," I said. "Can't we
do this another evening? I don't want to spoil this great—"

"I gotta do this today, Jodi. Before I lose my nerve. Please?"

Every nerve in my body wanted to protest, but something told
me that if I didn't go, Denny would go by himself. I sighed. "I'll
go. As soon as we eat supper, okay?"

He shook his head. "Don't think I can eat. Maybe when we get
back."

So I pulled out Sunday's leftovers for Josh and Amanda,
tanked up Denny and myself with some fresh coffee to take along,
and headed for Clark Street.

We pulled into a parking space across the street from Adele's shop about six-forty. The white twinkle lights around the shop's window had been replaced with multicolored ones and wound with silver tinsel, giving a festive holiday air to the shop. Through the window, we could see a customer still in the chair getting a comb-out. And so we sat, motor running so the car didn't get too cold.

I had no idea what we were going to say when we got inside. But maybe MaDear wouldn't remember a thing about the previous incident, wouldn't even recognize Denny. After all, sometimes MaDear even forgot who Adele was! That would be the best scenario of all, as far as I was concerned. We could all just start over, clean slate.

The customer left about ten minutes later, calling back cheery good-byes. Denny turned off the engine and we got out, walking across the street hand in hand at a break in the traffic. We both hesitated at the door, then Denny pulled it open.

42

The air was warm with the pungent smell of hair perm—and cinnamon. A wreath of cinnamon pinecones hung on the inside of the door, underneath the bell tinkling our arrival. A gospel version of "O Come, All Ye Faithful" pumped out of the small speakers above the wall of mirrors.

Adele's other hairstylist—Takeisha, if I remembered her name right—looked up from the counter where she was writing in the log book. She looked slightly puzzled. "We're closed in ten minutes, but I'd be glad to give you an appointment."

"No, that's all right," Denny said. He cleared his throat. "We actually just came to see Adele Skuggs for a moment."

The young woman turned to give the familiar yell—*"Adele! Someone to see you!"*—but at that moment Adele herself appeared. Her short "natural" was no longer red but black tipped with gray, which looked like a mat of tiny silver springs. I tensed, not sure what she would do. Yell at us? Throw us out?

She did neither. Just looked at us, surprised. Finally she spoke. "Jodi and Denny Baxter. What can I do for you?" Her tone was calm but guarded.

"Adele, could I please see MaDear?" Denny spoke quickly, as though afraid he'd lose his nerve. Adele started to shake her head, jingling the big gold loops in her ears, but Denny rushed ahead. "Adele, this is so important. Tell her . . ." His grip on my hand tightened. "Tell her it is the man who killed her brother, come to ask forgiveness."

I whipped my head around to stare at my husband. I opened my mouth to cry, *"No, Denny!"* but the words stuck in my throat. My brain was scrambling. We should have talked about this! Why feed into the old woman's delusions? How would that help? Didn't MaDear need to see that Denny was *not* the evil man who killed her brother? Wouldn't that lay this whole mess to rest?

Almost as if I'd said my thoughts aloud, Denny said, "That's what MaDear thinks. We have to start there." He was speaking to Adele, who was staring at him, lips parted, revealing the small space between her front teeth.

To my utter astonishment, Adele suddenly said, "Well, hang up your coats" and motioned for us to follow her. At the doorway to the back room she held up her hand for us to stop. Then she went inside, and we heard her say, "MaDear, the man who killed Uncle Larry is here. He has something he wants to say to you."

I sucked in my breath, but the salon did not erupt into mayhem. In fact, all I heard was mumbling, something like, "Huh. What he want?" A moment later, Adele motioned us into the back room.

MaDear was sitting in a wheelchair, hunched birdlike over a lapful of curlers and rollers, picking them over, like she was sorting green beans. She looked up sharply as we came in, eyes flashing.

She stared at us angrily for a moment, then her lip began to tremble, and I thought she was going to cry. It may have been only a few seconds, but it was like time slowed to slow-frame . . . and suddenly I saw Jamal and Hakim's mother sitting there, confronting the person who had killed a loved one. *This isn't just about Denny.* I, Jodi Baxter, was "MaDear's white man" to that other mother. We could talk till we were blue in the face—Denny really wasn't that guy; it really was an accident that killed Jamal—but generations of racial division, injustice, pain, and distrust made subtleties hard to distinguish, facts almost irrelevant.

Suddenly I realized what Denny wanted to do and why. *Jesus gave us the way to break the legacy of sin . . .*

Denny let go of my hand and knelt down beside MaDear's wheelchair. I knelt down with him, kneeling low so that she was looking down on us. "Mrs. . . ." Denny looked up at Adele, searching for MaDear's real name.

"Skuggs," said Adele. "Sally Skuggs."

"Mrs. Skuggs," Denny continued, his voice husky, "what I did was wrong and evil. You have every right to be angry. But I have come to ask if you could forgive me. I . . . I can't bring your brother back, but I ask you to forgive me for how we white folks wronged your people, and your family in particular."

The room was hushed. No one spoke. Somewhere I could hear the melodic words to "What Child Is This?" softening the electricity in the air. And then MaDear reached out and patted Denny on the head, tears streaming down her face.

My own eyes blurred, and I groped for a tissue in my skirt pocket.

"I knew yo' mama," MaDear said, stroking Denny's hair. "My mama took care o' you when you was no bigger'n a sucklin' pig, she did. But after Larry was dragged off, found hangin' the nex' day, yo' mama couldn't look my mama or me in th' eye. She done *knew* it was you and yo' daddy and yo' uncle. But ta look us in th' eye an' admit it . . . she couldn't do that. Couldn't do that." MaDear shook her head sorrowfully. "Went to her grave, she did, not knowing we woulda forgiven her for what her menfolk did if she'd asked us to."

Denny's shoulders were shaking, and I handed him a wrinkled tissue. MaDear just kept stroking his head. "Now the son comes," she mused, almost to herself. "Yes, sonny, I forgive you. Big load off my mind."

Suddenly I felt her thin, bony hand reach for mine. "This yo' woman, sonny?" She took my hand in her own and peered closely at it. "What? These hands like chicken claws! Nails a mess, all dry . . . Adele!" She looked up at Adele, who was standing speechless, leaning against the refrigerator as if she needed something to hold her up. "Adele!" MaDear screeched again. "Take this child and do somethin' with these hands. You be ashamed to let her walk outta here with hands like that."

She let go of my "claw" and flapped her hands at me. "Go on—shoo! Soak those nails. Get some paint on 'em." MaDear wagged a maternal finger at Adele. "An' don't you go chargin' this child nothin' either." She mumbled, "All the years I put food on yo' table an' clothes on yo' back, yo' can do one lil' favor for me. Huh." And MaDear started picking through the curlers and rollers in her lap.

Denny blew his nose, and we stood up. Adele and Denny and I just stared at each other. None of us knew what to say, but I had a lightness in my spirit I had never felt before and thought I might just float away.

Adele broke the silence. "Well, come on. If MaDear says you need your nails done, Jodi Baxter, we better do 'em. She's the boss—right, MaDear?"

"You got that right!" MaDear yelled then fell back to studying her lap.

Adele started moving things around at one of the nail chairs in the back room. "Adele, it's really all right," I whispered. "I know you close at seven and weren't expecting us."

"Sit." Adele lowered her bulk onto the stool in front of the little table and poured liquid into a bowl. "Soak."

So I sat, lowering my fingers into the soothing liquid. Denny blew his nose again and took a seat in the corner, resting his elbows on the chair arms and making a tent with his fingers. Watching.

"Takeisha!" Adele yelled toward the front, finally taking my hand from the liquid and starting in on my cuticles. "Turn that music up!—stop jerking, Jodi, or I'm gonna jab you."

I closed my eyes and smiled as "Go Tell It on the Mountain!" in rich gospel beat suddenly took over any need to talk. In my mind I began composing an e-mail to a bunch of crazy, praying sisters. They were never going to believe what God had done today!

On the other hand . . . sure they would.

Book Club Questions

1. The theme of *The Yada Yada Prayer Group* (Yada Yada #1) was *grace*—discovering what it means to be "just a sinner . . . saved by grace." What do you think is the main theme of *The Yada Yada Prayer Group Gets Down?* Why?

2. With whom did you empathize more in the incident at Adele's beauty shop: MaDear or Denny? Why?

3. The Yada Yada prayer group was traumatized by a crime. Have you or someone close to you ever been the victim of a crime? If so, how do you feel toward the perpetrator? If you had a chance for a face-to-face meeting, what do you think would happen? What would you want to happen?

4. How did Yada Yada's decision to visit Becky Wallace in prison affect the different sisters in the prayer group? How did it impact Becky Wallace?

5. If you were the mother of Jamal Wilkins—the boy who Jodi Baxter killed in her car accident in Yada Yada #1—how would you feel to discover her relationship to your other child? How does this discovery affect (1) Jodi? (2) the mother? (3) the child?

6. Jamal's mother can't forgive Jodi, even though Jodi asked for forgiveness at the end of Yada Yada #1. How does this affect Jodi? If the person she has wronged won't forgive, how can she ever be free of the guilt? However, if Jamal's mother does choose to forgive Jodi, what would that forgiveness look like?

7. What prompted Denny's response to MaDear in the final chapter? Why do you think his response was so healing? What questions does his encounter with MaDear raise for you about "repenting for the sins of others"?

8. Examine your own attitudes that may hinder fellowship with other groups of Christians. What is the most difficult or challenging area for you? What would it mean to repent of this attitude?

9. How might we "repent of" or "take responsibility for" past sins of our nation or people group? No matter what your race or ethnicity, what could *you* do to help bring about racial healing among God's people? How can we help each other?

10. Are there relationships in your own life—of any nature— that need healing through repentance or forgiveness? Whether you have "sinned" or "been sinned against," do you have the courage to take the first step?

Dear readers ~ If you would like the *real* "Yada Yada Prayer Group" (who inspired these novels) to pray for you about these matters, please e-mail me at Neta@daveneta.com. Bless you, my sisters!

For more information about the author and all three Yada Yada novels, please visit www.daveneta.com.

Find out how the Yada Yada Story begins . . .

I almost didn't go to the Chicago Women's Conference— after all, being thrown together with 500 strangers wasn't exactly my "comfort zone." But I would be rooming with my boss, Avis, and I hoped that I might make a friend or two.

When Avis and I were assigned to a prayer group of 12 women, I wasn't sure what to think. There was Flo, an out-spoken ex-drug addict; Ruth, a Messianic Jew who could smother-mother you to death; and Yo-Yo, who wasn't even a Christian! Not to mention women from Jamaica, Honduras, South Africa—practically a mini-United Nations. We certainly didn't have much in common.

But something happened that weekend to make us realize we had to hang together. So "the Yada Yada Prayer Group" decided to keep praying for each other via e-mail. Our personal struggles and requests soon got too intense for cyberspace, so we decided to meet together every other Sunday night.

Talk about a rock tumbler!—knocking off each other's rough edges, learning to laugh and cry along the way. But when I faced the biggest crisis of my life, God used my newfound girlfriends to help teach me—Jodi Baxter, longtime Christian "good girl"— what it means to be just a sinner saved by grace.

The Yada Yada Prayer Group ISBN 1-59145-074-8